The Other Path

Corinne Jeffery

One Printers Way
Altona, MB R0G 0B0
Canada

www.friesenpress.com

First Edition — 2023

This book is a work of fiction. All names and incidents are purely the product of the author's imagination. Any references to historical events, organizations, establishments, and locales are intended only to provide a sense of authenticity and are used fictitiously. Any resemblance to actual characters is a subtle blending of real and fictitious persons; where reality ends and fantasy begins is blithely indistinguishable. All other characters, and all occurrences and dialogue are drawn from the author's imagination and are not to be construed as real.

ISBN
978-1-03-916727-8 (Hardcover)
978-1-03-916726-1 (Paperback)
978-1-03-916728-5 (eBook)

1. FICTION, LITERARY

Distributed to the trade by The Ingram Book Company

The Other Path

To- Kathy and Kevin,

Enjoy reading my "What if..." story.

Corinne Jeffery

March 4, 2023

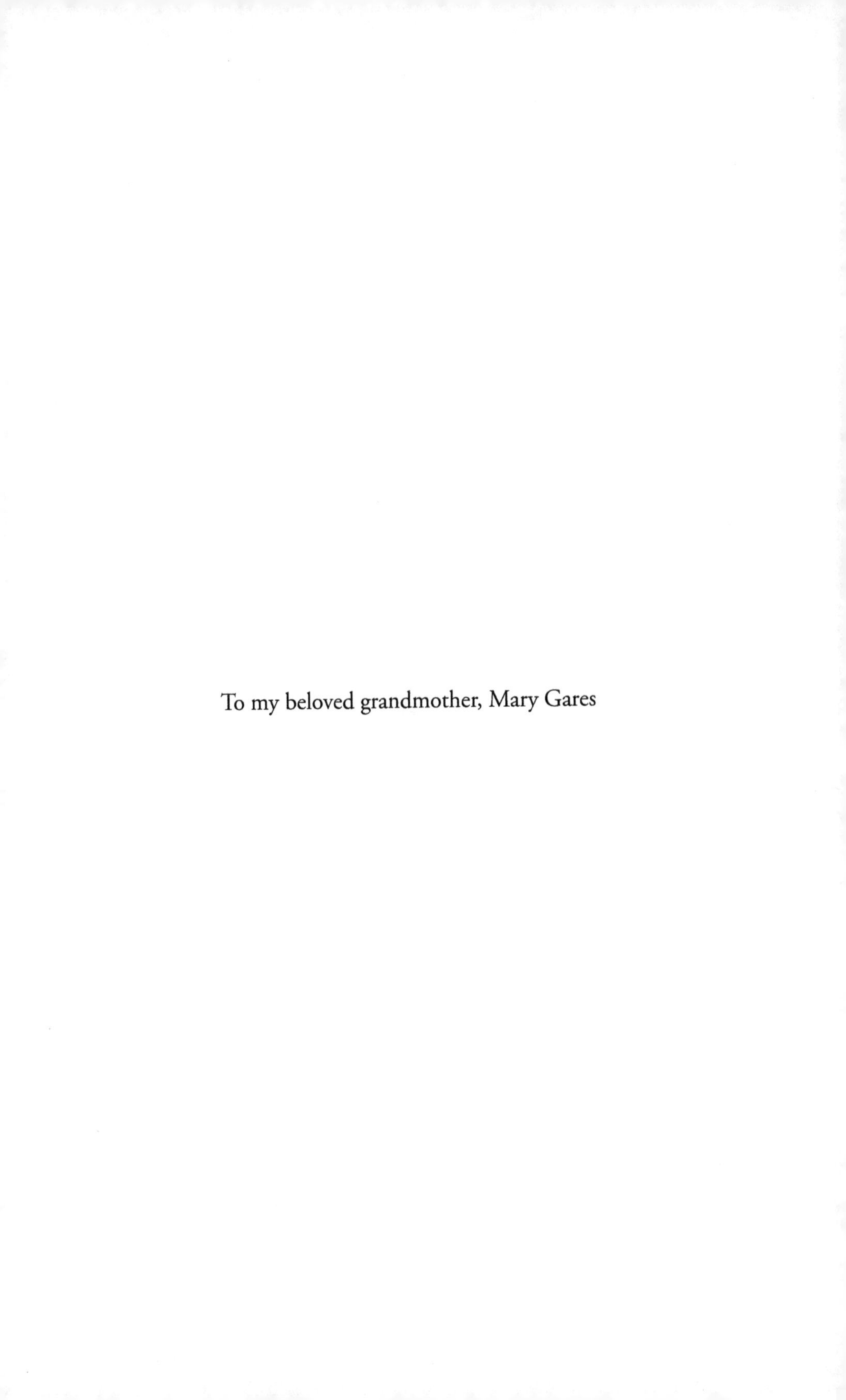

To my beloved grandmother, Mary Gares

It is what I do.
It is what I love.
It is who I am.

✵

Prologue

Somewhere nestled in the recesses of her mind the haunting image of a young man still lingers. Though, now more and more often long-forgotten memories were surfacing, with an exquisite gold ornate engraved bracelet soon becoming her most recurrent remembrance, and she would be transported far away for unknown lapses each time.

It was invariably while Alyssa was relaxing on her tempered glass panel railing cedar deck at the front of her home that she would reminisce about her decision more than fifty years ago. In August of 1966, her choice had seemed ordinary, and she anticipated that their lives would proceed just as they had planned. What had rendered her resolution extraordinary was that over the duration of five decades, Alyssa had never been able to unearth the reason that their assiduous arrangements had become unravelled. She would be the first to acknowledge though, that Susan's prediction had been undeniably correct.

Now in the twilight years of her remarkably healthy lifecycle, could regret be the reason that frequent, albeit vague recollections were struggling to emerge? Or, was Alyssa simply wondering how her life might have unfolded had she chosen the other path, at what she would irrefutably deem her decisive crossroads? Beyond the shadow of a doubt, Alyssa Rainer would be far from the first, and certainly not the last to question, "What if…?"

~ 1 ~

On Sunday, August twenty-eighth, during the almost twelve-hour train ride from Brandon to Saskatoon, Alyssa gave little thought to the outcome of her decision. Throughout her young life, whenever she had initiated a new endeavour she would begin with a carefully devised plan that she would then invariably find the way to bring to fruition. Instead, Alyssa spent most of the time, when she was awake, focussing on what lie ahead, and became increasingly invigorated by anticipation of her future.

Elaine had left Virden two weeks ago. Once she resigned from her position as the senior nurse at the Health Unit, she had returned to St. Laurent for a visit with her aging mother and younger brother. What a stroke of good fortune that 1966 happened to be the year when the Manitoba Department of Public Health was replacing their fleet of vehicles, and had accepted Elaine's offer to purchase the 1960 2-door Ford Falcon sedan she had driven since she had been hired.

Whereas Elaine could drive to Saskatoon within seven or eight hours, Alyssa had yet to graduate from nursing training and could not leave with her. Ever since the vehicular homicide of her older brother, she would no longer travel by bus and elected to purchase a train ticket. It was not long before Alyssa was mesmerized by the rhythmic clicky-clack of the swiftly paced wheels of the train along the railroad track and lulled into reminiscing about her new friend.

As much as she had not been looking forward to staying the last two weeks of April with her mother and three younger sisters in the dismal house where she spent as little time as possible, Alyssa was eager to begin her affiliation at the health unit. She had determined that she was not keen on working in a hospital, and public health nursing could present as an appealing option.

From the moment, Alyssa was introduced to Elaine she experienced a feeling of rapport with the attractive, impeccably dressed woman with the dark black hair, and smiling brown eyes. Her spontaneous offer to join her in the staff room for a cup of coffee of course heightened the warmness of her welcome. Clearly a much more relaxed approach to the work day than on the hospital ward where nurses were expected to hit the floor running as soon as the prerequisite report was finished.

Seated across the table and observing her more closely, Alyssa began to wonder if Elaine was Métis. Her copper-coloured complexion, high cheekbones, and open countenance brought her paternal grandmother to the forefront of her mind. Long before the first day had come to an end, she was convinced that Elaine shared other similar characteristics, specifically her quick tendency to laugh, and her agreeability with her father's adoptive mother.

Alyssa would never forget the day when she had met her paternal grandmother and great-grandmother. She would be nearly seven years old before she ever encountered any person who was not white, although prior to her family's move to Manitoba last winter, she had not been anywhere other than her maternal grandparents' farm, where she had spent almost the first six years of her life, or their current home in Melville. The subsequent summer when her father had decided to take his family to visit his parents in Amaranth, Alyssa's interest was immediately piqued when her mother said, "No damn way. I'm not taking my kids to stay with any filthy Indians."

"What makes you think they're any dirtier than the bloody krauts?" was her father's instant reply, and yet another parental argument was underway. Their quarrels were so frequent, loud, and essentially defined how they spoke to each other most of the time, that Alyssa not only tended to tune them out, but also would leave the house whenever the weather permitted. However, on this occasion although she had stepped out of the kitchen, she remained within earshot.

Who are these Indians, and what are they to my father? Alyssa thought. To the best of her recall, her dad had never spoken about his mother or father, and she was beginning to wonder, in light of her mother's derogatory remark if it was because they were Indians. Yet, he was white. Not at all like the pictures she had seen in books where the men usually had long hair, were brown-skinned, and wore two or more feathers in a headband. Though even as a young girl, Alyssa realized that if her father's parents were Indians, they would hardly be dressed as in the few photos she had seen.

By the day of their departure for Amaranth, her three siblings were as equally excited as Alyssa, although if the truth were told, for dramatically different reasons. Whereas her brother and two sisters were anticipating swimming and playing on the nearby Halls Beach on Lake Manitoba their father had told them about, she was almost beside herself with curiosity about why the Indians were 'dirty.' Once again, her imagination was running wild. Alyssa was envisioning that her father's family lived in a large tepee with a mud floor and could only bathe in the lake during the summer.

Of course, there was no tepee to be found even though at one juncture while her siblings were enjoying the beach, Alyssa set off on a solitary walk around the hamlet of Amaranth in what proved to be a futile search. She then had to reconcile herself by surreptitiously scouring every inch of the small two-bedroom bungalow in pursuit of the elusive dust bunnies, unsightly spills on the floors, dirt piled up in the corners. However, the more Alyssa looked the more she discovered that the small, quaint home was spotlessly clean and impeccably tidy.

Indoor plumbing was not a feature, but then neither was it on her grandfather's farm nor in their current house. The only home where Alyssa had enjoyed the luxury of running water, a flush toilet, and a bathtub was her grandparents' two-bedroom bungalow. Presumably during the winter months, her father's relatives bathed in much the same way as the Rainer family by warming water in receptacles on the top of the kitchen stove, before pouring it into a galvanized iron washtub for the weekly Saturday evening bath. Although the three adults were elderly, every time Alyssa approached them, she could not detect the slightest unpleasant odour.

What she did become aware of though, when speaking with each of them in turn, was the calm, courteous way that they had listened to her, and she began to experience a deep feeling of tranquility, which, in particular surrounded her grandmother and great-grandmother. She had less opportunity to converse with her grandfather, but in the day and a half of their initial stay, never once did she hear a raised angry voice. Their home was not only immaculate, but also peaceful.

Regardless of how long she lived, Alyssa would never understand why her mother had been so pejorative about her father's family. It would be many years later before she realized that on the succeeding four occasions when she had visited her adoptive grandparents, their quiet dignity and warm acceptance had become progressively more apparent.

~ 2 ~

As her two-week affiliation was drawing to a close, Alyssa silently lamented that she would soon be saying good-bye to Elaine. They were returning to the health unit on Thursday afternoon after making three home visits when Elaine said, "Your time with me has just flown by. I've seldom had nursing students come to Virden, but now if I receive requests from others, I'll readily accept them."

"Thank you. I was just thinking about how much I'll miss seeing you when I return to Brandon on Sunday."

"Since our professional relationship is ending, would you like to continue as friends? You must come home on a regular basis, and we could get together for coffee or a meal. As a matter of fact, are you busy on Saturday? My mother is taking the bus tomorrow to visit me for the weekend. She thinks that I don't eat properly, and she's cooking beef stew and bannock for supper. Would you care to join us?"

Chuckling, Elaine continued, "She wanted to bring a jack rabbit for her pot but didn't think the driver would allow her to transport it on the bus. But then, I would have hesitated to ask you because you've probably not eaten wild meat."

"Actually, I have although I didn't know what it was before I had eaten it, or I doubt that I would ever have tasted it. My adoptive grandmother, whom we were meeting for the first time, prepared supper for my family of six. We enjoyed a rich flavourful stew of succulent meat and plentiful garden vegetables, served with bannock. We were all surprised when my Cree grandma revealed that we had just eaten rabbit. To be truthful, the only one who denied it was delicious was my mother. All the way home the next day, she ranted about being tricked by those 'Indians' and she was never consuming any food in that house again. My older brother who had hoped we might get to try different foods could not understand why she was so angry. Yes, I would like to come on Saturday and meet your mother."

"I'm sure if you ever have a free weekend, I could pick you up in Brandon on my way to St. Laurent to visit my mother. She would be delighted to prepare rabbit stew with dumplings for you. And, of course, she would also serve bannock. I doubt that you've ever eaten it fried and dunked in chokecherry syrup."

As Elaine was speaking, Alyssa wondered if she would still be brave enough to try the meat. It might be an entirely different matter to know what she was about to eat, especially since as an adult she was not nearly as adventuresome, or as hungry as when she was a child, although bannock dipped in syrup made her mouth water. On the other hand, she could hardly believe that Elaine was inviting her home for a weekend. "As it happens, I've the May long weekend off, and I don't have any plans."

❋

When Alyssa returned to Brandon following the final affiliation of her three-year training program, she was convinced that she wanted to seek employment as a public health nurse when she graduated. She knew that the hours of work, with no shifts or weekends required, would be a desirable position, and decided not to wait for the career fair before sending off her application to the Manitoba Department of Health.

As the month of May flew past with hospital shifts, review classes, and studying for the State Board Examinations, Alyssa was starting to question whether she could afford the time to go away for three days. If she were honest though, because she had not heard anything from Elaine since she left Virden on the Sunday afternoon at the end of April, she was starting to wonder if the invitation still held. Alyssa always tried to say what she meant and to mean what she said, but she had been burnt too many times by people who extended insincere offers, or made empty gestures.

Just when she convinced herself that Elaine had forgotten her, Alyssa was called to the telephone in the student lounge. "Hi, Alyssa. Can you be ready to leave by noon on Saturday? I've some chores to finish and plan to leave Virden no later than eleven in the morning. It'll take us a little over two hours to reach St. Laurent, and my mother will have supper prepared."

Alyssa was looking forward to meeting Elaine's brother, Samuel, and especially to seeing Rose Hurren again. She recalled how she had become perceptive, only moments after being in the elder woman's presence of an aura of serenity, which enveloped her that was so reminiscent of her adoptive grandmother and great grandmother. Alyssa had always enjoyed visiting with them, but eventually her mother's prejudice won, and without any explanation the family abruptly stopped going to Amaranth before she was eleven years of age.

✵

Seated in the entrance of the residence, Alyssa was peering out the large window of the front door when Susan came rushing down the stairs. "Hi, Alyssa, you didn't mention you were going home for the long weekend, although I must say that I'm surprised since you just spent two weeks with your mother."

"Actually, I'm waiting for the senior nurse from the Virden Public Health Unit to pick me up. I'm spending the weekend with Elaine and her family in St. Laurent, and she's supposed to be arriving shortly."

"You didn't tell me you had plans. Or, come to think of it, that you had made a new friend during your affiliation. My, haven't you become close-lipped, since you usually tell me everything? So, what's going on?"

Glancing at her, Alyssa realized that she was beginning to resent Susan's possessive tendencies toward her. More and more as graduation was approaching, she seemed to think she owned her, but Alyssa knew that she dared not consider this proclivity to be mutual. Though, fortunately before she allowed her mind to twist into a knot she thought, *Since I've told Susan so many times that she was my very first, and will always be my closest friend, her acquisitive characteristics are only natural. And, she has been so good to me.*

Now that Alyssa was gaining confidence and at last learning to trust others, she was ready to forge ahead and develop new friendships. Still, there was something about her budding relationship with Elaine that Alyssa could not yet grasp, which might be the reason she had chosen not to apprise Susan. She could not put her finger on what it was and when reality did strike much later, Alyssa would be taken completely by surprise.

"Sorry, Susan, you know me. Once I start studying for final exams I disappear into my hiding place and bury my head in books. Actually, I was surprised that Elaine suggested we continue to get together when my affiliation came to the end. I liked her, but this weekend will probably be the last time I'll see her for a long time. No doubt you're going home to be with Bryan and your parents."

~ 3 ~

Memories of her paternal grandparents' home flooded her mind when Alyssa stepped over the threshold into the small two-bedroom cottage near the shore of Lake Manitoba in the municipality of St. Laurent. As was her wont, prior to going with Elaine, she initiated research to discover that the municipality was located approximately fifty miles northwest of Winnipeg and had a unique cultural heritage. The region comprised the villages of St. Laurent, home to the highest concentration of residents and services, and Oak Point, both of which were exceedingly popular during the summer because of their beautiful sandy beaches.

The coat of arms of the RM of St. Laurent, bearing the motto Ayangwamisita, a Cree-Ojibwa word meaning "Be safe" and the name of the municipality in French, reflects the community's Métis and Francophone roots in addition to its cultural diversity. It began as a fishing destination when Métis families arrived from Pembina to settle in 1824. The community acquired its name when a missionary, Charles Camper, established the Catholic parish in 1858, and received municipality status in 1882.

And, as the images on the coat of arms revealed, the municipality's cultural, economic, and family life was rich, vibrant, and diverse. The community had historically been known as a place where its habitants could work, play, and raise their family in French, English, and the traditional Michif language. A few short weeks ago when Alyssa had met Elaine's mother, her Métis heritage had been confirmed, and once she completed her study of an area of the province that she had scarcely been aware of, she had a much better appreciation of Elaine's nature.

Rose, as she had soon asked Alyssa to address her, was standing at the open door when they drove onto the gravel drive. "Welcome to my humble home. I hope you don't mind that I am burning three braids of sweetgrass which represent love, peace, and harmony in homage to your visit."

Momentarily rendered speechless, Alyssa recovered enough to say, "Thank you, Mrs. H…Rose. I'm honoured. I remember the first time when I became aware of the sweet scent of one of your sacred plants."

"Please come in and sit. I was just making a pot of sage tea, and wonder if you would like to try it. Traditionally, my ancestors would have offered you another one of our four sacred medicines, tobacco that was first and for everything, but I don't have any in my house. Was it Elaine who introduced you to burning sweetgrass?"

The subsequent two hours seated at the small round table in the tiny kitchen of the cozy abode were the most serene that Alyssa could recollect for a long time. The faint smell of the fresh sweetgrass mingled with the aroma of meat roasting in the oven of the cast iron stove. Shortly after Elaine had joined the other two women, a young man still an adolescent sat down on the fourth chair. He did not interrupt Alyssa's narration about her adoptive Indigenous grandmother and great grandmother listening as attentively as did his mother and sister.

Possibly for the first time in her life, Alyssa had an opportunity to tell someone with any interest that she had been fascinated when she learned that her grandfather had delivered her father and his older brother to the house he shared with the two women. The elderly Caucasian fisherman had apparently found the two pre-adolescent boys in a dugout along a country road, and had taken them to his wife's mother's home where the three adults resided in the village of Amaranth on the other side of Lake Manitoba, the fourteenth largest lake in Canada.

Years ago, during one of their rare family visits when the elderly women were relating the story of how the Creator sent the two boys to them because their home had not been blessed with children, Alyssa's mother had rudely remarked, "Well, I would have been a hell of a lot better off if they had been left in that damn ditch." Both of the Indigenous storytellers had recoiled into silence, the tale came to an immediate end, never again to be broached by them.

"It had been our last trip to see my paternal grandparents, and I always felt saddened that I didn't learn more about what precipitated my father's strange circumstances, until shortly before I left home at seventeen. For whatever reason, he never spoke about his biological parents and why they had abandoned him and James, with the exception of one evening when he had asked me to help him filet the pickerel he purchased in Amaranth for his sporadic fish sales. As unfair as it may sound, ever since I've often speculated that he could not accept responsibility for his additive and erratic behaviour because his parents had deserted him. Yet, he had clearly been loved by the folks who rescued him." During the ensuing silence, as Alyssa basked in the calm, warm acceptance she was experiencing with the Hurren family, she was again confounded by her father's rejection of his adoptive relatives.

Elaine brought her out of her contemplation when she asked, "Alyssa, would you like to stroll down to the shore of the lake?"

Seated together on a large flat rock overlooking the clear water, the two women enjoyed the tranquillity of their surroundings. In a quiet voice, Elaine confided, "I don't know who my father is, and Sam's stayed briefly until my mother was visibly pregnant. Then he too abandoned us, and she raised the two of us alone. Both of her parents died before I was born, and as their only living offspring, she inherited the house. She has a couple of aunts, uncles, and many cousins who fortunately shared food, chopped wood, and did whatever they could to ease her burden. Life was hard, but Sam and I always knew that we were loved."

"We were always poor, although we never needed to be if my father could ever have persisted with any one of his money-making schemes, and then not blown it all on alcohol. I never felt loved by either of my parents, and whenever they were at home together it was like living in a war zone. I've a hunch that the love and tranquility in your home went a long way to compensating for the deprivations you faced being reared by a single parent." Alyssa said.

"You're entirely right. Long before I became an adult, I realized that my mother often went to bed hungry so that Sam and I would have enough to eat. On the subject of which, we should go back and help with supper preparations."

By the time they returned indoors, Sam had just finishing setting the table, and Rose was on the verge of lifting a heavy roasting pan from the oven. "Wait, Mum. I'll carry it over to the table." Elaine offered.

Each of the four resumed the same chair they had previously occupied, bowed their heads as Rose said grace, before she asked Alyssa to pass her plate. It was soon returned to her laden with fluffy dumplings, a variety of vegetables, and a generous serving of succulent scented meat. Alyssa recalled that Elaine had mentioned her mother was going to prepare a rabbit stew for her. Now what could she do? Still, the meal looked and smelled delicious. She could hardly offend this gentle courteous woman who had welcomed her into her home.

She waited until Rose had filled four plates, and placing the last in front of her, sat down at the quiet table. All heads turned toward Alyssa. She sensed that none of them would begin to eat until she had taken her first forkful of food. *Be brave and focus on the flavour, not on what it is*. Alyssa thought. She speared a slice of carrot, placed it into her mouth, and began to chew. It was tasty. She cut off a piece of tender meat, munched on the juicy morsel, and then began to eat in earnest. She soon realized how hungry she was, that the stew was scrumptious, and before long was asking for another serving.

From that moment onwards, Alyssa endeared herself to Rose Hurren. After she helped Elaine with the cleanup, she joined the family in playing their favourite card game. The evening passed all too quickly, as did the weekend. Sam had relinquished his sister's bedroom back to her and was happy to sleep on the couch in the living room.

❄

It was sometime during the early hours of Sunday morning when Alyssa awoke to find Elaine snuggled the full length of her body. She dared not move. Was Elaine cuddling her because she had taken the lion's share of the feather quilt? Alyssa had never felt this excited before, not that she had ever lain in bed with another person's body nestled so near to her. Before she left home to begin nursing training, she shared a double bed with one of her younger sisters, but they slept as far apart as possible so that they seldom touched one another. Now she realized how good it felt to have Elaine huddled close side by side, as if she were seated in her lap. Alyssa found she was too aroused to go back to sleep.

Time elapsed. Elaine changed her position moving onto her right side, and Alyssa slipped stealthily out of the three-quarter bed. She was still tingly all over and would spend most of the day in a trance. Although she drank two cups of coffee before they departed, she remembered little neither of the drive to the St. Laurent Parish nor of the church service. Alyssa did not become more alert until she had consumed a hearty breakfast of scrambled eggs, and fried bannock dipped in chokecherry syrup.

In the late afternoon the two friends were on their way returning to Brandon when Elaine asked, "Have you had any success with your job search?"

"A public health nursing position appears to be out of the question. Not surprisingly with only hours during the day, and every weekend off, there is hardly a registered nurse who isn't seeking such a desirable job. I received a letter of outright rejection from the Manitoba Department of Health, but at least the Province of Saskatchewan recommended that I apply to Saskatoon City Hospital, which is currently hiring new graduates. Also, they'll keep my application on file in the event that an opening becomes available."

Elaine momentarily took her eyes off the road to glance at Alyssa. She hesitantly asked, "Do you think that you'll apply to nurse in Saskatoon?"

"I've already sent my application. My grandmother has a brother in the city, and she will telephone my uncle and aunt to ask if I could stay with them until I find an affordable place to live. My grandma always told me how pretty Saskatoon is with the Saskatchewan River flowing through the city."

When a prolonged silence infiltrated the interior of the car, Alyssa glimpsed at Elaine and waited. At last she responded, "What a coincidence. We were so busy over the weekend I never had a chance to tell you that I've resigned my position at the Virden Health Unit, effective the end of August. I'm beginning my Bachelor of Science in Nursing at the University of Saskatchewan on September 12th. It looks like we both could be in Saskatoon this fall. You'll be working just across the river from where I'm going to school, not more than a fifteen-minute walk apart. I haven't found anywhere to live yet, so what would you think about us sharing an apartment?"

"I had no idea you were leaving public health nursing. I don't suppose that there is any point in re-applying to the Province of Manitoba. Good heavens, what am I thinking? I would go out of my mind living in Virden. Actually, I was planning to look for room and board accommodation, but if you were serious about us living together, I would love to give it a try. As a beginning practicing nurse, my salary will be at the bottom level so the rent would have to be reasonable."

"That suits me just fine. Although I qualified for a bursary from the Métis Nation of Canada, which fully covers my tuition and books, the monthly stipend for all other expenses is barely adequate. Sharing rent and the cost of food would benefit both of us, and with my savings I might not have to look for a part-time nursing position right away. When do you think you'll hear back from City Hospital?"

"Hopefully soon and when I do, I'll let you know. When are you planning to leave for Saskatoon to start looking for an apartment?"

"I've a couple of referrals from the Director of the Nursing Faculty that I'm going to check out when I drive to Saskatoon over the Dominion Day weekend. One of them does have two bedrooms so I'll look at it first. I don't suppose there's any chance you could get another long weekend off. Would you be prepared to have me make the decision?"

"Actually, I'm spending ten days with my friend, Susan, at her aunt's cabin at Clear Lake right after we finish our State Board Examinations on Wednesday afternoon, June 29th."

"What a great way to relax after three gruelling years of nursing training. I'll do my best to find us a suitable place to live together in Saskatoon, if you trust me."

"Of course, I do and as soon as I'm accepted for the position on the surgical ward at City Hospital, my future will be decided. You can't believe how relieved I am that we've settled everything. Thank you, Elaine."

~ 4 ~

A deep feeling of peace permeated Alyssa's soul after Elaine and she had made their definitive plans, and she immediately booked a one-way ticket on the train from Brandon to Saskatoon for the day she was leaving the Nurses' Residence for the final time. She would give any of her personal possessions that she did not want to take to her mother when she returned to Virden the evening after the graduation ceremonies. With a *tabula rasa*, Alyssa Rainer was ready to begin a life of independence and freedom, at last totally liberated from the clutches of her domineering mother.

Then she met Eric. It was on the Friday following her visit to St. Laurent that Barbara had dashed after her at the end of class. "Hey wait up, Alyssa. Are you busy this evening? I was going to ask you this morning, but you didn't come to the cafeteria for breakfast, and I couldn't find you before Mrs. Casselman started the review."

"I'm on the night shift and just grabbed peanut butter and jam on toast for lunch. As soon as it's the supper hour, I'm going to eat and then get some more sleep. I haven't caught up from my weekend off."

"That's too bad. My boyfriend has a ball game at six o'clock, and one of his team asked him if he could arrange a blind date for the evening. I think that you would like him. Eric is attractive, and he's a second year university student at United College in Winnipeg. I know that you prefer men who are intelligent, and there will be hot dogs and fries to munch on during the game."

"Thanks, Barbara, but not this time. I would have to be back here by shortly after ten to get ready for work."

"Surely it doesn't take you that long to get into your uniform. He might meet someone else, and I'm not kidding you, Eric is tall, dark, and handsome. If I weren't going out with Mike, I would date him. At least come to the game and meet him, even if he has to bring you back to the residence early for your night shift."

Alyssa had always enjoyed playing baseball, but was not fond of watching the game, not that she was much of a spectator of any sport. She preferred to learn how to play and then with her competitive nature, typically became skilled at whatever contest was afoot. However, Barbara cajoled her until finally her offer of springing for her supper convinced her. The truth was Alyssa seldom had much in the way of spending money, the reason she usually could not indulge in any fare, and was limited to what was provided in the cafeteria.

The classmates arrived just before the team were walking onto the field to warm up for the game. Barbara quickly called out to the player heading out to the pitcher's mound, "Hi, Mike. We came early hoping you could introduce Eric to my friend, Alyssa, before you start to play."

"Sure. Since he is our catcher, he won't get much practice until I start throwing the ball."

✵

The evening passed all too quickly. Alyssa could not remember watching baseball when it had been so enjoyable. Barbara had been spot-on about Eric. Not only was he easy to gaze upon, but he was also a natural, and when his team reigned victorious, he was selected the player of the game. Although, Barbara had come through with her agreement to purchase her a hot dog, when the fellows suggested they find an A & W, Alyssa realized that after consuming little food all day, she was still hungry.

It was with a sense of relief that not only did Eric have his own car, but he also accepted that they would need to leave before ten o'clock to return to the residence. A teen burger and an order of onion rings that they shared, was just what Alyssa needed to energize her for her shift on the medical ward. She wished that she were back on the surgical floor where most of the patients had an analgesic at bedtime and then slept through the night. With not much more than four hours of sleep this morning before class, she envisioned a long night on medicine with older patients who were generally more restless and awake needing attention.

When Eric asked if he could see her again, Alyssa's mood lightened. She was glad she had decided to go on the blind date. From the moment they had been introduced, she felt there was something special about him. Eric had dark hair, deep brown eyes, and a pronounced copper tone to his skin. What were the odds Alyssa would meet another individual of Métis ancestry within two months, after living almost twenty-one years of her life without encountering individuals, with the exception of her father's adoptive mother and grandmother, who were not Caucasian?

Three evenings later, Eric called, and was perceptively relieved when Alyssa came on the telephone. "Finally, I've been able to get through. I tried all last night, but the line was always busy."

"I'm glad you're persistent. We only have three incoming telephone lines for a residence that houses over a hundred female students, so it's little wonder it took you awhile to place this call. Have you had any more ball games?"

"We did and it seems you picked the best one to attend. The team we played two evenings ago trounced us. But, I suspect you're allowed a very limited amount of time for our call, and I wonder when you have an evening off. Maybe, we could have a bite to eat and then catch an early movie. Mike has suggested that if it could be arranged, we double date with him and Barbara."

Timing was to their advantage. With the State Board Examinations looming, the Class of 1966 had completed all their scheduled shifts on the hospital wards, and were returning fulltime to the classroom for in-depth review of the five major nursing specialties. As gruelling as the next three weeks were no doubt going to be, every student was off on the weekends. Their first evening in the company of Barbara and Mike was enjoyable, although before the women were delivered back to the residence near the curfew hour, Eric had quietly asked if just the two of them could get together on the following Saturday afternoon.

They were no sooner seated in his second-hand 1959 Chevrolet Impala than Eric said, "I don't want you to think that I don't like your classmate, and although Mike is also a university student, he goes to Brandon College, lives at home, and apparently his parents pay his tuition and books. His summer employment is just to earn spending money. However, I have to pay all my costs for university, as well as my living expenses. In fact, I had to work in Northern Manitoba for more than two years before I could start attending United College in Winnipeg. As much as I would like to take you out to nice restaurants and other exciting places, even movies on a regular basis, I'm sorry but I have to save most of my money."

"You don't need to apologize for that. If it were not for my meagre monthly stipend and regular financial support from my cherished grandfather, I wouldn't be able to buy toothpaste. Brandon is a city of beautiful parks. I love nature hikes, especially through old forests, and there is no better place that I like to be than outdoors."

"Hey, that's great and once in awhile, I could even spring for a teen burger. The other thing I need to mention is that I'm studying to rewrite two courses I failed at the end of my year, so it sounds like we both will have a busy summer. Still, I'd like to see you as much as possible, if that's okay with you."

❋

Often on the weekend Eric drove six miles south of the city, and they strolled along a variety of pathways in the "Blue Hills of Brandon," so nicknamed because of their distinctive colour seen from a distance in the summer time. Alyssa was delighted with the trail system through the gentle rolling hills and aspen-oak parkland in the beautiful forested area, although it was soon apparent that she was far more enamoured with hiking than Eric. Nonetheless, the moderate slopes were conducive to conversations, and the more he was getting to know Alyssa, all the while careful not to reveal his escalating feelings to her, the more he was becoming convinced that she was the woman for him.

Just weeks after they started dating, Eric invited Alyssa to drive to Oakville to meet his parents. His invitation followed right on the heels of Susan's suggestion that she ask Eric to drive to Clear Lake to spend the first Sunday of the classmates' ten-day vacation with them, and her fiancé, Bryan. Before long, Alyssa began to sense her relationship with Eric was progressing far too quickly, and began to feel so pressured that she needed to step back to contemplate where it was potentially leading.

Finally, she did acquiesce to Eric's repeated requests that they spend a weekend with his parents. Alyssa liked him, much more than any of the other men she had dated over the past three years. She had entered nursing training vowing that she planned to be a career woman with no intentions of ever marrying, not after being a reluctant witness to her parents' marriage from hell. During her first year when Judy's cousin proposed, she tried to be gracious in her refusal of Kerry before she bolted. Then, began a spree of double dates arranged by one classmate or another, but the minute any of the men started to become serious, Alyssa promptly ended the relationship. On the other hand, could she be reading too much into Eric's invite? After all, he had yet to complete his second year of university.

The weekend passed without a hitch. Alyssa was warmly received, and the most notable characteristic she observed had been that there was a lot of laughter. Then less than three weeks later while exploring another picturesque trail through the blue hills, Eric said, "Could we sit down on this knoll and enjoy the scenery for a few minutes."

Alyssa was reaching her stride and was hesitant to lose her momentum until glancing at Eric, she noticed the earnest expression on his handsome countenance. Had something happened to him? Although he mentioned that he was not keen on climbing, the slope they had chosen this afternoon was nothing if not gentle. It occurred to her that the sooner she discovered what his issue was, the quicker she could determine where this particular path would take them.

"Are you okay? Surely with all your baseball this elevation is hardly winding you, and I've a sense that this pathway goes through an old forest. My, you do look serious."

The minute she settled down on the grass beside him, Eric gazed intently into her eyes before saying, "If I don't ask you here and now I know I'll lose my nerve. Alyssa, will you marry me?"

~5~

The world became silent. The breeze ceased to stir. Songbirds no longer chirped. Time stood still. She felt like she was plummeting into a void. Alyssa could neither hear nor speak. It was as though she had slipped through an aperture. She knew not where she was, and she was afraid.

Finally, she became aware of Eric grasping her shoulders. "I didn't mean to upset you. Alyssa, can you answer me please? I've never seen anyone behave like this. Are you okay?"

Giving her head a vigorous shake, blinking her eyes while looking around her, Alyssa slowly regained her awareness. "What did you say, Eric? Here we are outdoors on a beautiful day enjoying a hike along a scenic trail, and out of the blue, did you ask me to marry you? I've hardly known you for two months. Is this your idea of a prank? If you hadn't been so solemn, I would have laughed. Instead, I found myself in some place that I had never been before."

"I'm sorry. I thought you would have had a pretty good idea when I took you home to meet my parents and sisters."

In truth, Alyssa had had an intuitive feeling, but as she most often did, she had chosen to ignore it. Perhaps if she had not, she would have given herself time to reflect about her response. At last she replied, "We scarcely know anything about each other. I've yet to reach the age of twenty-one, and I haven't graduated or started my career. I grew up in a highly dysfunctional family, my mother was a tyrant, my parents had an acrimonious divorce, and I can hardly wait to begin a life of autonomy and freedom. I've repeatedly vowed that I was never planning to get married. I'm sorry for my behaviour. My utter surprise must have put me into shock. Even I'm astounded by the magnitude of my unusual reaction. Could you please drive me back home? I need to be alone and to regain my equanimity"

✵

Neither spoke another word until Eric was nearing the nurses' residence. "Does this mean you don't want to see me again?"

Choosing her words carefully, Alyssa said, "I think that we both need some time and space. I can't help wondering if your proposal was little more than a spur of the moment request prompted by the beauty and tranquillity of our surroundings. Although I don't want to speak for you, Eric, I don't think that either of us is in any position to get married right now. I know that even if I should agree to become your wife, it would be at least a couple of years in the future. I've had very little autonomy in my life, and as soon as I graduate, I plan to exercise the freedom and independence of making my own choices, which I've never been allowed to do." At the final moment, she stopped herself from adding what she was also thinking, *And, the last thing that I intend is to have a man tell me what to do.*

Meanwhile, Eric had stopped paying attention after Alyssa's comment about where they were, instead reflecting, *It had nothing to do with the peacefulness of our environment, and everything with what a perfect place it would have been to make love to you.*

"Hey, are you listening to me?" Why don't we wait and get together next Saturday? The last three weeks of August are going to be full of grad events, and I would still like you to be my escort, as we had planned."

"So, in the meantime you just want a date for all your outings, is that it?"

"My upcoming activities will give us time and opportunity to get to know each other better, how we both interact in social settings, and an awareness of our relationships with others. You have to admit that other than your ball games, we've been solitary during the occasions we have been seeing one another. Thanks for driving me back. I'll be on the front stairs at one o'clock next Saturday."

Alyssa made a quick exit from the car. She sensed that Eric was lingering, almost as though he wanted to start an argument and put her on the defensive. She was insightful enough to realize that if she became emotional, she might well react and say something that she would later regret. Once she was inside the residence, she waited at the door for five or six minutes before partially opening it to ascertain that Eric had driven away.

Although she had qualms about whether she would ever see Eric again, she had to get outdoors. She must commune with nature, preferably amongst trees, tall ones if she could find any. Alyssa needed to cogitate upon what had happened to her on the crest of the hillock, to try and put it into perspective, and to fathom a possible meaning of the strange occurrence. It had been eerie, but yet in a way there had been something revealing about it.

Never before had Alyssa experienced anything so bizarre. Nor, at the same time had she ever felt such an ungrounded fear. Had she had a seizure and momentarily lost consciousness? Was there something wrong with her that had caused her to be panicky? She could arrange for one of the physicians at the hospital to examine her. But what would she say to him? How could she describe her responses, other than that she had acted like a fool? Because that is what she was now thinking, and furthermore she would not be at all surprised if Eric had come to precisely the same conclusion.

After wandering about a large nature park several blocks from the hospital for the better part of three hours, Alyssa was no closer to answering her questions. She did though, feel much better, and began to wonder why she was focusing on an issue over a seemingly short lapse of consciousness that had never occurred before and hoped would not again. Perhaps, she should focus less on what had given rise to her odd behaviour, and ruminate about how she felt regarding Eric's precipitate proposal.

It took only a few moments for Alyssa to wish that he had not asked her to marry him. She liked Eric, maybe loved him, if she even knew what it felt like to love a man, but not now. Not just when she was on the brink of becoming her own person. She might come to relent on her oft-stated adolescent vow to remain single and pursue a lifetime career, especially if her budding feelings for Eric did indeed progress to a deep abiding love. Alyssa was reassured when she mused that for centuries it had been said 'absence makes the heart grow fonder,' and if she were hired by City Hospital in Saskatoon, their affection for each other might well be confirmed.

At any rate, Alyssa would have to wait and see if Eric returned next Saturday. She hoped that he would, both for pragmatic reasons – it could be a little late to find another date for all her graduation activities – and for future possibilities. But enough pondering, the day was waning and she should start back to the hospital, and determine what the cafeteria had to offer for her evening meal, since there was not even a teen burger on the horizon.

~6~

The level of excitement was escalating at the beginning of August, the final month of the three years of nursing training. On a late Saturday afternoon the residence was virtually empty. Not expecting to find anyone to join her for dinner, Alyssa had just entered the connecting tunnel to the hospital when she heard footsteps ahead, but could not see who it was. "Hey, wait up. If you're on your way to the cafeteria, we could eat together."

Stopping and turning around, Susan was pleasantly surprised. "What are you doing back so early, Alyssa? I thought you were spending the evening with Eric?"

"I was on the verge of asking you the same thing. What happened to your plans with Bryan?"

"His father was rushed to the Melita Hospital after falling off the roof, and his mother telephoned to ask Bryan to come home. I'll be glad when we'll be living in Winnipeg so she can't expect him to be available at a moment's notice. Of course, he wanted me to go with him, but since I've seen him every evening this past week, I thought I would enjoy some time to myself. Where's Eric? Since you two only tend to get together once or twice a week, I hardly expected to see you."

"I'm starving, so let's have something to eat first."

Later when the two friends were seated on a bench in the small park adjacent to the hospital grounds, Susan had reached the end of her patience. "Tell me, what's going on? Have you and Eric had a falling-out?"

"I'm not sure that I would call it a quarrel. We were walking along a different trail in the blue hills when Eric wanted me to sit down with him for a few minutes. Then he quite literally blew me away by proposing marriage. After hours of walking alone this afternoon, I concluded that his impetuousness could be nothing more than a flight of fancy."

"How did you answer – yes or no? I'm dying to know."

"I didn't respond in either the negative or the affirmative. Instead, I asked him to return me to the residence."

A sudden stillness descended upon the women. A slight breeze rustling through the nearby popular trees was cooling the blistering summer air, birds were chirping, squirrels were squeaking, but they sat silent. After nearly two years of working interminably to gain Alyssa's trust and become her friend, Susan was only too aware of the predicament that Eric's impulsive proposal would have created for her.

"Wow. I can imagine your response. On the few occasions I've seen you two in each other's presence, you both look like you enjoy the other's company, especially that Sunday at Clear Lake. To be perfectly frank, I have the impression that Eric is smitten with you, and I've also noticed you seem to be infatuated with him. But marriage? Heavens above, it took you the better part of two years to accept that I truly cared about you. How long is it since you met Eric?"

Suddenly remembering her peculiar reaction, Alyssa thought, *Actually, I doubt that you have the slightest idea how Eric's proposal affected me since I am nowhere near figuring out what transpired. And, although you're my closest friend, I'll never tell you, or for that matter, anyone else. It was far too idiosyncratic to ever verbalize.* Rather she said, "Precisely my point. We've only known one another for a little more than two months. As well, the minute I hear from City Hospital, I'm on the telephone to Elaine to confirm that we'll be sharing an apartment in Saskatoon."

"When were you going to tell me? The last I knew was that Judy, you, and I were on our way to Winnipeg. It doesn't sound like you were successful in getting a public health nursing position in Saskatchewan either, so why didn't you just apply to hospitals in Winnipeg, instead of Saskatoon? What has come over you since you met that senior nurse?"

"What are you implying? Elaine asked me to consider sharing accommodations, not go steady. To my mind, that's a quantum leap. Perhaps, you could enlighten me regarding your thoughts."

Susan knew only too well that when Alyssa became haughty in her manner of speaking, it was time to back off. Also, she was acutely aware she could never win if they became engaged in word games. And, the absolute last thing that she had any intentions of doing, during the final month they seemingly would have together, was to embroil Alyssa in an argument. Susan was not only feeling annoyed that Alyssa had not discussed her change of plans with her, but also her resentment toward this new friend had increased considerably.

Reaching over to fondly place her hand on Alyssa's arm, Susan said, "I'm hurt that you haven't let me know you're not coming to Winnipeg. But, enough about me. Do you have any idea what's going to happen with you and Eric – are you still dating, or did you two break-up?"

"Your guess is as good as mine, and we'll likely both have to wait until one o'clock next Saturday."

"Well, if Eric does show up, I think that one of the things you need to do, if you're to have any hope of determining your true feelings for each other, is to spend more time together. Given that you have less than one month before you go your separate ways, once a week just doesn't cut it. My aunt is having a garden party next Sunday. I'll ask her if Eric and you can join Bryan and me."

~7~

Shortly before one o'clock, Alyssa looked up from her novel just as the old green Chevy turned into the driveway. When he stopped, Eric reached across the front seat to swing open the door for Alyssa. "Hey, I'm right on time. I was worried I might be late, because there was a section I wanted to finish studying. I tried telephoning, but as always it was impossible to get through. How was your week?"

"Hi, Eric. My week was surprisingly busy. It's funny how we thought that with exams over, we would be able to relax and enjoy some free time, but we're busy with a plethora of graduation activities. I'm glad you're making those two supplementary examinations a priority, even though it must be difficult with working fulltime and your hectic baseball schedule."

"On the subject of baseball, I've a game at seven o'clock, and I wonder if you want to come and watch. Maybe, we can grab a hot dog and coke at the stadium before I begin to play."

When Eric turned onto the highway toward the blue hills, Alyssa was on the verge of suggesting that they find a different trail than the one they had started last Saturday. However, he drove past the trailheads and continued on a sparsely gravelled road that looked as though they would encounter little traffic. Reaching an encircling grove of popular trees, Eric brought the car to a stop.

"Where are we? I don't see any hiking paths around here."

"Could we just sit on the grass for a while and visit? We never seem to take any time to talk and get to know each other better. In a month you'll be a registered nurse, and I would like to have some idea of what you're planning to do."

As much as Eric was accurate about them seldom being sedentary to converse, Alyssa was instantly concerned that he wanted to revisit the subject of marriage. Still, if she outlined that she was relocating to Saskatoon to become a surgical nurse at City Hospital, he would have a more complete understanding of her personal aspirations. "Okay, but I want to go for at least an hour or two walk before your game."

They were under the shelter of the trees when Eric moved closer toward Alyssa and began to kiss her. Pulling back she said, "Is this your characteristic prelude to conversation, or have you hoodwinked me?"

"Oh, I thought you rather liked that." Eric replied as he reached for her again and positioned her on his lap. His kisses became more ardent, and his lips were soon on her neck with his hands touching her breasts as he lifted her light t-shirt. Before she could stop him, his right hand had slipped down the front of her shorts and underpants. Within minutes Eric had surpassed Alyssa's limit of necking and petting with any man. To her consternation, she was very much enjoying the sensations he had so readily aroused. Her body was soon coursing with desire. She might be inexperienced, but Alyssa knew only too well where this situation could lead. She had to stop him.

With all the strength she could muster in both her arms, Alyssa pushed Eric away, immediately stood up, and walked briskly toward the road. Struggling to his feet Eric called after her, "I'm sorry. I got carried away. Please stop. I never had any intention of going all the way. Please believe me. You just looked so sexy I couldn't help myself. I promise I won't pull such a stunt again."

"Please drive me to one of the hiking trails."

Once back in the car, Eric was subdued as Alyssa searched for a trailhead parking lot with a number of vehicles. "Pull in here. You can wait while I go for a hike. I'll be back in an hour. You can use that time to think about your devious behaviour. I intend to assess if there is any hope or purpose in continuing to pursue a relationship with you."

In the end, Alyssa walked for the better part of two hours. She was banking on the premise that if Eric had decided to leave her, there would be other hikers still in the hills to give her a lift, at least back to the outskirts of Brandon where she could catch a bus. She recognized that she was taking quite a risk, but she needed to evaluate that should Eric have waited, how contrite he was about his deception. The slightest indication of insouciance and they were done.

She was furious. He seemed like a decent guy, but she had been totally unprepared for the swiftness of his advances. His knowledge of the isolated destination suggested that he had been to the location before, and if he had indeed scouted the area, he planned his deceitful behaviour. Did he think that she was a brazen woman, ready to engage in wanton activities with just any man? Or, had he been confident that his marriage proposal would pave the way for him to take advantage of her? If that were the case, his lack of remorse would reveal not only his insincerity, but also his duplicity.

More than an hour had passed and Alyssa had scarcely been aware that she was walking, never mind enjoying the ambiance of the nature trail. But, she had to regain a modicum of her equanimity before she returned to the car. She was also disappointed. She usually was a good judge of character and in addition to liking Eric, she considered him to be reputable. Over the initial two months of their relationship, he had given her every indication that he was honest, hardworking, and responsible. What had come over him?

On the other hand, Alyssa had to admit that not only did she have no experience, but also her knowledge of human sexuality was seriously deficient. She had not needed any of her classmates to remark how incredibly naïve she was. She was acutely aware that other than what had occurred between the animals on the farm – hardly an appropriate exemplar – and scenes from romantic movies, Alyssa was completely in the dark about the act of coupling. Could Eric's sexual overtures simply have been a natural manifestation of his feelings for her?

A flicker of memory flashed through her mind of something she had once read that for many men the act of lovemaking was often their way of expressing affection. For a man, love meant meeting a woman's desires and having his needs met as well. Regardless of whether it was true, the sad reality is that it was always, and many times alone, the woman who had to bear the brunt of the ultimate consequence of copulation.

Alyssa had been almost eight years old when her youngest sister was born. She had first asked her mother, then when she was unresponsive, her grandmother where babies came from, and how long it took for one to arrive. About the only piece of information that she had ever been able to glean was that they usually appeared within a period of nine months. Then, knowing the date of her parents' anniversary and also of her older brother's birthday, Alyssa had readily calculated that her mother was with child some months before she married.

Suddenly an unforgettable scene near the end of her first year of nursing training surfaced before her eyes. It had been a Sunday afternoon and

Stephen, a nice young beau had invited her for a drive in the country. Time had slipped by when Alyssa realized they were approaching the Town of Virden where her mother and sisters lived. Against her better judgement, she agreed to stop for a brief visit. The minute they entered the house her mother had yelled, "What are you doing here? Who the hell is he? I'm not sending you to Brandon so you can get knocked up and be saddled with an illegitimate brat for the rest of your life."

Her embarrassing behaviour was no surprise to Alyssa, but it had brought a rapid end to her relationship with Stephen. By the time Alyssa had entered high school, she knew beyond the shadow of a doubt that her mother did not trust her. She had never been allowed to date, or even to attend any of the extracurricular activities during the three years of her secondary schooling. Little did her domineering mother know though, that when she reached puberty, Alyssa had vowed she would wait until she was married before engaging in sexual relations with any man. The world would have to come to an end before Alyssa Rainer would ever duplicate the same mistake as her mother and ruin her life.

As soon as she could see the parking lot Alyssa noticed that Eric's car was still there, although he was no longer seated in it. Glancing around she observed someone seated under the boughs of a tall conifer. Scrutinizing the figure in more detail, she could not honestly recall that she had ever before seen anyone looking quite so dejected and forlorn. Slowly approaching Eric, Alyssa quietly said, "Thank you for waiting. Time slipped away. I know that I'm much later than I planned to be."

"I wouldn't have blamed you if you had found a ride to the residence with someone else. I'm so sorry. I'll drive you back right now."

"Wait a minute. It's perfectly clear to me that your remorse is genuine, Eric, and I accept your apology. I believe that you'll keep your promise, so let's start over and enjoy the ball game on this beautiful day."

If Alyssa were being honest, a significant aspect of her decision to continue dating Eric was practical. The last month of training was chock-full of social functions and she certainly wanted an escort, especially a handsome one, who with the exception of earlier today had been courteous and fun. Also, she sensed Susan was very keen on her courting Eric, as she may have intuited that Alyssa had deeper feelings for him than she had had for most of the other men she dated over the past three years. As well, Alyssa did not relish returning to the residence and telling Susan that she was bowing out of her aunt's garden party.

The balance of their date passed without incident. Rather than eat at the stadium before the game, Eric suggested that they dine at the A&W where they would have comfortable chairs in an air-conditioned restaurant. Not wanting to appear too anxious to forgive and forget, Alyssa waited until after the game on their way back to the residence to ask Eric about double dating with Susan and Bryan tomorrow afternoon.

Eric could hardly believe his ears and quickly said, "Sure. What time do you want me to come for you?"

"Susan mentioned her Aunt Francis was expecting a lot of guests, and suggested the four of us arrive in one vehicle to minimize the amount of traffic vying for parking. Bryan will pick you up around one o'clock."

Sunday afternoon was gorgeous with radiant sunshine and a northerly breeze blowing through the towering conifers strategically situated around Francis' spacious backyard garden, making the day very pleasant. Twenty to thirty people were gathered on the lush verdant lawn near the tables overflowing with finger foods, punch bowls, soft drinks in ice buckets, and kegs of draft beer. While mingling with her guests, Francis kept an eye out for her niece. She was particularly eager to see Alyssa, Susan's friend who had spent a week with her at Clear Lake for the past two summers.

To Francis' surprise, as much because of the lateness of the hour as by her request, Susan had telephoned last evening to ask if she could bring Alyssa and her boyfriend with her and Bryan today. Several weeks had passed since Francis extended the invitation to her niece, and now she wondered why she had waited until literally the eleventh hour to express her entreaty, especially when she suggested that she bring some of her classmates Susan had adamantly refused.

✵

That afternoon when they arrived at Eric's boarding house, he climbed into the backseat of Bryan's Ford Mustang and whispered to Alyssa, "I should have brought my own car. What if we want to leave early and have some time to ourselves before your curfew?"

"Hush, don't be ungrateful. Besides, I thought that you would like this cosy seating arrangement?"

Initially the foursome stayed together chatting about the beauty of the garden, the number of people, and the spread of snacks and drinks. When the conversation turned to the excitement of the upcoming graduation events, the guys drifted away. Bryan was planning on getting to know Eric because they were likely to be spending considerable time in each other's company during the next three weeks. Whenever he tried to engage Eric in small talk, he readily agreed before once again gravitating to the food tables and especially to the kegs of beer.

At first Bryan joined him in consuming a healthy portion of the appetizers and alcohol, until he began to consider maybe Eric had not had a chance to eat anything yet that day. Soon though, it was the quantity of beer he was drinking that began to alarm Bryan. The heat of the afternoon was blistering, the beer refreshing, but as the hours passed the thought that kept flitting through his mind was, *Wow, I'm glad that this guy didn't drive his own vehicle here.*

Finally with hesitation, Bryan went in search of Susan intending to apprise her of the situation. Alyssa was talking to Francis, and he stealthily pulled Susan aside. They agreed to remove Eric surreptitiously. The ruse was that Eric was feeling lightheaded and wanted to go home. Susan found Alyssa. Together, they thanked her Aunt Francis while Bryan told Eric they were leaving.

As they had pre-arranged, Susan got into the backseat with Alyssa while Bryan directed Eric into the passenger seat in the front of the car and then locked the door. Once they arrived at Eric's place of residence, Bryan planned to escort him right to his room and put him to bed to sleep off his overindulgence. If Alyssa was aware of how inebriated Eric was, she did not give the slightest indication. For once since Susan had met Alyssa, she appreciated the extent of her close friend's naiveté.

~ 8 ~

The month of August became a blur. When the Faculty of Nursing did not have a celebratory event planned for a particular afternoon or evening, it was as though Bonnie considered it her moral obligation to organize a class party, whether or not her parents were away from home. Then she was adamant that as many as possible of her closer friends be in attendance. Most likely, had it not been for Susan, Alyssa would not have been invited, and if anyone had ever thought to ask Eric, he would have been quick to identify that his preference was not to go.

Eric was only too aware that his time with Alyssa was running out. From the moment they met, he had been captivated with her and knew that she was the woman with whom he wanted to spend the rest of his life. Although, following her weird reaction when he asked her to marry him, he realized that he had been much too hasty. Two months of dating was clearly not long enough time to determine if he was the man for her. But, what else could he have done, particularly now that she had mentioned she was leaving for Saskatoon within the month?

One way or another Eric simply had to ask Alyssa again. He was practical enough to recognize that he would need, at the very least, to complete his Bachelor of Arts degree, and find employment before he would be in any kind of financial position to support a wife. After he was introduced to Alyssa, his motivation to study and pass the two supplemental examinations had increased exponentially. It became perfectly clear that his only option was to be starting his third and final year at United College in Winnipeg come September.

For the briefest period of time, Eric wondered if only he had been a better student, he could have transferred to the University of Saskatchewan. However, he was soon chiding himself for being so unrealistic – how could he ever have afforded such a major move, and would Alyssa have freaked out once more with another of his impulsive decisions? On the other hand, Eric was beginning to realize Susan liked him, and maybe even thought that he might be a good match for Alyssa. Why else was she keen on them always double dating with her and Bryan?

What if he played along, could he eventually convince Susan to become more of an ally? To be honest, Eric had expected that as the repercussion of his behaviour at her aunt's party, she would hardly want to go out with him and Alyssa again. Yet, no one had made any comment and Susan kept insisting that they join her and Bryan, although thereafter Eric asserted that he would drive his own car. He was not fussed about Bonnie's parties, but he had to admit that the food and beer were plentiful, and before long he developed the habit of whisking Alyssa away early enough that they would have ample private time before her curfew.

While Eric was soon congratulating himself on the economy of their entertainment, Alyssa was alarmed by the increasing intensity of their necking and petting. She was aware that Eric usually consumed two or three bottles of beer, but since she did not drink alcohol, she was confident she could maintain control. What she had not counted on was that with his amorous advances, she was becoming as aroused as he. Before long every evening became a struggle to avoid sexual relations. Alyssa began to think that the end of August could not come soon enough.

❋

The weekend before graduation, Eric said, "Let's drive to Oakville and visit my folks. We could leave on Friday right after I finish work."

Alyssa instantly responded, "The Class of 1966 are having a graduates-only barbeque that evening, and I've no intention of missing our last all-girl get together."

"Well, can we go on Saturday then? Every evening next week, I plan to be very busy cramming for my exams."

Alyssa was on the verge of saying that the next ten days were also extremely hectic for her, but then the thought occurred to her, *Why not? At least at your parents, I won't have to fend off your advances.*

"Okay, as long as we don't have to be on the road before noon. Our instructors have extended our curfew until midnight, and I plan to sleep late. If we go Dutch, maybe we could grab brunch before we leave?"

It was a sweltering afternoon by the time they were on their way, although with all the windows rolled down the breeze kept them comfortable. Now that they were going to Eric's parents' farm, Alyssa was glad to get out of the city. Ever since that Saturday afternoon when Eric had first become passionate with her, they had not returned to the Brandon Hills. She wondered whether it was because they had such a plethora of social functions, or that she was hesitant about being so alone with him. At any rate, Alyssa was missing the country and began to anticipate the chance to commune with nature.

They had no sooner arrived and expressed their salutations to his mother and father than Eric said, "Why don't we head out for a walk to Ma's garden and pick any remaining raspberries left on the brambles?" Not for the first time since Eric arrived at the residence, Alyssa thought that he was being more focused than was typical, and she was becoming increasingly skeptical about his motives. Still, she enjoyed eating fruit from the vines and away they went.

The ripe raspberries were plentiful, and Alyssa even found succulent strawberries in the adjacent patch. Before long however, Eric was suggesting they stroll along the grassy roadside, until they would come to a small pasture that had not been cultivated. The notion of being in a meadow alone with him again raised Alyssa's suspicions to the point of unnerving her. Was she being paranoid, or did Eric seem to be even more determined about having his way with her? At least, he had not had any beer today, which she often considered loosened his inhibitions.

Sensing her hesitation, Eric said, "There is a shady grove of poplars, and I just want to get out of the sun for a few minutes before we return to the house, okay?"

What could she say without revealing her heightened apprehension about his intentions? Alyssa was becoming overwhelmingly torn between her feelings for Eric, and breaking her oath of abstinence before she was a married woman. For her such self-restraint was the only proven way to prevent pregnancy, and even love could not eradicate her morbid fear of having a baby prematurely, or worse, out of wedlock. And, Alyssa no longer trusted that either she or Eric would be able to exercise enough control to stop in time.

A patch of grass in front of the tall trees was a comfortable place to rest, and when he had convinced Alyssa to be seated, Eric kneeled beside her and said, "I love you, Alyssa, and I want you to be my wife. Will you marry me?"

Although Alyssa was not expecting a second proposal, fortunately on this occasion she did not experience as drastic an outcome as she had during Eric's first request. Still, she was silent for several minutes before she responded, "Over the past month, I've come to love you, Eric, but I have not changed my mind about answering your question at this time. Neither of us is in the slightest financial position to get married, and to rush into such a significant lifetime decision under our existing circumstances would surely result in disaster. And, if you're entertaining any thoughts that I could support us until you establish a career, it is not going to happen. In addition to working fulltime, I intent to take university evening classes to begin studying for my Bachelor of Nursing degree. Did you hear any of my comments about not getting married for, at best two or three years?"

"I heard all of it, but I just can't help how much I want you." Eric replied reaching to take Alyssa into his arms. But, she was too quick for him rising to her feet and walking rapidly back to the road. She continued until she had returned to the safety of the yard. Glancing behind her, she was glad to see that Eric had not followed her. She needed to be alone and try to regain her composure. She could not ever remember feeling so wretched. Why had she come? If only she knew Eric's mother better, as uncharacteristic as it would be, she might have been tempted to cry on her shoulder. Instead, Alyssa sat down on a tree stump on the side of the house in the shade.

After a hasty supper with his parents, they returned to Brandon. Neither said a word. A single thought kept coursing through her mind, *How I can overcome my abject desolation one week before graduation, the day of freedom that I have been striving for my entire life, is beyond my comprehension*? By the time they were nearing McTavish Avenue though, Alyssa realized if they were going to say another word to one another, she would need to initiate the conversation.

"I'm sorry I ruined your visit with your parents. I've little doubt that I'm afraid of making a commitment to you, Eric, but I need time to resolve several profound issues from my abusive upbringing, and the abysmal model of marriage between my parents. You may choose to consider that I'm being selfish, but my struggling to achieve independence and self-actualization is real. I think that one of my more notable attributes is loyalty, and before I consent to marry you, I want to be confident that I can honour the well-known phrase from the marriage liturgy, "Till Death Us Do Part." Does my reasoning make any sense to you?"

"Wow, I had no idea that you thought about things so deeply."

"And, that is precisely why we need much more time to learn about and accept each other – our beliefs, expectations, hopes, and dreams. I've always been serious and responsible, and it is highly improbable that I'm going to suddenly change drastically and view life from a frivolous perspective now."

"Will we see one another again? I know that I've been coming on strong, but we only have a little more than a week before you move to Saskatoon. I really want to marry you."

"Good heavens, Eric. I'm not going to the end of the world. The actual distance between Winnipeg and Saskatoon is less than five hundred miles. Since I'll be earning a monthly salary, I could save money for the bus trip that takes about twelve hours, and I'm sure if I ask Susan about staying with her and Bryan, they'll give me a place to sleep. Creating opportunities to see each other will hardly be insurmountable."

"But it's been great being together every evening this past month. That's what I'll miss when you're gone."

"Well, this upcoming week will give you an idea of what spending less time together will feel like come September. Our instructors have advised us that we're going to be very busy with final classes, cleaning out our rooms and lockers, packing all our belongings, rehearsals, and last minute preparations for graduation, and we are not to plan a host of social activities."

"Will I see you tomorrow, and am I still going to your graduation next Saturday?"

"Of course, you're my date for the afternoon ceremony and our celebratory dinner. On Sunday though, I'm going to begin going through my things, but I'll telephone you if I'm available."

~ 9 ~

When Alyssa was inside, she rested her back against the heavy door and breathed a sigh, although she was not sure whether it was of relief or of hope. She had no idea how long she leaned against the aperture through which no one entered or left. The residence was like a mausoleum, and she realized that if she started her chores this evening, she could make great strides toward completing them. But, she was not in the mood. Since she had a book in her purse, she decided to sit on the bench in the treed park across the street and read before the light of day began to wane.

Though, once she was comfortable Alyssa never opened her current novel. Her mind was racing with questions and self-recriminations regarding her lack of preparedness that Eric might ask her to marry him again. During the past month, had she so thoroughly convinced herself that his initial proposal had been expressed, quite literally in the heat of the moment, with little likelihood of it being repeated? Was Eric's approach nothing more than a carrot dangled in front of her to entice her to engage in sexual relations?

How Alyssa wished that she were not so incredibly naïve. If her mother had not forbid her to date before she had left home, beyond a doubt she would have been more aware not only of male sexuality, but also of her own. Over the last three years she had certainly done her share of dating, albeit most of her socialization was with the groups of students who accepted the frequent invitations by bus to the Air Force base in Rivers, or the Army in Shilo. They were always treated with the greatest of respect, and entertained royally in the respective Officers' Club with fine dining and ballroom dancing. Individual encounters beyond the officers' facility were prohibited, and unobtrusive chaperones were always in attendance.

During her first year of training, Alyssa had only gone on single dates with Kerry, who invariably invited her to his home for family dinners, and Stephen whose courting came to a sudden end after the brief dreadful meeting with her mother. However, it was subsequent to a Friday evening house party at Bonnie's that Alyssa would learn her most perilous lesson about dating.

The next day she had received a telephone call inviting her to a matinee movie on Sunday afternoon followed by dinner at the Royal Oak Inn's Echo Restaurant. Alyssa could not recall the man who extended the invitation and was on the verge of refusing. Daniel assured her that he was an old friend of Bonnie's family, and he would be certain to have her back to the residence hours before her curfew.

On this occasion Alyssa did not heed her intuition, although by the end of the precarious day, she had vowed never again. A matinee and a meal at an upscale restaurant had considerable appeal when contrasted with a boring day in residence and a typically unsavoury supper in the cafeteria. She agreed and was ready when Daniel came to the door to announce his arrival, but then she hesitated. Her niggling feeling resurfaced when she saw him. When she stepped outside she thought, *Oh, what is the matter with me? It's a beautiful day, and we're only going to public places where there will be lots of people.*

Alyssa was so entranced with the luxury of the most beautiful automobile she had ever ridden in that it took her several minutes to realize they were headed in the wrong direction. "Where are you going?"

"I stupidly left my wallet on the bedside table, but fortunately we have plenty of time before the movie so I can pick it up." Arriving in front of a motel on the outskirts of Brandon, Daniel turned off the car and continued, "In fact, we've enough time to go in for a refreshing drink before we need to leave."

Alarm bells began clanging in her mind, but now what could she do? The vehicle had power windows, and rather than sitting outside in the blistering August sun, Alyssa decided to follow him. Inside, she sat down on the corner of the sofa closest to the door and lit a cigarette.

Sitting down on the edge of the bed, Daniel remarked, "Hey, what the hell are you doing? I thought nurses were supposed to be healthy. Do you mind extinguishing that weed? I'm allergic to smoke."

Alyssa did not care to speculate what this man, whom she suddenly realized she did not recognize intended to do, but the ringing in her head was becoming louder. She knew that she had to immediately find the way to get out of the motel and impel him to drive her back to the residence. That was it! She would chain smoke until the room became blue, if necessary, and she lit another cigarette from the butt. "I'll stop when we're outside getting back into your car so you can return me to the nurses' residence."

"We're supposed to be on a date. Be damned if I'm taking you back already."

"Unless you want to explain to the manager of this establishment how the fire started, you will do exactly what I say."

"You're crazy! There's no bloody way that you're going to smoke in my new car."

"That will depend solely on you. If you don't take me straight back to 150 McTavish Avenue as of this minute, there is no telling what I might do."

"Let's get out of here. I'm not wasting any more of my time, or a penny on a nut like you. What the hell did Bonnie set me up with?"

When Alyssa climbed into the passenger seat, she held her package of cigarettes and her lighter in her hands ready to ignite on the slightest indication that Daniel was not following her instructions. During the tense twenty-minute ride she paid close attention to each passing street sign. She barely breathed until she saw the hospital in the distance. The second the vehicle was stopped she was out the door and running up the stairs to the safety of the residence. On her way Alyssa vaguely heard, "The next time you go on a blind date, have the decency to tell the unsuspecting man that you're a lesbian."

Once inside Alyssa sought the familiarity of one of the comfortable chairs in the front lounge. She was stunned. She was beyond belief that she had put her personal safety in such jeopardy. Had she really been so stupid? Why had she accepted the invitation and then willingly gone into the motel? As soul-destroying questions threatened to overwhelm her, on the spur of the moment, Alyssa Rainer decided to block any and all thoughts about what could have happened in that situation, most importantly the worst-case scenario, from forming in her mind.

Instead for once in her life, she chose to congratulate herself on the quick thinking of using her unhealthy smoking habit for her defense, rather than to wallow in self-chastisement. From that moment, Alyssa promised herself to only double date or to socialize with pre- arranged groups of her classmates, which she held to until her second date with Eric Easton almost three months ago.

~ 10 ~

She could not believe her good fortune for a change. Imagine renting the upper level of a one and a half story house on the prestigious riverfront Spadina Crescent, one of Saskatoon's most beautiful and oldest streets. Elaine had been strolling along the paved path overlooking the South Saskatchewan River when she came to the crescent and noticed the elegant houses. She decided to cross over the road and check out the homes more closely. To her amazement, just then a blonde haired lady was striving to place a sign 'Loft for Rent' in the front window.

Not for one minute did Elaine consider that whatever the owner was about to rent would be affordable, but what harm could there be in asking? Walking toward her she said, "Hello, my name is Elaine Hurren. I was wondering if you might like some help."

"How lovely of you, my dear. I don't recall seeing you before on my crescent. My name is Helen Symonds and I would appreciate your longer reach."

Smiling, Elaine replied, "I believe that's why I offered, although I'm new to Saskatoon and am looking for an apartment for my friend and me."

"If that is the case, why don't we wait with the sign? You can tell me what type of accommodations you're searching for over a cup of tea under the shade of my veranda. Please have a seat and I'll be right back"

On the front of Helen's home was a large welcoming patio with several comfortable deck chairs, some with matching footstools. What an appealing place it would be to begin a warm day with her morning coffee. Elaine glanced around at the row of towering conifers on the side of the house before claiming a lounge chair, and was immediately taken into the charm of the well-maintained attractive home with its exquisite scenic river view.

When Helen returned with tea and scones, Elaine leapt to her feet saying, "Here, let me help you. My, those look delicious." She hoped that her growling stomach had not given away the fact that she had yet to eat today.

"No, dear please stay where you are. The tray isn't heavy, and I'll take the chair on the other side of the table. During the clement seasons of the year my daughter, Mariah, and I always ate our meals on the veranda, so I'm an old hand at carrying various sizes of receptacles." Helen replied deftly setting the tea service down.

"What a lovely name. She was a lucky girl to grow up in this beautiful home."

"She's a splendid girl, although Mariah would laugh if she heard me still calling her a girl. She is now a grown woman, has graduated from Medical School *Summa cum laude*, and is completing her residency in Cardiology at the Royal Jubilee Hospital in Victoria, British Columbia, but she'll always be my little girl."

"Where did Mariah study medicine?"

"Our only child was about to begin her Bachelor of Science Degree at the University of Saskatchewan, when Ray and I decided to refurbish the loft so she could live at home and walk across the river. Mariah had just been accepted into the Faculty of Medicine, when her father died suddenly with a heart attack. We were both devastated, but at least I still had her here with me. I was grateful when she started her medical degree, and then her internship that she decided to stay. I think that she not only loved the loft her father had so devotedly renovated for her, but she also appreciated the proximity to the school and the hospital, with the heavy expectations and demands of becoming a doctor. However, since Mariah left for Victoria last fall, all my friends have been hounding me to sell my beloved hearth and home, but I just can't bring myself to leave my lasting memories."

"I don't blame you in the slightest. I also imagine that you and your home could be compelling incentive for Mariah, when she finishes her residency, to return and set up her practice in Saskatoon. If I thought for a moment that my friend and I could afford to rent your loft, I would never help you put your sign in the window."

"Let's talk about that. Why don't we begin by you looking at my fully furnished loft for rent?"

It was as though Lady Luck was on the verge of shining her countenance upon her. Elaine was careful not to pinch herself and break the spell. From the moment Helen led her through the foyer to the elegant light oak carpeted staircase ascending into the upper half story, Elaine was captivated. An open cosy sitting room with a large window revealing the fast flowing water of the South Saskatchewan River greeted her when she reached the top step. Sinking into one of the La-Z-Boy Recliners she said, "What a stunning view. Already, I love your loft."

"I haven't even shown you the large bedroom with a walk-in closet, the full bathroom, or the smaller room that Mariah used as her study and den. Oh dear, it just occurs to me that I was so busy talking I never asked you what kind of accommodations you were seeking for you and your friend."

As Helen guided her through the other rooms of the fully furnished immaculate garret, Elaine became more enthusiastic with what she was seeing. "This would be perfect if there was a kitchen for us to prepare our meals."

"Well, what if we agreed upon room and board accommodation? If the two of you have your own furniture, I could arrange to store all of this in the spacious lower level of the house."

"Would you consider furnished lodgings and meals for two people? That would be ideal for Alyssa and me. I know that she doesn't own a single piece of furniture because she's graduating next week as a registered nurse, after having lived in a residence for the past three years. I left my position as the senior nurse at the health unit, and either sold or gave away what little I had before travelling from Virden. I only brought what I could of my personal possessions – books, clothing, family pictures, and my precious mementos in the backseat and trunk of my car. When we planned to live together in Saskatoon, we realized that we would need to rent an apartment with at least some furniture."

"I love to cook and bake, but there is nothing more boring than preparing meals for one person. Also, you would be more than welcome if either of you wants to assist in the kitchen, or with the shopping, on occasion. And, you could avail yourselves of the washer and dryer in the laundry room on the main level. I would be delighted to share my home with two young nurses. Tell me, where will each of you be working?"

"The day before I left, Alyssa telephoned to confirm that she was offered a position at City Hospital on the surgical ward, and I relocated to Saskatoon to begin my Bachelor of Science in Nursing at the University of Saskatchewan. Both of us would be within walking distance to our respective destinations."

"That settles it then. I've never had a paying lodger before, so in your consideration in 1966, does a hundred dollars a month from each of you sound to be a reasonable amount for your room and board?"

"Thank you, Mrs. Symonds. For me, and I shall also speak for Alyssa, I think that is a very equitable payment for our accommodation. If I may, I'll give you my hundred-dollar deposit until Alyssa arrives on the first of September, when I'm confident she'll be pleased to provide the same amount. Or, do you prefer that I pay her portion right now?"

"Please call me Helen and yours will be just fine. You can start to move in whenever you want, but where did you leave your car?"

"I can? Is this really happening? It's like a dream come true. Was it only two hours ago that I parked my car in a parking lot under a bridge and decided to walk along the river?"

"It seems to me that we were meant to meet, my dear. Now, why don't you help me make us some lunch before I join you for my afternoon stroll to pick up your automobile?"

~11~

The residence was so quiet on Sunday morning when she awakened that Alyssa decided to have coffee and toast in the student kitchen before she began to sort out her belongings. Sitting alone at the table a feeling of melancholy threatened to engulf her. Yesterday when she told Eric that she loved him, was she being honest? What did it really mean to love a man? Alyssa had, at best minimal feelings for her father since as far as she was concerned, essentially his only claim to being her parent was biological and over the years, she had heard his heated arguments about its veracity. She had experienced brotherly love, and deep respect, admiration, and affection for her grandfather, but she had never before felt passionate love for a man.

More and more she was convinced that for Eric, sex was equated to love and with little regard for its consequences. Long ago Alyssa had calculated that her mother had barely turned nineteen when she delivered her first-born son. Then, in rapid succession she had birthed three daughters within three years whom she basically neglected, leaving their upbringing in their grandmother's hands. To her mother, parenting had been the bane of her existence and had culminated in destroying her future. Remarkably, Alyssa did want children, but planned and not for several years to come. Under no circumstances, was she going to ruin her life, or the lives of her offspring.

Yet, within three short months she and Eric were becoming closer and closer to crossing that unbidden boundary every time they were in each other's company. How could she fend him off when she was soon as aroused as he? As the solitary morning marched on, her pensiveness began slipping into desolation. Alyssa had to move, to get her act together, and to stop dwelling on her relationship with Eric. After all, there was a shining light at the end of the tunnel since in nine days she would be on the train to her career in Saskatoon.

She was on her way to the third floor staircase when the student telephone rang, and it was for her. Now what were the odds of that happening when she was bar none the only student in the lounge? "Hi, is that you, Alyssa? Am I ever glad you answered the phone? I've some incredible news."

"If you had been five minutes later, your call would have rung endlessly into oblivion. I think that the entire residence has emptied for this weekend before graduation. Please do tell your exciting information."

As Elaine imparted an update on her search for their living arrangements, Alyssa was increasingly challenged to listen attentively and not interrupt. "Wow, Elaine, I thought you were leaving Virden on Friday morning, and you have not only arrived, but you have also discovered what sounds like accommodations made in heaven."

Chuckling, Elaine said, "I know. I'm being very careful not to dispel the enchantment of Helen, her fairy-tale home, her location, and best of all, her proposal for us to share lodgings and meals with her. Actually, I've confirmed for both of us, and just as soon as we enjoy blueberry pancakes and bacon on her veranda overlooking the river, we're walking along the path to fetch my car. I'll begin my marginal unpacking once we've fairly determined which one of us will occupy the bedroom with a double bed, versus the den with a three-quarter bedstead. Any ideas about how we might reach a distance decision?"

"Were I standing beside you, I would suggest that we toss a coin. Perchance, is Helen with you now?"

"She's sitting on the same sofa as me. Will you permit her to take your toss and what will it be?

"Let's do the best of three and my choice is 'heads,' okay?"

Seconds later, Elaine was back on the line. "You've won, so what is your preference? I did forget to mention that we would be sharing the bathroom."

"I'll take the large bedroom, please."

In the background, Alyssa heard a lilting voice say, "No worries, my dears. There's a half bathroom with a shower in the foyer just before the stairway that I never use. We can designate it for you, Elaine, and there is a shower and bathtub on the lower level. With four bathrooms for the three of us, I can't think that we'll ever encounter a problem."

"So, Alyssa, grab a pen and paper. Here is your new address – 1154 Spadina Crescent East, Saskatoon, Saskatchewan and the telephone number is (306) 665 - 2507."

Buoyed by Elaine's masterful resolution regarding where they would live in Saskatoon, Alyssa bounded up the stairs to begin sorting through her personal possessions. Now that her plans were coming together, her mood was lifting, and if she got herself organized she might even telephone Eric. She was eager to discuss with him how they could manage a distance relationship, with the possibility that before this time next year, after he had completed his Bachelor of Arts degree in the spring, he might consider relocating to Saskatoon.

No doubt, the onus of maintaining their liaison would fall upon Alyssa. She cared enough for Eric, and was determined to stay in touch that she would willingly communicate on a regular basis – write letters, place telephone calls, and travel to and from Saskatoon and Winnipeg. Indeed, it made perfect sense since she was moving into the ranks of wage earner, while Eric had, at least one more year of being a student. What was he planning to pursue once he had graduated? It dawned on Alyssa that she did not have the slightest idea.

It was yet another reason for them to have time away from each other. Perhaps with verbal and written interactions from afar, they might start to share their dreams, hopes, and plans about building their future. When they had started dating more often, they spent progressively fewer hours talking and getting to know one another, and more time necking and petting in the backseat of Eric's Chevy. From Alyssa's perspective, the escalating sexual tension between them was eroding rather than enhancing their relationship.

When she had packed most of the items that she wanted her mother to store in Virden, Alyssa ran down the stairs to telephone Eric. "Hi, there, are you busy studying or would you like to drive out to the Blue Hills? I've some exciting updates about Saskatoon to tell you."

Hesitantly, Eric replied, "Would you like to get a bite to eat first? I've been at the books all morning and skipped lunch."

"Sure, and it will be my treat. We received our last stipend this past week since we'll have graduated and left the residence by the end of the month."

At the A & W the more Alyssa told Eric, the more animated she became and the more subdued Eric was until at last in a quiet voice he asked, "But, what about us?"

Alyssa could not believe her ears. Had Eric heard a single word that she had said about how she would work diligently to continue their courtship, perhaps for less than a year? Surely their bond of love could endure for such a short period. She was even more surprised when he said, "I don't have time to go for a hike today. Will you be alright if I just take you back to the residence so I can carry on studying?"

Alyssa was still sitting on the park bench when Bryan returned Susan to the residence. Spotting her she walked over and sat down. "Hey, you're back early. I wasn't expecting you to arrive from Oakville until much later. Why so glum?"

Should Alyssa take her closest friend into confidence one last time? Would Susan, who always seemed to see life so clearly, understand her dilemma? At any rate, she would certainly have an opinion, but Alyssa had a strong feeling that she may not want to hear it. Truthfully, her decision was made and she was not going to change her mind, regardless of how much pressure, from either Susan or Eric, she had to endure. Still, Alyssa not only needed to apprise her best friend of her address in Saskatoon, but she also wanted to ask whether she could stay with Bryan and her when she returned to Winnipeg for visits with Eric.

"I've been on an emotional roller coaster for the entirety of the weekend, which makes for a long story. Are you sure you want to hear it? But if you do, Susan, could you please wait until I'm finished before you say anything?"

It had been a long time since Alyssa had been this serious with her, possibly dating back to their first year of training. Good heavens, what could have happened to cause her to be so distraught since Susan had left for Melita on Saturday morning? Would life ever be free from interminable upheavals for her beleaguered friend? Attempting a modicum of comic relief, Susan said, "I promise to barely breathe."

How much time elapsed during Alyssa's narration, Susan would never know. Almost from the beginning, she could envision the pitfalls for Eric and her being able to maintain a long-distance relationship. Nonetheless, she understood that the reality of a happy marriage was so far beyond Alyssa's comprehension that she would never ever change her future plans for a man. It was axiomatic that at this crossroads in her life, her decision was absolute, and there was not a single word that anyone could express that would alter her course. Come what may, eight days from now Alyssa Rainer would board the train to follow her chosen path, which Susan feared would forever remain untrodden upon by Eric Easton.

Silence reigned supreme. Even though Susan had vowed she would not interrupt, she was struggling with accepting that she could not articulate anything, which would have the slightest impact on Alyssa. At last in a peculiar trembling voice she said, "I've kept my promise, but now I must speak my mind if I'm ever going to be able to live with myself for the rest of my days. Neither you nor Eric has two pennies to rub together, and I just know that what I'm going to tell you, Alyssa, is the truth. Should you persist with your decision to get on that train next Sunday and leave for Saskatoon, instead of seeking an impromptu move to Winnipeg, you two will never see each other again."

~12~

The undercurrent of the final week of nursing training for the Class of 1966 was bittersweet. On the surface, one and all were excited to the point of being giddy. They had done it. Thirty-nine students had achieved the pinnacle of success and were on the cusp of graduating as Registered Nurses. For three long years, they had yearned for this celebration, and now that the day would soon be upon them, none of the students wanted their time together to come to an end.

Oh, never during the days and the evenings which were filled with accolades, activities, pleasures, and festivities. It was not until eleven o'clock when they returned to the residence, still abiding by the curfew, when they gravitated to the third floor lounge. As each of them sought a favourite chair, during long moments of silence, a state of nostalgia settled upon their shoulders, and they all knew that the cause was far from trivial. For Alyssa, melancholy had always been a complex emotion that not only brought a feeling of sadness, but also a time of reminiscing and savouring her memories. But, during her last week as a student nurse subsequent to Susan's succinct prediction, Alyssa Rainer's touch of poignant pleasure was jettisoned by the much-needed opportunity for reflection and contemplation to reclaim her peace of mind and to soothe her despairing soul.

As throughout her life, Alyssa had not reached her decision lightly. She was not only aware of the possible drawbacks of a long-distance courtship, but she could also appreciate the many promising advantages. She was optimistic that if their love were true, together they would overcome any potential obstacles. And, the actual period of separation could be as short as nine to ten months. Once Eric had graduated with his degree, whatever employment he decided to pursue could be as obtainable in Saskatoon as in Winnipeg. Alyssa had always been confident that believing makes everything possible.

❋

During the week before the afternoon and evening celebrations on Saturday, Alyssa and Eric had scarcely seen one another. It was also Eric's final week in Brandon, and he had been just as glad his baseball team missed the playoffs. His two supplementary examinations were scheduled for the Tuesday and Wednesday mornings of August Thirty and Thirty-first, and if he had not been so desperate for the money, he would have quit working to spend all day cramming for his finals.

Whenever he had any free time Eric needed to be alone. His feelings of ambivalence about Alyssa leaving for Saskatoon continued to escalate. Why had he even considered that she would change all of her plans just because he had proposed twice? In so many ways, Alyssa was right. They had only known each other for three months, she was almost three years younger than he, and neither could afford to get married.

When Eric was being honest, he realized that they did need much more time to get to learn about each other's aspirations, traits, and desires. He did not even know if Alyssa wanted a family, although he recognized within short order that she had virtually a morbid fear of getting pregnant. With good reason it seemed since he had been sexually attracted to her so quickly, and their making out was becoming increasingly heated. At first, Eric had been confident that Alyssa would stop him in time, but either he had become more persistent or she more aroused. On many occasions this past month, when their necking resulted in heavy petting, they had come much too close. And, Eric Easton could not live through the ultimate consequence – again.

By the time the weekend arrived, Eric was becoming reconciled to Alyssa's departure. He knew he would miss seeing her, but he was certain that she would follow through with her plans of staying in touch with him. He had studied late every evening from Monday to Friday, so he could enjoy both Alyssa's graduation ceremony on Saturday afternoon and then the evening celebratory dinner.

Saying good-bye was not one of Eric's strong points and he decided to wait until after he had given Alyssa her graduation gift before telling her that he was driving back to Winnipeg as soon as he awakened on Sunday morning. He had splurged on a beautiful gold bracelet engraved with her name and the date of her graduation. Eric was hoping that she might also think of his present as symbolic of their engagement, but he was not asking. He had learned his lesson, and he would wait until Alyssa was ready to commit.

~13~

The afternoon ceremony was stunning. One by one, the full name of each of the thirty-nine registered nurse graduates of Brandon General Hospital's Class of 1966 was announced, and every woman proudly walked across the stage to receive her diploma and graduate pin. Dressed completely in white from the cap on her head to the smartly polished white shoes on her feet, each RN resembled a veritable angel of mercy. The twelve spectacular red roses in full bloom, gracefully carried in their arms, provided a dazzling contrast. And thirty-nine graduates beamed with joy and dignity. After every Registered Nurse's name had been called, they were asked to form a group on the stage for their class photograph, and the collective image of brilliant red on pristine white was radiant to behold.

The celebration had been so touching it was doubtful that there were many dry eyes in the auditorium. Eric had always been uncomfortable with expressing his emotions, but there was such an aura of perfection and hope enveloping the group of young women that he was surprised when a tear slipped down his check. He was so glad that he had changed his mind and decided to come. At the beginning of the week in his bitterness, he was stubbornly determined not to attend any of Alyssa's graduation activities. Let her find out how rejection felt. Now Eric would not have missed this afternoon for the world.

When the class filed off the stage still in alphabetical order, and began to search for their beloved family and friends, Eric could not have been more proud. As he was approaching Alyssa, it occurred to him that he had not given a moment's consideration to the fact that her family members would surround her. She had not indicated that she was expecting any other guests, and quite frankly, Eric had been so absorbed in having her meet his parents and siblings, he had never suggested they visit hers. How could he have been that self-centred? No wonder Alyssa needed time. It was just unfortunate that they would be five hundred miles apart.

When Alyssa had spoken about her family, she essentially only talked about her much-loved grandparents and how sad it was that her grandfather had died in February, just months before she was to graduate. Now within brief moments of being introduced to her family, Eric realized how accurate Alyssa had been about her mother, and he also understood why she cherished her grandmother.

Instantly, she had ensconced Eric in a hug reminiscent of one from his maternal grandma who lived in Oak Point. How long had it been since he had visited her? Was it before he had left to go to Churchill to work more than four years ago? How could he have been so remiss? Eric did remember telling her that the only way he would ever be able to attend United College in Winnipeg was by seeking employment in Manitoba's Far North, and she had urged him not to worry about her. Still, meeting Alyssa's loving grandmother spurred him to commit to going to see her the afternoon following his last exam.

As soon as the faculty and the hospital-nursing administrators had served afternoon tea, the graduates boarded a bus to be transported back to the residence, for most of them, one last time. Not for Alyssa, however. When at length, she had finalized all her preparations for Saskatoon she arranged an appointment with Miss Brannon. The Class of 1966 were expected to gather their belongings and vacate their respective room no later than five-thirty on the afternoon of Saturday, August 27th. Where would Alyssa spend the night before her Sunday morning train departure? Explaining her situation to the Director of Nursing was not quite as formidable as three years earlier when she had requested that, although she did not meet the entrance minimum age requirement she be accepted into training on August 26th, 1963.

Seated in Miss Brannon's office, Alyssa came straight to the point. "I'll be completely packed, have my bed stripped, and only ask that I be able to sleep on one of the sofas in the student lounge on Saturday evening. I'll order a taxi cab to be at the front door for seven o'clock on Sunday morning to take me to the train station, and I assure you that no one will be any the wiser."

"Well, Miss Rainer, you're a sharp little cookie. I've often marvelled at your resourcefulness. Please leave the bedding, blankets, and pillow on the couch, and I'll ask Mrs. Smith to gather them before she finishes work."

❋

The evening passed far too quickly. Eric was showered and ready to put on his best suit, at least thirty minutes before he needed to pick up Alyssa. He waited though, to remove it from the cleaners' lightweight plastic bag, sitting in his small second floor boarding house room in his underwear with the window wide open on the breezy August late afternoon. Eric had already determined that he would arrive early and once he collected Alyssa from the residence, he planned to suggest that they sit on the park bench while he gifted her bracelet, in the hope she would don it for the evening.

❋

"Oh, Eric, thank you. What an exquisite ornate bracelet. No one has ever given me jewellery before in my life. I've always found beauty and splendour in nature, never expecting that I would be the recipient of such a stylish present. I'm going to wear it right now. But, you shouldn't have. Your earnings are for your last year of university and maybe a trip to Saskatoon next spring."

"I'm glad you like it. I was hoping you would put it on. And, don't worry I'll shovel sidewalks all winter to earn enough money to come and see you."

The auditorium had been transformed into an elegant dining hall with seating for eight at each table. When they were being ushered toward the Rainer family, Alyssa noticed that there were only seven place settings and chairs. Feelings of grief surfaced as Alyssa reflected how poignant her beloved grandfather would have found all of the proceedings of this momentous day. She would always revere him not only for his lifelong encouragement, but also for his gift of money every three months over the past two years that had allowed her to enjoy some of the pleasures of youth.

The dinner of succulent roast beef, Yorkshire pudding, and all the trimmings had been served when the formal speeches and the presentation of awards were commenced. As the dance was about to begin, and her family were preparing to depart, Alyssa's mother presented her with mother-of-pearl cufflinks engraved with the initials RN, one letter on either side of the medical insignia. Alyssa was quick to acknowledge that it was the nicest present that she had ever given her.

As she was leaving, her grandmother remembered to dig in her purse and gave Alyssa a card of congratulations. She enveloped her in one of her ensconcing hugs as though she would never see her again, and thanked her granddaughter over and over for inviting her to her nursing celebration. Much later when Alyssa opened the card back in the stillness of the residence, she was astonished to discover five crisp one hundred dollar bills.

At last, Alyssa and Eric found Susan and Bryan at a table with two remaining chairs. While Eric confirmed that they could be seated, Alyssa sat down beside Susan who scarcely acknowledged her. She was still deep in conversation with Stacy, when Alyssa suggested to Eric that they join several of their classmates already on the dance floor. As the hours passed other than a brief salutation, Susan had all but ignored Alyssa, until even Eric was beginning to wonder why her closest friend was being so distant.

At first Alyssa was hurt by Susan's obvious slight, especially when she could hardly wait to show off her new bracelet, but then she became annoyed. Although the past week had flown by Alyssa just realized that since her dire prophecy on Sunday, Susan had hardly spoken to her. Had she been waiting for her friend to heed her pending doom about her and Eric? Did she expect that her stony silence would spark all of Alyssa's assiduous plans to spontaneously combust?

At any rate, it was not going to happen. Alyssa was not anything if not resolute though, before long she began to fret about whether she would have a chance to ask Susan about staying with her and Bryan during the weekend of her twenty-first birthday on November eleven. It was nigh onto ten o'clock when Susan and Bryan simultaneously rose from their chairs as though on cue.

Reaching to hug Alyssa, Susan said, "We want to make it home to Melita before the bewitching hour, so we'll say goodnight. Enjoy your train trip to Saskatoon and whenever you need a place to crash in Winnipeg, give us a call, okay."

"Thank you, Susan and Bryan. My best wishes for a lovely wedding, a splendid weekend, and a memorable honeymoon. I'll be thinking of you and sending fond vibes over Thanksgiving.

"If you weren't so stubborn, you could still be one of my bridesmaids." Susan flung at Alyssa as she marched out the door.

"I'm sorry, Susan. Drive safely."

Alyssa remained standing. As she watched Susan leave the building, she firmly fixated her image in her mind's eye. She had no idea how long Eric had been talking to her before she finally heard him. "Are you alright, Alyssa? Why were you apologizing to Susan? She ignored us all evening and then when they were leaving, she became snarky with you. Does she expect you to come all the way back from Saskatoon in a little over a month for their wedding?"

"It's a long story. Maybe we should get ready to leave." Even in the diffused lighting, Eric could see how sad and deflated Alyssa was, and he wished that she would not have to stay with Susan and Bryan when she came to visit him for her birthday.

Even though the graduation had been exhilarating and memorable, it had been long and tiring. After working all day and studying every evening during the week, Eric was ready to take Alyssa back to the residence. On the verge of being overcome with melancholy, when he arrived at the front door, he left the car running, walked around to the passenger door, and took Alyssa into his arms. After a long, deep, and satisfying kiss, Eric gazed into her eyes and said, "My mother always told me – when it is time to go, just go. Alyssa, I'll see you in November."

A dim lamp shone on a cozy bed made on the sofa in the far corner of the student lounge. Slipping into a trance, Alyssa removed her pyjamas and her attire for the next morning from her suitcase, before undressing, packing her party clothing on the top, and closing the lid. Becoming comfortable, she focused her mind on her long-practiced relaxation techniques so she would not reach a state of analysis paralysis reviewing all the details of the eventful day when she thought, *I have done the best thing, right? I promise to always remember these words of wisdom – the hardest choices in life are not between what is right and what is wrong but between what is right and what is best.*

~ 14 ~

Miss Brannon had apprised Mrs. Smith about their Saturday evening guest. Alyssa awoke to her gently shaking her shoulder, "It's six in the morning, Miss Rainer. I've placed your coffee and toast on the table beside you."

Struggling to recall where she was, Alyssa sat up with a start and nearly struck the night housemother on her lowered head. "I'm sorry I nearly knocked you out when I need to be thanking you, Mrs. Smith. This is such a nice surprise."

"No, you should thank Miss Brannon. She insisted that I wake you, and she told me to make your breakfast in her office. So you better get up and have it before your taxi arrives. After you warned that Markham girl, I knew you were a kind person." And, Mrs. Smith was gone with her large flashlight still in hand.

✵

The sun was shining radiantly when Alyssa stepped out the heavy front door one final time. It was the perfect start to the day earmarked for following the new path of her life, and for becoming her own person. Long before she was an adolescent, she had been convinced that she was born ready to make tough choices and to take responsibility for her actions. Alyssa Rainer had vowed that throughout her life, she would heed her cherished grandfather's counsel – you have the right to be you and to go wherever you want with confidence.

Later with a novel on her lap, she sat staring out the window waiting for the train to take her away. Ever since her first sleepover at her grandparents' home in Melville, where their two-bedroom bungalow was situated directly across the street from the Canadian National Railway, she had loved the sound of train whistles and of the engines shuffling back and forth in the rail yard. Alyssa was four years old when her grandmother had taken her to the doctor's office for a tonsillectomy and adenoidectomy in the afternoon. Although she had been drinking fluids and eating ice cream, by evening her throat was raw and sore. While her grandma rocked her in her arms, Alyssa had fallen asleep to the rhythm of the interminably moving locomotives.

The golden wheat fields of the Saskatchewan prairie were streaking by when the clickety-clack of the metal wheels on the track lulled Alyssa into sweet repose. Awakening several hours later, she could scarcely believe the time. Climbing the steps into the train, she thought that she was full of vim and vigour, but the excitement, ambiguity, and melancholy of graduation week had clearly taken its toll.

Her pressing need for the moment was to find the lavatory. Then she was ready to consume some of the snacks she had purchased at the train station before boarding. Aside from the short trip from Brandon to Virden on a number of occasions, Alyssa had never travelled by train and was captivated with her experience. There and then, she promised that one day she would take the journey through the Rocky Mountains to the west coast of Canada. From all the photos in books that she had ever perused, the splendour and majesty of the mountains and the beautiful blue of the Pacific Ocean were sights to behold.

The balance of the day passed in peace and tranquility. There were only a few other passengers who seemed to be equally besotted with their rail excursion. A serene silence permeated the rail car. Alyssa was so content to sit and be in the moment that not once did it occur to open her book to read. As the day began to wane and the sun was beginning its slow descent below the horizon, she readied herself for her departure.

When she arrived in Saskatoon shortly before seven o'clock in the evening, Alyssa was saddened her trip was ending. She was hoping Elaine would meet her. She was doubly pleased when she stepped onto the platform at the station to be greeted not only by her, but also by Helen. Regardless that she had not showered in the morning, each of the women gave her a warm hug. Her new sprightly, tall, slender, stylish, blonde-haired landlady said, "I'm so pleased to meet you. Welcome to our lovely city. After twelve hours on the train, Alyssa, you must be ready for some real food, and I'm taking both of you to The Bessborough for dinner."

Entering the foyer of the grand hotel, Helen's guests were awestruck by the splendour of the historic building, one of Canada's grand railway hotels. Helen began their edification as the two young women continued to gaze about at the ceiling moulds, the elegant furniture settings, and the terrazzo floors. "My father was one of the engineers hired by the Canadian National Railway in February, 1930 to begin construction of this chateau style structure, with further inspiration drawn from castles in Bavaria. Before and after its completion, he often brought me here with him, and I've always considered The Bessborough my palace. And, we're being hosted in my favourite restaurant in the whole of the city – the Garden Court Café."

Dinner was a delightful two hours of introductions, sharing of information, and the consumption of delectable locally sourced food. Helen was well known and fondly received by the maître d' and everyone in the bistro. Elaine was overjoyed Alyssa had finally arrived, and was already as delighted with Helen as she had been from the moment of their first meeting. Yet, Alyssa was different in a manner that Elaine could not interpret. During all their previous interactions she had presented as being innocuous to the point of naiveté, but now seemed to have acquired an aura of worldliness.

Too impatient to wait until later this evening when they were alone in their loft, Elaine decided to use an oblique approach to try and ascertain what she was not grasping. "I gather you have had an eventful three months since we last saw each other. Graduation as a Registered Nurse is a momentous occurrence, isn't it?"

"It was one of my most memorable days ever, and aside from now being a Registered Nurse, I have not only met the love of my life, but also he has proposed marriage, twice. Eric is starting the third year of his Bachelor of Arts degree at United College in Winnipeg. When he graduates next spring, he might relocate to Saskatoon. Not to mention, he is tall, dark, and handsome, and decidedly the man for me." Alyssa said with uncharacteristic merriment as if the magnitude of her feelings were engaging her fully for the first time.

"Congratulations, my dear. Isn't that delightful, Elaine?" Glancing at her, Helen suddenly experienced a wave of foreboding when she noticed the look on Elaine's face. What was wrong? She appeared as if someone had just kicked her in the teeth. How very odd? Alyssa's news was exactly the kind that elicited excitement and accolades from other young women of marriageable age. Thinking that it was just her being overly sensitive, Helen decided to forge ahead with a recommendation, which had just crossed her mind.

"Thank you, ladies for providing such wonderful companionship for dinner. May I suggest now as we prepare to leave, Alyssa and I walk the short distance along Spadina Crescent while you bring the car, Elaine."

Fortunately, Elaine had mastered the technique of quick recovery long ago and replied,

"After sitting on the train for nearly twelve hours, I'm sure you would enjoy stretching your legs, Alyssa. It's a gorgeous evening with scenic paths along the river in a beautiful city, with Helen's home located on one of Saskatoon's most exquisite streets. Please take your time. I'll wait until you return to help carry in your suitcases."

She needed to be alone, the longer the better. She was shattered. How could she ever have been so mistaken? She was convinced she had read all the signs accurately. Otherwise, she would never have asked her to come for the weekend. That night in bed Alyssa had cozied right into her body as though they were meant to be. Then, she had been in a trance for the entire next day. Had she exhibited the slightest indication of repulsion that would have been it? Oh, Elaine knew she would have to be patient, to go slow, to allow her to adjust, and to accept, but she was confident that with the passage of time they would become one. Now what…?

~15~

Returning from their walk, Helen had been about to point out her new home when Alyssa spying the numbers under the veranda light from the street remarked, "Oh, is yours that picture perfect white house tucked in by the grove of conifers? I love it and I bet our loft is in the upper half story, isn't it, Mrs. Symonds?"

"My dear, did I neglect to ask you to call me Helen? I'm so happy the charm of my little house appeals to you. Your enthusiasm reminds me of my daughter, Mariah, who always viewed her home as an adult-sized dollhouse compared to the other monstrosities on our crescent. I hope you'll enjoy living here as much as she did."

Alyssa was enchanted with Helen. She seemed such a gentle, cheerful, and kind soul that she could have predicted on the spot they would develop a positive bond. For starters, terms of endearment were virtually foreign to Alyssa and she could become used to them very quickly. Those early years of unsuccessful striving for her mother's approval had unfortunately initiated Alyssa's predisposition of becoming a consummate people pleaser, and try as hard as she might, she had not succeeded in overcoming behaviour that she had since learned was a reflection of her insecurities and lack of self-esteem.

❋

Seated at the picnic table on the veranda the three women were enjoying a cup of tea with cookies when Helen asked, "Do you expect your young man to visit you for Christmas, Alyssa? I have two extra bedrooms on the lower level, so even in the unlikely event that Mariah doesn't have to work during the holiday season, he would have a place to sleep."

"That's very kind of you. I'll include your offer when I write my first letter. I'm planning to take the bus, only because it is quicker than the train, to Winnipeg for my birthday over the Remembrance Day weekend. I'll be staying with one of my nursing friends and her husband."

This time when Helen glanced at Elaine, her face was a mask not revealing any emotion, which also seemed peculiar. What would prevent her from wanting to hear the news about her friend's budding love life? In the short time Helen had known Elaine there had not been the slightest indication that jealousy was one of her personal traits. *Oh, stop it. I'm reading far too much into Elaine's innocent behaviour, especially when Alyssa is totally oblivious to there being anything unusual in her friend's response.* She thought as she lifted the teapot to serve her newfound boarders a second cup.

"No thanks, Helen. I'm going to take my dishes into the kitchen before I unpack my suitcases. Elaine is going to show me around Saskatoon tomorrow before I begin work on Tuesday morning at seven o'clock sharp."

"That's okay, Alyssa, I'll help Helen to give you some time to sort out your room and become familiar with our loft."

By the time Elaine climbed the stairs, Alyssa was sitting in one of the comfortable chairs in the loft peering out the large window at the silhouette of the flowing river. "Wow. You did a fantastic job of finding us a place to live – congenial landlady, prime location, beautiful home, and affordable room and board accommodations, which I think will work perfectly for both of us and let's hope for Helen as well. Thank you, Elaine. Here's the two hundred dollars I owe you for the deposit and the month of September. I do want to ascertain though, that you're okay about occupying the den rather than the bedroom."

"You won the toss fair and square, Alyssa, and I'm not one to complain. Actually the study has a large table and a desk chair that I'm going to need much more than you."

"I haven't had a chance to tell you I'm taking an evening class at the university. As soon as I had my job confirmation, I applied to enrol in an Introductory English course and just received my acceptance before I left Brandon."

"It seems you have a lot of news to share. In the five months I've known you, not once did you breathe a word about having a serious boyfriend, or that you were contemplating marriage."

Surprised by the terseness in Elaine's voice, which she had never heard before, Alyssa chose her words carefully. "I guess you could say Eric and I had a whirlwind romance. We only met at the end of May, the weekend after I spent with you and your family in St. Laurent."

When it was apparent that Alyssa was not about to elaborate further, Elaine decided not to push. Truthfully she was encouraged, hoping that the hasty relationship might prove to have been a summer fling. Earlier that evening when she recovered from her shock and devastation, Elaine had sat on the veranda attempting to regain her composure. But, instead she found she became resentful and angry, although she could not decide whether to blame herself or Alyssa. Had she made a precipitous decision regarding Alyssa's preference, or was the woman so totally unaware of her own sexuality? In retrospect, she had always warmly received Elaine's fondling – a gentle caress on her shoulder, an arm intimately slung around her waist, a light touch on her cheek, and she never had the slightest hesitation about an embracing hug.

~ 16 ~

Alyssa could not believe how the sphere of her life in Saskatoon revolved in such extraordinary propinquity. Three minutes to City Hospital, five minutes across the river via the walking bridge to the University of Saskatchewan, four minutes to The Bessborough, not that she expected to become a regular patron. Had the stars aligned and her trajectory been determined by fate? Still, all too often when Alyssa was slipping into sleep a niggling thought would surface, *Will the time come again when I question whether I was meant to choose this path to Saskatoon*?

Life at 1154 Spadina Crescent East soon settled into a pattern of defining tasks, setting boundaries, and developing harmony as the three women became more knowledgeable about each other's expectations, needs, and capabilities. Within two weeks during a telephone call with Mariah, Helen had said, "I hope you can come home for Christmas and meet my two fine young ladies. You wouldn't believe how pleasant it is have them coming and going, and also to have someone to converse with at mealtimes. I'm certain you'll quickly agree that I've chosen wisely."

When would her bubble burst? Alyssa had never expected that life could be so enjoyable, so sweet, and so serene. On Monday morning after Helen served Elaine and Alyssa cereal, coffee, and toast, they were off to visit some of the highlights of Saskatoon, the largest city in the province, which straddles a bend in the South Saskatchewan River in the central region of Saskatchewan. As her grandmother had told her, the city was beautiful capturing the splendour of the natural scenery astride the banks of the major fast-flowing river.

Feelings of camaraderie soon resurfaced between the two women. Elaine was more than ready to resume, at least their friendship following the rude awakening she had experienced yesterday. She had had a difficult time falling asleep last night, becoming quite irrational as the hours dragged by, at one point on the verge of going into the next bedroom. She wanted to shake Alyssa awake and demand to know just what game she thought she was playing. Fortunately, Elaine reined in her errant emotions in the nick of time, with a severe admonishment to exercise much better control in the future.

Following a fairly long driving tour throughout the heart of the city, Elaine said, "Before we explore the university this afternoon, may I suggest we grab a bite of lunch? The other day when I was driving around, I happened upon 8th Street and discovered that since the 1950s it has been named 'The Street of Dreams' for several Saskatoon restaurants. There's an A&W, so why don't we treat ourselves to a teen burger and onion rings?"

The mere mention of A&W brought Eric to mind and Alyssa became lost in thought. He should have finished his first supplemental exam by now, and she was sending up a little prayer that he had passed it, when she heard. "What do you think?"

"Sorry, would you be okay with trying another of those places. It sounds like there might be some interesting history behind this street, and maybe someone could enlighten us."

"Sure. I noticed a drive-through or eat-in restaurant with the interesting name of Dog 'n Suds. It would be nice to get out of the car and sit at a table."

When they had finished eating, Alyssa promptly opened her wallet and paid the bill. "This is on me, Elaine, to thank you for finding Helen and 1154 Spadina Crescent East."

❊

The women spent the entire afternoon walking around the University of Saskatchewan campus. A plethora of trees – maples, aspens, oaks, ash, and the ubiquitous poplars were beginning their seasonal transition to brilliant yellow, orange, and red autumnal colours. Historically, the unique architectural plan had called for the university buildings to be constructed around a green space known as *The Bowl* with the planting of abundant trees to accentuate the picturesque grounds.

The Collegiate Gothic style of architecture was breathtaking to behold. Alyssa's research into the university's history revealed that the original buildings were constructed using native limestone – greystone – that was mined north of the campus. Over the years, this greystone became one of the most recognizable signatures of the University of Saskatchewan. When the local supply of limestone was exhausted, the contractors turned to Tyndall stone, which is quarried in Manitoba.

"I love this campus. The University of Manitoba had already accepted me, but this spring during a conference in Saskatoon, on a whim I embarked upon a tour and became enthralled with the unique architecture and the spectacular setting of Saskatchewan's University. Given the proximity of St. Laurent to Winnipeg, it made far more sense to stay in Manitoba so I could help my mother, but for once, since it will be less than two years, I decided to indulge me. I'll soon be twenty-five and other than a work-related function, I haven't travelled outside of my home province."

"Every second summer, it was my turn to spend a week with my grandparents. They made sure to take me to Katepwa Beach in the Qu'Appelle Valley and to Regina to visit some cousins. But, that's the extent of my travels. This is a stunning campus, and I think that my grandma was right about Saskatoon being a much prettier city than Regina. When I see Eric in November, I'm going to convince him to search for a position in Saskatoon as soon as he graduates with his degree."

Glancing sideway to gaze at her, Eileen could not help but notice how animated and flushed Alyssa became whenever she mentioned Eric's name. Cupid's arrow with the golden point must have struck Alyssa with full force. During their initial conversations, Eileen had been astonished by how adamantly Alyssa had expressed her disdain for ever getting married, and yet now scarcely more than three months later, she was aglow with any reference to the man who had swept her off her feet. Not surprisingly, Eileen was experiencing a deepening sense of wonder that Alyssa had even arrived in Saskatoon at all.

~ 17 ~

The weeks were flying by and with November rapidly approaching, Alyssa was feeling compelled to telephone Eric. On her second evening in Saskatoon, seated at the small desk in her bedroom, she had penned her first letter to let him know that she had arrived safely. Initially, she could hardly contain her excitement when she was describing the quaint loft that Eileen had discovered for them. However, when Alyssa recalled the rundown apartment Eric had mentioned he lived in over the course of the past year, she decided to tone down the many attributes of her current place of residence.

Other than the street address Eric had given her, Alyssa did not have the slightest idea of what area of the city, or the type of accommodations he would be renting during the upcoming year. She did remember Eric telling her that United College was right in the heart of Winnipeg on Portage Avenue, the city's oldest and major arterial route. She also recollected that he wanted to stay as close as possible to the campus so he could walk when the weather was clement, or take the bus, rather than having to pay the parking fee for his car. Eric had laughingly alluded to the fact that since the college is in the older part of Winnipeg, and the majority of the student rentals are dilapidated, it was not uncommon to have a resident rat or two.

Similar to other members of his family whom Alyssa had met, Eric had what she could only regard as a strange sense of humour, tending to chuckle about the most unusual things. The first few times any one of them had laughed about a negative occurrence to someone, and she had queried why, the standard response was, 'it's better to laugh than to cry.' Alyssa was much too serious to grasp how laughing about another person's misfortune was humorous, so she did not know if Eric actually did have rats visiting in his apartment, nor did she ever want confirmation. It had crossed her mind not to ask Eric if the address on the piece of paper he had given her before she left Brandon was the same as his previous year.

When it was nearing the end of September and she had yet to receive a reply from Eric, Alyssa began to wonder if he had written the information correctly. During her first four weeks in Saskatoon, she had already mailed him five letters. No doubt, Eric was busy settling into his living accommodations and classes, but then so was she. From that Tuesday morning when she had arrived at City Hospital twenty minutes before seven o'clock, she felt that her mind and body had become engaged in the steepest learning curve of her life. Alyssa soon became aware that the expectations and requirements of a qualified Registered Nurse were considerably more pressing than those of a student, although during training they had all thought they were severely put upon by the nursing staff.

From the beginning of her Tuesday evening class at the university, Alyssa immediately recognized the advantages of having been an avid reader during her youth. The required reading list for the first year English course was extensive, but fortunately she had read the majority of the books, many of them more than once. As soon as the semester was underway, she became enthralled with the professor's interactive method of teaching, and the animated discussions that she rapidly perceived would become the norm. It would not be long before Alyssa Rainer would come to realize that she would far rather pursue a degree in English Literature than in nursing.

In her subsequent letter to Eric, Alyssa was sharing how her preference was changing, when it occurred to her that during those three intense months with Eric, she had only briefly mentioned she was planning to continue her education at university, and to complete a degree in nursing. Now she wondered how he viewed her aspiration when getting her to marry him seemed to be his only priority. As the days passed and she had yet to receive any correspondence from Eric, Alyssa became more and more convinced that her tough decision of opting for the best thing – rather than choosing between 'what is right and what is wrong but what is right and what is best' – had been very wise.

On Wednesday, September 28th exactly one month following her departure from Brandon, arriving home from work Alyssa found her initial, and what she would eventually come to learn, her only letter from Eric. Once she was comfortably settled in one of the recliners, she began to slowly open the epistle, wanting to savour her first news from Eric in four weeks. Since the envelope was thin, Alyssa was not expecting an abundance of information, but was amazed when she saw that less than one-half of the page had been written on – essentially asking her how she was doing, informing her that he had passed both of his supplemental exams, and promising that he would write more just as soon as he had time.

She could not believe her eyes. Was this Eric's idea of a joke? Would she receive his 'real' letter in tomorrow's mail? Alyssa was miffed, to say the least. After she had written five lengthy letters imparting all of her news, he could not even fill one page. It was clear that Eric did not like putting pen to paper, but this skimpy note had not been worth the stamp. So much for staying in touch. She would wait to see if an actual letter arrived before she would correspond any more with him. However, days and then weeks came and went, and still she did not receive any further communication.

Time was becoming of the essence. Alyssa had asked for the Remembrance Day weekend off in preparation for her journey to Winnipeg. The head nurse had been less than pleased with her most junior staff person's request, but relented when she had overheard her telling a colleague that she was going to visit her fiancé. The end of October was looming and Alyssa's feelings had been vacillating between anger and concern. Finally, she had broken her resolve and written Eric two follow-up letters, but still nothing.

Had something happened to him? Had he lost her address? Did he still want her to come? She needed to know so she could telephone Susan and Bryan to ascertain if she could stay with them. She could hardly make that long bus trip when she did not have the slightest idea whether Eric would be expecting her. Then it was Friday, October 28th. Halloween was just around the corner, and by the beginning of November it would be too late for Alyssa to confirm any plans. She could no longer wait. As soon as she arrived home from her day shift that Sunday evening, she sought Helen's permission to place a long-distance telephone call to Eric in Winnipeg.

After more rings than Alyssa dared to count, she returned the phone to its cradle. Rather than sit alone up in the loft, she decided to join Helen and Elaine in the family room where they were enjoying coffee. As she always did, after two or three sips of the refreshing brew from the porcelain cup Helen handed to her, Alyssa felt better. She had long ago perceived that the other two women sensed she was experiencing a breakdown in communication with Eric. When Helen brought in the morning mail, she always displayed it on a small oak table in the foyer, and Elaine invariably returned from the university much earlier than Alyssa, subsequently the absence of correspondence for her was obvious. On the other hand, both women had willingly mailed her letters on many occasions.

Nonetheless, Helen and Elaine were each blessed with the soul of discretion, and neither had ever breathed a word. During a lull in their conversation, Alyssa chose to take them into her confidence. "Well, another fruitless attempt to reach Eric. It's as if the man has disappeared off the face of the earth. He personifies the summer admirer – in Brandon he could not stand to be away from me, but the minute I leave it is as though I do not exist. Sorry, I realize that I sound petulant, but I'm so frustrated with not being able to communicate with him. Helen, may I please try to reach him again? I need to ascertain my plans for the November long weekend within the next few days. When your telephone bill arrives, please total the amount I owe you."

For some time, Helen had been aware of Alyssa's anguish and had experienced many moments when she wanted to throw her arms around her young boarder to commiserate. Her excitement about her fiancé, if indeed they were engaged, had over the past two months steadily eroded until Alyssa scarcely mentioned his name. Fortunately, she enjoyed her new home, remained enthusiastic regarding her nursing position, and especially about her course at the university. Now gazing fondly at Alyssa, Helen said, "Of course, you may use the telephone whenever you want, my love."

Elaine recognized only too well that she needed to show her support, but aside from not knowing what to say, she was quite frankly having ambivalent feelings. The more she realized Alyssa was presumably not receiving mail from Eric, the more she hoped that their fling had just been a summer romance. Elaine appreciated she was being selfish, but perhaps as time passed there might be a chance for her. She did manage to express, "I'm sorry, Alyssa. I'm sure if you keep calling, you'll eventually talk to Eric. Thanks, Helen for the coffee, but unless I want to get behind in my reading, I'd better scurry to my desk."

❋

Three evenings later around ten o'clock, Alyssa decided to try yet again. As during her numerous other attempts, she let the telephone ring incessantly until to her amazement she heard Eric's voice. "Hello, why do you keep calling here so late at night? People might want to sleep, you know."

"Hello, Eric. This is Alyssa Rainer telephoning from Saskatoon. Please stay on the line. I must talk to you."

"Alyssa, is it really you? You've no idea how terrific it is to hear your voice, but you couldn't have called at a worse time. I just got out of the shower and I'm standing here dripping water all over the floor. Can I towel off and call you back?"

"No, Eric. You absolutely cannot. Ages ago I lost track of how many times I've tried to reach you, not to mention all the letters I've written. I have little, if any trust left that you'll telephone back, and I need to know if I'm still coming to Winnipeg next weekend."

"Wow. It is the beginning of November, isn't it? Hey, look something has come up. A bit of a situation has arisen from when I worked in Northern Manitoba that I have to deal with now. This month is not a good time for you to visit. I'm really sorry, Alyssa. You won't believe how much I was looking forward to seeing you, but I just can't until I have worked out this problem. Tell you what, as soon as it's resolved, I'll telephone you and rearrange getting together. Have a happy birthday, and I'll call you as soon as I can." The line went dead.

❋

Alyssa would never know how long she sat at the small desk in the foyer staring at the phone before she accepted that Eric had given her the brush-off. She just could not believe it. Was this the same man who after two months had proposed marriage, not once but twice? He did not even sound like the guy she thought she was in love with, not to mention, debating whether to change all of her carefully prepared career plans. What could possibly have happened that was more important than her travelling to Winnipeg to spend her birthday with him? And, he thought that she would ever trust him again?

Her disbelief soon transitioned into annoyance. Then, she was only too aware that she would not settle into sweet repose for some time. Quietly climbing the short flight of stairs into the loft, she noticed the glow of light coming from under Elaine's closed door, before slipping into her bedroom to retrieve a novel she had just started. Alyssa returned downstairs, turned on a reading lamp in the corner of the cozy family room and tried to unwind, but to no avail. She had laid the book on her lap, although she never opened it. Instead, she kept remembering not only Eric's words, but also the tone of his voice. A situation that had occurred more than two years ago was hardly an explanation. It was an excuse.

When at last Alyssa sought the comfort of her bed, her analysis paralysis shifted from anger to melancholy. She had been so excited about going to Winnipeg to celebrate her birthday with Eric, as well as visiting with Susan and Bryan to hear about their wedding and to see all the photos. She knew beyond a doubt that Susan would have been a gorgeous bride, but she was still waiting for her to send some pictures. At the back of her mind, Alyssa appreciated she would likely have had to fend off Eric's advances, but even that might have been fun. In the early hours of the morning, Alyssa realized that she was missing him more than she ever thought she would, and she had been eagerly anticipating Eric taking her into his loving arms again. When Alyssa finally slept, she dreamt she was ensconced in one of her grandmother's legendary hugs.

Walking home from work that afternoon, Alyssa's thoughts returned to her dream, and on the spot she determined she would visit her grandmother for her birthday. At first, she debated whether she would mention her change of plans, but within minutes knew that she had no desire to deceive Helen. They had readily established such rapport that Alyssa could feel the older woman's angst with regard to what was occurring between Eric and her. Honesty was the only recourse. On the other hand, Elaine seemed to share but a modicum of Helen's interest in her relationship with her fiancé, which Alyssa was finding increasingly surprising. She had also noticed that her friend was becoming more and more detached from her, and decided to spare her the details of her distressing telephone call with Eric.

~ 18 ~

Spending her twenty-first birthday with her grandmother was inspired. It took Alyssa some time to convince her that she was planning to board the Thursday afternoon train in Saskatoon on November 10th and would arrive in Melville after nine o'clock that evening. When Grandma had understood she said, "You are coming to stay with me for your birthday. So, should I ask your Uncle Norman to pick you up at the train station and bring you to my house?"

"No, Grandma, please don't bother Norman. I'll take a taxi. I just want to visit with you. I'm still feeling sorry I had so little time to be with you when you came to Brandon for my nursing graduation, and we'll have two days completely for us."

"It will be like when you were a girl, except your grandfather will not be here. I am still missing him, and it will be nice to have someone to cook meals for again. Just come to the front door, instead of walking all the way around to the back. I will leave the light on. Alyssa, do you want me to keep supper for you?"

"Thank you, Grandma. I'll buy a sandwich before I board the train, but if you have any of your chicken and dumpling soup, I would love a bowl to warm me up on a cold winter night. I can hardly wait to see you."

When Alyssa arrived in Melville she had to wait for the ticket agent to ring for a taxi. It was nearing ten o'clock. She was worried that her grandmother might have gone to bed. The minute the driver pulled up in front of the two-bedroom bungalow on Third Avenue, she paid the fare insuring a healthy tip. She was so relieved to see the outside light still on that she opened the door, and was out of the vehicle before it had barely come to a stop. Dashing up the flight of three steps, Alyssa peered through the small side window before knocking gently on the door.

Her grandmother was seated in her rocking chair in the small-enclosed annexe that her grandparents had added to the front of their home many years ago. Alyssa took a few moments to rest her gaze lovingly upon her, knowing this trusting elderly woman would soon bestow one of her hugs that would make everything right with the world. Not wanting to spook her, especially since she had probably heard the car door closing, Alyssa tapped on the aperture to let her know that she had arrived. Instantly, Grandma was on her feet welcoming her into the warm cozy house she had made her home for the past sixteen years.

"I'm sorry to be this late, Grandma. I never thought that there would not be taxicabs at the station when the train pulled in, until I realized I was the only passenger to disembark. I think the ticket agent must have had to wake up the driver since it took him so long to come. What time do you usually go to bed? Please don't bother about making me anything to eat."

"Your soup is warming on the stove, and I will cut you a thick slice of the bread I baked this afternoon. You are never a bother to me, Alyssa. I am just so happy to have your company. I will serve it while you take your valise to the second bedroom."

The moment Alyssa was wrapped in her grandmother's arms she could feel the tension and stress that she had harboured for over the past week slowly begin to recede from her body. Noticing how inviting the eiderdown quilt folded back on the three-quarter bed looked, if it had not been for her grandma's homemade chicken and dumpling soup, she would have crawled between the sheets. Placing her luggage on the adjacent chair and hanging her coat in the closet, Alyssa was soon seated at the round kitchen table savouring one of her grandmother's favourite culinary delights.

✵

Alyssa awoke from a deep restorative sleep, her first full-uninterrupted repose since the abruptly severed telephone connection with Eric, to the delectable scent of baking wafting through the little house. She had no idea what time it was, but she remembered her grandmother telling her that she would prepare her breakfast whenever she was ready to get out of bed. Before they retired last evening, Grandma had become quite talkative, "Do you like working as a nurse, Alyssa, and do you wear a white dress and that cap on your head? I will never forget going to your nurses' graduation. I still tell all my friends about you walking across the stage when your name was called. Your grandfather would have been so proud of you, just like I am."

"I can't tell you how saddened I was that Grandpa did not live long enough to celebrate with me, but I'll always be grateful you came. Since I've not had a chance to say this to you in person, Grandma, I want to thank you for your generous graduation gift. I couldn't believe it when I opened your lovely card and saw that Grandpa had signed it from both of you. He must have made the arrangements with his banker to withdraw the money, and have given you the card dated for August 27th, 1966 months before he died."

"Your grandfather had wanted to give you your card last Christmas because he seemed to know his Maker would call him home before you finished your nursing training, but Mr. Schmidt at the bank explained what he could do. Your Grandpa had also arranged with Frieda and Norman to take me shopping at the beginning of August to buy a new dress, hat, coat, shoes, and purse which I stored in my closet, along with your gift until it was time for your mother to pick me up to go to Brandon. And, Alyssa there was no way I would ever have forgotten to give you your graduation gift."

"I know you and Grandpa have always celebrated everything that is important to me. You have been here for me my entire life. On the way to Melville, I realized since I live in Saskatoon, I could visit with you much more often. In fact, I would like to come the third week of December on my days off and we could have an early Christmas together, just the two of us again."

"You can stay with me whenever you want to come. If you need help with your train ticket, tell me. Your grandfather also made sure I have plenty of money to spend."

❋

The time with her cherished grandmother was balm to Alyssa's soul. Each morning she sat down to toasted fresh bread slathered with homemade jam and two fried eggs, which try as she might, she would never be able to duplicate throughout her life. As well as baking her favourite prune plum coffee cake for her birthday, Grandma must have remembered all of her preferred meals, which she then prepared for either dinner or supper. When they were not eating and visiting, each gravitated to her favourite chair, Alyssa to read, and her grandmother to crochet while enjoying the peace and serenity of her cozy home.

From the moment, Alyssa had curled beneath the quilt on Thursday evening she felt as though once again she was cocooned in the love she had invariably received from her maternal grandparents. When she became old enough to analyze, she incessantly attempted to determine how her mother could view children as nothing more than a burden, but any logical answer had remained beyond her grasp. It did occur to her many times that throughout her adolescence her grandparents had strived to compensate her and her siblings with the care and affection, which was never forthcoming from their negligent parents. Alyssa had long ago decided that if ever she should be blessed with her own children, she would role model her grandmother as the embodiment for mothering.

For three consecutive nights, Alyssa slept so soundly that she scarcely wrinkled the bed linen. Over the course of the two and a half days, she savoured such delicious German cuisine that the restoration of her taste buds, following three years of institutional food, begun by Helen was irrefutably concluded. In her grandmother's calming presence as they whiled away the hours chatting, reminiscing, sitting side by side in silence, Alyssa could feel her equanimity gradually seeping back into her heart, mind, and soul. By the time she left just before eleven o'clock on Sunday morning and Grandma walked the two doors up the street for church, Alyssa Rainer knew that whether she heard from Eric and whatever plans they made for next month, she would return so the two women could rejoice together in an early Christmas celebration.

~ 19 ~

During the train ride home Alyssa's thoughts kept returning to Elaine. When had they started to drift apart and what was causing the rift between them? She remembered how overjoyed Elaine had been when she greeted her at the station upon her arrival in Saskatoon. Then suddenly during dinner Elaine's countenance clouded over, and she had become taciturn while Helen and Alyssa engaged in the balance of the conversation. Regardless of how she tried, Alyssa could not recall what she might have said or done. But, Elaine had been increasingly distant ever since. What had they been talking about at that juncture? Perhaps, if she were to let her mind wander to the rhythm of the wheels on the track it might come to her.

Alyssa awoke with a start. How could she have fallen asleep after the blissful repose she enjoyed last night? She had been dreaming about Eric. Could that be it? Had Elaine's cheerful demeanour turned disconsolate when Alyssa was enthusing about being proposed to by the love of her life? But, why would Elaine not be elated for her? Could she be jealous that her younger friend had a fiancé, when she seemingly did not have a boyfriend? Considering this possibility, Alyssa readily ruled it out as the reason, thinking that Elaine probably had her share of men interested in courting her. She was attractive, intelligent, successful, and had likely left any number of broken hearts behind in Manitoba when she chose to pursue a university education in Saskatchewan.

Of course, both women had been exceedingly busy since their relocation to Saskatoon, adjusting to a myriad of schedules, activities, and changes in their lives. Many times they were like ships passing in the night with Alyssa rising before the light of day, and Elaine studying well into the late evening. However, unless she was working an afternoon shift, both of them joined Helen for dinner in the comfort of her attractive kitchen. Dialogue was light, congenial, and usually focused on the daily happenings of one or another of the threesome. The rapport amongst the group was enhanced the more they were in each other's presence, with Helen especially benefitting from the recurring interactions with two bright energetic young women.

Had Helen become a buffer between the friends? She was so affable that it would have been near impossible not to come to regard her in the most favourable light. When the three were together she brought out the best in Elaine and Alyssa, and any potential tension disappeared like the mist coming off the South Saskatchewan River early in the mornings when she walked to City Hospital. Nonetheless, when alone in their loft the roommates scarcely spoke to each other beyond monosyllabic responses, and Alyssa for one was missing their conversations. In truth, after three years of living in a room with two or more classmates in a residence overflowing with women, any pretense of camaraderie was sorely lacking.

A sudden perspicacity of her grandmother's day-to-day reality surfaced in Alyssa's mind. Now that grandpa was gone, did she wake every morning, attend to her household chores, and then wait in vain for someone to telephone, or in the rare circumstance come to visit her? Little wonder she was so talkative when Alyssa had arrived on Thursday evening and often throughout much of their visit. She had regularly written letters to her grandfather, but since grandma could not read English, and Alyssa could not write German, she resolved then and there to telephone her once a week. Her Christmas visit would become the precedent that she would duplicate at least every three months whenever she had two or more days off from the hospital. And, as soon as she encountered Elaine, she was going to suggest that they set aside time for a coffee or lunch date.

❋

By the time Alyssa arrived at the train station, Saskatoon was mounting the peak of a blizzard with blustery winds whirling about large flakes of snow until visibility was all but nonexistent. Before she departed, she had received instructions from both Elaine and Helen to telephone for a ride home upon her return. In all conscience, Alyssa could not ask either of them to come out in such a storm and was quick to race to the taxi waiting at the end of the platform. She reached the door just moments ahead of a man intent on the same pursuit.

"To what part of the city do you need to travel? In view of the inclement weather, maybe we could share what appears to be the only available cab. I'm going to Spadina Crescent close to City Hospital."

"How fortunate. I need a ride to King Crescent only one block over. Actually, you look familiar. I'm certain I've seen you in the cafeteria at the hospital. Do you happen to be one of the employees? I'm David Singer and my fiancée, a registered nurse and I both arrived here from Manitoba at the beginning of September. Cheryl works on the Pediatric ward at City Hospital, where in my medical studies at the University of Saskatchewan, I'm often referred to visit patients."

Once they had given their respective addresses to the driver, she said, "My name is Alyssa Rainer. Happenstance seems to be the order of the day. I relocated to Saskatoon from Brandon at the end of August to begin work on the surgical ward at City Hospital. During my second year of nursing training, I affiliated at the Children's Hospital in Winnipeg for two months. Perchance, is your fiancée's surname, Sheps?"

"As a matter of fact, I'm engaged to the vivacious Cheryl Sheps, a recent graduate of the Children's Hospital. Don't tell me that you two know each other? Good heavens, talk about a plethora of coincidences."

A smile crossed Alyssa's countenance as she thought, *So, Cheryl did find her doctor to marry, and not surprisingly, she had chosen well.* David Singer was Jewish, tall, well-built, handsome, and already during their brief encounter, she considered him to be courteous and amiable. Her mirth was heightened when she wondered how Cheryl's outspoken father had quizzed him during their introduction. Beyond a doubt, David would have fared much more favourably than she when Cheryl had taken Alyssa to their extravagant home for dinner. Not about to divulge the slightest indication for her inner glee, she replied, "I agree with you. Cheryl is a vibrant individual. Please tell her that for the third time we find ourselves under the roof of the same hospital, although I believe now we will strive to be more appropriate in our behaviour. She will know instantly the raison d'etre for my comment."

"I can hardly wait to tell Cheryl about meeting you. I'm going to King Crescent to have dinner with her at her aunt and uncle's with whom she's residing until we get married next September. What shift are you working tomorrow? Surely you two can reconnect either at the hospital or walk one block over when the storm abates."

"Just out of curiosity what is the house number of Cheryl's relatives? I share a loft with a friend at 1154 Spadina Crescent. I'm on days for the next week and if we miss each other in the cafeteria, maybe she could stop on the third floor on her way down from the fifth."

"Well, if this storm had not intervened I daresay that fate would have brought Cheryl and you together either at the hospital or in the neighbourhood. She lives at 1127 King Crescent. You can walk down the back lane to see one another. Here we are at your address. Don't worry about the fare, I'll pay when the driver delivers me, and you can get Cheryl's lunch one day. Thanks for sharing your cab. I look forward to seeing you again."

Alyssa had scarcely climbed the stairs when the front door opened, and a relieved Helen ushered her into the warmth of her home with a gentle hug. "Thank God, you found a taxi. Elaine couldn't wait any longer and has just gone upstairs to grab her purse. Toss off your boots and let her know that you have arrived safe and sound."

"Thank you, Helen. I'm so glad she has not ventured out. I think our cab driver drove by rote memory taking the chance that there were no other vehicles on the streets because it was impossible to see." Alyssa replied as she dashed through the foyer up to the loft.

They met on the landing. Elaine was so grateful to see Alyssa that without thinking she enveloped her in a heartfelt embrace, which lasted far longer than she had intended. When she realized she quickly released her saying, "I was convinced you were going to be stranded at the station, and I could not imagine you spending the night in that old building."

"I appreciate you would go out on a night like this for my sake. All the way home on the train I kept thinking how much I miss the warmth and ease of our friendship."

"I know. We've both become so busy with our respective pursuits that we haven't made time for our lives to intersect. Belated happy birthday, Alyssa. On your next day off, I would like to invite you and Helen out for lunch. I can't take you to the Bessborough, but we shall find a venue that is a little more upscale than Dog 'n Suds."

~20~

Christmas was fast approaching. Every moment her mind was not focused on work, or when conversing with others, Alyssa's thoughts turned to Eric. Would he telephone or write a letter to follow up with what was happening with him? She knew beyond a doubt that with her schedule there was no way she could journey to Winnipeg over the holiday season. Furthermore, at all costs she would keep her promise to her grandmother, and had already called her to confirm that she was coming on December 19th for three days. There was little she could do, but wait. And, wait she did, while wavering between feelings of angst and anger.

When Elaine asked her to join them for lunch to celebrate Alyssa's birthday, Helen had anticipated that she would be included, and her reply was instant, "Thank you for the invite, but you two friends have had so little time together since you arrived that you need to catch up. On Sunday I'm planning a special dinner with a black forest cake, and then we'll all rejoice in Alyssa reaching the age of majority."

As soon as her last morning class on Thursday ended, Elaine left the campus arriving back at Spadina Crescent shortly after noon. She had driven to the university and appreciated that Alyssa was peering out the glass window of the front door when she pulled onto the street. Once she was seated Elaine said, "I discovered another restaurant on Broadway I've wanted to try. I'm not sure my pronunciation is correct, but it's called Weczeria. Several of my classmates say it is the best café that Saskatoon has ever had with good farm-to-plate values and a focus on regional cooking with local ingredients. Would you be interested in going there?"

"Sure, that sounds like a good idea since we seem to gravitate to Broadway Avenue. It's kind of you to take me for lunch, Elaine, although we could go Dutch given that you're a student."

"Thanks, Alyssa. Mostly I'm looking forward to spending time with you and rekindling our friendship. Even though I've met many other students, while we're on campus our only topics of conversation are related to courses, assignments, and how we're ever going to handle the workload. Since we've moved in together, we scarcely speak to each other. I miss our animated discussions and I miss you."

Elaine had fortuitously found a parking spot close to the restaurant, and because Alyssa wanted to delve deeper into her remarks, she waited until they were seated at a table. When they had placed their order she said, "I think that we're both at fault for the essential breakdown in our communication. Naturally, we've been adjusting to all the changes in our respective lives, but when we're at home, I believe we enjoy interacting with Helen so much that we don't allow time for us. She's an appealing astute woman and I suspect before we rented her loft she was quite lonely. I've also missed our camaraderie."

On the one hand, Elaine was pleased that Alyssa had chosen to refer to her previous comments, while on the other she wondered if she might have come across as needy. She was still feeling the glow from her hug on Sunday, and her mood had been lighter all week. When Alyssa suddenly changed her travel plans for her birthday, Elaine had speculated ad nauseam about what could have motivated her decision. Was it possible she and Eric had had a parting of the ways? Would it be prudent to ask? Dare she have hope? Instead, Elaine considered that it might be wise to wait and see if Alyssa made any reference to what had happened.

"I couldn't agree with you more about Helen. She's delightful, defying any conceivable negativity about 'the landlady.' Actually though, change is the operative word in your comment. I don't think that I anticipated the requirements for the nursing degree to be so onerous, or maybe it is just trying to cope with becoming a student again after years of being out of school. Are you finding working fulltime and being a part-time learner challenging?"

"I certainly did during the month of September, but now I'm familiar with the routines and am getting to know my coworkers, I've become more comfortable. As far as my English course, I've read all of the requisite novels, most of them several times, and I can write the essays any time. I've always loved Literature, and I'm contemplating completing a degree in English rather than pursuing my nursing degree."

"That would be quite the transition. Within my first month I'd concluded that university consists of all-embracing expectations, unrealistic reading, and excessive writing. Since you're planning to get married in the near future, I wonder what Eric might have to say about all the additional schooling."

"The way things are going, or should I say not going, marriage could be a considerable distance down the road. After he all but dismissed me on the telephone, I haven't the slightest intention of initiating communication with him. Even if Eric rang to ask me to come during the Christmas holiday I couldn't request the time, and I'm not likely to make that trip across the prairies in bleak midwinter. To be perfectly candid, my reticence with you this past while is primarily attributable to my being out of sorts with what is happening with Eric. I'm sorry, Elaine."

"Oh, I can't let you shoulder the entire fault, Alyssa. I forfeit my sense of balance whenever I become overwhelmed learning to cope with new responsibilities. I'm enjoying our lunch, and may I suggest that we plan to set aside time once a week to touch base with what's happening with us."

"I would like that, Elaine. Once I've my schedule, we can select a time that works for both of us. We don't always need to go out especially during the winter, but could have coffee in the cosy confines of our loft."

Alyssa's birthday lunch became a celebratory affair when the owners of the family restaurant served a complimentary slice of a double-layered chocolate cake with two forks after the main course. At the juncture when Alyssa had excused herself to use the lavatory, Elaine motioned for the waitress to request she be presented with the combined bill. During their conversation she identified the reason for their outing, with both women subsequently enjoying the surprise dessert and singing to conclude a delicious repast.

Helen was pleased when her two endearing 'girls' returned home in high spirits. She had been noticing that Alyssa was often withdrawn during their interactions at mealtimes as the Christmas season was nearing. Helen knew that there had not been any letters waiting to be mailed, or any further requests to place long-distance telephone calls. Nor had Alyssa once mentioned Eric's name. The older woman remembered a conversation with her about her grandfather's stoicism, and she suspected that Alyssa's dearth of any emotional manifestations, whether shedding tears or outbursts of anger, was the result of her emulating the man who had been her lifelong source of inspiration and love.

Not surprisingly, Alyssa confined the full expression of her feelings to the privacy of her bedroom. On occasion, Elaine could hear quiet sobs vacillating with slamming drawers through the walls, but unlike Helen, she was not touched by concern. May God forgive her? She realized that if Alyssa and Eric had broken their engagement, she was more likely to remain in Saskatoon and continue to live in their loft with her. Alyssa's excitement about reconnecting with a friend from nursing training last Friday evening, especially with Cheryl's wedding planned in the city next September, also heightened Elaine's conviction that she would be less motivated to return to Manitoba. Over time with gentle and steady commiseration, Elaine might succeed in winning Alyssa's love.

~ 21 ~

Once the three-day blizzard had moved on, the temperature dropped until the air was so frigid that opening the front door felt like stepping into a deepfreeze. Alyssa thanked her lucky stars she had purchased an Eddie Bauer down-filled jacket and sturdy warm boots with her first paycheque. Bundling up with a woollen toque covering her head, and a scarf around her neck and face with only her eyes exposed, she was prepared for whatever the unpredictable prairie winter would bring forth. Elaine's fortuitous discovery of Helen's loft within a three-minute walking distance to the hospital however proved to be the most auspicious of all.

On Wednesday morning squeezing on to the crowded elevator for her coffee break, Alyssa literally came face to face with Cheryl. "You always did have great timing. I was going to stop on the third floor on my way back to Pediatrics, but now we can begin catching up in the cafeteria. Firstly, I want to invite you to dinner at my aunt and uncle's on Friday. David has to work, thus presenting us with a perfect opportunity for a long overdue chinwag."

Chuckling, Alyssa instantly inquired, "Do I need to prepare to be interrogated before I'm served any food to eat?"

"Not to worry, my Uncle Jacob is the antithesis of my father. Aunt Vera is my mother's younger sister, and as I recall you and Rebecca interacted famously, so come ready to have an enjoyable evening. If you're on the day shift on Friday, why don't we meet in the foyer at the main entrance of the hospital and walk to King Crescent together? And, it seems that you owe me lunch. Whenever the temperature moderates we'll have to schedule a day to feast at the Bessborough."

"Leaving the wealthy milieu of your parental home and becoming independent have had little impact on your perspective on how the rest of us live, I hazard a guess. Nonetheless, I'll honour my word to David, and we'll set a date." Alyssa replied humorously as they left to return to their respective wards.

❋

Vera not only shared Rebecca's temperament, but also could physically have passed as her twin. She welcomed Alyssa into her elegant home with arms reaching to help remove her winter wear. Jacob soon joined her at the front door to offer his assistance to Cheryl, before both were invited into the family room with a blazing fire in the hearth. Alyssa and Cheryl were no sooner seated than Vera said, "I'm ready for my late afternoon coffee, which has just percolated. Would you care to join me, or perhaps you would prefer a hot toddy?"

"I'll have a cup of coffee with cream and sugar please. I've discovered that I'm allergic to alcohol and avoid drinking it at all costs." Alyssa replied. Cheryl chimed in, "Thanks, Aunt Vera, I'll have the same. Would you like help?"

"You two get comfortable and cozy after your busy day at work. Jacob will wheel in the coffee cart when I'm ready."

Within minutes, Jacob appeared pushing a vintage Danish Teak Trolley laden with four china mugs, a silver coffee percolator, serving plates, and two different desserts. "Terrific, you've been baking this afternoon." Cheryl exclaimed. "Alyssa, you must sample both the honey cake and the macaroons now because if I know my aunt, she'll have prepared another delightful treat to serve after the roast chicken with all the trimmings."

Had it not been for the coffee, both young women would have dozed off in front of the fire when Vera and Jacob vacated to the kitchen and dining room respectively, amid refusals for any assistance. Alyssa's week had been long and tiring, with another three shifts before she was scheduled for two days off. Then and there, she resolved she would not be late returning home subsequent to an acceptable interlude after dinner. Of course, she forgot that 'the best laid plans of mice and men often go awry.'

❋

It was nearing nine o'clock when Cheryl invited Alyssa up the stairs of the two-storey house to view her room. "Would you mind if I took a rain check? I'm bushed and plan to be asleep at a reasonable hour."

"We won't be long. I haven't had a chance to show you my engagement ring. I keep it in a small wall safe because I wouldn't dream of wearing it to the hospital when I nurse on a children's ward. David's father owns Peoples Jewellers in Winnipeg, and he had my ring set exclusively designed for me."

The ring blew Alyssa away. Cheryl clarified that the elongated centre diamond was 2.01 Carats, the first two side antique oval cut diamonds weighed 1.13 Carats, and the second two were each 1 Carat. The five exquisite diamonds were mounted in 18 K gold. Alyssa could not imagine ever removing the ring from the safe much less wearing it to work in a hospital. She was so stunned that all she could utter was, "David has designed and presented you with an incredible ring." Under her breath though, she mumbled, "It's a prodigious leap from the gold bracelet that Eric had engraved for me."

"What did you say? Who is Eric? Are you implying that you're engaged? You haven't mentioned a word about having a fiancé. You're not leaving here tonight until you tell all."

"I'd no idea your hearing was that acute? It's a long and unresolved story that I don't have the energy to relate this evening. It'll have to wait until our luncheon."

Cheryl studied Alyssa for several moments in silence before saying, "I'm surprised that in less than a year you've forgotten how tenacious I am. So, you're well-advised to begin."

Recalling how insistent Cheryl had been when they discovered they were sharing another affiliation, this time at the Brandon Hospital for Mental Diseases, Alyssa realized that she had no recourse but to recount her relationship with Eric. She was determined, however she would stop her update with his graduation gift, and his request she consider the bracelet as a token of their engagement. Then she would be on her way back to Spadina Crescent.

If Cheryl had not been listening so attentively, which was uncharacteristic of her, given her propensity to interrupt and ask questions, Alyssa might not have become as immersed in relating her brief courtship with Eric. When she was nearing the end of her narrative it was as though all of the questions, anxieties, and trepidation that she had been suppressing suddenly surfaced, and she was as surprised as Cheryl when she erupted into tears. She huddled her body into itself, drawing her knees up in the sofa chair in an attempt to cope with the outburst of her feelings.

Cheryl silently approached, sat on the side of the chair, and gently placed her arm around Alyssa's shoulder. She remained in that position until her sobbing subsided before asking, "Do you want to talk about what's happening?"

Snuffling, it took Alyssa several minutes before she said, "That's just it. I don't know what is taking place with Eric. Inhaling a deep breath, she explained the sequence of events that had occurred since they had expressed their farewell on the evening of graduation, and how she had been waiting for Eric to telephone her as soon as he had solved his problem, whatever it might be. After a second thought Alyssa lamented, "I'm afraid that Susan's prophecy is coming true."

"Refresh my memory please. Susan is the attractive blond who practically shadowed you in Winnipeg, but then wrote you off because you were going out and having fun with me during my three months in Brandon. Good heavens, what did she predict?"

"To make a long story short, I was a fool to pursue my confirmed nursing position in Saskatoon, and arranged room and board accommodations with my friend, Elaine. Instead during our last week in training, I should totally reverse all of my plans and relocate to Winnipeg, even though other than her and Eric I didn't know another soul, I didn't have a job, and I didn't have a place to live. Her rationale was that since neither Eric nor I had 'a single penny to rub together' as she so eloquently expressed, we would never see each other again. Now the question that keeps coursing through my mind is could Susan have been right?"

"Wow, what heavy foreshadowing to lay on you at the last minute. Little wonder you've been overwhelmed with worries and fear. However, Saskatoon and Winnipeg are hardly on the opposite coasts of Canada, and as you've just shared you were prepared to shoulder the majority of the correspondence and travel since you do now have a salary. But, of course it's difficult, if not impossible when Eric chooses not to reciprocate. I'm not sure that with a friend like Susan you need any enemies. She wouldn't be discouraging him, would she?"

Alyssa became still. She sat in silence for long moments. At last she said, "That's interesting in light of another dilemma I've been wrestling with since Eric terminated our telephone conversation. Before she left Brandon, Susan had offered that I could stay with her and Bryan whenever I returned to Winnipeg. When I realized I wasn't likely to hear from Eric in time to finalize my trip, I rang Susan to let her know that I was not coming. Much to my amazement, the operator came on the line to identify the number was no longer in service. I tried a second and a third time, knowing it was the only quick way I had of contacting Susan. I'm beginning to think that anyone I know who went to Winnipeg has disappeared into an abyss. Nevertheless, I can't believe that Susan would do anything to thwart Eric from persisting with our relationship. She liked him and right from the time we met, she professed that he was my soulmate."

"I'm sorry, Alyssa, that I pressured you into sharing your complicated life situation and being responsible for upsetting you. Would you like something to eat or drink before Uncle Jacob and I bundle up to walk you home, whenever you're ready? By the way, why would you travel that distance by bus, rather than fly from Saskatoon to Winnipeg?"

Never for a moment would Alyssa have expressed the thought that coursed through her mind, "*Oh, what a difference to one's perspective money does make*?" Instead she said, "I neither intended to unload all my cares and woe on you, Cheryl, nor to monopolize the conversation. I didn't give you a chance to tell me anything about what is transpiring with you, and especially when and how you met David. He impressed me as a lovely man, and he is a doctor – perfect for you. I'll express my thanks to your aunt and uncle for a delightful evening and be on my way. I wouldn't dream of dragging you and Jacob outdoors on such a bitter night to walk one block."

"Safety in numbers. We'll escort you to your front door to make certain you're inside and then return home together. I'll regale you with David's and my story next Wednesday when we enjoy lunch at the Bessborough."

~22~

The Christmas season came and went. The temperature across the prairies moderated in time for travellers to feel confident about venturing forth to visit family and friends. December had been a busy month at Spadina Crescent filled with excitement, plans, longings, and despair. Helen was ecstatic that Mariah was coming home during the holiday season and bringing her beau to meet her. Had it not been that there were two bedrooms in the refurbished basement, for the briefest of moments, she might have asked her young ladies whether they would vacate their loft for eight days. She recognized such an expectation was entirely unrealistic, and decided that her daughter would not even allow the thought to cross her mind. Over the past three months, Mariah was pleased with her mother's revitalized enthusiasm and energy, and had expressed, during several different telephone conversations, she knew that it was undoubtedly attributable to her lodgers.

For as much as Helen loved her three girls, she was anticipating a male presence in her home once again. Bit by bit Ray's friends who had come by to check on how she was managing following his passing, no longer stopped in, and Mariah had been much too involved with medical school to entertain young men. Helen still hosted her female friends for luncheons and bridge games, but primarily in the afternoon. Yet, she had always enjoyed the company of the opposite gender, tending to be more vibrant and beguiling than if she were only hosting women. And, of course she had a vested interest in charming Steven. Helen so often fretted that Mariah would be too engrossed in her career to find time to marry and present her with grandchildren.

During her childhood and youth, Mariah had pined for siblings and regardless how much her parents included her in everything they were embarking upon, she never gave up asking for a brother or sister. It was not that she lacked for friends, invitations to parties, sporting events, or sleepovers, but that as she explained, in the evenings in the quiet of her bedroom she wanted to share the adventures of the day with her own kin. When she was old enough to understand, Ray and Helen apprised her of how fortunate they were she had survived her premature birth, and they were convinced that she was a blessing from God. In the midst of her preparations, a smile flitted across Helen's face with the thought, *Were Mariah not bringing Steven home she would most likely bunk in with Alyssa and Elaine in her former loft.*

❋

The timing of Alyssa's return from her visit to her grandmother on December 22nd dovetailed perfectly with Mariah and Steven's late afternoon arrival on the twenty-third of the month. Helen would take her automobile to the airport since it was large enough to accommodate Alyssa and Elaine, both of whom had indicated that they would like to go with her. She had been a little surprised that Elaine was interested, but in the past three days since the completion of her exams she had regained her relaxed pleasant demeanour.

Throughout the first semester of university, Elaine was often so tense that Helen worried whether she was going to cope with the strenuous academic requirements. It had been during Alyssa's visit to her grandmother in November that Helen acquired a heightened awareness of why Elaine was stressed about her course work. She was helping her wash the dishes and tidy the kitchen following a light supper of creamed chicken with vegetables and cheese biscuits when Helen said, "Are you planning to resume your studying this evening, or would you care to join me in front of the fireplace for a cup of tea and a sample of the fruit cake I baked yesterday for Christmas?"

"I would enjoy the time with you very much. For the past four months it seems that all I do is bury my head in books, and yet I never seem to catch up on my reading and assignments. I miss the tête-à-têtes with you and Alyssa. Unless she's working an evening shift, she is available to relax with you in your comfortable family room. I know that she's only taking one course, but she must be proficient about meeting the expectations."

"Alyssa has mentioned that she's enthralled with her English class, and having read all of the assigned books, completing the essays is hardly challenging. I've a hunch she has a natural talent and perhaps, writing is her true calling. She did share that her dream is to pen her own book, although she realizes she needs to make a living before she would be able to follow the path of an author."

"Often when I've been hunched over my desk, I've heard the murmur of your voices. I'll admit that I'm envious of the time the two of you spend together. Already you know more about Alyssa than I do, and are becoming closer to her than I am."

Helen wondered if she detected a note of jealousy in Elaine's words. Every now and then, her inquiring mind was skeptical about her sentiments toward Alyssa. Was she overprotective of her, was it about control, bordering on possessiveness, or was there a hidden depth to her feelings? Not for the first time and far from the last, Helen remembered Elaine's response to Alyssa's news about her engagement on the day of her arrival in Saskatoon.

She had never been able to decipher her unusual reaction, but she did notice that whenever Alyssa mentioned Eric and now the lack of his communication, Elaine feigned a paucity of interest.

Instead of slipping into more analysis about Elaine, Helen decided to avail herself of this opportunity to get to know her better and said, "It's possible that with Alyssa just finishing three years of studying and writing exams, it's easier for her to get back in the groove of school work. I think that by your next semester you'll have rediscovered your rhythm and won't need the same amount of time to meet the requirements."

"Thank you, Helen, for your kind words of encouragement. I certainly hope you're right because there is no way that I want to disappoint my sponsors. When my mother mentioned that I was planning to attend the University of Saskatchewan, the Métis Settlement of St. Laurent decided to subsidize me as the first member of the municipality to pursue higher education. I had been saving for years to study for my nursing degree, and their support is a godsend for me. Of course, I'm putting myself under considerable pressure because I would never want to let my community down."

"Ah, now I've an enlightened sense of why you're so driven. What an honour, but also what a responsibility. If there is anything that I can do to ease your load, Elaine, please tell me. For example, rather than assisting me prepare dinner or clean the kitchen, why don't you use that time to do your own work? Alyssa is younger and full of energy, and I could ask her to help me more. Then you could join us to relax, even if it was for shorter periods during the evenings."

In the calm and warmth of the moment, Elaine came ever so close to disclosing the real reason for her compulsion. If only she could tell someone she might not be so obsessed with Alyssa, perhaps eventually overcoming her feelings. Still, as empathetic as Helen was, Elaine wondered how traditional she might prove to be in her beliefs. Could she take the chance? The last possible outcome she was prepared to risk was endangering the budding relationship among the three women and their appealing living arrangement.

It had not been until her first year in nursing school that Elaine Hurren came to realize her relationship preference was the cause of her always feeling different. Over the subsequent years, she had never disclosed her proclivity to anyone, and she was not about to begin now with a conventional middle-aged woman.

~23~

Christmas at Spadina Crescent was enchanting. The magic began the moment Mariah spotted her mother in the arrivals waiting area and beamed her beautiful smile. As soon as she was near, she wrapped her arms around her as though she never wanted to let go. "Oh, Mama, I've missed you every minute I haven't had to concentrate on work." At last releasing her, Mariah turned to the two young women, introduced herself first to Alyssa and then to Elaine as she enveloped each of them in heartfelt hugs. "How lovely you've come to meet us. May I introduce you, Steven to three endearing ladies with whom we'll celebrate the love and joy of the Christmas season."

Mariah Symonds was blessed from the day she was born, and once held in her parents' loving arms she began to develop into the name they had bestowed upon her. They had long ago given up the slightest hope of ever knowing the delights of raising a family when to Helen's complete surprise a doctor diagnosed her as being pregnant. She was over thirty and for the first time in her life, she was so tired she could hardly muster the energy to get out of bed in the morning. At first, Ray thought that she had picked up the flu after they spent the September weekend with their friends at their summer cottage on Martin's Lake.

As the days became weeks, one month, then two, even Ray was becoming concerned with the steady loss of Helen's usual vim, vigour, and vivaciousness. She had seldom been ill in her life and subsequently rarely sought the services of a doctor. One of his colleagues from the office recommended his family physician, and the next day Ray insisted Helen accompany him to visit Dr. Ryner for a thorough physical check-up. He remained with her for the duration of the examination and the follow-up laboratory tests, his anxiety reflected on his handsome face, although nary a word crossed his lips. How could he ever carry on living if there were something seriously wrong with his beloved wife? When they finally accepted that they were not to bear children, Ray and Helen had become even more devoted to each other.

On Friday morning of the following week, Ray answered his telephone at work and was instantly agitated when he heard, "Hello, Mr. Symonds. This is Robert Ryner calling. I want to ask you to bring Mrs. Symonds to my office this afternoon at five o'clock. I've news for you."

As soon as their conversation was over, Ray rang Helen. Waiting for her to answer he wished he had inquired whether the 'news' was negative or positive, and realized that he had not because he needed Helen to be with him when he received the results. In addition, he knew he must downplay the alarm that was beginning to surface in his mind and be nonchalant when she asked what the doctor had said. "Hi, Helen, I was just dashing off to a meeting when the doctor's office called to ask us to meet with him this afternoon. I'll be home to pick you up before four o'clock. Love you."

Approaching their tenth wedding anniversary, Helen was well aware that when her husband attempted to be blasé with her, it was because he wanted to minimize whatever instance of reality was about to rear its ugly head. She also knew he treated himself to a late afternoon cup of coffee with a small sweet at the office to carry him through the balance of his workday. Helen was dressed and waiting in the shade on the front veranda, with a carafe of coffee and a piece of freshly baked rhubarb cake as the day was reaching the designated hour.

Still trying to lighten the mood, Ray climbed the four steps onto the veranda and said, "I may have to make a habit of arriving home at this time of the day. Is that my favourite cake you're offering me? How lucky can I be?"

Ray and Helen continued to engage in light-hearted conversation from the minute he had come home, during the half hour drive, and as they waited in the doctor's office. All the while, each was running through a mental checklist of what could possibly be wrong with Helen. When they were welcomed into his office, Dr. Ryner seemed unusually cheerful compared to the dire prospects, which Helen and Ray had been considering. "Please have a seat. I'll not keep you in suspense any longer, particularly since I suspect that I may have favourable information for you. Mr. and Mrs. Symonds, your lives are about to be altered significantly in approximately seven months when you become the proud parents of a baby girl or boy."

They were stunned. Neither knew where to look nor what to say. Dr. Ryner's 'news' had not made an appearance on either of their lists. Quite frankly, the results of the laboratory tests and the potential diagnosis had been exclusively negative in both of their minds. Perhaps, it was fitting that Helen was the first to break the ensuing silence, "Are you telling me that I'm going to have a baby? How can that be? All these years and I could never become pregnant. Are you certain? I just can't get my hopes up to have them come crashing down when you determine that it is something else."

"I appreciate your skepticism, Mrs. Symonds, especially as it is later in your life, so I had the lab repeat your test to positively confirm that you are indeed with child. Your others results are equally positive and I'm delighted to give you a clean bill of health. You're remarkably fit, and you've just now affirmed that becoming a mother has long been an aspiration of yours. Congratulations Mrs. and Mr. Symonds."

❋

The years flew by much quicker than either Helen or Ray would ever have preferred. They lived in a neighbourhood where the majority of the residents were older than the Symonds. As a consequence, there were virtually no little playmates for Mariah until one or the other of their friends and neighbours enjoyed visitations from their grandchildren. Nonetheless,

Mariah Symonds was never lonely, she was known to everyone, and was lovingly referred to as 'Little Miss Sunshine of Spadina Crescent.'

Helen was invariably asked why she had chosen the name Mariah for her long-awaited daughter and never tired of explaining its multiple origins. She would always begin by saying, "I had discovered the name derives from the Ancient Greek names 'Mariam and Maria' found in the New Testament meaning 'beloved, wished for child.' Ray and I had yearned for our own child for almost ten years and when we had given up hope, I became pregnant. In our search for girls' names, we came across 'Mariah' with other possible genesis, such as the Latin 'Star of the Sea' signifying 'like the wind.' We both loved the sound of Mariah along with its different meanings, and decided it was the name we wanted to christen our daughter feeling that she would aspire to all of its connotations."

Though as the years passed with Mariah maturing and blossoming into a beautiful human being, in her heart and soul, Helen came to believe that "the Lord is my teacher" from the biblical derivation was the wellspring whence Mariah's humanity originated.

~24~

As Christmas Day was drawing to a close, Alyssa and Elaine had retired to their loft. Neither was ready to bring the surreal evening to an end, and simultaneously gravitated toward her easy chair designated months ago by tacit agreement. In an ethereal voice Alyssa mused, "During the ensuing hours since I arrived home from work at the hospital, I've felt as if I were being blessed by the truest spirit of Christmas that I have ever experienced. In the simplest of moments love shone brightest and we were immersed in hope, joy, and peace, all of which have been woven into the tapestry of Mariah Symonds' soul."

Long moments elapsed when in a *sotto voce* Elaine said, "I had no idea your spirituality reached such depth or that you were so eloquent. Often throughout the day, I felt otherworldly, but I would never have been able to express what I was feeling as succinctly as you. Thank you, Alyssa."

"My grandfather was a devout Lutheran, and my grandmother will be until she joins him in the hereafter. The only time that I ever attended church was when I happened to be in Melville. The service was entirely in German, and although I could not understand a single word, combined with the resonance of a magnificent pipe organ, being with my grandparents in worship was the most memorable occurrence of my upbringing. They not only imbued me with an abiding faith, but also with lifelong gifts of love and inspiration."

"I gathered you must be very close to your grandmother, given that you've visited her twice in as many months. Would she have been alone for Christmas?"

"My mother and three sisters were going to drive to Melville yesterday, and will probably return to Virden in a day or two. I did explain to Grandma I had to work today, but I'll telephone her before my evening shift tomorrow and also speak to my mother. Throughout my childhood, we always had Christmas dinner with my grandparents. Grandma worked so hard to prepare all the food and to buy us our only presents, but invariably my acrimonious parents would initiate their never-ending arguments and ruin the festivities. When I arrived last week, Grandma had roasted a chicken with all the trimmings. The two of us had the most enjoyable and peaceful Christmas of my life."

"I did call my mother this morning. This is the first year that I haven't spent Christmas with Mum and Samuel, and they both had to apprise me how much I was missed. Although we never had much, my mother always succeeded in making us feel the joy and peace of the season. Every year there was just the three of us, but love permeated our tiny home. The older I get the more I realize what a special person my mother is. When I complete my nursing degree, I'll return to St. Laurent to be with her as she ages."

"I believe that you and I might already represent a significant application of the words of a renowned American educator, author, orator, and advisor to several presidents of the United States. I often think about one of Booker T. Washington's poignant quotations, *Success is to be measured not so much by the position that one has reached in life as by the obstacles which he has overcome.* I do wonder though, how much more likely I would be to self-actualize and to achieve my true potential in life, if I had been as fortunate as Mariah to be born and raised by parents like Helen and Ray Symonds."

❋

As the holiday season was coming to its inevitable end, Helen realized that she dreaded Steven returning to Victoria as much as she did Mariah's departure. She could not have been more pleased with her daughter's choice, and prayed their relationship would eventually culminate in them becoming lifelong partners. He was so much like Ray in temperament, mannerisms, and even appearance that Helen could hardly believe her eyes and instincts when first they had been introduced. It was uncanny and she let slip an audible gasp when she saw him approaching at the airport. For several moments she had wondered if her mind was playing tricks on her. Steven Lancaster could have been a version of Ray in his younger years.

The more time Helen spent with Steven, the more memories began to flood her mind throughout the day and her dreams during the night. The thought surfaced that Mariah may have been initially drawn to him because of the resemblance to her father, until she remembered Ray was thirty-seven when she was born, ten years Steven's senior. Aside from seeing pictures in their bedroom and in the living room, Mariah would only have been vaguely aware of their physical similarities. Concluding that mother and daughter shared a proclivity for character judgement, Helen decided to not only enjoy Steven's presence, but also to savour the reminiscences of her many happy years with Ray.

Alyssa had been the first person with whom Helen consulted regarding the date that she would plan to invite Mariah's friends and colleagues for an open house. She was the only one working during the holiday, and she did not want Alyssa to miss any of the preparations or activities of the day honouring her daughter. Although Helen would not ask, she suspected that Alyssa seemed detached from the excitement and revelry not so much because she had to work the days of the Christmas weekend until Tuesday, but rather that she was thinking about Eric. It had taken little time for Helen to realize that Alyssa had a prodigious memory, and she would not have forgotten her fiancé had also been invited to Saskatoon for the season.

No doubt there were many times, if only for some male conversation, when Steven would have been more comfortable with the presence of another man in the household. However, it was not really Steven that Helen was concerned about, but rather Alyssa. Over the course of the last four months, she had become extremely fond of the young woman to the point of starting to think of her as though she were her second child. How unusual that other than visiting her grandmother, Alyssa had not heard from anyone since she arrived? No telephone calls, no letters, not even Christmas cards from family or friends, and saddest of all, nothing from a man who apparently had proposed to her. Yet, Alyssa Rainer was a congenial, kind, and sensitive person so willing to please others that Helen could make no sense of it at all.

~25~

Winter returned with a vengeance on the first day of the New Year. Overnight the temperature dipped to minus thirty-seven degrees. Neither Steven nor Mariah would allow Helen to drive them to the airport. Then their flight out of Saskatoon was delayed by four hours for the airplane to be de-iced. When at last they arrived in Victoria, a deluge of rain was turning to sleet causing poor visibility and icy roadways. Mariah waited with their luggage in the terminal while Steven stood outside trying to hail a taxicab. By the time he succeeded, with a strong wind constantly blowing his umbrella upwards he was drenched. Once in the vehicle, he gave the cab driver the address of his apartment.

Steven settled back against the seat before turning toward Mariah and saying, "I'm sorry, darling, but I need to get home as soon as possible and change out of these soaked clothes. I've such a crazy busy week ahead of me that I couldn't cope with becoming ill. I'll give you my bed and sleep on the sofa. In the morning I'll drive you to the residents' hall with plenty of time for you to get ready for your rounds. With the care package your mother so kindly sent we should have more than enough food for dinner, and probably for a satisfying breakfast."

"That's a good idea, Steven. I'll be relieved to be indoors and out of this inclement weather. We could both do with a relaxing evening and early to bed for a change. And, I'm quite prepared to sleep on your chesterfield."

Steven was on the verge of suggesting that they could both fit comfortably in his double bed, but Mariah had made her feelings about premarital sexual relations abundantly clear. When she invited him to her ancestral home for Christmas, she had been explicit in her explanation that there were two bedrooms with ensuite bathrooms in the developed basement of her mother's house, and under no circumstance would she accept nocturnal visits. As desperately as Steven wanted her, he would never risk being disrespectful of Mariah by seducing her in the middle of the night, and especially not when he was an invited guest in her mother's home.

The first time Steven had noticed the same look of yearning in Elaine's eyes, he was startled. They were seated around the dining room table after enjoying a sumptuous Christmas dinner, and he had been gazing at Mariah with unadulterated love until his longing began to pulsate throughout his body. Steven knew that he needed to avert his attention before she felt his eyes on her and happened to glance at Elaine. He immediately realized that she was equally fixated on Alyssa with urgency as perceptible as his. Elaine must have felt him staring at her because she abruptly turned in his direction. He had just barely managed to look away.

Within a second, Steven's thoughts shifted from his feelings for Mariah to the presumed plight Elaine would encounter if she chose to pursue the object of her desire. He was confident his love for Mariah was reciprocated. Once they returned to Victoria, Steven planned to take her to the Brasserie L' Ecole, the celebrated French restaurant in the city and propose to her. Likely by this time next year when they returned for Christmas, Mariah would be wearing a beautiful diamond ring on her left hand and she with her mother would be well underway to planning for their wedding in May, following the completion of her residency in Cardiology.

Steven had little doubt though, that Elaine could expect a similar journey of excitement, planning, and culmination to wedded bliss if she followed her heart. He took a few moments to observe the other three women around the table, and suddenly it dawned on him that he was the only person to have the slightest awareness of what was emerging within Elaine. At first, Steven considered it odd that a man would be perceptive of her feelings toward Alyssa until he began to put the situation into perspective. Helen was as loveable and benevolent as Mariah had enthused ever since he had met her, and her daughter was a mirror image sharing her traditional values and beliefs.

Not much, if anything in Helen Symonds' life would ever have precipitated her to think about or to question human sexuality, and likely neither would Mariah with both parents having been devoted role models. However, Steven was convinced that the last individual in the room to have even a modicum of knowledge of Elaine's ardour was the recipient. Alyssa had to be one of the most innocent and naïve young women he had ever met in his lifetime. Often when they were together as a group, she was reserved seldom initiating conversation, until a topic happened to be introduced that resonated with her. Once Alyssa began speaking though, she was soon immersed in narrating, becoming less diffident and more animated until she became mesmerizing. Silence would descend upon them as they listened with rapt attention. She possessed an extraordinary gift of entrancing those around her bringing them into her sphere of consciousness. Unbeknownst to her, Alyssa Rainer was a natural storyteller.

Was she, on the other hand, aware of her impact on others and more specifically of how they felt toward her? Discreetly glancing back and forth between Elaine and Alyssa, Steven suspected Alyssa was oblivious of Elaine's deepening feelings for her, and never that what she was experiencing went beyond viewing her as a friend. A memory flashed through Steven's mind chilling his body as though he had stepped outdoors clothed in nothing but his underwear. It had been years ago now since Daniel had invited him to spend the weekend with him at his parents' cottage at Thetis Lake.

Daniel Pratt had moved into his neighbourhood late in August the year that Steven was starting Grade 6. He was looking forward to being in the senior class at his elementary school, as would Daniel, who was one month older. Over the preceding five years of schooling, Steven had formed a clique of close buddies, but he still remembered that it had taken him time to develop his circle of friends. Within days of meeting him, Steven planned to pave the way for Daniel into his group. They had arrived on the school grounds, introductions were made, and by the time the bell rang, Daniel entered the sixth grade with four classmates who would become his friends until their high school graduation.

Steven and Daniel were both accepted into the Bachelor of Science program at Victoria College, and their close friendship continued with them now sharing transportation. But, for all the time the two men spent together, it was not until the summer after their first year of college at the lake that Daniel had declared his love for Steven. It was a bolt out of the blue. God forgive him, he was stunned. Steven racked his mind, but over the past eight years, it had never once occurred to him that Daniel had passionate feelings for him. Yes, he loved him in the same way as he felt affection for his other buddies, but Steven knew beyond the slightest doubt that his ardour was exclusively directed towards the fairer sex.

When Daniel hanged himself in the basement of his parents' home three days after they had returned from the cottage, Steven was overwhelmed with guilt. Canadian law considered suicide a criminal offence and the police, and the coroner were called to the house. Before long, the entire neighbourhood learned of the tragedy. Furthermore, when Daniel's parents identified that Steven had recently vacationed with their only child, he was taken to the police station and questioned, for hours. Throughout the nightmare, Steven steadfastly maintained that he could neither, nor would he speculate about what had driven Daniel to take his own life. It was hell. The police did not believe him. Daniel's folks blamed him. His own parents were dubious about what had transpired during the two weeks at Thetis Lake. Long after he had come to terms with his death, Steven would be haunted by the certainty that over the course of eight years, he had been utterly oblivious of Daniel Pratt's true feelings for him.

~ 26 ~

Seated in the Garden Court Café of The Bessborough Hotel on a bitterly cold Tuesday during the second week of January, Alyssa was at last fulfilling her pledge to David Singer. She had arrived early to check her hair was in place and she had properly donned her apparel. In time, Alyssa had remembered that Cheryl was always such a fashion plate, and although she could never afford to dress like her, she had known precisely how she would spend her grandmother's Christmas gift of one hundred dollars. When she had returned from Melville she ventured to Klassique Designs, the 2nd Avenue downtown dress store.

Sipping on a glass of ice water she noticed Cheryl the moment she entered the restaurant, as did most of the other patrons. She was wearing a gorgeous classic style three-quarter-length Mahoney mink coat with a matching fur cap that had to have cost a small fortune. Cheryl made it apparent when the

Maître d' escorted her to the table she intended to retain possession of her outerwear, "Thank you, I'll wear my coat for now." She did remove her hat and placed it on the table before lowering herself into the proffered chair.

"Hi, Alyssa, you're looking lovely. Quite a change to see each other out of our proverbial uniforms, isn't it? Don't you find it chilly here by the window, although I do love this seating for its spectacular view of the river?"

"I booked this table for that specific reason. When I arrived in Saskatoon, my landlady, Helen, introduced my roommate and me to The Bessborough and this is her favourite table. I've never seen you so elegantly attired. I love your coat and it seems so do a few others. You've turned every single head in the restaurant."

Alyssa had planned to tease Cheryl about having to work several extra shifts in order to earn enough money to cover the price of their lunch, but when she saw her, she decided to forego her jesting. Cheryl looked so glamorous that rather than chiding her, Alyssa considered she should be grateful to be seen in her presence in the most upscale hotel in Saskatoon. Would she ever cast off the carry-overs from her dysfunctional upbringing? Thanks to her domineering mother, there were still too many times when Alyssa believed she was inferior to those people who occupied a higher social status because of their money and position.

"Shall we start with a glass of champagne to celebrate two friends getting back together?" Cheryl asked, perusing the wine menu. "I don't think that I ever did mention how excited I was when David told me he had met you."

"Please order whatever strikes your fancy. Once we said our good-byes in Brandon, I thought that our paths would never cross again. You can imagine my astonishment when David identified you were his fiancé, although I was not at all surprised he's studying to be a doctor. Let's decide what to eat because I'm dying to know when you became engaged."

"Great. Here is our server now. Could we please both have a glass of

Dom Perignon, and then I'll have a bowl of lobster bisque before the Prime Rib and Yorkshire pudding. I'll wait and decide about dessert later."

Without batting an eyelid, Alyssa replied. "That sounds delicious. Please bring me precisely the same." She refused to allow herself to think about the cost of their luncheon, although now she wished she had saved more of her grandmother's gift. It had been simple enough to request additional shifts during the holiday season, but when she resumed her English course last Tuesday evening her flexibility was curtailed. Determined not to convey the slightest indication of her possible quandary, Alyssa resolved to slip to the lavatory at the earliest opportunity and verify the exact amount of cash she had in her wallet. Similarly, she chose not to reflect upon viable options in the event she fell short.

"Before I tell you about David, I've a quick question for you. Did you hear anything from Eric over Christmas? I've been dying to find out."

"It's a good thing my answer is short since you promised to tell me about your courtship with David. Do you realize that right up until we parted ways in Brandon last February, not once had you breathed a word about David Singer? No I didn't. So it's your turn."

Following a toast to renewed friendship while sipping on the champagne, Cheryl began. "My father and David's are lifelong business associates. Even though we socialized with his family on a sporadic basis, David left home to attend the Foundation Day School at the Beth Tzedec Synagogue, a private Jewish Junior High School in Toronto when he was twelve. His father was determined that he would become a Rabbi, and subsequently enrolled him as one of the inaugural students in The Anne & Jacob Tanenbaum Community Hebrew Academy of Toronto, a private Jewish High School established in 1960. I'd met David often when he was a boy, but as time passed I didn't see him for years and forgot about him."

Cheryl paused in her narrative as their server skilfully placed a bowl of steaming soup in front of each of the young women. "Thank you. I love lobster bisque to be piping hot." She then consumed the entire serving in silence. Only when she was finishing the last spoonful from the bottom of the delicate porcelain did she continue, "It was near the completion of my first year of nursing training when I encountered David quite by accident, and I mean literally. I was dashing out of a patient's room with his lunch tray and almost dumped it into his lap as he was coming through the door. I expected him to chastise me, but instead the most handsome man I had ever seen kept staring at my name tag. Before I could apologize, he asked me if my father's first name was Maximilian.

"Fifteen minutes later we were seated in the cafeteria having coffee. He remembered the occasions he accompanied his parents to my home for dinner, but other than when we were sitting at the table he spent his time with my older brother, Adrian. I'm almost a year to the month younger than David, so I would have only been about eleven when he left Winnipeg. At best, we had vague memories of each other, although David had vivid recollections of my father. During his final year at the Academy, his parents flew to Toronto for the express purpose of convincing him to register in the Rabbinical Seminary of America based in Kew Gardens Hills, Queens, New York. David would have none of it, instead announcing that he planned to become a doctor and was conditionally accepted into the Bachelor of Science program at the University of Manitoba."

"I doubt that many people would ever forget meeting your father. Are you telling me you reached that scope of conversation during your coffee break? If you did, you must have been seriously late returning to the ward." Alyssa remarked with candour.

"Of course, we didn't. Those details were expressed later as our relationship developed. David asked if he could call me and I gave him my telephone number. Within a week, he invited me out for dinner and before long we were dating regularly. Since David had years of study ahead of him before he would qualify as a Pediatric Neurologist, we decided to be discreet about our budding romance. I never told any of my classmates so please understand why I couldn't tell you."

"I'll say. I had to find out you were engaged from a stranger I offered to share my taxicab with at the height of a blizzard."

Cheryl was on the verge of retorting she had not heard about Alyssa's fiancé until there were substantial questions about its continuance, but recognizing her comment would be crass she bite her tongue. "To my surprise, David was waiting at the bus depot in Winnipeg when I returned from the infamous Brandon Hospital for Mental Diseases that bitter winter day. He invited me to join him at Rae & Jerry's Steak House. We were no sooner seated on the plush red chairs than the waiter arrived with a bottle of the champagne we've just enjoyed. As he removed the cork, I kept glancing at David and wondering what was transpiring. I didn't have long to wait. When we were alone rather than raise the flute, he reached into his suit jacket and proposed to me with my exquisite engagement ring. And, there you have it."

A magical stillness surrounded their table overlooking the frozen South Saskatchewan River. Neither of the two friends seemed eager to disrupt the tranquillity of the moment. Time passed. The silence continued until the Maître d' quietly approached. As he calmly stood beside the table he, too, must have perceived the peacefulness emanating from the guests. At last in a serene voice he spoke, "It is not my intention to hasten your departure, but only to let you know that you may leave whenever you are ready without concerning yourself about payment. The charge for your luncheon was covered before I escorted you to this preferred location."

~27~

When Alyssa opened the door, Helen greeted her with a welcome message. "I'm so glad you're home. I received a call from the secretary of the English department earlier this afternoon. Your professor telephoned the university to explain she was ill and cancelled the evening class. I was beginning to think that you were going to stay with Cheryl until it was time for you to go to the campus. Perhaps if your friend wouldn't mind, you could give me her aunt's number. You might have visited longer had I been able to telephone you."

"That's a smart idea. I'll ask Cheryl the next time I call her. Before she dropped me off she did invite me to go to her home, but we had had such a marvellous lunch, I decided to come back and savour the time we enjoyed together. Have you ever felt how sometimes if you overextend a pleasant event it can lose its lustre? Besides, I thought that since I had class I would have to return into that deep freeze twice more."

"I know precisely what you mean, my dear. Do you want to be alone or would you care to join me for a cup of coffee to warm up?"

"Although I can't imagine that I would need anything, I would love coffee. Sharing the pleasure of an exciting occasion can also enhance the experience, don't you think?"

"Have a seat in the family room and I'll pour the coffee. I can hardly wait to hear about your luncheon."

❋

The ambient glow and cozy warmth of seasoned oak logs blazing in the fireplace enticed Alyssa to sink into one of the comfortable wing-backed chairs positioned around a small table near the front of the hearth. Settling in she realized just how much she loved this house and although she relished her English class, she was relieved that she did not have to face the elements again this evening. Once more, she felt grateful to Elaine for her fortuitous discovery of Helen and her lovely home. Now into the fifth month of their choice living arrangement while waiting for Helen she started to think, *I cannot believe how fortunate I've been since I persisted with my decision to work and live in Saskatoon. I still keep wondering if I'll ever hear from Eric Easton, but look at what I would have forfeited had I changed all my plans for him.*

"You're looking very pensive, Alyssa, although rather than savouring your memories of lunch, the frown on your face implies that your thoughts are disturbing your tranquillity."

Accepting the steaming mug, Alyssa replied, "I can't believe how perceptive you are, Helen. I sometimes think that you're reading my mind."

"For the moment why don't you stop thinking and enjoy your coffee. I've often considered that for a young woman you are much too serious. I was pleased with how serene you were when you arrived home. Start from the beginning and tell me everything about lunch with your friend. Then later if you still want to share what's on your mind, I've no plans for the evening and as it happens neither do you."

Coming to the end of her detailed narration, Alyssa said, "I think that when we finished our coffee and crème caramels, both of us were on the verge of slipping into a food trance from our overindulgence. I was so relaxed that I had even stopped worrying whether I would have enough cash for the cheque when the strangest thing happened. The Maître d' appeared and in a *sotto voce* expressed that our luncheon and gratuity had been paid. There was no hurry and we were free to leave by our own volition. I immediately thought that Cheryl must have arranged the payment, but she vehemently denied knowing anything about it. You didn't happen to pay for our lunch, did you, Helen?"

"As gracious a gesture as that was, I can't take credit for it. I didn't know you were buying lunch for both of you. From the way you have described Cheryl's coat and engagement ring, it sounds to me as though she should have been the one springing for your costly meal."

"I was buying Cheryl's lunch as reimbursement for David covering the cost of the taxi from the airport in November. She has expensive tastes, although during a shared affiliation in Brandon, she paid each time we went out on one excursion after another. Beyond a doubt, Cheryl has lived a charmed life, and I believe the magic will continue with her being extraordinarily unaffected by danger or difficulty. I'm just happy she's my friend and that some of her pixie dust has been sprinkled on me, especially this afternoon with such an unexpected surprise. Cheryl is going to ask David when she telephones him if he was our Fairy Godfather, otherwise it may always remain a mystery."

"You can't imagine how happy I am for you that Cheryl has come back into your life, Alyssa. I sense that although you're always careful not to allude to him, you're still very distressed by the lack of communication from Eric. May I be candid with you, my dear?"

"I would prefer that you were, Helen."

"I was saddened to the point of feeling your pain when the Christmas season came and went, and as far as I know you never heard from anyone. Not only was there nothing from Eric, but also not one of your family members or friends were in touch with you. It is beyond my comprehension. I love you as though you were my daughter, and yet you were ignored as though you're an orphan. I must say you put up a stoic front, but underneath that façade is a sensitive, eager to please, and I suspect, a diffident person who wonders why whenever you become close to others, they leave."

Poignant silence descended and permeated the cozy room. Tears sprang to her eyes and yet Alyssa did not cry. Taking time to compose herself eventually she said, "Thank you, Helen, for caring enough to permit me to be honest. Throughout my youth, I was raised on an isolated farm where my siblings and I were expected to do most of the chores. I was neither allowed to make friends nor to date, so that other than in school, I never interacted with girls or boys my age. I soon became self-reliant deriving my pleasure from reading any book I could get my hands on, hiking in nature, and walking amongst trees. It hadn't taken me long to realize that I was at my best when I was on my own, and gradually I began to think that I was different from my classmates, a misfit, if you will. By the time I was an adolescent, I was uncomfortable in a group, and I became convinced that with the exception of my grandparents, I didn't need other people."

Alyssa lapsed into stillness as though she was deliberating just how much she was prepared to reveal. Helen was beginning to perceive that the young woman was only scratching the surface as she tried to be factual, while avoiding any suggestion of self-pity. At last, Alyssa continued, "It was not until I started nursing training when several of my classmates decided to socialize me that I began to realize I could have fun with friends. Oh, at first, I was hopeless – nervous, tongue-tied, and I didn't even know what small talk meant never mind how to make it. On the other hand, I could sure make mistakes, lots of them until eventually I was able to relax and be myself. And, I began to learn that there were others who appreciated my liveliness and what they called my quirky sense of humour."

"As I recall, when you first arrived you mentioned that although you couldn't attend her wedding, a classmate named Susan had asked you to be one of her bridesmaids. She must have been a close friend. Did you hear from her at Christmas?" Helen cautiously inquired not wanting to sound as though she was prying.

"Whatever has happened with Susan is almost as strange as not hearing from Eric. She promised to send me pictures of her wedding, and I still haven't received those either. Susan was terrific to me during training, taking me on my very first vacation for a week at the end of our second and third year to her aunt's cottage at Clear Lake. However, she was also the one who was adamant that I move to Winnipeg because if I were stubborn enough to come here, Eric and I would never see each other again."

"Good heavens, Saskatoon is not that far away. You were hardly relocating to either one of our beautiful coasts, unlike my darling Mariah."

"I knew Eric was putting himself through university, so I was prepared to travel back and forth, and even do most of the letter writing. Now I suspect that the distance between Winnipeg and Saskatoon has nothing to do with why I don't hear from Eric Easton. I'm beginning to think that he just wanted to have sex, and he didn't have the slightest interest in marrying me. Oh, I'm sorry. Did I actually say that out loud?"

Chuckling Helen replied, "You don't have to apologize, Alyssa. You're an attractive, bright, appealing young woman, and I wasn't born yesterday." At the same time another thought was coursing through her mind that she never had any intention of verbalizing. *I have a strong feeling that your loft mate shares the same* predilection *for you.* At that moment, Helen glanced at the grandfather clock in the corner and said, "Goodness, look at the time. I better get the ham and pea soup I made yesterday on the stove to heat before Elaine comes in from the freezing cold."

~28~

Instead of lessening the wind was gusting harder at five o'clock than when she had walked to the campus that morning. Elaine was starting to think that being so close she did not need to drive her car to the university might not be such an advantage after all. She did not envy Alyssa having to be out in this blustery frigid weather following her class at ten o'clock in the evening. The sudden thought of Alyssa elevated her mood, especially when she realized that two weeks after Christmas, to the best of her knowledge, Alyssa still had not heard from Eric.

The warmth emanating from the family room greeted her as soon as she opened the front door. She stood in the foyer taking time to enjoy the scent of oak logs burning in the fireplace before removing her heavy outerwear. It reminded Elaine of her mother's house, even though the wood would have been burning in the cast iron stove in the kitchen of her small home. Perhaps, over the weekend she would have a chance to present her proposal to Alyssa about driving back to Manitoba together at the beginning of May. If she could convince her to take her two-week vacation then, Elaine could be available to work summer relief at the hospital for three-and-a-half months before university started in the fall. On Monday she would start submitting her application.

When Elaine peered around the corner of the entrance she glimpsed Alyssa gazing into the glowing embers. "You're looking very pensive and too relaxed for someone about to face our inclement conditions. I expected to find you agonizing over how many layers you would need to put on to maintain some semblance of warmth on your walk to the campus."

"Hi, Elaine, I'm glad you're safely home. I didn't hear you come in."

"But, I did and you took long enough to get your coat and boots off for me to make a pot of your favourite peppermint tea." Helen said, carrying a tray, which also contained fresh carrots, celery, sliced apple, crackers, and an assortment of cheeses. "I thought you both would like a snack while I'm reheating the soup."

"Thank you, Helen. I'm going to wrap my hands around the cup as soon as I have poured the tea. Have you eaten, Alyssa?"

"For once on a Tuesday evening we can have dinner together. My English professor is ill so my class has been cancelled, I must say to my delight. Later I'll start reading my next assigned novel in the comfort of our loft."

When Helen returned to the kitchen, Elaine filled a small plate and hungrily began to eat. While she was enjoying her snack, Alyssa rose from her chair, stoked the dying coals, and placed another log on the fire.

"Did you make it out to have lunch with your friend?" Elaine asked as she sipped her tea. "You don't seem very hungry, so my question might be rhetorical."

"Cheryl and I had a sumptuous three course lunch. Although I can hardly believe I could eat again, as soon as I've rebuilt this fire, I intend to join you." On the spur of the moment, Alyssa decided that she would not share any of the details of their visit. Later she would again wonder why she so often felt the need to be circumspect about discussing her and Cheryl's relationship with Elaine.

As it happened, Alyssa's lunch date with her friend was far from uppermost in Elaine's mind. She had immediately recognized what an opportune instance it would be to make her pitch about summer vacations. "My last examination is on April 28th and I'm intending to leave for Manitoba on May 1st returning on the fourteenth to be available for work on the subsequent Monday. Why don't you take your two-week holiday at the same time so we could travel together and share the driving and expenses?"

At first, Alyssa was not only surprised that Elaine was planning so many months ahead, but also by how assiduously her proposal had been formulated. She continued to nurse the fire back to life. Something about Elaine's question was bothering Alyssa, but she had yet to grasp it. When flames began to devour the twigs and bark she had tossed on the fire, she realized it was Elaine's assumption that she found disquieting. She was aware she had been asked, but what could have made her think she even wanted to go to Manitoba, or why before summer had come to the prairies?

As if reading her mind, Elaine said, "I'm sorry, Alyssa. I obviously considered you would be eager to seek out Eric as soon as he finished his university year. I didn't allow any flexibility for when you preferred to return to Manitoba."

Keeping her voice calm, Alyssa replied, "Truthfully, I'm so over Eric Easton that I don't care if our paths ever cross again, and for that matter, if I have anything to do with any other man. Besides, I've no intention of going to Manitoba during my vacation. I plan to meet with my ward supervisor about adding one week of leave without pay to my paid holiday time. I'm going to register for the three-week fulltime English course on campus to be offered during the summer term."

It was all Elaine could do to keep her feelings of glee from being mirrored on her face. Alyssa's words filled her with overwhelming anticipation. She had been hoping for weeks Alyssa was getting over her infatuation with Eric for in her heart, Elaine was convinced that her love for a man she had known for three months could only have been transitory. How could she possibly have considered him to be her true love? It had obviously been nothing more than Alyssa's attempt to quell her escalating doubts about her sexuality. Reflecting back, Elaine recalled how she had scarcely met Alyssa before she became aware that she had little respect or apparent preference for the opposite sex.

It might also have been a case of Alyssa climbing on the proverbial bandwagon. As typically happened subsequent to the completion of three years of Registered Nursing training, during which students were not permitted to marry before graduation, many young women arranged their nuptials forthwith of the memorable event. There likely was little doubt that after Alyssa had been invited to several weddings within months, she felt pressured to find her own fiancé and progress to the ensuing life milestone. Now that Alyssa was no longer intent on marriage, Elaine was confident that if she proceeded with patience and affection she could, as time elapsed, enlighten her regarding her true inclination and ultimately become the recipient of her love.

~ 29 ~

How long could the brutal weather last? This winter with Alyssa and Elaine to take care of her home, Helen did not have the slightest qualm about travelling to Victoria. During Sunday dinner the third week of February she excitedly said, "Another joy of having you two lovelies live with me is that I've booked an open-ended ticket to visit Mariah come Tuesday. I've had quite enough of the prairie climate and intend to stay with her for at least a month. First thing tomorrow I'll do a substantial grocery shop to make sure you have enough food staples to keep you going, and for everything else that you need, I'll leave cash. Mariah had pleaded with me to spend time with her last year, but I wasn't comfortable about entrusting the care of my house to a neighbour."

"Lucky you, can I come in your suitcase?" Elaine teased while thinking how appealing it would be to have Alyssa all to herself.

Ever serious, Alyssa replied, "Although we'll miss you, I'm sure we'll manage to keep your home running smoothly."

❋

Throughout the ensuing weeks, Alyssa was primarily scheduled for evening and night shifts. She worked a total of five days during the time Helen was away. Elaine's anticipation of returning home from class to partake of afternoon tea in front of the fireplace, before together preparing and sharing a cosy dinner soon became nothing more than a fantasy. Alyssa was gone for three of the available evenings by the time Elaine arrived home, leaving a note letting her know she had walked across the street to visit with Cheryl. Was Alyssa deliberately avoiding her? Did she realize Elaine's intentions and was choosing to continue to deny her repressed attraction to women?

By the time the almost five weeks had passed before Helen returned, Elaine was more frustrated than she could have imagined. In fact, she had seen Alyssa less than when Helen was at home. Any attempt to develop intimacy with Alyssa had been thwarted. Elaine was finding it increasingly challenging to be in such close proximity in their loft. She was beginning to debate whether she should consider looking for new living accommodations following her trip in May. Perhaps, she also needed to accept that Alyssa was lost to her and transfer her affection to a more willing candidate. There was hardly a dearth of women in her nursing degree classes on campus. Still, Elaine had become fond of Helen, felt very comfortable in her home, and loved Alyssa beyond measure.

The end of Helen's sojourn to British Columbia heralded the beginning of an unusually early spring on the prairies. By mid-April when the snow began melting and the bright colour of crocuses started shooting up through the dirt, the avid gardeners in Saskatoon were both amazed and skeptical. To her immediate neighbours it was as though Helen Symonds was a Pied Piper chasing the chill of winter on its way, and setting an example with the ubiquitous flowers that had been coming into bloom all over Victoria when she departed. When it was apparent that the warming weather was not a false start, everyone became caught up in spring fever.

No one could have been more aware of the moods, physical, or behavioural changes one might experience coinciding with the arrival of spring, nor happier than Elaine to be reaching the end of April. The past eight months had been gruelling. Once she rediscovered her stride in the hallowed halls of learning, she had poured herself into her studies as much to succeed as to sublimate her desires. She often disputed Alfred, Lord Tennyson's quotation, "In the Spring a young man's fancy lightly turns to thoughts of love." In her mind, she always considered the sentiment equally applicable to women, never more than this year, so much so that she left for Manitoba the afternoon of April 28th within an hour of the completion of her last examination.

~30~

The open road was the balm to her soul that Elaine had been seeking since Christmas. It was fortunate she was an accomplished driver because once she was on the outskirts of the city her body and mind went numb. As the miles sped by she became robotic in the handling of her vehicle as though she had slipped into a trance. Only the greening countryside captured her full attention as she motored along the two-lane highway, which had surprisingly light traffic for the beginning of a weekend. The next morning, Elaine awoke with a start in a roadside motel in Yorkton, realizing that she had little recollection of her two hundred and four mile journey from Saskatoon.

Looking around the shabby room, Elaine could not believe that when she had crashed on the bed for a short nap upon arrival, she must have slept right through the night on top of the covers fully dressed. The rumbling of her stomach confirmed she had not eaten and she was quick to make her exit. The sun was rising over the horizon and she soon spotted a Husky Gas Station with an adjacent restaurant. Hot coffee never tasted so welcoming. She ordered bacon, scrambled eggs, toast, and hash browns before the waitress could bring a menu. As she waited for her breakfast to be served, she wondered if she had ever been so exhausted or ungrounded in her life.

When Elaine was growing up her mother had taught her to believe that their values and traditions were gifts from the Creator. Her teachings emphasized that she should live in harmony with the natural world and all it contained. Most importantly, her mother and aunts taught Elaine how to be grounded and centred in the core of her being so she could listen from her place of connection to the Spirit that Lives in All Things. Only then could Mother Earth guide her with what she needed to know for her self-care.

As a youth, Elaine could always be found playing in the small grove of white Aspens and Jack pines behind her house. She loved the outdoors whatever the season – the trees, the animal life, the vegetation, and the forest floor itself. In nature, Elaine was at peace, never lonely, sad, or fearful, directed by, connected to, and made whole by Mother Earth – a child of the universe. Up to Grade 6 whenever she shared her treasures from the woods – berries, acorns, mushrooms, and colourful bird feathers – her classmates gathered around her curious to see her latest discovery.

Still, Elaine was beginning to sense that she was different from the other girls in the small one-room schoolhouse. She attributed the disparity to the fact that she had never met her father. There were other families in the village where the head of the household came and went, but as far as Elaine could remember few men ever darkened the door of their tiny dwelling. When she was six her mother returned from the hospital in Stonewall with her baby brother, but there was no adult male presence in the home on the outskirts of St. Laurent.

It was when Elaine was bussed to the two-storey high school in Warren to begin Grade 7 she started to suspect that her divergent tendencies sprang from another source. With students arriving from outlying farms and villages in the surrounding communities, Elaine was excited about making new friends. When they had returned to the classroom there was a sudden shift in the conversation. During every recess and lunch hour all the girls could talk about was boys – who is the cutest, which one has the strongest muscles, who will you let walk you home, which of us will be the first to be kissed?

Other than her younger brother, Elaine knew little and had even less curiosity about the adolescent members of the opposite sex. She had bathed

Samuel enough times to be aware of the differences between her body and that of the opposite gender, but she had given precious little thought to the reason. On occasion, Elaine had overheard her mother and aunts refer to "the birds and the bees" and she did have questions about how she was created, but she had never bothered to ask. She was strangely disinterested in babies and their procreation as though she knew that she would never birth any of her own.

If the truth were known, Elaine was much more captivated by the pretty, well-dressed, soft-spoken girls in her class than with the boisterous boys. She would have preferred talking to her classmates about the books they were reading, what their science project would be, how much more they would learn about history, geography, and mathematics. Soon they began to chide Elaine that there was something wrong with her. It was only natural for maturing girls to develop friendships with boys.

With her early start, Elaine arrived in St. Laurent in time for lunch. Samuel was the first to hear the crunching of tires on the gravel road at the side of the house. He went racing to the window and excitedly said, "Ma, Elaine is home already." And, he was out the door. Rose returned the pot of soup she was carrying to the table back to the top of the stove to follow him. It had been more than eight months since Elaine had left them to move to the next province, and she had been sorely missed. Samuel, in particular had not understood how his sister could even consider not being with them for Christmas. Never before had their small family circle of three not been together to celebrate the birth of Christ.

Rusty, their Heinz 57 dog who had aged over the winter reached the car just as Elaine was opening the door. After scratching the family pet's ears, she rose and peered lovingly at her mother and brother. She had been longing for this moment from the first mile of her journey home. With respect Elaine approached Rose first even though she knew Samuel was chomping at the bit to hold her close in one of his legendary bear hugs. Noticing he had filled out during the time she had been away Elaine said, "Hi there, little brother." She braced herself when he came rushing toward her.

Towering over her Samuel chuckled, "It has been awhile since you could call me that and not after this long cold winter. Even though I went out regularly to check my trap lines, and shovelled the snow for many of our elders, I spent too much time sitting around and eating. As soon as the snow started to melt I began walking for miles, but it's a lot easier to put on the pounds than it is to take them off. I've been trying to get into shape because now that you're home at last, I'm returning to Portage La Prairie to continue with my apprenticeship program to become a lineman with Manitoba Hydro."

Taking a quick glance at Samuel, Elaine wondered if she had detected more than a hint of resentment in his remarks. Not only his umbrage, but also that he had been a lineworker came as a surprise to her. He had only been twelve when she left for nursing school followed by years of employment in other parts of the province. Whenever Elaine returned home for a visit, Samuel was overjoyed to see her. She always thought that he wanted to stay in St. Laurent with their mother. But then, how well did she know him? How much, if any consideration had she given to what his dreams, plans, ambitions were for his future?

Aside from fishing and trapping, there was little to hold the young people in the village. Most of them, she included made a hasty exodus to the nearby cities to seek employment or to pursue higher education. Why had she taken it for granted that Samuel would be content to remain? He had never fared well in school, but the outdoor installation and maintenance jobs of the power lines would suit him to a tee. Elaine realized that she was long overdue in getting to know her brother as an adult, instead of the excitable youth who usually focused on what she had been doing, rather than sharing what was important to him.

As soon as she had cleaned the kitchen after lunch she said, "Hey, Samuel, let's go for a walk in the woods."

"Sure. I'd like that and I could burn off some of Ma's bannock and jam. Rusty will also appreciate the exercise."

As she had so often felt while strolling amongst the budding Aspens, Elaine experienced the peace and serenity of spring permeating her soul, and she had to concentrate on speaking with Samuel. "Wait up, you two. I've been sitting in a classroom for the past eight months, and I'm the one who is unfit. Tell me about your studying to be a lineman?"

"I started the program last May, but when you won the scholarship to study at the university in the fall, I had to give it up to spend the winter with Mama. I really liked the job and because I seemed to be a natural, my boss told me that if I were back by May 1st this spring he would let me continue with the program. By the way, since you made it home early could you drive me to Portage tomorrow?"

"I'd be happy to and maybe Ma would come with us. We could make a day out of the trip. I'm surprised you never mentioned you'd sought employment with the hydro, but now that I think about it, I realize what an appropriate choice it is for you. You've always loved working outside and you certainly don't have any fear of heights."

"I don't recall you ever asking. It has become near impossible for me to make a living from my trap lines. I'll be lucky if I make five hundred dollars this year and with the over-trapping, lower prices for the furs, and government policy, my income will continue to decline. Someday I would like to get married, not that there are many young available women left in the village, and raise a family, but what could I offer?"

"Your best offering is you, Samuel. You're a fine young man – kind, responsible, hard-working, respectful, loving, and the list goes on. I imagine many women are attracted to you, but you make a valid point about options for earning a living."

"You can't believe how glad I am you've come home to stay. My boss made it very clear that once I return, I'll have to be prepared to work throughout the whole year. No taking five or six months off for the winter."

Elaine's heart skipped a beat. She was delighted Samuel was opening up to her, but she was dismayed he was under the misconception she had come back to St. Laurent to live. Surely, he remembered her degree was of two years duration. As much as she did not want to limit his expressing, she knew that she had to clarify her situation forthwith. "You give the impression that Mama needs one of us to reside with her. In fact, Samuel, I'm visiting for two weeks, and then I have a nursing position at City Hospital in Saskatoon before I resume my degree at the University of Saskatchewan in September. Maybe this time next year, I'll be coming home to stay."

"After fourteen days, you're leaving again and this time for more than eleven months?" Samuel stopped walking and turned to look at her with disbelief, which quickly became anger. "It's always about you, isn't it Elaine? You don't give a damn about what I want to do, and you never have. How could whatever I want to study be as important as your precious nursing education? You were always the smart one, while I was the dud, so it doesn't matter if I sit and rot in this godforsaken hellhole."

When Samuel started to hasten his pace, Elaine caught him by the arm and said, "Please wait. I understand why you're upset and also what's motivating you to learn a trade, but who is insisting that you stay here? Mama assures me she's healthy and she's perfectly capable of living alone throughout the winter. After all, she has two sisters here and this 'hellhole' as you call it is actually a supportive close-knit community, probably much more so than the majority of others. For whatever reason, Samuel, I think that you're the one who is underestimating Mama. She would neither expect either one of us to live with her, nor would she appreciate it if we made that choice for her sake."

Time stood still as Samuel stopped in his tracks. Elaine waited. She knew that her brother needed to ponder ideas before he would speak his mind. After several minutes he said, "You could be right, Sis, about Ma not wanting you or me to spend our lives in St. Laurent to look after her. Come to think of it, she has always been a strong independent spirit. She did raise the two of us without our respective fathers and she did a pretty fine job, if I say so myself. I'll tell you this though; I intend to be there for my children if I'm ever blessed with a family. Sorry, I sounded off at you. So, will you drive me to Portage La Prairie in the morning, but I don't think that Ma will come with us. I know she has afternoon plans with her friend, Sadie, in Oak Point tomorrow."

~31~

By the early light of dawn, Samuel was awake and had prepared coffee for both of them, before Elaine would be driving him out of the sleeping village. The previous evening they had agreed to breakfast together when they arrived on the outskirts of the prairie city, and then after delivering him to his boarding house, Elaine could be on her way back to St. Laurent. Arriving home the day before she was expected had given rise to her family's anticipation of having her taxi them to their desired destinations on Sunday, and she certainly did not mind. A vehicle was still such a novelty for her mother and brother who were quite accustomed to walking, or taking the bus to wherever they needed to travel.

Long before she was ready to crawl out from under the quilt her mother had provided for the sofa bed along the far wall of the house, Elaine could hear Samuel quietly moving about the kitchen. Exhausted as she was, her conscience had not permitted her escape into sweet repose. Samuel had been so insightful. Every word he had spoken was accurate. From the time Elaine started school, she realized that the only way she could break out of the cycle of poverty and hardship, which had trapped her mother and her sisters in the Métis Settlement along the eastern shore of Lake Manitoba, was through education. Why had it not once crossed her mind that such a fundamental truth had equal application to her brother? How could she have been that selfish?

They were outside on the doorstep when Elaine handed the keys to Samuel and said, "Would you like to drive? I presume that you have your licence now."

"I do, but I thought that I wasn't allowed to drive this car."

"Oh, that was last year when it was a government vehicle. When I resigned my public health nursing position at the end of August, I was approved to purchase the car outright because the government was changing its fleet. And, last spring you didn't have a driver's licence as I recall."

"No, I didn't. My boss, Jake, is a good guy and one of the first things he did was teach me to drive on his own truck. He told me that long before I finished my apprenticeship program, I would need to drive to work sites."

"I'm glad you decided to become a lineman. You sound like you've found your niche, and the provincial government is a good employer. I want to apologize about how obtuse I've been all these years, Samuel, regarding your aspirations. I can't imagine why I thought that you wanted to be a trapper and fisherman. There is no viable way of earning a living in our small village."

"It's okay, Elaine, your determination and hard work have inspired me. I know you must also worry about what will happen to Mama as she gets older, but I guess we'll have to cross that bridge when we come to it."

Again, Elaine was surprised by the perceptiveness of her younger brother. Mama had been the other reason she had remained awake until the wee hours of the morning. Before she left to become a nurse, her mother often asked if she were interested in any of the boys in high school and if she wanted to date. Elaine would always change the subject quickly and with the passage of time, she had stopped her inquires. Elaine wondered if she ever did succeed in convincing Alyssa of her feelings and she became her lover, how she would explain her choice to Mama. Did she have any awareness of same sex relationships, and would she understand that her daughter was a lesbian? Elaine knew it was entirely possible there might come a day when her mother would need to live with her, and could she be open-minded enough to accept her female partner.

Although Elaine arrived back in St. Laurent well before noon, the minute she approached the driveway her mother had the front door open, her hat on her head, and carrying her coat on her arms. "Hello Ma. What's your rush? I'd like to have a bathroom break and a cup of coffee before we dash off to see Sadie."

"Just after you and Samuel left Sadie telephoned to ask me to come earlier. Her grandson had to change his plans and drive back to Winnipeg to return his daughter to her mother before four o'clock. Could we please just go? Sadie doesn't want me to miss meeting her grandson and her first great-grandchild. She said she would have lunch ready."

"Okay, Ma. You get into the car and I'll be right with you."

Snailing along the lake road which was sorely in need of a grader to fill in all the ruts from the spring runoff and to level the ground, Elaine was reminded that it could take as long as thirty minutes to drive the seven or eight miles to Sadie's home. There had been no way that she would have refused her mother, but she was worried about taking out the bottom of her car. No wonder Sadie's grandson wanted to get on his way back to Winnipeg.

"Thank goodness you made it. Come in please, Rose and Elaine. Meet my grandson, the one and only member of my family to ever go to university, and he graduates in May. This is Mr. Easton and his daughter, Natalie."

"Hi, as no doubt you've noticed my grandma is just a little proud. Please call me Eric."

Time ceased. She could not see. She could not hear. She could not speak. The floor collapsed. She was falling…Alyssa's betrayal cast her into an abyss.

His body shuddered. What was happening? He was seized by a memory. Not long ago Alyssa Rainer had stared at him with that same vacant look.

✵

From far away a faint voice, "Come sit beside me, child. Sip some water. Who is this spirit you have brought with you into my home?"

✵

Her soothing presence revived her. Her mind cleared. Elaine returned to Sadie's small two-room house. She remembered her mother's friend was the healer for the Métis Settlement in the St. Laurent community. "I'm sorry. I don't know what came over me. Please give me a few moments and I'll be fine."

Soon they were seated around the table as Sadie served venison stew with vegetables from her root cellar, and fried bannock. Silence fell upon the room as everyone consumed the delicious lunch as though none had eaten a scrape of food for the day until seated in Sadie's kitchen. Even Natalie sitting beside her father was dipping her fry bread into a small bowl of the traditional meal. What questions any of them might have had regarding the bizarre incident were never asked. Elaine felt each of the three adults surreptitiously glancing at her at different times during the repast, but she persisted in eating as heartily as the others.

The two aging friends ushered the young people outdoors as soon as dessert of golden brown oven baked bannock bread with wild berry jam had been enjoyed. When they were on the step Natalie said, "Let's play hide-and-seek again, Daddy. The lady can count to ten and we'll go into the trees behind the house."

Laughing, Eric replied, "Do you remember Grandma said her name is Elaine. Maybe we should ask her if she wants to play with us. Then if Elaine agrees, let's not tell her our hiding place."

Releasing his hand, Natalie walked toward Elaine, who had now fully recovered from her shock, and said, "Pretty lady, can you start counting?"

Twenty minutes of running around the woods and back to the front steps achieved the exact effect that Eric had had in mind. Natalie was tired and likely as soon as they started on the way back to Winnipeg, she would fall asleep in the back seat of his old Chevrolet. "After each of us has one last turn, Natalie, we'll go into the house to say good-bye to grandma and her visitor before we go back to the city."

Against all odds she had liked him. Eric was respectful to his elders, polite to her after a devastating beginning, thoughtful, and loving toward his daughter. No reference had been made to the child's mother. Elaine could only speculate about the circumstances between her parents. Did she even want to know? Was the child related to the 'situation that had arisen from when Eric had worked in northern Manitoba,' which Alyssa had shared with her when they started having regularly scheduled coffee dates? Whatever the reality, Elaine knew beyond a doubt that Alyssa did not have the slightest awareness Eric might have been married, perhaps still was, and certainly not that he was the father of a three or four-year old daughter.

Throughout her two-week vacation, Elaine could not help but ruminate ad nauseam about what, if anything, she would do with the vital information that she had happened upon in relation to Eric Easton. Her initial overwhelming reaction had been a reasonable indication of the impact that the knowledge might have on Alyssa. Would it be kinder to tell her the truth, or to keep the facts a secret from her? On the one hand, if she apprised her, once Alyssa had recovered from the shock, loss, and anger, would she say to hell with men, and become more responsive to Elaine's amorous overtures. On the other, did she want her on the rebound? Was it possible that ignorance could truly be bliss?

~32~

The day before she was returning to Saskatoon, Elaine telephoned Helen to apprise her that she would be home in time for supper. "It's thoughtful of you to call, dear. How was your holiday? Alyssa is working her last day shift tomorrow before starting three evenings, and we're planning to have barbequed hamburgers for dinner. Will that be okay with you? I don't know if you're aware she's leaving on Thursday morning to visit her grandmother."

Their Sunday evening barbeque would be the last time in more than the two subsequent weeks that the three denizens at Spadina Crescent would all eat together. By the time Alyssa departed for the train station, Elaine had left for work. It was as though destiny was transpiring to insure that the friends' path would not cross as they fulfilled their nursing responsibilities at City Hospital. Long before Alyssa had returned from Melville, Elaine had become so immersed in the necessity not only of adapting to fulltime hours, but also as summer vacation relief, adjusting to the requirements of whatever ward she happened to be posted to at the beginning of each shift.

Summer was fast approaching, and when Alyssa was not working additional hours to earn extra money to compensate for her week of leave without pay, she was reading the books identified on her class syllabus. Achieving a grade of A+ on her first university English exam added impetus to an aspiration that she had already verbalized to almost everyone with whom she spoke on a regular basis. Alyssa began to formulate a plan – a five-year proposal for continuing to work fulltime while completing a Bachelor of Arts degree in English Literature. She appreciated her life would border on being frenetic, but she determined that if she enrolled in two evening courses and a summer session completing three requirements each year, then in her proposed period of time, she would graduate with her first degree.

❋

Her recent journey to Melville heightened her resolve. From the moment, Alyssa had arrived on Thursday afternoon until her mother and sisters joined them for supper on Sunday evening, as always her grandmother and she had found peace and tranquility in each other's company. The ambiance of the small bungalow vanished however, as soon as Emily stepped through the door. She had given her mother a cursory hug and then springing into an attack on her eldest daughter said, "Well, look what the cat dragged in. None of us thought we would ever meet up with the high and mighty registered nurse again. After all, what could possibly make us think we were anywhere near as important as your precious boyfriend that you went to visit for your birthday and for Christmas?"

"It's nice to see you too, Mother. You chose a beautiful day to drive across the prairies. Right from the onset, let me clarify that as the most recent staff nurse on the ward, I had to work through the holiday season. Maybe, by next year I'll have earned a vacation over Christmas." Turning from her, Alyssa greeted her three younger siblings.

"What the hell do you think you're doing? I'm not finished with you. Why didn't you tell me you were coming to Melville that week in December so I could have brought your sisters to see you then?"

As Alyssa matured more and more often whenever she was conversing with her mother, she tried to bite her tongue. Nonetheless, the challenge was daunting, and she did not always succeed. "I doubted that either you or they would have been interested in celebrating Christmas a week early, so I chose to enjoy the season with Grandma. Since you didn't acknowledge my birthday, I surmise that you must have forgotten I'm now twenty-one and can make my own decisions." On that note, Alyssa walked away and began talking with her youngest sister.

Refusing to allow her mother to upset her equanimity, Alyssa maintained her distance for the balance of the evening. Until she had seen the Mary Poppins movie with Cheryl in Winnipeg during her affiliation at The Children's Hospital, she had always considered that she owed other people an explanation. Now if ever she were tempted, Alyssa would remind herself of Mary's famous quotation, "First of all, I would like to make one thing clear: I never explain anything." Furthermore, Alyssa had no intention of presenting her mother with an opportunity to ask and gloat about

Eric Easton.

The visit with her sisters was short, but in truth with their dysfunctional upbringing any spirit of camaraderie among the four siblings had most often been replaced by competition. For unknown reasons Alyssa would never unearth, this tendency had heightened dramatically when she left home for nursing training. There seemed to be some strength to the bond between the two youngest, but the antagonism from the sister who was fifty-one weeks, to the day, younger than her had decidedly increased its intensity. By the time Alyssa went to bed that evening, she was grateful for her early departure time in the morning when, other than Grandma, the rest of her family would likely still be sleeping.

The clickety-clack of the wheels on the track lulled Alyssa into a quiescent state. She often wondered if it was the stillness, which permeated her soul that accounted for her preference of travelling by train. During her return to Saskatoon cloaked in serenity, she began to analyze whether she derived any pleasure from seeing her mother, or even her sisters. Had they ever enjoyed each other's company, or was getting together little more than a familial obligation? Since Alyssa had lost touch with Eric, and equally surprisingly with Susan and Bryan, and with minimal incentive to relate to her family, she could not imagine why she would take the time or expense to journey to Manitoba.

Long before the train reached the outskirts of the city, Alyssa affirmed that regardless of how hectic her life would become, she was going to proceed with her five-year plan. She would continue her visits with her grandmother, at least every three months, she would nurture her relationships with Elaine and Helen, and she would value the spontaneity of Cheryl's friendship. The reality that she would have little time or interest to consider the possibility of meeting a man barely registered on her radar screen. The longer Alyssa reflected upon pursuing her degree in English Literature, the further she envisioned where her path could take her until the vision of attaining a Doctor of Letters began originating in her mind.

~ 33 ~

Preparations were well underway for Cheryl and David's wedding on Tuesday, September 19th. As soon as Alyssa had finished her summer university course, which she aced, she devoted time to learning about Jewish nuptials. She was thrilled beyond measure Cheryl had asked her to be one of her bridesmaids. Alyssa suspected that Cheryl was breaking from tradition with a gentile being included in the bridal party, but she was not about to ask. From the time, Cheryl ordered bacon and eggs when they had met for brunch, she realized that her Jewish friend stepped to the tune of her own drummer.

Since the two friends had reconnected in Saskatoon, Cheryl was not nearly as extravagant or flamboyant as she had been during their previous encounters. Now, Alyssa wondered if she had simply been trying to lighten her perpetually serious demeanour and convey that she was allowed to have fun. Much like Susan had throughout their three years in training. As Cheryl's wedding day drew nearer, Alyssa was missing Susan more and more. She had never understood why Susan had not sent the pictures she had promised, unless almost a year later she was still annoyed that Alyssa had declined coming to her wedding and subsequently could not be one of her three bridesmaids. Furthermore, why had Susan not mailed Alyssa a change of address card and her new telephone number since she was the one to have moved?

In the midst of the feverish bridal activities, Alyssa arrived home on a Monday afternoon as Helen was answering the ringing telephone. "If you please wait, Alyssa is just walking through the front door and could be with you momentarily. Aha, here she is now."

"Hello. Yes this is Alyssa Rainer. To whom am I speaking?"

"My name is Mary MacDonald. I'm the assistant director of the Saskatchewan Public Health Department. I've an application on file from you dated May 2, 1966 for a public health nursing position in Saskatoon. Are you still interested in being interviewed for employment with us in that city? I've had a sudden opening which I need to fill as soon as possible."

"Thank you for contacting me. I would very much like to be considered for the position. I'm currently a fulltime staff nurse on the surgical ward at City Hospital, and I'm required to give two weeks' notice."

"As it happens, Miss Rainer, I'm at the University of Saskatchewan visiting with a friend, but if you have any immediate availability we could meet at the nursing faculty office before she and I leave for the evening."

"If you don't mind me appearing attired in my after work clothes, I could be with you within the half hour."

"Perfect. I'll see you soon and thank you for your responsiveness."

Waiting until she was well away from the nursing office, Alyssa responded with a hop, skip, and jump the exact moment Elaine happened along the corridor. "Hi, sorry I didn't mean to knock you over in my excitement. What are you doing on campus?"

"I was about to ask you the same question. How ironic that our paths seldom cross at home, but we bump into each other here? Do you have time for coffee to enlighten me?"

Seated at one of the last outdoor tables at Louis' Loft on Campus Drive Alyssa replied, "I've just been hired as a public health nurse at the Saskatoon Health Unit starting on Tuesday, September 12th. The office is all of fifteen minutes from Helen's, and as you know, one of the perks of being employed by the provincial government is a vehicle. Now in little more than a year, I'm not only indebted to you for my unbelievable proximity to everywhere I ever needed to go in Saskatoon, but also for teaching me how to drive. Would you like something to nibble on with your coffee? It's my treat."

"Congratulations. Lady luck is certainly shining her countenance upon you. There can be little, if any, doubt in your mind about how apropos it was that you chose to follow your path to Saskatoon." Elaine glanced away hardly believing that she had repeated the word 'path' which was clearly on her mind. It had been months since she had met Eric and his daughter, and she had yet to disclose the most plausible reason that he would have severed all communication with Alyssa. Deep in her heart, Elaine accepted Alyssa had every right to know, but still she persisted in withholding the critical information she had so blindly stumbled upon in Oak Point. She kept telling herself that she had never found a moment when just the two of them were together. Now was definitely not the time.

"I just realized that I haven't eaten since breakfast. I would like a tea biscuit. What were you saying regarding a question you had some qualms about asking Miss MacDonald? My mind was wandering – if I don't soon get back to studying, I'll be right back where I was last year."

Not for the first time since her return from Manitoba, Alyssa wondered why Elaine would suddenly become distracted. But once again, rather than heeding her intuition, she reiterated, "I was saying that by the time I arrived for my interview, she had already calculated that if I gave my notice at the start of my shift tomorrow, I could be available in two-weeks on Tuesday at nine o'clock. Even though her computation was reassuring regarding my being offered the position, I debated how I could ask her for a day off after one week of employment. Since I've always considered that the truth is the most effective approach, I explained I was to be a bridesmaid at a Jewish wedding on the subsequent Tuesday. Fortunately, she was very curious why the nuptials were planned for a Tuesday. Once I had elucidated her, Miss MacDonald was most cooperative and did offer me the job. She also identified that a letter of reference from a Miss Elaine Hurren, the senior nurse from my two-week public health nursing affiliation carried substantial weight in her decision. It seems that I owe you huge thanks."

"You're welcome. So, tell me why do Jews marry on a Tuesday?"

"I started to read about Jewish wedding ceremonies, but soon became bogged down in their numerous customs, laws, and traditions. I did learn however, that for many Jews Tuesday is deemed an auspicious day to get married, as well as to begin a new business, move to a new home, or start a new adventure because in the Torah's story of Creation, the parashah, Tuesday is the only day that God describes as "good" not once, but twice. It is a day not only to find love, but also to celebrate it. Since I'm still ignorant of their practices, I've decided that I shall employ my tried and proven method of observing and then following what everyone else is doing."

That was it. That was how Alyssa always seemed to adapt to every situation, to have the uncanny ability to blend seamlessly into any social environment. No wonder initially she would present as being quiet and reserved while paying close attention to everyone's cues, until she could imitate the behaviour of others. How very clever. She is a Chameleon! Elaine thought as she gazed at her roommate from a different perspective. Suddenly glancing at her watch, Elaine said, "Oh, look at the time. We better start on our way if we're to be home to help Helen prepare dinner."

Strolling along University Bridge across the South Saskatchewan River, Elaine was still marvelling about her heightened awareness of Alyssa. It dawned on her she knew very little about what had happened during her upbringing that could account for her ingenuousness, but if she were as guileless as she invariably claimed to be, where had she learned how to become such a subtle mimic? St. Laurent was little more than a speck on the map of Manitoba, Elaine had also been subjected to minimal social and emotional experiences, but yet she could hardly profess to any measure of the naïveté that she attributed to Alyssa. How could the love of her life be so gifted when acquiring cognitive skills and knowledge, but so credulous in her interactions with others? Elaine began to seriously consider that she was sparing Alyssa from a profound loss of innocence by choosing to keep Eric's lies and deceit from her.

~34~

September had all the portents of being a splendid month. After Alyssa tendered her resignation to the head nurse on the surgical ward on Tuesday,

August 29th she began marking off the last evenings she intended to work for some time. Nonetheless, she was not prepared to sever all of her ties with City Hospital, and did agree that she could be telephoned occasionally for relief on Statutory Holidays. What was most appealing to Alyssa was that she would no longer need to juggle shifts with her university classes, closely followed by the freedom to regularly engage in exercise at the completion of her workday.

Her grandmother had been spot-on when she described Saskatoon as a beautiful city, although it was hardly likely she would have been aware that it was known as "The City of Bridges," appropriately named due to the five structures that spanned the South Saskatchewan River. Last fall when Alyssa and Elaine arrived to reside with her, Helen encouraged her young boarders to stroll along any or all of the bridges for splendid views of the province's gorgeous and diverse landscape. However, as they adjusted to their changed life circumstances and busy schedules, in addition to an early onset of winter, other than crisscrossing University Bridge neither had had the opportunity to do much sightseeing.

Not so this autumn. One of Alyssa's first resolutions when she became employed as a public health nurse would be to work out every day, and eventually stroll along the walkways of each of the existing bridges in Saskatoon. Seizing the opportunity to spend intimate time in the outdoors where Alyssa gloried in the beauty of nature, Elaine planned to join her regularly. However, the afternoon when Helen offered Alyssa the use of Mariah's bicycle, she realized she could cover considerably more distance on each of her excursions and promptly switched her daily routine to biking. Since there was only one bike, once again Elaine would be thwarted in her scheme to be alone with Alyssa. Would Elaine ever have the chance to persuade her young friend to follow her heart?

❋

The morning she was to appear at the Saskatoon Public Health Office on

Idylwyld Drive, Alyssa was awake before the sun came over the horizon. She was still pinching herself that she was the successful candidate and had landed the job of her dreams. Sleep had not come easily when she had finally turned out her reading lamp, and although the night was short, she awoke bursting with energy. As soon as she finished breakfast and was dressed in a smart new outfit, Alyssa was about to leave when Helen said, "You look like a ray of sunshine in that lovely orange skirt and floral blouse, my dear. But, you've at least an hour before the office opens."

"Yes, I know but I just can't wait inside and fidget about for that long. It's a glorious day, and I'm going to stroll both ways across University Bridge before I arrive at the health unit."

Pacing herself, Alyssa reached her destination fifteen minutes before the designated time and pushed open the heavy oak door. Although she could hear people chatting near the back of the building, the reception area was empty. She was glancing at the pictures of nature scenes on the wall when she heard a soft voice say, "Good morning. I'm Jean. I'm sorry to have kept you waiting."

"Not at all. I'm early, one of my more dominant traits. I'm a nature lover, and I've had an opportunity to study the lovely photos. My name is Alyssa Rainer. I'm looking forward to meeting Miss Kennedy."

"Welcome, Alyssa. I'm glad you appreciate the paintings. I requisitioned them when I started to work here in the only area of this beautiful building without windows. Irene will be with you shortly."

Alyssa's first impression of the senior nurse would remain with her throughout her life. When Jean escorted her to Miss Kennedy's office, she felt as though she stood in the doorway for at least twenty minutes before the austere looking woman behind the desk lifted her head from what she was reading, rose to her feet, and peered at her through Coke-bottle horn-rimmed glasses. She was tall and as thin as a pencil, dressed in a drab grey blouse and charcoal skirt that was in sharp contrast to Alyssa's brightly coloured attire. Her deep voice surprised her and for a moment Alyssa did not process her direction.

"Take a seat, or are you planning to stand and stare at me for the next hour?"

"Thank you, Miss Kennedy. I'm Alyssa Rainer, and I'm reporting for duty as your new public health nurse."

"I heard Jean's introduction. You're to address me as Irene. The medical director, Dr. French, insists that everyone working in this health unit is to be called by their Christian name, with the exception of him. I've been reviewing your curriculum vitae to ascertain what qualifies you to be employed in a position for a mere six days before being granted a day of leave. I'm surprised by Miss MacDonald's unusual dispensation, but I assure you that you won't receive any such special consideration from me. I'm assigning you to Nutana, the original settlement of the city of Saskatoon. Now follow me. I'll take you to your desk and introduce you to the other eight nurses, the two health inspectors, and Dr. French when he arrives."

The nurses occupied an elongated office housing nine desks and chairs approximately six feet apart each with a two-foot vertical window on the left side of the building. When they entered eight seated women stood in unison, turned to their collective right and said, "Good morning, Irene."

Beginning to wonder if she had enlisted in an army regiment, Alyssa focused on remembering her colleagues' names. Fortunately as soon as Irene walked through the row of desks indicating that the empty one was her workstation, and introduced her staff of nurses, she made a hasty departure. The woman nearest to Alyssa's desk pulled out the chair and gestured for her to have a seat. "I'm Gayle, and I'm sure that in your state of shock you don't recall my name, but once you've resumed breathing, we'll meet one another with a much more pleasant approach."

By the end of the day, Alyssa remembered everyone's name, had begun to organize her desk, and to study the map of Saskatoon to familiarize herself with the subdivision where she would provide community nursing with Gayle, and another amicable woman called Cynthia. She was informed that by the late 1950's the advent of newer subdivisions, shopping malls, and chain stores had drawn commercial activity away from the traditional businesses in Nutana. Soon the neighbourhood had fallen into decline with large impoverished families living in rundown single detached dwellings, and apartment-style multiple unit lodgings. However, because of the travelling distance and the complexities of the residents' health needs, each of the three public health nurses was assigned her own vehicle.

After lunch Jean reviewed the contract and details of driving a government car. Dan, one of the health inspectors accompanied Alyssa to the staff parking lot to check on the specified automobile's registration, insurance, and fuel level before the two of them journeyed to Nutana. As Alyssa drove she paid close attention to the street signs in the event that she could be on her initial home visit alone as early as tomorrow. Not that she regretted her absence, she had not seen Irene for the balance of the day, and was beginning to wonder if the senior nurse would be the one responsible for her orientation. Alyssa found herself hoping that she could just tag along with Gayle or Cynthia until she had acquired the specific prerequisites of her new position.

At five o'clock when her colleagues were leaving the building, Alyssa realized that she was fatigued. It was Jean who reminded her that she could drive her assigned automobile home and to her amazement, she decided to follow her suggestion. Was she weary because of her restless sleep the previous night, or had she been overwhelmed by the expectations and activities of her first day? The very idea of not walking the short distance when she had fully intended to stroll for an hour before eating dinner was close to being foreign. Still, when she pulled up and parked on the street in front of 1154 Spadina Crescent East, Alyssa Rainer experienced a feeling that at last she was on the path she had been searching for since graduation as a registered nurse.

❋

A sharp rap on the passenger window abruptly brought Alyssa out of her reverie. She had no idea how long Elaine had been standing by the curb, nor had she noticed when she had parked on the street if she had been sitting on the veranda. Before she could slide across the seat to unlock the door, Elaine knocked again. *This is exactly an expression of her possessiveness that is beginning to irk me.* Alyssa thought.

"Are you going to flaunt your success all evening, or are you going to come in and help with dinner? My, but the sun is shining on you, Alyssa. Not only do you get the job, but you also get a vehicle on your first day and a brand new one at that." Even as the words slipped out of her mouth, Elaine recognized that she was again alienating Alyssa. Try as hard as she might, she could not seem to endear herself, but instead was persistently estranging their relationship. She knew it was her frustration that Alyssa was so obtuse about her true feelings toward her. When was she going to wake up, realize that she was in love with her and stop playing games with Elaine's emotions?

Deciding not to dignify Elaine's sarcastic comment with a response, Alyssa said, "I'm on my way right now. I was reviewing the names of my eight colleagues and where they sat in our shared office. I spent the afternoon driving around Nutana with Dan, a health inspector to become familiar with my assigned area, and when we returned everyone was leaving for the day. How were your classes?"

She came so close to blurting out, *I don't want to talk about school. I want to discuss us. When will you stop scratching the surface and acknowledge how deeply you love me? I only have eight months left in Saskatoon. We need to start making our plans to be together.* She gazed intently into Alyssa's eyes, but she could not see the slightest reflection of the passion that was burning in her own. Instead what Elaine observed was the annoyance that she had felt emanating from Alyssa when she chose to gloss over her remark. What must she do to elicit an admission of love and desire from this woman about whom she spent so many of her daytime hours yearning, not to mention every night in her dreams?

~35~

The magnitude of her newfound independence afforded with a government vehicle, and every weekend off became apparent as Alyssa was planning to visit her grandmother for Thanksgiving. She had begun by checking the train schedule, which tended to undergo frequent changes when it occurred to her that she now had an alternate method of travel. When Jean had explained the contract for the new turquoise blue Ford Fairlane Sedan that had been assigned to her, she was astounded. In addition to being allowed to drive the car back and forth to work, Alyssa was permitted to put on a maximum of five hundred personal miles every three months. In the event that she exceeded the allowable limit, she would be required to reimburse the extra mileage at a reasonable rate. Subsequently, if she walked to the health unit every day as she had intended, her travel allowance would be nearly enough to make a return trip to Melville.

Given that it would be getting dark by five o'clock when she finished work on Friday, October 6th, Alyssa decided she would leave early on Saturday morning. They had been enjoying a beautiful Indian summer since the beginning of the month, but with the unpredictable weather on the Canadian prairies she preferred to drive during the light of day. If she were on her way by seven o'clock, she could reach Melville in time to have a late lunch with her grandmother. Her mind was suddenly alive with possibilities. What if when Alyssa telephoned Grandma about her upcoming plans, she suggested they drive to Neudorf in the afternoon to visit Great-Aunt Katherina, Grandpa's youngest sister? She was one of her favourite relatives, but since she had lost her vision, she seldom travelled. Alyssa had not seen her in years.

And, why should her grandmother prepare a turkey dinner with all the trimmings for just the two of them? Uncle Norman and Aunt Freda were on a river cruise in Germany, her mother was apparently working, and her three sisters only visited on the rare occasion when Emily deigned to make what she categorized the 'long trip' to Melville. Instead, Alyssa would make a reservation at the new restaurant in town and treat her grandmother to an evening out. She appreciated that prior to her return to Saskatoon, Grandma would insist on preparing one of her yummy meals of smoked sausage, cabbage rolls, and perogies before they enjoyed her delectable apple cinnamon coffee cake. Beyond a doubt, Alyssa knew that she could convince her beloved grandmother to wait until Sunday lunch so she could savour her delicious cuisine all the way home.

As soon as Alyssa was on the thoroughfare, she realized that she was embarking upon what would become one of her lifelong passions. Other than when Elaine had been teaching her, she had never been in control of an automobile, much less travelling alone along a hectic highway inundated with a plethora of semi-trailers. To her surprise and utter delight, Alyssa was neither nervous nor anxious. Rather she took to the open road like an eagle to flight – relaxed, confident, and free as if she were soaring through celestial skies. Her driving aptitude seemed so automatic and her mind so focused that she soon found herself thinking about what was occurring in her life as she sped by the stubble of the prairie fields.

More and more, Alyssa was becoming concerned about her relationship with Elaine. Since she had returned from Manitoba in the spring her attitude towards her had completely changed. She would vacillate between being very chummy to the point of possessiveness, and presenting as superior and detached as though she was privy to some truth that was of the utmost importance to Alyssa. There were several times when Alyssa had had the feeling that Elaine was on the verge of sharing some vital information with her, but then she would suddenly turn away and become as closed as a clam. Furthermore, Alyssa was still ruminating over Elaine's unusual behaviour when she had returned home after her first day at the health unit.

Once Alyssa had turned off the engine, she remained seated in the Ford Fairlane. She was lost in reflection as she philosophized about how her life had unfolded throughout the past year. She was on track with her long-term goals, albeit she had changed her chosen field of study electing to pursue a degree in English Literature rather than in Nursing, and she had obtained her preferred employment. It dawned on her that she seldom gave any thought to Eric Easton, other than occasionally wondering whatever had happened to him. Alyssa reminisced how last autumn she had hoped that once he was finished his degree in the spring he might consider relocating to Saskatoon to pursue his career. Conceivably they could be in the throes of planning for their wedding during the subsequent year. Though, was that actually the choice she wanted? She had spent so much time during her adolescence maintaining that after her parents' marriage from hell, she did not have the slightest interest in devoting her life to a man "till death us do part."

❋

On the other hand, being in the bridal party for Cheryl and David's nuptials had proven to be a thrilling experience. Alyssa had only attended one wedding, her uncle and aunt's when she was eleven years old. She did not have the slightest idea of the role of a bridesmaid. It was early into the preparations when she asked Cheryl, "Why is a Jewish girl born in Winnipeg getting married in Saskatoon? I can't imagine that your parents are happy about your choice."

"I must say that in a short time you came to know Rebecca and Max very well. As it happens, it was not my decision. Simon, my favourite uncle has been the Rabbi at Congregation Agudas Israel Synagogue in Saskatoon for the last forty years. As soon as I was born he made my parents promise that he could marry his first niece. They never thought it would ever come to pass until last September when David was accepted to do his residency at the University of Saskatchewan Hospital, and I chose to accompany him to Saskatoon. My father, of course wasn't going to honour his wife's sister's husband's vow unless before we moved, David and I pledged that we would return to reside in Winnipeg with the birth of our first child."

"And, you did? Your family ties must be exceedingly strong."

"That is the understatement of the decade. In the event that David and I had dared not to agree to my parents' oath, and coincidently to his folks as well, none of them would arrive for our wedding or acknowledge our marriage. So, my dear friend, know that whenever the birth of our first baby is imminent, we'll be returning to Manitoba. If David hasn't completed his medical studies, he'll be joining us later."

"Wow. That level of adherence to family obligation is beyond my comprehension. I can't begin to fathom what would force you to accept such strict personal stipulations in relation to your life."

"Please, don't go there, Alyssa. It is what it is. Can you come for supper to my aunt's on Friday before we leave for the Shabbat Service? And, also on Saturday morning could you arrive in time for all of us to go to Shacharit and the subsequent Kiddush luncheon."

Cheryl's family, with the exception of her father's intense questioning on their initial meeting, had always warmly received Alyssa. She was quick to acknowledge that in her parents and in her aunt's homes, there was an aura of love and acceptance. Often she wondered if there had been much controversy about Cheryl asking her to be one of her bridesmaids, but she had never perceived the slightest concern during her increasing interactions with her relatives, or with David's. She was enjoying learning about Jewish culture in a spirit of openness and trust, and she was not about to jeopardize her relationship with Cheryl, or any of her family members. After all, what did Alyssa know about familial responsibility, commitment, and affection other than from her grandparents?

"Thank you for the invitations. I would not miss any of your wedding preparations for the world, Cheryl."

~36~

Had it not been for Gayle and Cynthia, Alyssa's adjustment to the role of a public health nurse, particularly in the downtrodden district to which they were assigned, would have been a nightmare? Her first two weeks were a blur, until she wondered that if she had not been so focused on the excitement of Cheryl's wedding, she might have been more attentive during her so-called orientation. There had been an activity scheduled every evening from the day Alyssa had started at the health unit, and the hour that she was climbing into bed became later as the days of the week progressed. She had no idea whether the number of festivities were related to Jewish's traditions, or because Cheryl's family had a propensity to celebrate, but Alyssa felt duty bound to participate in all of them.

From the beginning of the ceremony, Alyssa had been fascinated by the various customs and stages of the Jewish wedding process. As soon as they were gathered in the synagogue, she wished that she had been more diligent when she had decided to study the more common Jewish traditions – their names, their meanings, and their sequencing. She did remember some of them including breaking the glass, Yichud, the ceremonial banquet, and especially that dancing was a major feature of Jewish nuptials, beginning with a number of special customary dances by the guests in front of the seated couple to entertain them. Whether it was the lateness of her return to hearth and home, or the extent of the many intriguing wedding rituals, she could not fall asleep until the wee hours of the morning.

It seemed as though she had scarcely surrendered to sleep when the ringing of the alarm rudely awakened her. Oh, how she wished that she had had the foresight to ask Mary MacDonald to have the Wednesday after Cheryl's wedding off as well. But, Alyssa had been so afraid she would jeopardize the Assistant Director's offer of the position that it was with trepidation she even dared to request the day of the nuptials. Although she had only consumed a small glass of wine all evening for the toast to the bride and groom, she felt groggy, more from a lack of repose than from alcohol. She could hardly wait to rush down the short flight of stairs to brush her teeth and gargle with mouthwash.

After she had finished her morning hygiene and opened the door of the bathroom off the main floor hallway, Alyssa's nostrils detected the most desirable aroma to start any morning. Her landlady was standing at the entrance to the kitchen with a mug of coffee. "I heard you get home in the wee hours, my dear, and I suspect you could use some java to clear the cobwebs from your mind."

"Thanks, Helen. How right you are. I'm sorry I woke you, especially now since you're my knight in shining armour. I'll drink this upstairs while I get ready for work."

Going out the door some time later, Alyssa grabbed a slice of toast with peanut butter to eat on her walk to work. Once again, she considered how fortunate it was that when she had won the toss for the bedroom, she and Elaine had agreed the loft bathroom adjacent to the den should be compensation for her, and unless she wanted to bathe rather than shower, Alyssa would use the half bath on the main floor. This was not the first time Helen had greeted her at the bottom of the stairway with a cup of steaming coffee prepared just as she preferred so she could savour it while she dressed. And, the more Alyssa learned about Helen Symonds the more she accepted that it would not be the last.

Alyssa arrived late – three minutes after nine o'clock. Pushing open the heavy door, she was congratulating herself when she came face to face with Irene. "I knew there was no way that you would make it in on time after partying most of the night. And, no you aren't going to sit in the staff room drinking coffee for the next hour trying to wake up. Come to my office now."

Heading to the senior nurse's work area, Alyssa could not believe her ears. During the previous six days of employment she had scarcely seen Irene, but today she urgently needed to meet with her. Was she trying to set her up? Almost three hours later, Alyssa was convinced that Irene had deliberately waited to review the most boring details of an orientation to public health nursing as a test of her alertness. Would Irene have a question period before releasing her for lunch? She was starving. Alyssa was already teetering on the brink of hypoglycemia without so much as a hard candy in her purse.

At one minute to twelve, Irene dismissed her with the same abruptness as she had greeted her. "Here are the names of the baby visits you've been assigned for today. You better eat and get on your way."

Hurrying back to the nurses' office, Alyssa was relieved Cynthia and Gayle had returned from their morning calls. As soon as they saw her Gayle said, "Well, there you are. We were wondering if at the eleventh hour you had also asked for today off. Do you want to join us for lunch outdoors in the picnic area to enjoy this beautiful autumn weather? Both of us are bursting with curiosity about Cheryl's wedding."

Following a shared collegial repast, and home visits to three young mothers and their sweet babies with whom she established rapport, was able to answer many of their questions, and to offer encouragement, Alyssa returned to the health unit with her equanimity restored. She waited until it was precisely three minutes past five o'clock before she started to clear off her desk and leave the building. After a brief chat with Helen and a quick change of clothes, she hopped on the bicycle to explore more of the Meewasin Trail, which she had discovered ran along both sides of the South Saskatchewan River, winding under bridges, and through beautifully landscaped parks and natural areas.

There were many aspects of public health nursing Alyssa was already beginning to enjoy. In particular, she appreciated the freedom of working in the community, the virtual independence of determining the time and order of her visits, and the interaction with families in their homes. Alyssa instantly accepted that she was a guest wherever she went, and in her hosts' environment her clients had every right to make their own decisions. No longer was she in charge of a patient with whom she would provide the specified nursing action, but rather she recognized individuals could exercise preference in their health care. Alyssa could offer information and advice, but whether the recipient would act upon it was not her choice.

This approach which she viewed as promoting autonomy, self-care, and self-actualization was much more consistent with her personal philosophy and with her commitment to encourage, support, and edify effective health practices to suit individual needs. Very early into registered nursing training, Alyssa had realized that she might be considered an ivory tower idealist in her delivery of patient care as she strived to maintain her characteristic standard of perfection.

Furthermore, within the week she had come to know and to like the personnel, bar one who comprised the team at the health unit. Then, public health nursing also had its auxiliary benefits – a workweek from Monday to Friday, days only, and the keys to a new automobile with the generous accruing allowance of personal miles.

~ 37 ~

Long before any of them were near ready for the season, Christmas had become the topic of conversation among the compatible trio living at 1154 Spadina Crescent East. On the last Friday in September, the women were taking advantage of a balmy autumn day by enjoying a light supper on the veranda. As evening twilight was beginning, Helen said, "This has always been my favourite time of the day so I've waited to share my wonderful news. Mariah telephoned this morning to invite me to join her and Steven for Christmas at The Empress in Victoria, arriving on Friday, December

22nd in time for afternoon high tea. My reservation at one of Canada's grand railway hotels extends through to Sunday, December 31st . Could I please attend their wedding ceremony on Wednesday, December 27th at four o'clock? It is reminiscent of Cheryl's nuptials on a week day don't you think, Alyssa?"

"What a perfect Christmas present." Alyssa replied. Elaine offered her congratulations and asked, "Are you surprised that Mariah isn't coming home to get married?"

"Initially, I was taken back thinking they were making a precipitate decision when she identified that much to their astonishment for the second successive year they both have the week between Christmas and New Year's off from the hospital. By organizing their wedding mid-week, they would have four days to fly to Vancouver for a short honeymoon. Then, when I check out of The Empress on Sunday morning, Mariah has asked if I would move into her apartment for the month of January until her lease is up. Upon their return from the mainland, they'll be living in Steven's townhouse, and she's hoping I can help pack and clean before she officially vacates. Now, my lovelies tell me your plans for the holiday season."

To be perfectly honest neither of Helen's young boarders had given much thought to Christmas, although it would have been a safe wager both of them cherished fond memories of the delightful time they had enjoyed when Mariah and Steven visited last year. Glancing at each other, Elaine and Alyssa shrugged their shoulders conveying uncertainty. Looking from one to the other, Helen said, "I know you'll manage even if you decide to stay in Saskatoon with the same arrangements we had last March, and we'll have an early celebration before I fly to the coast."

Elaine was the first to reply. "Could we please celebrate before Sunday, December 17th?"

"After the fuss my mother and Samuel made during the summer about me not coming home last Christmas, I've been considering that I might drive to Manitoba as soon as I finished my exams. If I do, I would like to be on the road early that morning."

"What about you, Alyssa? Since many offices close at noon on the last day before the holiday begins, you'll probably finish on the Friday I leave. If you're both available on Saturday, December 16th we could plan our Christmas for that day."

"After my mother's ire about not spending Christmas at Grandma's last year, I've been debating whether I would chance taking my car to Melville, rather than the train. But, if you're confident about driving all the way to St. Laurent, Elaine, surely I can manage a five-hour road trip during the winter. I'll leave on the Saturday morning after you, Helen. Since I'll be the last to depart, I promise to make sure that the house is safely locked, the water turned off, and whatever else you require done."

"Terrific. Then we're set. I'll also make a detailed list so I don't forget to attend to all the essential arrangements for the month of January in terms of leaving money for groceries and bill payments. Now, I'll depart with my mind at peace, and my heart ready to rejoice in the glad tidings of Christmas and my only child's wedding. Thank you, my dears for being so amenable."

It was as though finalizing their plans for Christmas hastened the coming of the end of the year. Spadina Crescent was a hub of opening and closing doors as the three inhabitants pursued their various activities, with Sunday dinner soon proving to be the focal time for them to gather. Now that Alyssa worked from Monday to Friday and Elaine was on campus every day of the week, they often arranged to share a quick bite at Louis' Loft on a Tuesday or Thursday before her evening class. During these cozy tête-à-têtes, Elaine was drawing closer and closer to Alyssa and was becoming hopeful for what the month of January might bring with only the two of them in residence.

Upon awakening, Elaine's first action on the morning of December 17th was to glance out the large picture window and was pleased to ascertain that the skies were clear. Fortified by a full breakfast and snacks to consume along the way, she was on the Yellowhead Highway by eight o'clock. She hoped to be in Yorkton by noon, to stop for gas and a quick bite to eat before continuing on her journey. If all went according to plan, she could be driving into her mother's yard as the sun was sinking below the horizon.

Traffic was steady, primarily with transport trucks, which Elaine had never minded on the highway when it was not storming. By and large in fair weather, the drivers observed the speed limit, and if there was ice or snow on the road, the multiple wheels of the heavy vehicles helped to break it down thus improving the safety of the paved surface. Elaine had always found driving relaxing and as the miles passed, she could feel the tension ebbing from her body. Never before in her life had she so fully appreciated her capacity to sublimate her desires into the much more acceptable pursuit of knowledge. She was confident her examination results would reflect her ability to focus, but now as she was starting to unwind her yearning for Alyssa returned with a vengeance.

The longer she was on the highway, the farther she was away from her, the more Alyssa occupied her mind. Elaine could not stop thinking about her. She had to make a deliberate effort to pay attention to the highway. She might have been better off if driving conditions were less favourable, then she would have needed to concentrate more on the task at hand. When Elaine arrived in Yorkton, she decided to purchase a large cup of coffee, which no doubt meant she would have to make an additional stop. Nonetheless, she knew that she had been functioning on adrenaline and required the natural stimulant to improve her mental acuity, or she could become lost in her daydreams.

Twilight was turning to dusk when Elaine reached St. Laurent. She loved coming home to this little community where a profound feeling of peace would begin to permeate her body as soon as she glimpsed the sandy beaches along the lake. This evening though, as she was on the verge of yielding to the pleasurable sensation, insight as bright as a bolt of lightning illuminating the sky flashed through her mind. Elaine grasped beyond a doubt that when she did succeed in convincing Alyssa to become her life partner, she would never consent to relocating from Saskatoon to Portage La Prairie. With Samuel living in the small prairie city to work for the hydro, and Elaine realizing that she was not likely to return to Manitoba, it dawned on her that she would need his help persuading their mother to leave her childhood home.

If she thought it would take considerable effort to prevail with Alyssa, Elaine knew that it would pale in comparison to the fight they would have on their hands with their mother. Both of her offspring appreciated Rose's deep roots in the traditional Métis Settlement. Elaine always planned to search for a nursing position in Portage once she completed her degree. Then her mother could reside with her during the long bitter winter, and go back to her home on the shore of Lake Manitoba to enjoy the more clement seasons of the year. Furthermore, she could not begin to imagine what she was going to tell her mother or her brother about what was prompting such a dramatic change in her life. Still, she could not wait any longer.

When she had received the letter from her mother to tell her that Samuel had brought a young lady home to meet her, Elaine quickly read her joy between the lines. Rose Hurren was the last woman of her vintage in St. Laurent who was bereft of a grandchild. Although she never asked her about her personal life, Elaine often saw the questioning look in her eyes, which had become more haunting this past May when they met her friend Sadie's great-granddaughter. How could she tell her mother she loved a woman and had no intention of ever having a child? Elaine's only hope was the weather would remain mild. She would stroll into the nearby forest in search of her soul, and find the words to reveal her sexual preference to her mother. Thankfully, Samuel was not coming home until Christmas Eve giving her a week with just the two of them.

❋

From the moment Elaine met Tara Weiss, she understood why Samuel was so taken with her. She was as sweet as she was pretty with blond hair, blue eyes, and a fair complexion. Elaine had not been in her presence long before she realized that her physical appearance reflected an inner beauty. From her arrival, she was kind, cheerful, considerate, and particularly solicitous towards Rose, whom she was only meeting for the second time. For a playful young woman, Tara's perception, sensitivity, and acumen conveyed that she was wise beyond her years.

The five days the foursome spent in the small house were the most tranquil that Elaine had experienced for years. She slept with her mother, and Samuel willingly bequeathed the bedroom he had moved into years ago after his older sister had left for nursing school to Tara, while he returned to his original roost in the living room. Each morning whoever awoke first arrived in the kitchen, turned on the coffee percolator, set out the mugs, and essential fixings. Necessary chores were initiated and finished scarcely without anyone aware of their completion, and then hours gave way to relaxation, enjoyment, and celebration. The Christmas goose was on the table, grace said, the festive feast consumed, gifts opened, games played, and before any of them wished, the day was done. Never was a cross word heard, an unpleasant glance seen as the family cocooned within the walls of the cozy hearth and home.

When Samuel and Tara were ready to depart, none could believe the serene camaraderie they had felt during their time together. It would have bordered on irreverence had Elaine dared to broach the subject of her sexuality. The unpleasant topic had no place in her ancestral home with a mother who had bestowed upon her children such a gift of inner peace. Why had she not taken this devoted woman into her confidence before her brother and his girlfriend had arrived? Yet, all that her solitary wandering in the woods had accomplished was to convince her to wait. Had she been hoping, if not for support, at least understanding from her younger sibling? Elaine had relinquished her religious beliefs years ago when she became aware that the Catholic Church viewed sexual activity between members of the same gender a sin. Knowing her mother was a devout believer, whatever could have possessed Elaine Hurren to consider making her revelation during the season celebrating the Christ child's birthday?

~38~

On the morning of the last day of the year, Elaine awakened with a sense of foreboding. She had planned to be on the road by eight o'clock, but was disheartened when she glanced out the tiny unfrozen section of the kitchen window. All she could see was whirling snow. The forecast had been for light flurries, but in the pre-dawn darkness, the world was a blur of white. Nonetheless, she arose and carried on with her waking activities hoping that by the time it was daylight there would be an improvement in visibility.

Carrying a cup of coffee to the table, Elaine was about to be seated when her mother came into the kitchen. "Good morning, my girl."

"You're up early, Ma. I'm sorry if I woke you. Sit down and I'll pour you some coffee. I don't like the look of the weather, so I'm going to wait until later before I start out."

Peering through the same pane of glass, Rose said, "My goodness, there appears to be a full-blown blizzard raging outside. Surely you aren't thinking of leaving until it has cleared?"

"I'm sure in the daylight the snowstorm won't be as threatening, especially once I'm beyond the Interlake Region. I have winter tires, sandbags in the trunk, a snow shovel, and I'll drive slowly until I reach the main highway."

"You've been away from this district too long. You can't be serious about driving in these conditions, Elaine?"

"Ma, I've driven these roads for many years. I must get back for school. Classes begin on Tuesday, and I've lots of preparations including making sure that there's food in the house. Remember I mentioned Helen is visiting her daughter in Victoria for the month of January. If the inclement weather persists, and I need to break up the journey I'll stay in Yorkton. I'll telephone you whenever I've safely arrived at a destination."

Not wanting to allow her mother to increase her anxiety level, Elaine returned to the map of Manitoba she was studying. She had clearly written her route with large lettering on a piece of paper for a quick reference once she was behind the wheel. Even with reduced visibility, Elaine considered that she would not encounter much difficulty along Highway 6, but she would need to keep a sharp eye for her left turn onto Highway 68. The subsequent sixty miles of winding road through the Lake Region and The Narrows, the only place where Lake Manitoba was traversed by the use of a bridge, could be challenging. However, once she reached Sainte Rose du Lac and was on Highway 5, no doubt the storm would have moderated and she would be well on her way.

Finally in exasperation when Rose realized that she was not going to convince her daughter not to embark upon such a foolhardy and dangerous trip, she stood up from the table. "At least, you'll have a nourishing meal before you leave. I'll make you eggs and pancakes now, and pack some sandwiches and a thermos of coffee for the road. You can fetch your old quilt from the closet along with some candles and matches. Samuel always travels with provisions and a blanket when he comes to see me."

The morning light marginally improved the distance that Elaine could make out ahead of her when she went outdoors to pack her car. The heavy woods darkened the area surrounding her mother's house and once she started to drive it became clearer, albeit she could still only see ten to twenty feet in front of her. Shortly after she turned left at the stop sign on to the highway, she spotted the faint taillights of another vehicle, possibly a small truck. If she could get close enough and follow in its tracks, she should be able to keep sight of the road in the squall. She accelerated and when she quickly caught up, she realized that the half-ton pickup could not be travelling more than twenty miles an hour.

Fortunately, Elaine had accurately calculated the distance between her village and Highway 68. Before leaving she had mentally added it to her existing odometer reading so that she would know when she was approaching the left-hand turnoff. She had no idea how long she had been on the road when she noticed the flashing of the left turn signal light of the truck. An instant check of how many miles she had travelled verified that she would be able to continue to follow the driver ahead. What luck? She thought that Highway 6 would have been much easier than it had proven to be. Several times she did consider returning to the safety and warmth of her mother's home.

Within the first five miles, Elaine came to the realization that Highway 68 was all but impassable. But, it was too late to alter her course. No doubt the truck driver had also grasped the situation – it was impossible to turn around and return to Highway 6. Suddenly, she noticed the truck's hazard lights were blinking. Elaine was certain the driver was sending her some kind of a warning sign, but what? Was the person trying to indicate that he would escort her along the treacherous road? She drove marginally faster until she was almost right behind the vehicle. Although the intermittent flashing was something of a distraction, it did improve Elaine's visibility of the highway and how far she was from the rear of the truck.

Hours slipped by, the blizzard whorled, the convoy inched along, the bridge at The Narrows was painstakingly crossed, and eventually the lights of Sainte Rose du Lac could be seen in the distance. As suddenly as they had come on the hazard lights went off. After another few miles the truck's right hand signal light began to flash. Before long the streetlights revealed a two-storey structure. Elaine drove up alongside the truck when it came to a stop in front of the Ste. Rose du Lac Hotel and Motel. From the moment she shifted the car out of gear, she went numb. Finally, loud insistent knocking drew her attention. As she began to roll down the window she heard a man's voice urging, "Turn off your engine and come with me."

Once they were in the lobby of the quaint old establishment, he extended his right hand saying, "My name is Henri. If you're like me, the first place you need to visit will be the lavatory. It's on your left and then come back to the desk."

Several minutes later when Elaine returned and approached Henri, she said, "Thank you. I owe you my life. I'm Elaine Hurren, and if you had not become aware that I was following you, I would be lost in the Interlake region somewhere between St. Laurent and here."

"More likely, you would have veered off the road or the bridge and onto the frozen lake. As much as I was a damn fool to be out on the highway under these conditions, at least I knew my way, but you're a stranger in these parts. You should have stayed at whatever place you started. I've just made a reservation for you with Pierre, the owner of the hotel. I know the motel rooms are newer, but once we bring in your belongings from your car, he is under my orders not to let you leave the building until it is daylight and the storm is over. His wife, Dolores, will make sure you have meals while you're a guest in the hotel. I'm leaving for my home three streets over. You can thank me by never doing anything so risky again."

Still shaking once she was safely in her second floor room, Elaine tried to calm her nerves by gulping the coffee in her thermos. Dolores had offered to bring her a tray with food and drink, but she politely declined, explaining she had a prepared lunch with her. Elaine was desperate to be alone. Her stomach was in such a knot that the last thing she wanted to do was eat. She had checked her watch when she was in the washroom and could not believe that it was nearing three o'clock. She had been gone for five hours, her mother would be frantic, and she needed to call her.

The receiver was picked up before Elaine was even sure the telephone had rung. "Hello, Elaine. Is that you? Tell me. Where are you?"

"Yes, Ma, it's me. Please take a breath before you hyperventilate. I'm safe and sound in a hotel room in Sainte Rose du Lac. I've decided to wait out the blizzard. I won't get back on the highway until it has passed." Expecting her mother to say, "I told you so." Elaine quickly asked, "How have you spent your day?"

"You can't imagine? I've been sitting here by the telephone fretting about you. I haven't been able to think or do anything but worry and fear for you."

The next morning dawned bright and clear, albeit cold. The wind had ceased to blow and visibility was restored. The moment the sun rose over the horizon, Elaine was ready to leave after a hearty breakfast, a packed lunch on the seat beside her, and a tank full of fuel. At best, she had a six-hour journey ahead of her. She only intended to stop for a washroom break and gas in Yorkton. Other than a skiff blowing across both lanes, the highway was free from snow, although she was wary of black ice and of the potential danger that it created. For the balance of the most harrowing driving trip of her life, Elaine stayed intensely focused while two oaths were formulating at the back of her mind. Never again would she ever venture across the prairies during a Canadian winter, and once she had returned safely home, she was not waiting a minute longer to declare her undying love for Alyssa.

~ 39 ~

She made it. The sun was dropping below the horizon as she reached the outskirts of Saskatoon. It would only be a matter of fifteen to twenty minutes before Elaine would be parked outside Spadina Crescent, in time to help Alyssa prepare dinner. After a casual meal she would suggest that they retire to the living room in front of a fire. As they relaxed staring into the flames, Elaine would move closer to Alyssa on the sofa and speak of the love that had been blossoming in her heart for almost the past two years.

For once the street was not overrun with parked cars, and Elaine was able to come to a stop directly in front of 1154 Spadina. When she gazed toward the house she realized that it was in darkness. One dim light illuminated the numbers and it was the outdoor fixture of the veranda. Where was Alyssa's vehicle? Had she not made it back from Melville? It was not yet five o'clock. Even if she had gone to the health unit for the afternoon to catch up on her charting she would have walked. Surely though, Alyssa would be home soon, and Elaine would surprise her by having dinner ready.

The hours passed, Elaine prepared and ate dinner, unpacked her suitcase, and still no sign of Alyssa. With time marching on, she became more and more worried. She decided to have a relaxing bath to ease the tension that was seeping back into her body. She was beginning to appreciate how her mother must have felt yesterday. After reheating the bath water on three occasions, Elaine got out of the tub before she began to look like a prune. As she towelled herself off, she realized how exhausted she was and crawled into bed.

❋

Noticing Elaine's car on the street, Alyssa remembered she had forgotten to leave her a note that she was working an evening shift at City Hospital. Actually, she expected her to arrive home last night and then with Cheryl's impromptu invitation this morning to lunch at the Bessborough, she had dashed out of the house to meet her on time. Whereas she was glad Elaine had returned from her long trip, apparently without any mishaps, Alyssa had not considered it necessary to keep her in the loop regarding her whereabouts.

Alyssa had been looking forward to a hot bath, but unless she broke house rules and used Helen's bathroom, she would have to wait until tomorrow morning. Instead she slipped into the kitchen, prepared a mug of hot chocolate, and with only a reading light turned on relaxed with her latest novel in the living room. Once she unwound from the hectic demands of the hospital and her eyes were growing heavy, Alyssa climbed the stairs. She was soon sound asleep in the comfort of her double bed.

With a start, Elaine sat straight up in bed. Alyssa was lost in the blizzard. She had veered into a snow bank miles out of Melville and was the only vehicle on the highway. It would be hours before she was found. *Have I been dreaming*? Elaine thought as she flung off the covers and raced to Alyssa's bedroom. *Was the door closed when I walked by earlier on the way to my room*? She could not remember and she had to know.

Stealthily turning the knob, she pushed the door open and with moonlight streaming through the large front window, Elaine was able to discern the shape of Alyssa's body stretched horizontally under the duvet. She was immersed in such sweet repose. If only she could join her. What if she were to lie down, just for a few minutes until Alyssa's warmth had chased away the nightmare? She would be ever so quiet and then sneak away before Alyssa even knew she had been in her bed. As she crept closer, Elaine could see that she was facing the wall, and lifting the quilt she slipped in beside her.

It was heavenly. When Alyssa did not stir, Elaine snuggled up to her until their bodies fit like a satin glove. She had been daydreaming about being with Alyssa for almost two years now, longing to hold and to love her in this cozy bed. Before she could stop herself, Elaine started to touch her hair, to stroke her back and shoulders until somehow without being aware her left arm slid over Alyssa's side and her hand found her breast to caress. At the same time, Elaine began kissing the back of her neck. She was beyond being able to leave.

"What the hell do you think you're doing?" Alyssa said pulling away from her interloper. "How dare you come on to me when I'm sleeping?" As it happened, she had been in the depths of a dream about Eric. At last he had convinced her just to sleep with him, while promising he would stay on his own side of the bed. When it was becoming so real that Alyssa began to feel aroused, she suddenly awoke. When she realized it was Elaine she shouted, "Get out of my bed right now."

"Oh, Alyssa, give up your pretenses and stop playing games already. You know you've wanted me just as much as I yearn for you ever since that weekend you came to St. Laurent with me. We're alone for the whole month and then when Helen returns home, we'll just have to be careful not to rouse her curiosity, since she watches you like a hawk."

Bounding out of bed and throwing the duvet off Elaine, Alyssa ordered, "Leave this minute. You're as crazy as a loon. I can't believe you've been lusting after me all this time. We're done. I don't want anything more to do with you."

"Once you realize what you're saying, you'll come begging me to take you back, and I won't be around. Then you'll wish that you hadn't played so hard to get. Believe me, there is no one else who will love you as much as I have these past two years."

Grabbing a pillow, Alyssa started to swing it at Elaine. "Get the hell out of my bedroom and never come back again." Elaine glared at Alyssa one last time and strode into the open area of the loft. The minute she was gone, Alyssa rushed to the door, slammed it shut, and positioned her straight-backed chair under the handle.

~40~

The last time she recalled glancing at her alarm clock it was almost five in the morning. When she finally awoke it was nearing eleven o'clock. Alyssa had had no intention of sleeping so late. Then she remembered the sordid scene with Elaine. She still could not believe that the woman she had respected, admired, and yes, loved as a friend, had been after her body. How strange that she had been dreaming about being in bed with Eric, when instead it was Elaine, although they both had the same objective. If the solemn truth were told, Alyssa Rainer spent little time and less energy thinking about having sex with anyone.

Suddenly she was taken back to that horrible day in the basement of her grandmother's house in Melville. At first, Alyssa had been excited and even haughty that her brother, and their older cousin, Orville, had let her play hide-and-go-seek with them, but had excluded her younger sisters. Before long though, the boys had coaxed her to accompany them into the darkened potato bin for a new game. Orville placed an old sack near the door and told her to sit down on it. Initially she was hesitant, but he reassured her they were taking a little break because he wanted to show her brother something.

"Go ahead and lie down. You know your grandma would have washed that bag." Orville said. Alyssa was tired from running around her grandparents' large backyard and decided to rest for a few minutes.

Her eyes shot open when she realized Orville had lain down beside her on the rug sack. Then, before she knew what was happening he pulled down her underpants and was on top of her. "Don't move. I just want to see if we fit together like a bug in a rug."

Soon Orville became very excited as he began shoving himself into Alyssa. "Stop it. You're hurting me." Alyssa shouted. When it had no effect she appealed to her brother, "Get him off me. Why are you just standing there?"

"Stop yelling. Nobody can hear you. Don't be stupid. I'm showing your brother what to do when he wants some nooky. That's the reason boys are born first – so they have younger sisters to satisfy their urges."

As quick as Orville had started he was finished. He scrambled off Alyssa, grabbed her brother by the arm, and when they left the potato bin he laughingly said, "There now you know how it's done."

Alyssa was so ashamed. She felt so dirty. She wanted to scream, to sob, to confide in someone, but she did not even really know what had happened. Who could she ask? Or, whom would she tell? She did not want her grandmother to know. Her mother would never believe her, or worse would say that she made the boys do it. Her older brother had always been her favourite, he could not do anything wrong. Alyssa was only ten years old, but yet again she was on her own. What would she do now? At last, when she could move she sat up to experience something sticky between her legs. What was it? Looking down she saw red. Then she realized she was bleeding. The only cloth she could wipe herself with was the sack. She wanted a scalding bath to cleanse away the blood, the dirt, the shame, the guilt, but she dissolved in tears knowing that it was not possible.

The memory spurred Alyssa out of her bed and into the shower at the bottom of the stairs. She turned on the water as hot as she could. Even when it became icy cold, the recollection of that abhorrent day – minutes that changed her life forever, still poisoned her mind. She had never told anyone. After they returned home she gave her brother a wide berth. On several occasions when they were doing their farm chores, he had come upon her and pretended to be nice. Alyssa had never trusted him again and immediately got as far away from him as she could.

Could she ever trust another person again? Alyssa remembered how pleasant Orville had been before persuading her to go into the potato bin. What had she done to spur him on, to make him hurt her? It had to be her fault. Why did she provoke people and turn them against her as her mother had repeatedly asserted? She had always justified her physical cruelty by telling Alyssa she had a big mouth and was a born troublemaker. On the other hand, when someone was being kind, was it just so they could take advantage of her? Isn't that what had happened with Eric? And, now it had occurred with Elaine?

Not once over the course of the past twelve years had Alyssa ever grasped the truth – she had been the victim, not the perpetrator of all the abuse, which she had endured. At long last, Alyssa Rainer realized beyond the shadow of a doubt that Orville had raped her. Still, would her dark secret sear her soul until the end of her days?

~41~

Had she left? When she was dressed Alyssa quietly stepped into the open area. Glancing out the window she noticed Elaine's car was no longer on the street. She stopped and listened, giving her full attention to every sound the house emitted. Aside from the occasional creak caused by the wind, all was silent. Alyssa tiptoed back down the stairs to the kitchen, glancing into the other rooms until she arrived at the counter with the coffee pot. It was cold and clean. Convinced that at least for the moment she was alone, she made coffee and toast for her late breakfast.

After she had eaten and was relaxing at the table, she spotted the newspaper on the floor in the entrance hall. It was warm when she gathered it up, confirming that it had been brought into the house some time ago. Had Elaine gone out, then parked on the driveway, and returned to her bedroom, or was she still away? Alyssa stealthily retraced her steps, climbed up the staircase, walked toward the den, and peered around the doorpost. Silence prevailed. But, something was amiss. There was a vacancy about the bedroom that gave her an eerie feeling. It was more than the fact that Elaine was not present in the room. Alyssa turned on the overhead light. It was then that she noticed the desk, the bedside table, and the top of the dresser were bare and wiped clean. She dashed to open the drawers and to the clothes closet – all empty. It was as though Elaine had never been in the room.

How was it possible? What time was it when Alyssa had locked her out of her bedroom? At best, it could not have been more than eight or nine hours ago. Could Elaine have removed her belongings and packed them into her car in such a short time? A thought raced through her mind. What had she done with her house key? Alyssa flew down the stairs and checked the front door. It was locked. Slipping on her boots, she opened the door and searched the mailbox. Finding an envelope, she retreated into the house and tearing it open discovered Elaine's key, still on the chain that Helen had provided to both of her boarders when they had moved into her home.

Now what? A plethora of questions began bombarding her brain. Where would Elaine have gone to live? It was presumably possible to vacate a dwelling place within hours, but how does one find another home so quickly? When would Elaine telephone, or write Helen to advise her that she had terminated her residency at 1154 Spadina Crescent? Was it likely Alyssa would be held accountable for paying the full rent for the room until Helen could find another boarder? How could she afford to pay two hundred dollars a month? She did not care whether she ever saw Elaine Hurren again, but would she have the courtesy to apprise Helen about her precipitous departure? What would she have said? Questions continued to flit through her mind, until Alyssa realized that she would have to wait before she would have any answers.

As it transpired, she did not wait long. Alyssa was in the kitchen eating breakfast before leaving for work at the health unit the next morning when the telephone rang. "Hello, Alyssa. How are you? I'm so glad I caught you before you left, but I won't keep you. I need to speak with Elaine, please."

Knowing that she would need time to explain the current situation to Helen, and she did not want to be late Alyssa said, "Elaine's not here, Helen. May I please telephone you as soon as I return from work this evening?"

"Since Elaine always arrives home from the university before you, could you please leave her a written note to ring me? Thanks and have a lovely day, my dear."

Before the nurses had left for their Christmas break, Irene had told them to prepare for a day in the office when they returned to the health unit. She did not want any home visits – the staff was not to be getting in the way when people were readjusting back to their routines. Alyssa thought this edict worked well for her given that she was having a challenging time concentrating on the tasks at hand. She would just start some paperwork when her mind wandered to what she was going to impart to Helen. What if Elaine had not telephoned her yesterday, or still not during the course of today? Where would Alyssa begin to describe what had occurred in Helen's home in the early hours of Tuesday morning?

After a brisk walk home, Alyssa went straight to the telephone table and chair in the foyer. She picked up the receiver and just as quickly returned it to the cradle. Although this conversation had been preying on her mind all day, she still did not know how much she was going to reveal to Helen. Yesterday's profound realization that she had been the one who was victimized reminded Alyssa of the last line in J.D. Salinger's *The Catcher in the Rye* – "Don't ever tell anybody anything. If you do, you start missing everybody."

Ever since Alyssa read the novel, she had pondered Holden Caulfield's quotation. What did it mean? Was he suggesting that when a person becomes close to others and begins to build intimate bonds, the relationship would eventually end in heartbreak and loneliness? Was that the reason she had invariably preferred to be aloof and distant – to detach from others as a protective measure, while suppressing her emotions? Was it fear that if she expressed her feelings, shared her experiences, thoughts, and desires the other person would take advantage of her, or worse, use them against her? Would she ever learn to trust others, to trust her?

Analysis paralysis was setting in when the shrill of the telephone brought Alyssa back to the present. Answering it she was not at all surprised to hear Helen say, "Hello, Alyssa. As much as I would enjoy speaking with you, I must talk to Elaine. Is she in at the moment?"

"I'm sorry, Helen, but Elaine is no longer here." Seldom ever at a loss for words, Alyssa hesitated before saying, "I know the truth will out, so I'll tell you right now that Elaine has chosen to move out of your home."

"Well, that makes the picture a little clearer. Just before I rang you this morning, I had a call from my bank manager. Near closing yesterday, Frank had had a telephone message to ring Miss Elaine Hurren. When he followed through, she requested him to stamp "Stop Payment" on her cheque dated for January 3rd when I tried to cash it. Little did I know that I would be aiding and abetting her the day I had suggested my lovelies could postdate their cheques. Thank you, Alyssa, yours has been duly deposited. Now, could you please tell me what has happened?"

"I was not only surprised that she had left, but also amazed by how quickly and stealthily she was gone." Alyssa paused. Helen waited. Several moments later, Alyssa continued, "There was an incident, but I would prefer not to speak about it over the telephone."

"Are you alright? Would you like me to come home sooner, Alyssa?"

"No, Helen. I wouldn't dream of asking you to change your plans. I have Cynthia and Gayle at work, and Cheryl, if I need anything. Also, I'm looking forward to beginning my first evening class tomorrow, and my other course that starts on Tuesday. Though, thank you for offering."

"I heard you, Alyssa, when you expressed you didn't want to talk about what happened, but I would just like to ask one question, if I may. Did Elaine make advances toward you?"

Helen could hear Alyssa gasp at the other end of the receiver and gave her time to respond. "How did you know? I never realized for a moment that she wanted me to be her lover, although she accused me leading her on. I'll admit that I'm naïve, Helen. As you know, I was raised on an isolated farm and my mother didn't allow my sisters or me to date. I didn't start to go out with boys until I went into nursing training, but even in a residence full of women, it had not occurred to me that there was such a thing as a lesbian – I looked it up in the dictionary yesterday. I just thought we were friends, like all my other girlfriends."

"Oh my poor guileless girl, Elaine did come on to you. I can't say that I'm surprised. I couldn't believe how she mooned over you, and I often wondered about her intentions. I still have plenty to do before I've helped Mariah clean out her apartment, but if you want me to return to Saskatoon before the end of the month, please let me know. Does Elaine still have her house key?"

"No, she did have the decency to leave it in the mailbox. Do you want me to send you another cheque for one hundred dollars to pay her share of the room and board?"

"Absolutely not, don't you worry your sweet head about money? We'll work everything out when I arrive home. And, I think that you'll be fine for groceries. Remember I left several dishes in the freezer for you to eat. I know you'll manage, Alyssa, and I'll see you on Sunday, January 28th at the airport."

Once Alyssa returned the telephone to its cradle, she remained seated deep in thought. She was relieved that Helen not only believed her, but also was ready to support her with her offer to come home earlier. Looking ahead, Alyssa realized that January could be a long lonely month until Helen returned to Saskatoon, but she would keep herself so busy she did not have a minute to think about Elaine. Then, the insidious self-sabotaging tape in her head began to clamour, *Do I really think that Helen would still consider me so innocent if she knew what I was doing in that potato bin when I was ten?* STOP IT! Alyssa shouted as she leapt from the chair.

For the moment at least she was glad that she was alone in the house. Would Alyssa ever be able to break the vicious cycle of undermining herself with her destructive thoughts? She was beginning to realize that the only way to change her negative mindset and to alter her inner voice would be to believe the truth about what had occurred in her grandmother's basement. In a flash of clarity, the Biblical verse John 8:32 came to her and permeated her soul with peace – "And ye shall know the truth, and the truth shall make you free."

Even the weather was ready to welcome Helen Symonds home. Alyssa was as excited as she had been as a child when she found out that Grandma and Grandpa were coming for a visit. As she had so often then she could not settle, but on Saturday evening rather than try to sleep she made herself comfortable in the living room in front of a fire. Alyssa had started to read

Leo Tolstoy's masterpiece *War and Peace 2* and was eager to discover what would transpire between Count Bezuhov and Natasha.

There were only embers remaining in the fireplace when Alyssa coming to the end of a chapter, closed the novel, and climbed the stairs to her bedroom. Many times throughout the past month she had felt lonely rambling about the house as its sole occupant, but never once did she regret that Elaine was unequivocally gone. She loved being able to leave her door wide open at night to enjoy the light from the moon shining through the large loft window. As soon as evening classes began she had taken advantage of the desk and chair in the den, even though she realized she would have to relinquish her newfound study area when Helen selected another boarder.

The sun was streaming through the skylight when Alyssa awoke. The blustery wind that had been whistling through the window and doorframes when she went to bed had ceased. The house was serenely quiet. It had neither seemed as cold when she crawled out from under her cozy quilt nor when she opened the front door to retrieve *The StarPhoenix*. Could the largest city in Saskatchewan be experiencing a 'January thaw' with Chinook winds from Alberta causing a temporary warming trend? Or was Helen bringing the much more clement weather from Victoria where flowers were beginning to bud home with her?

❋

"Over here, Alyssa." Helen waved as soon as she entered the arrivals waiting area. The minute she reached her, she enveloped Alyssa in a huge hug. "It's lovely to see you, my dearest."

Ensconced in Helen's arms, Alyssa felt as safe and free as she always did when she was with Grandma. Now, learning to forgive herself she knew beyond a doubt that neither Helen nor her beloved grandmother would ever have faulted or judged her. Both older women would have been shocked and horrified, but empathetic, and they certainly would not have condemned her. Still, Alyssa grasped that she could never bear her soul to either one of them. Years ago, even when the assault had occurred, she knew that she could not wound her grandmother to the core of her being by telling her the truth. If only her brother had not been present during her ordeal and worse yet had not come to her aid, she might, at least have taken Helen into her confidence. But, when he had been killed in a vehicular homicide, Alyssa Rainer vowed that her redemption could not, under any circumstance, come at the ruination of his short history.

~42~

Spring had come early that year. Helen's return from Victoria had indeed heralded the arrival of unusually temperate weather. February had passed quickly. March not only came in like a lamb, but also went out like the young woolly mammal. By the beginning of April, the citizens of the city were ready to plant their flowers and vegetables. Early in the morning of Good Friday, Alyssa had left to spend Easter with her grandmother, and Helen was donning her gardening clothes when the doorbell rang.

"Hello, Helen. You're looking very well."

Never expecting to see her again, Helen could not find a single word to say. She must appear as though she had lost her mind as she continued to remain motionless and stare at her visitor.

"It's Elaine. I'm sorry to have startled you. Do you have a few minutes to speak with me?"

Recovering at last, Helen said, "Let's sit on the veranda. Since the weather has been so warm we put out the deck chairs at the beginning of the week."

"Thank you, Helen. My exams finish near the end of the month, and I'll be leaving for Manitoba the afternoon I've written the last one. I didn't want to go without saying good-bye and paying the money I owe you."

Now, Helen did look at her with a genuine lapse of memory. Fortunately, before she had to acknowledge it, Elaine continued, "I've brought you the hundred dollars in cash I owe you for January's rent. I'm sorry I had to stop payment on the cheque then, but I needed the money to put down as a deposit for a room at the college dormitory."

The mention of Elaine's cancelled cheque loosened Helen's tongue. "Well, I must say I'm surprised to see you, although not on a weekend when you likely surmised that Alyssa would be visiting her grandmother. She never spoke about what had given rise to your abrupt departure, but my intuition has advanced a fairly plausible reason. In future, may I suggest that you strive to be more accurate when reading people? There is little doubt in my mind Alyssa is one of the most naïve individuals that I've ever met, and furthermore she tends to live in her ivory tower where human sexuality seldom enters. Thank you, Elaine, for coming to say good-bye to me. Please use the hundred dollars to enjoy your trip back to Manitoba."

If Elaine's first departure from 1154 Spadina Crescent East had been precipitous, her second was even quicker. She had never felt so dismissed in her life. But then, she had always known that Alyssa was Helen's 'pet.' Elaine recalled how she had met her former genteel landlady while walking along the street that morning nearly two years ago when the enchanting house had come into view. Over the past months she had missed Helen. She was hoping that not only was she at home, but also she would invite her to have tea and scones with her. Believing that she would be received amicably before her farewell, Elaine planned to ask Helen if she might take a few minutes to check she had gathered all of her belongings when she had made her hasty exit. What Elaine wanted was to immerse herself in the ambiance of the loft one last time and reminisce about her moments with Alyssa.

Remaining on the veranda until she was certain that Elaine was truly away, Helen went back into the house and locked her door. What audacity! How dare that woman return to her home where Helen had trusted and loved her until she had molested Alyssa? To her credit, she had never once spoken about what had actually transpired between her and Elaine during

Helen's absence. Alyssa's only acknowledgement occurred on the first of February when she handed her a cheque made out for two hundred dollars.

"What's this, Alyssa? I don't expect you to pay the full amount of rent for the loft. Before I arrived home, I had given considerable thought to whether I would bother to place an ad for another boarder. I meant to discuss my decision with you, but clearly I've neglected to do so. I'm sorry. I've no intention of bringing another person into my home to share accommodations with you. On the other hand, I did wonder if on your budget that I know is tight to cover your university courses, you could manage another twenty-five dollars per month."

"Oh, thank you, Helen. That's so considerate of you, although I think it would be fairer if I were to pay you an extra fifty dollars per month, going on the premise that when there were two of us, we each paid fifty for renting the loft and the balance for our board."

Chuckling, Helen answered, "Trust you to think in those terms, Alyssa. However, I've made up my mind. Please change your cheque to one hundred and twenty-five dollars, thank you very much."

Alyssa was so relieved that she would have the loft and the study area entirely to herself, she gave Helen an impromptu hug.

When it occurred to Alyssa she was eligible for three weeks of vacation with pay, she realized that if she registered for a spring evening course rather than the summer session, with careful planning she could allow herself at least seven days for a retreat somewhere. After she wrote the exam, Alyssa would then seek as many hours of work as possible at City Hospital, an achievable objective to cover for staff vacation time that she could for the first two weeks of her holidays to earn extra money. She did have enough sense to acknowledge that with fulltime employment at the health unit, four three-hour evening classes every week during May and June, followed by two weeks of hospital nursing, her schedule would be gruelling.

Since Helen mentioned that she was meeting Mariah and Steven for a train excursion through the Rocky Mountains, Alyssa had been intrigued. She had only ever seen the mountains in pictures, and began to consider the possibility of planning a driving trip to the ranges in Jasper National Park. With map in hand, she had determined that it was a nine-hour drive and with time calculated to stop for a meal and fuel, she would require a minimum of ten hours. Subsequently, if she were on the road before seven o'clock, she should arrive at her destination prior to the dinner hour.

The next step of her plan was to search for an affordable place to stay for seven nights. One February evening before class, Alyssa made her way to the travel agency in the Students' Centre on campus. A helpful agent soon provided her with brochures of accommodations and activities throughout the park. She was particularly enthusiastic about some cabins located five minutes from the townsite of Jasper at the end of a private road high in the Rocky Mountains, overlooking the calm crystal clear Patricia Lake.

Perusing a booklet, Alyssa discovered a fascinating lesson in Canadian history. During the 1940's, Patricia Lake was chosen as the location for the WWII top-secret project code-named Project "Habbakuk." This assignment was the vision of Winston Churchill who wanted to build a ship of ice that would allow airplanes to land, refuel, and continue on their missions of protecting merchant ships. Several factors contributed to the eventual demise of the Habbakuk. The key players in the undertaking believed it was no longer needed and in the fall of 1943, the fully operational Habbakuk was stripped of its reusable parts and sunk to the bottom of Patricia Lake, forever secret.

When the region was vacated, the area around Patricia Lake became an autocamp for travellers and campers. The original owners and builders, the Houg family eventually purchased the leasehold from Parks Canada in the mid 1950's and began to construct cottages, which they named Patricia Lake Bungalows.

Combined with the historical information, the promise in the brochure that Patricia Lake Bungalows, "offered a kind of peace and quiet that few have experienced, the provision of a place to commune in the beauty of nature, a home away from the daily stresses of life, and a haven to recharge body and soul," Alyssa was captivated. On the spot, she booked seven nights at one of the two original log cabins, arriving on the fourteenth of July and departing on the twenty-first of the month.

❋

It was love at first sight. Spring had steadily given way to summer, and Alyssa soldiered onward. She was no stranger to hard work. Early in her adolescence she had learned that she was defined by accomplishment. In the serenity of Helen's home and her loft, she felt the love and bliss that she had hitherto only experienced in her grandparents' presence. With no negative detractions, and becoming progressively free from the guilt and shame of her past, Alyssa's confidence and self-esteem soared. She began to reach her potential. There was little doubt though, that she was exhausted by the middle of July when she had concluded her arduous five month timetable, inclusive of completing her first year toward her university degree.

Fortunately, she had been scheduled for the day shift on Saturday, July 13th. Helen had thoughtfully planned a barbeque with prime rib steaks, mushrooms, and grilled potatoes, which she was prepared to serve whenever Alyssa was ready to eat. Given the choice, she decided to pack and prepare her car for an early start in the morning before enjoying a delicious dinner on the veranda. Helen was delighted that for the first time in two years, Alyssa, her other daughter had an opportunity to pursue a vacation beyond her regular visits with her grandmother. Helen expressed she was worried about her driving so far alone, although she knew once she arrived, she would be enthralled with all that she would experience.

As it happened, by the time Alyssa observed the mountains in the distance she was in awe and when she reached the entrance to Jasper National Park, she had to drive to a pullover site and exit her vehicle. Her sensorium was overwhelmed – the freshness in the air, the stillness of the location, the quiet of the surroundings, the rocky mountain sheep high on the peaks, the beauty and the majesty of the mountainous ranges to behold in every direction. For a woman who had never in her life travelled farther than two Prairie Provinces, Alyssa was beyond incredulous.

Approaching Jasper and instantly spotting several quaint buildings, which she would explore later, Alyssa decided before she stopped for anything to eat she would locate the cabin she had booked at Patricia Lake. Once registered, she followed the directions until she arrived at her accommodation. She stopped her car and again slipped into the stillness and tranquillity of the famed Canadian Rocky Mountains. Alyssa was motionless as she gazed at the small rustic log cabin that was to be her home for the subsequent week. The exterior was so apropos, and she had yet to discover the stone hearth, the cozy quilted double bed, and the comfortable reading corner near the entrance. The mere thought that this sanctuary was for her and her alone for seven days was Alyssa's idea of heaven, and she was taken into the soul of her spectacular surroundings.

It must have been the pristine mountain air – Alyssa had not slept so deeply since her childhood. She awoke as dawn was breaking and with coffee in hand was seated on the red deck chair in time to observe the sun rising over the lake. Then and there, she resolved that she would enjoy every moment of daylight in the park, until the last sunbeam disappeared below the horizon near her cabin. She planned shorter morning walks in the vicinity of the lake, with a two to three hour mountain hike scheduled in the afternoon beginning with Old Fort Point Trail.

Alyssa followed the park attendant's recommendation to start the moderately steep loop trail by climbing clockwise through an old forest overgrown with moss covering until a rocky outcropping was reached. The scenery was magnificent with the view the highlight of the hike – the Jasper townsite, valley and Athabasca River stretched in front of her and far in the distance, Alyssa could see the peaks of Pyramid Mountain, Mount Kinross, Cairngorm, Mount Kerr, and many more beyond.

On Friday Alyssa decided to embark upon the Whistlers Mountain Hike, a distance of slightly more than 4 miles with an elevation gain of 8085 feet to the summit. She wondered if she dared attempt the six-hour trek alone, until the park attendant assured her that the climb was well travelled with most people hiking one way and riding the SkyTram in the opposite direction. Alyssa did not have the slightest intention of getting on the highest and longest aerial lift in Canada, constructed in 1964, with two stationary track cables for support, and a haulage rope attached to the cabin for propulsion.

Following coffee and a lighter breakfast, Alyssa filled a backpack with enough food and fluids to sustain her for the day and drove to the parking lot by eight o'clock. At the west end, she found the trailhead and began the hike by entering a narrow path surrounded by dense bush. The climb turned sheer toward the boulder side, where the trail descended marginally before it switched back and forth with the grade becoming progressively steeper until close to the summit, hiking was perilous. The folly of wearing her Trackster running shoes versus hiking boots was clear as Alyssa had to squat to scale the rocky ground before reaching the tramway terminal. After she had signed her name in the logbook near the summit, she cautiously walked toward the edge of the mountain, wondering just how far she could go without slipping over.

Standing still atop Whistler's Peak, the pulchritude, the splendour, and the panorama of the Canadian Rocky Mountains was truly awe-inspiring. Alyssa knew that it was by divine intervention that she had ascended to this pinnacle of God's Creation. At that moment, she thought of her beloved grandmother. How she wished that she could have brought her on this trip with her, not to climb but to view the mountains. She had never travelled beyond Saskatchewan and Manitoba either, and it did not seem likely now unless Alyssa could convince her devout grandma that it would be providential for her to travel with her to Jasper next summer. There was no doubt whatever in Alyssa Rainer's mind that henceforth she would return to Patricia Lake Bungalows every year.

~ 43 ~

Come September it would be five years since Alyssa had relocated to Saskatoon, and changes were in the wind. Walking across University Bridge on the morning of May 25th after writing her final examination, she was in a melancholy mood. She had followed her academic plan to the letter, and would graduate in the autumn with her Bachelor of Arts in English Literature. She continued to live with Helen in her beautiful home, and by fall she would have been employed as a public health nurse for four years, while continuing to take additional shifts on the surgical unit at City Hospital. She returned to Jasper every summer, albeit she could never convince her grandmother to make the journey with her. All too often though, Alyssa still thought about Eric Easton.

Where was he? What had happened to him? Why had he severed all communication with her? For that matter, what about Susan and Bryan, and all the other friends she thought she had acquired during nursing training? To be truthful, Alyssa had not kept in touch with any of them, but then she had virtually one week every year when she was not employed while pursuing her studies. Maybe, she should not have tossed that surprise invitation to their five-year reunion in Brandon when it had arrived. For the first time, Alyssa might have been able to afford taking her full vacation rather than working the initial two weeks. Perhaps, she could have planned a trip to Manitoba.

Had she sacrificed too much in the quest for her university degree? Unbelievably on this bright summer morning, even knowing that she had aced her exam, Alyssa was well on her way down the path to a pity party. She began to wonder when she had perfected her proclivity for losing people. The trend had escalated at the end of last year when Cheryl and David apprised her that they were moving back to Winnipeg before the birth of their first child. The nursing staff had no sooner returned to the health unit after the Christmas break than Cynthia announced that she and Sebio were moving to Indianapolis at the end of June. They were beginning their family and wanted their children to share their American citizenship. Then in rapid succession, Gayle disclosed that Ken had been offered his dream position in his home city of Toronto, and they planned to be relocated before their baby arrived.

Within six months every person Alyssa had cared about in Saskatoon, with the exception of Helen, would be living in another city, each of which were progressively distant, and she was unlikely to see any of them again. They had been so supportive during these past years, cheering her on whenever she became snowed under with her strenuous self-imposed workload. Alyssa would receive her degree, but none of her friends could attend her convocation.

If she did decide to attend the reunion, it would be surface visits catching up with thirty-eight classmates and little chance for spending much time with any one person. It would be great to see Susan, even though she realized it would be highly improbable that she would have any current information about Eric. And, Alyssa knew that Susan was not above saying, "I told you so." No wonder Alyssa was feeling sorry for herself.

Sliding deeper into the pit she was digging, Alyssa nearly bowled over a pregnant woman walking in the opposite direction on the bridge. "I'm sorry. I neither intended to test your balance nor to push you over."

Chuckling, she replied, "Bloody hell, you talk like a Brit."

"No, I'm Canadian, but I must say your accent sounds like you are."

"Actually, I'm Australian, born and bred in Melbourne. I'm called Kathleen Sinclair and who may you be?"

"My name is Alyssa Rainer. I was born on a farm in Duff, Saskatchewan not far from here."

"Well hello, Alyssa. I can't remember ever seeing anyone look so gloomy on such a beautiful day in this picturesque city. I'm out for my daily constitutional and rather than throw yourself in the river, why don't we go for a coffee at Louis' Loft?"

❋

It was close to four hours later when the two women asked for their bill and prepared to leave. Coffee had become lunch, with more coffee to follow until Kathleen had said, "Well, I think that I'll walk over to Darren's office to see if he's ready to wrap up his week. We'll likely check out the menu at the Faculty Club, and you're welcome to join us."

"Thank you, no. I can't believe the hour. Helen will be wondering what has happened to me."

If Alyssa was having difficulty grasping that it was nearly four o'clock, she was beyond understanding how and why she had not only revealed, but also discussed the most confidential details of her life with a complete stranger. Her disclosure had started innocently enough. She recalled asking Kathleen when her baby was due to arrive. From such an ingenuous beginning, over the course of their visit, Alyssa had bared her heart and soul. How could she have been that forthright?

Kathleen had responded, "Other than sometime in October, I don't know when this baby is coming. We weren't planning to start a family because Darren realizes that he needs his doctorate if he's to be considered for tenure at the university. But, it is what it is."

"It must be a sign of the times. My three closest friends are not only pregnant, but also have all moved away." Alyssa replied with chagrin.

"Now I'm beginning to get an idea of why you looked so glum. From the absence of a ring on your left hand, you're not married. Is there a significant other in the picture?" Kathleen inquired.

There was something so open and genuine about Kathleen Sinclair that Alyssa surprised herself by saying, "I let the only man I ever cared about get away almost five years ago." She became silent. Kathleen waited. Then before Alyssa knew it, everything tumbled out – the story of their blind date, their instant bonding, the realization they shared similar backgrounds and aspirations, and the suddenness with which Eric proposed. She talked about her ambivalent feelings, her uncertainties, her negativity about marriage, and most of all, her inflexible decision that she would never allow a man to change the plans she had firmly put in place. Still, Kathleen listened. In a distraught voice, Alyssa expressed they had lost touch with each other, she did not know why, they had not communicated since November of 1966, the year she chose to come to Saskatoon instead of following him to Winnipeg. "It has only been recently I've come to realize that Eric might have been my one true love."

Both women were standing when Kathleen spoke her profound parting words, "You'll make one of two choices after you leave me today, Alyssa. You'll either be so embarrassed that you spilled your guts you will never want to see me again, or you'll become my lifelong friend. If you should choose the latter, you're welcome anytime at 1108 King Crescent."

The summer was full of surprises. When Alyssa arrived home, Helen was on the front veranda clearing the remnants of afternoon tea, where she often entertained her friends and neighbours during the day and evening. "Hello, my dear. I was beginning to think that you were off with friends celebrating your last examination and the completion of your degree."

"I wouldn't say that I was so much celebrating, as I may have met a new friend though, I have yet to make my decision."

Helen was on the verge of asking what she meant when she observed the pensive look on her face. From past experience, she knew Alyssa was deep in thought and that she would not divulge any information until, if ever, she were ready. Changing the subject, Helen said, "The mailman delivered two important looking letters for you from the university when Margaret and I were finishing our tea. I still have them here. Would you like something to drink while you open them?"

"No thanks, Helen. I've been drinking coffee all afternoon. I can't imagine why there are two. I've been expecting one from the English Faculty, but it's too early for my transcript." As she sat down on a deck chair, Alyssa tore open one of the epistles. "It's what I hoped. I've been accepted to begin my master's programme in the fall semester. So, what is this other letter?"

Opening the second envelope with more care, Alyssa began to read intently. Her face reflected surprise, incredulity, and as she glanced farther down the paper, a look of sheer delight. "Wow. I don't believe this. I've been awarded a fifteen hundred dollar scholarship based on my academic achievement to continue as a full-time graduate student in English Literature. Also, I'm the recipient of a twelve hundred and fifty dollar bursary awarded on the basis of scholarly merit and financial need. Good heavens, these two awards will not only cover all my university expenses, but also most of my living costs."

"Congratulations, Alyssa. I can't think of a single other person more worthy than you for either of these honours. I've always known that you're an exceptional student and how nice to receive such recognition from the university. In celebration, I'm taking you out for dinner, so name your preference, although I'll give you a hint that my favourite hotel restaurant is in the offering, my dearest."

By late afternoon on Saturday, Alyssa completely reassessed her summer schedule. She had booked her vacation at the health unit from July 5th through to the twenty-sixth of the month. With the exception of the Dominion Day Statutory holiday weekend, she had not firmed up any other dates for vacation relief at the hospital. Instead of committing for summer relief, Alyssa decided to take her full vacation and allow herself a three-week holiday before starting graduate school. Her registration at Patricia Lake Bungalows was for July 11th to the 25th. Subsequently, Alyssa had no definite plans from the fifth of July until she was due to arrive in Jasper.

What did she want to do with her week of newfound freedom? Should she drive to the reunion in Brandon before continuing on to Winnipeg to search for Eric Easton? If she could remember the location of his parents' farm somewhere east of Portage La Prairie, she could stop and ask them. But she had only been there twice, had not been driving either time, and did not have the slightest clue how to find their property. Alyssa might have searched for a listing in the telephone directory, but she neither knew their specific municipality nor his father's Christian name, since he had always been referred to as Pa.

Winnipeg was a much larger city with a total population that was nearly triple that of Saskatoon. Searching for Eric without a telephone number or an address would equate to looking for a needle in a haystack. No doubt he had progressed with his life – had married, started a family, moved to another city, or any other number of possibilities. Why would he have waited and pined for her when he could not write or return telephone messages five years ago? Had it simply been a summer fling, or were they fated to be star-crossed lovers?

To enjoy the balmy afternoon, Alyssa left her loft and joined Helen on the veranda. As it happened she was perusing a map of Alberta, when suddenly a plan began to crystallize in her mind. Much to her surprise the distance from Saskatoon to Banff National Park was less than it was to Jasper. "Did you know that it is closer to drive to Banff than to Jasper?"

"I believe it is by more than an hour, although I think that it is much farther if you decide to drive to Regina to connect with the Trans-Canada Highway. An alternative route is to leave Saskatoon on Highway 7, which turns into the #9 when you cross the border into Alberta, and continue until you reach Highway 2. Either way you need to drive through Calgary to continue on or to access the #1, which takes you to Banff. We always drove the shorter and more scenic cross country route whenever we drove to the park to visit my cousin."

"With my unexpected windfall, I've decided to take three weeks of vacation. During the first week, while I still have my government car, I would like to tour around Banff National Park before driving the Icefields Parkway on my way to Jasper. But, it will depend on whether I can find a reasonable priced place to stay in Banff."

"I've a proposal, Alyssa. How would you feel if I came to Banff with you and we both stayed with my cousin, Marjorie? She's always asking me to visit and she has plenty of room. Then, I might coax her to drive me back to Saskatoon to do some sightseeing, or I could take the Greyhound bus home while you continue on your way."

"Do you mean that? I would pay for my room and board for the week just like I do with you, Helen."

"Don't be silly. We would both be her guests. Why don't I call her right now? What date are we planning to arrive? "

While Alyssa continued to study a brochure for likely excursions around Banff, Helen disappeared into the house. By the time she returned, Alyssa had discovered multiple hiking trails – Johnson Canyon Lower and Upper Falls, Lake Louise and Lake Moraine Shoreline Trails, the Lake Agnes Tea House Hike, and many more than she could ever hope to climb.

Twenty minutes later, carrying a tray with two glasses of iced tea, Helen shared, "Marjorie is positively delighted we're coming. She's already making plans."

"Thank you. I was concerned that my budget wouldn't cover the cost of a week in Banff, as well as my trip to Jasper. What a splendid summer this will be. You're so good to me, Helen."

"My dearest Alyssa, we're good to each other."

~44~

The more she thought about her the more she wanted to take her up on her invitation. But, Alyssa realized she could not wait too long. She had experienced considerable chagrin about revealing her innermost feelings and secrets to Kathleen Sinclair and at first had decided she would forget that they had ever met. But, she intrigued Alyssa. She not only liked her Australian accent, but also her manner of speaking, her satirical sense of humour, her perspicacity, and her candour. Besides, Alyssa had never known anyone from the "Land Down Under."

Timing could be a factor. July was shaping up to being a very busy month for Alyssa. If she prolonged arriving at 1108 King Crescent until August, there was a reasonable possibility that Kathleen would have forgotten her. Fortunately, she had been scheduled for a day shift on Sunday, July 3rd and returning from the hospital, she decided to stroll down Kathleen's street before going home.

Reading the house numbers, she was surprised when she found the small two-bedroom dwelling perched on an oversized lot surrounded by towering trees. There did not appear to be any sign of life within and when she rang the doorbell, there was no answer. Alyssa was ready to leave when she heard a voice, "If you're not soliciting, come around to the back. As you can surely imagine, it's much cooler in the shade of my own forest than inside my tiny domicile."

"It's you, Alyssa Rainer. Welcome. I was wondering when you were coming. Inside the back door there's a small refrigerator with canned drinks and beer, if you're so inclined. Please grab what you want before having a seat under the boughs of this lovely willow."

Returning with a Diet Coke and a glass with ice, Alyssa claimed a lounge chair opposite Kathleen. "It's so bloody hot, and a word of advice. Make sure you're never coming up to the third trimester of a pregnancy during the high temperatures of summer."

"Thanks for the drink. It wasn't until I was walking home that I realized it was this hot. It was cool this morning when I went to work. How are you feeling other than sweltering? If I remember correctly your baby is due some indeterminate date in October."

"I've nothing to complain about except for feeling as big as my house."

Glancing around, Alyssa was astounded by the size of the backyard and the number of trees. "I'm amazed by the disproportion between the land and the lodging of your property."

"Precisely the reason we purchased it as soon as we saw the location with its proximity to the river. Eventually we intend to demolish this house, and construct a large two-storey Cedar home that I've already designed. I'll also be the Builder/General Contractor."

"I don't recall you mentioning that you're an architect. You're going to be one busy lady when you begin your project."

"I'm not an architect, although not by my choice. I've always had a flair for designing and building, but the only post-secondary education my chauvinistic father would pay for was a teaching certificate. He maintained that university was wasted on a girl. For the short time she would work before getting married and having babies, becoming a teacher was good enough. As soon as I graduated I accepted a teaching job in Norway House, Manitoba, and I've never been back home. As it happens, my younger brother is now studying to become an architect at the University of Melbourne. You better believe there was no way on God's green earth that I was ever going to marry some bloody patriarchal Aussie."

Since Alyssa had monopolized the conversation during their initial encounter, she was not about to interrupt Kathleen when she was disclosing her personal history. "When the Rossville Residential School in Norway House was closed on June 30, 1967, I was flying to Winnipeg on one of the two private airlines, Perimeter Air when I met Darren. He'd been assisting the Cree Nation with the proposal and funding for the development of a new school in the Frontier School Division. He asked me to have dinner when the airplane landed, but I had a connection to Toronto. During my two years of teaching, I'd saved every penny I had earned and was about to travel around the world for ten months. Not to be daunted, Darren gave me his business card and private telephone number, asking me to let him know when I was on my way back to Canada."

Highly unlikely when Eric and I could not maintain communication beyond two months when we lived five hundred miles apart in adjacent provinces. And yet? Alyssa thought as she waited for Kathleen to continue.

"Almost a year later prior to my return to Winnipeg, I telephoned Darren's office and left a message with his secretary with the time that my flight was landing at the International Airport. At arrivals to my incredulity, I heard someone calling my name and there he was. Was I glad to see him? I was starving, exhausted, nearly broke, and didn't know a single other person in the city. We went for dinner, Darren invited me to his place, the sex was great, and we shacked up in his apartment in St. Vital for the next three months…that's where I had seen you before. The day on the bridge I thought that I'd met you previously, but I couldn't remember where. You lived in the suite across the hall with your husband. He usually stopped to chat with me while I was on the front steps waiting for Darren to come home from work. You often said hello and asked me how I was doing, but you were always too rushed to stop and visit. Your hubby did introduce himself, and although I rarely forget a face, I'm dreadful with names."

"Sorry, you've clearly mistaken me for another person. I haven't the slightest idea where St. Vital is, much less have lived there."

"We conversed at least a dozen times, albeit we didn't exchange names. You look exactly like her – same height, same size, same mannerisms, and same tone of voice. She could be your identical twin."

"That's bizarre. I don't have a twin. It couldn't have been me. Even though I know that St. Vital is a subdivision of Winnipeg, the only time I was ever in the Capital City was in 1964 when some of our nursing training instructors took a group of students from my class there for pizza and to see the movie, "The Sound of Music."

"Well, then she must be your alternate self. Come on don't look so astonished. Have you never had anyone tell you that you're the spitting image of another person they know? There are plenty of people who believe there is a parallel dimension that exists concurrently with our own, although they never intersect with each other."

"I can't believe that for a microsecond. I'm one of a kind as unique as are you. I know who I am. I would never want some 'other self.' Heaven forbid there could be another person like me. But you haven't told me what happened after three months?"

"Darren proposed, I accepted, we had a quiet wedding with his mother, his aunt and uncle who acted as the witnesses, and we moved to Saskatoon. Say, look at the time. Darren will be home soon. Would you like to join us for barbequed hamburgers?"

"Thanks, but I must dash. My landlady and I are planning our sojourn in Banff next week. When I return near the end of July, I'll invite you over to meet Helen. She's the most endearing woman other than my grandmother that I've ever met."

"Yet another characteristic shared by your alter self in St. Vital." Kathleen laughingly replied. Walking across the back alley, it occurred to Alyssa that her new friend had a tendency to convey parting shots.

~45~

In order to take advantage of the Ford Fairlane before she had to hand over the keys, Alyssa chose Friday, September 10th as her last day of employment with the health department. She planned one last driving journey leaving as soon as she finished work on September 3rd, to visit her grandmother for the Labour Day weekend. Graduate classes did not commence until the subsequent Monday, and she was never above utilizing any opportunity to earn money. At any rate, Alyssa was so well rested following her blissful three weeks in the mountains that she was eager to meet the challenges of being a fulltime university student.

Alyssa had ambivalent feelings about resigning her position at the Saskatoon Health Unit. She would miss many of the clients she had worked with for years in the Nutana subdivision, but since Gayle and Cynthia had left, she shared little camaraderie with any of the other nurses. And, she was more than happy to say farewell to Irene Kennedy. Alyssa had often thought that Dr. French was an alcoholic, although she would always appreciate his full support when she had proposed establishing a family planning clinic in Nutana, and then he essentially approved hours of her time to work with the Saskatchewan Department of Health to develop and operate it. Alyssa's fondest memories of her community nursing career were of the many women she had rescued from reproducing prolifically.

✵

From the moment, Helen had unexpectedly given her a set of keys to her new automobile one of Alyssa's major adjustments had been alleviated. She loved having a car over the past four years, even if it came with restrictions, but she realized she would have to wait until she graduated with at least her master's degree before she could consider purchasing her own. It had been on their drive to Banff when Helen mentioned she had ordered a 1971 Ford Escort that would arrive sometime upon their return. "I know how much you like to drive, Alyssa, and I've bought a compact vehicle for both of us to use."

"You're a gem, Helen. I would have missed not having a car, although I'd confirmed the Grey Hound Line's schedule to Jasper next year for my annual trip to Patricia Lake Bungalows, and I'd go back to taking the train to Melville. Still, I appreciate that you're planning to allow me to drive your car. I was blessed the day I met you."

Since Helen regularly visited Mariah and Steven in Victoria for five to six weeks every winter, she had realized that Alyssa would need access to her vehicle while she was away. In so many ways, the young nurse had come to fill the void left when Mariah married Steven. Between their busy respective medical practices, they could return less and less to Saskatoon. Helen's hope that Mariah would eventually come back to the city of her birth had long been forgotten, but she was not ready to give up her home with all its memories to relocate to the island. She loved the expansiveness of the prairies and felt closed in by the ocean and the mountains.

Helen had often thought of Alyssa as another daughter, and their week in Banff cemented the bond between them. Even the trip across the neighbouring prairie had been enlightening with her coming to appreciate what a skilled driver Alyssa was, and how much energy she had wasted worrying about her solitary excursions. Helen had been so relaxed that she napped for over an hour, a feat she had never achieved even when Ray was at the wheel. Marjorie liked Alyssa the moment they met, and the week the three women spent in her cottage sped by suffused with enjoyable conversations, delicious meals, drives and hikes in the mountains, laughter, fun, and games until all too soon it was time for Alyssa to continue on her way.

The Sunday afternoon before Alyssa started grad school, she arrived on the veranda with her friend, Kathleen. Helen was reading when she heard a voice with which she was not familiar, "I've always liked a house with a front porch, much more preferable than being stuck at the back where one can't spy on the passersby."

"You share my exact sentiments. From your accent you must be Kathleen. Alyssa has mentioned that she was going to introduce me to her Australian friend. I'm Helen. Let me welcome you and offer you young ladies a glass of freshly made lemonade."

Two hours later, Helen asked Kathleen if she would like to telephone her husband to join them for dinner. "Early this morning before the day became a scorcher, Alyssa and I prepared salads – potato, bean, and Greek to go with cold chicken, and we have enough for an army. I'm afraid though, that ice cream will have to suffice for dessert."

Lying in bed that night, Helen understood immediately why Kathleen Sinclair had become Alyssa's latest friend. She was outgoing, affable, bright, and funnier than any one she had met in years. It was patently obvious Darren adored her and was delighted that a baby would soon arrive. How nice they had asked Alyssa to be their child's godmother? She often wondered if Alyssa would ever stop working and studying enough to date a fellow, much less to consider marriage. What impact had that unfortunate incident with Elaine have upon her? Alyssa always seemed to be focused on achieving, not unlike her own daughter. Helen feared Mariah and Steven might become so wrapped up in their careers there would not be any grandchildren on the horizon. At least, since Kathleen lived one street over, she was convinced that she would soon have an opportunity to cuddle an infant. Before succumbing to sweet repose, Helen Symonds decided that she would frequently include Kathleen and Darren in her widened circle of young people.

~46~

If Helen often reflected that Alyssa might have been considered obsessive before, her decision was readily confirmed once she began her graduate studies. She was frequently out the door prior to Helen having awakened, and she was an early riser. Returning, as the dinner hour was pending she allowed all of thirty minutes to eat and talk about her classes before retiring to her loft with an armful of books. It was not until Friday evening of the initial week that Alyssa assisted Helen with the cleanup of the kitchen and joined her on the veranda to enjoy the autumn evening.

"What a pleasure to have your company, Alyssa. This first week has been reminiscent of when Mariah started in pre-med. I've missed chatting with you, although I suppose I was spoiled during the summer, the only one you hadn't been taking courses."

"I'll admit that I was both enthralled and overwhelmed by my introduction to becoming a fulltime student. It's one thing to study part-time for only two courses, but quite another when I began to grasp that I now have five totally different subjects, and five professors each believing they're the only one with expectations. As I always do, I started my transition by thinking I must accomplish everything instantly. If this week hadn't come to its timely end I might have spiralled out of control. I've a hunch that my most important learning might be how I'm going to maintain balance."

"Now that's insightful, my dear. Mariah tended to be an equally intense student. We soon reached an agreement that if I sensed she was starting to unravel, I would suggest a time out. We would go for a walk, have a coffee, or take a short drive into the country, weather permitting, until she became calm again and could put her studies into perspective. How would you feel if we used the same approach?"

"You're infinitely wise, Helen, and I would appreciate your objectivity. All my life whenever I've embarked upon an activity that fascinates me, I'm inclined to go overboard to the point of becoming compulsive. How kind of you to be prepared to help me remain centred?"

As it happened, Kathleen soon became Helen's ally in making sure that Alyssa did not bury herself in books. During the last month of her pregnancy she was unwieldy, lonely, and scared. She had never been particularly close to her mother, but as her due date approached, she wished that she were not halfway around the world. Kathleen had taken prenatal classes, read as many books about labour and delivery, and the care of newborn babies as she could digest, until she had surpassed cerebral satiation. However, she had multiple questions to which she could not find the answers in books – would her baby be normal, could she handle the pain of giving birth, would she cope with looking after her infant, would she be a good mother?

Kathleen still walked every afternoon albeit for a much-shortened distance, confined primarily to the neighbourhood. She did not dare stroll across University Bridge for fear of her labour starting prematurely. It had been over a week since Kathleen had seen anyone other than Darren and precious little of him, since he was spending eight or nine hours every day at the university. She never thought that she would ever wish she were back home in the large house in Melbourne, surrounded by the several women of her extended family who had birthed babies, and suddenly she missed them. They would no doubt jest with her and recount dismaying stories of their own experiences, but she would eventually obtain the answers she was seeking.

Turning the corner onto Spadina Crescent, Kathleen thought she saw movement on the veranda. Would Helen welcome her if she were not accompanying Alyssa? She appeared to be alone, and Kathleen did not have to go onto the patio in the event she was busy. As it transpired, Helen spotted her coming and waved to her until they were within hearing distance. "Hi, there I thought that might be you, Kathleen. Would you care to join me for a cup of tea?"

Helen insisted that Kathleen sit on the chaise lounge and elevate her legs while she disappeared into the house. Carrying a tray laden with blueberry scones, butter, rhubarb jam, and a pot of tea, Helen returned saying, "I baked these this morning hoping someone would come along to share them with me. I'm so glad it's you. When I was in the last trimester of my pregnancy with Mariah, I could eat at the drop of a hat. How are you feeling, my dear?"

"Cumbersome like I'm carrying around a twelve pound baby. The mere sight of food makes me hungry and your scones look yummy. How is Alyssa? I've seen neither hide nor hare of her since your lovely dinner."

With a chuckle, Helen replied, "Nor have I, other than on the weekend. During the week university completely devours her. She doesn't even walk or ride her bike on these gorgeous autumn evenings. In fact, I was just thinking that I might enlist you to help me save Alyssa from herself."

"No worries, Helen, you can count on me. I've never met a more serious young woman than Alyssa. Does she have a boyfriend or ever go out on a date? It's funny though, you were thinking about me helping you, when I came to see if you might assist me. My mum and I were always at loggerheads when I was growing up, but the closer it gets to my baby's arrival, the more I wish she were on the next street. I was raised by my extended family in our home in Melbourne. There were so many adults that I hardly had a chance to get near my brother, who is seven years younger than me. Nor did I ever babysit. Now I've a hunch that what I need to know is not found between the pages of any book."

"Anyone who has prepared as diligently as you, Kathleen, and who asks such insightful questions is bound to be a loving mother. It has been so long since I've held a baby that I can hardly wait for your little one to be born. You may rest assured I'm fully anticipating becoming a surrogate grandmother, and I'll be here for you whenever you need me."

"Thank you, its little wonder why Alyssa is so fond of you, Helen. I'm delighted you'll be my child's grandmother. In short order, you and Alyssa are not only alleviating my loneliness, but also my desire for extra arms to hold my baby. Darren is so busy teaching and taking preliminary course-work in preparation to begin his doctorate that I scarcely see him. In terms of saving Alyssa from a premature death by books, the first thing we'll do is find her a nice young mate."

"That may not be as easy as you might think. I'm not one to tell tales out of school and I'll only mention this to you once, Kathleen, but I think that it's fair you're aware of it. The year Alyssa was graduating as a registered nurse, she had accepted a position at City Hospital and had registered at the University of Saskatchewan as a part-time evening student. Then three months before her training finished she met a young man on a blind date, a student at United College in Winnipeg. A few weeks later he proposed to her. Her plans for the future were firmly in place, notwithstanding she was prepared to travel back and forth, and to initiate most of the ongoing telephone and written communication – in short, Alyssa believed their long-distance relationship could last for nine months until he had completed his final year at university. Two months later, by the end of November she never heard from him again."

"That must have been crushing for Alyssa. Not only is she solemn, but also she's very sensitive. Thanks for telling me. I promise that it will be our secret."

"Alyssa is a special young woman with an enduring sense of responsibility. Of course, she blamed herself for not changing her plans on the spur of the moment to follow him to Winnipeg, even though she had no place to live, no job, and only the money that her beloved grandmother had given her for graduation. I'm thoroughly convinced that she has worked so hard these past five years to seek atonement for abandoning her one true love."

Kathleen became still lost in reverie. Helen was beginning to think that she was starting labour when she finally said, "Life is so bloody mystifying. Three years ago when I was living with Darren in a subdivision of Winnipeg, I often chatted with a young woman outside, but she was always rushing and never stopped long enough to tell me her name. Not that it would have mattered because I'm not likely to have remembered – faces I seldom forget, but not names. The woman was the exact replica of Alyssa – everything about them was identical."

Kathleen paused before continuing, "It wasn't until the afternoon when Alyssa dropped in to see me that I remembered the Winnipeg woman so I told her about her doppelgänger. She was quick to enlighten me that she has been living in Saskatoon for the past five years, had never been to St. Vital, much less resided in an apartment across the hall from me with her husband. I thought that Darren might recall his name because he'd been one of his students in an accounting course he taught years before, but he couldn't remember either. Ever since I've met Alyssa the memory of that other woman haunts me."

Searching her memory, Helen could neither recollect Alyssa's young man's Christian nor his surname. How unusual that she had completely blocked both from her mind. It occurred to her that were Elaine still in the picture she could no doubt provide his full name and possibly more. For unknown reasons, she often thought that after Elaine returned from Manitoba the first summer, she had acquired some information about Alyssa's fiancé. On several occasions, Helen observed her furtively glancing at her loft mate on the verge of disclosing something of import, before noticeably giving her head a shake and then remaining silent. She had even attempted to surreptitiously solicit details of Elaine's trip home hoping that she would express what was on the tip of her tongue slip, but to no avail.

At last, Helen spoke, "In my youth I had been fascinated by the history of the ancient Greeks and Romans and when I started university, I began to study the Classics. I was particularly enthralled with a Greek philosopher, priest, historian, and essayist by the name of Plutarch who lived c. AD 46 – after AD 119. His best-known work, *Parallel Lives* is a series of biographies of illustrious Greeks and Romans, arranged in pairs to illuminate their common moral virtues, vices, and destinies. It's considered more of an insight into the human condition than a historical account. One of the ancient Greek's most famous quotations might well be, "It is not histories I am writing, but lives." However, I soon realized that Plutarch was far too complex for me. I completely lost interest in studying ancient history. Later on in my life, I recall reading about a much more intriguing concept called parallel universe. I'm wondering if this could be what you are alluding to, Kathleen?"

With mirth, she replied, "You and I are kindred spirits, Helen. That's precisely what I was referring to but when I hinted at the possibility to Alyssa, she adamantly declared that such an idea was absolute and utter nonsense. On the other hand having travelled around the globe for nearly a year, I believe that we are inhabitants of a weird and wonderful world with many more mysteries than we'll ever know."

"We do indeed share similar souls, my dear. But, now let's have a touch of reality. I must check on my roasting chicken while you follow me into the house and telephone Darren about coming to dinner."

"Only on one condition – you and Alyssa come to us on Friday for a barbeque."

~ 47 ~

The arrival of an eight-pound, seven-ounce baby on Thanksgiving Day strengthened the bond between the three women who lived in houses virtually separated by a back lane. The foursome of friends was seated around the oak table in Helen's elegant dining room peering out the large picture window revelling in the scenic view of the South Saskatchewan River. They were replete with a splendid roast turkey dinner and all the trimmings followed by homemade pumpkin pie slathered with whipped cream.

Leaning back in the captain's chair, Kathleen said, "Helen that was the most delicious meal I've ever eaten in Canada. I'm stuffed."

In a droll tone of voice without so much as a hint of a smile, Darren replied, "Yes, love, you are." While the three older adults were laughing, Helen noticed the questioning look on Alyssa's face. "Sorry if we're excluding you, my dear. In Australia when a woman expresses she is 'stuffed,' she means that she's pregnant."

Alyssa was saying, "Thanks for the elucidation, Helen. I'll make certain I never use that word again in reference to eating…" when Kathleen gasped, "I dislike eating and running but Darren, could you please dash home for the car. A pain like this can only mean that labour has started."

✵

Before midnight on October 11th, 1971, Craig Michael Sinclair boisterously arrived, and began to feed at his mother's breast while she was still on the delivery table. From the first day in the hospital it was as though he was establishing a precedent, which would firmly become his pattern when they were discharged. The nurses could not recall ever having cared for such a hungry baby and since he was in a bassinet in her room, Kathleen was putting him to her breast every two hours. Little did she realize that she would need to continue nursing him at such frequent intervals day and night once they were at home?

Initially, Kathleen's thesis was that if she fed Craig on demand throughout the day, he would have consumed enough to go for longer periods without nursing during the night. The infant quickly proved his mother wrong, until she began taking him to bed with her to lessen the interruptions to her sleep. Darren understood the necessity of Kathleen's approach. Since he could not give her a break from feeding Craig, he placed a cot in the nursery temporarily moving out of the master bedroom. The new parents were coping with their challenging situation until the public health nurse arrived unannounced three weeks after Craig's birth.

It was on a Thursday, the only afternoon that Alyssa did not have a class and could give Helen a reprieve. Since mother and babe had been discharged, either of the women had assisted Kathleen during many of the hours that Darren was at the university. Other friends came to meet Craig, but tended to increase the expectations on Kathleen, rather than to provide any relief from the baby's insistent demands.

When Alyssa opened the door to the nurse, her replacement at the health unit whom she had met on her last day she said, "Thank you for coming. Baby visits were always my favourite activity. May I offer you a cup of tea until Kathleen has finished nursing Craig?"

"In case you don't remember me, I'm Miss Adams. No, thank you. Why is she feeding the baby an hour early? The reason I plan my visits between scheduled feeds is so that mothers are available to hear my essential advice. Please tell Mrs. Sinclair to put the baby in his crib and join us."

If ever Irene Kennedy had a prototype it would be Miss Adams, not in appearance but most definitely in manner of speaking, attitude, and behaviour. Alyssa stared momentarily at her before she clarified, "Were you expecting Mrs. Sinclair to be nursing her baby on your schedule? Did you make an appointment for today's visit?"

"Surely you haven't forgotten already that all of our calls are drop-ins so the clients don't have a chance to distort what's actually going on. Now can you get the new mother? I've several other appointments."

Voices carried through the walls of the small house and before Alyssa could move, Kathleen appeared carrying Craig in her arms. "Good afternoon, Miss Adams. Thank you for your spontaneous visit, but I'm not in need of your advice. I breast-feed my baby on demand whenever he is hungry. Neither do I have any intention of putting him on a schedule nor of offering him any solid food until he is at least six months old. With the capable assistance of my husband and friends you may be on your way. Please record that all is well with mother and babe at 1108 King Crescent."

"Such a method of feeding is simply not recommended and can be injurious to an infant's health and well-being. I can't leave until I'm assured that you will put this baby on a four-hour feeding schedule and pablum before the end of today. Then, there is the follow-up of his bathing, skin care, sleeping accommodations, and immunization timetable. My, look at the hour, I'll have to go and return for the full morning tomorrow."

"Miss Adams, in the brief time you've been in my home, I've determined your methods of rearing a child are quite the opposite of the approaches that I'm accustomed to and which my husband and I intend to employ as we raise our son. In view of your marital status, I hazard a guess you don't have children of your own, and that your advice is derived from reading books rather than from any practical experience. Thank you for your time. Alyssa, could you please see Miss Adams out?"

Returning to the living room, Alyssa was pensive. *Good heavens, what have I done to all those young mothers that I visited over the span of four years.* From a distance she could hear Kathleen saying, "A penny for your thoughts."

At last, Alyssa came out of her reverie to reply, "I'm impressed, Kathleen, with how succinctly you expressed your intentions for parenting. I can't recall how many baby visits I made during my public health nursing days, but I know for a fact that not one of the mothers was as assertive and definitive as you. The truth is I was similar to Miss Adams. I was just thinking about the magnitude of possible repercussions from the same ill-informed advice that I passed along to young mothers. I don't have a clue about how to care for an infant. Everything I asked them to practice, I had learned from studying my Pediatric Nursing textbook. Oh, what a travesty."

Laughing, Kathleen exclaimed, "I can't imagine you marching into my home or any other, like a sergeant major and expecting someone to follow your orders. No doubt you genuinely tried to listen to and help those new mothers, Alyssa, so stop being hard on yourself. Now could you please bundle Craig into his warm togs, and take him for a very long carriage ride on this lovely Indian summer day while I collapse into bed alone for a change."

Their schedule for Christmas travel had been decided early that autumn. Alyssa's final class of the semester was Thursday morning, December 16th and she had booked her ticket to leave on the afternoon train. Helen had offered her the use of her car, but after four gruelling months of university, Alyssa was looking forward to the relaxing clickety-clack of the wheels on the track. She had not been to visit her grandmother since the September long weekend. Alyssa appreciated Helen's request to make the journey before she departed for Victoria on the Monday morning of December 20th.

Of course, Alyssa would get an earful of flak from her mother, and probably her sisters when she telephoned Melville on Christmas Day, but there was no way she was going to leave the Sinclair family without an extra pair of hands over the holiday season. Helen had been coaching her on the preparations for a turkey dinner and with Darren's help, they would set a festive table for the season. At first, Helen had considered not flying to Victoria until after the celebratory meal, but when Alyssa became confident that they would manage, Helen had booked her flight, returning on January twenty-third in the New Year.

Helen had originally considered leaving her return date open in case the Sinclairs needed her assistance. Four weeks was a long time for Kathleen to cope once her husband and Alyssa started back at the university, but when she suggested it, Darren said, "Thank you, Helen. You and Alyssa have been godsends for Kathleen and me these past months, but bit by bit we're resuming some semblance of our quotidian rhythms."

"If I were being honest, I'm not certain that I can endure going so long without cuddling your son. Before Craig was born, I had mentioned to Kathleen that I planned to become his surrogate grandmother, but the truth is I love him as though he were my own grandson. You're both such devoted parents that being included in his care is an honour. I want you to promise though, to telephone me, Darren, should Kathleen be in need. I've flight insurance and could jump on an airplane at a moment's notice."

Overhearing her comments when she opened the door to bring Craig back from a sleigh ride around the block, Alyssa was overwhelmed with affection for the endearing woman. Helen Symonds had a magnanimous heart and soul, and would love a houseful of children as well as their parents. And, Kathleen was unbelievable. How she could with practically no sleep and nary a moment to herself, still be so loving and solicitous with her insistent baby was beyond Alyssa's comprehension. She did remember studying about the mothering hormone, Oxytocin that was released into the mother and the baby's brain during breastfeeding, with the naturally soothing hormone promoting stress reduction, increasing confidence and calmness, and creating positive feelings in the nursing mother.

Nonetheless, not for a single moment did Alyssa think that she could ever become the assiduous mother Kathleen was proving to be. The more time she spent with her, the more her disquieting doubts increased until she came to the realization that no amount of Oxytocin would be enough for her to cope with the utter dependency and responsibility of caring for an infant. Alyssa always wanted children, and indeed this desire had essentially been her primary motivation for marriage. She had grown up deprived and had no intention of inflicting poverty on a child by becoming a single parent. Once again as on many other occasions, Alyssa Rainer was convinced that her decision not to alter her life plans had not only been wise, but also was her destiny.

~ 48 ~

Spring was upon them. Alyssa had written her last exam, proposed the topic for her thesis, met her graduate advisor, and excelled in all her coursework. In addition to being awarded a continuation of her scholarship and bursary, the faculty had invited her to become a teaching assistant providing tutorial sessions to a group of undergraduate students. Once she and Helen had finalized their dates to return to Banff and visit her cousin Marjorie, Alyssa could confirm her two weeks at the Patricia Lake Bungalows, and then provide a schedule to the head nurse on the surgical ward at City Hospital for vacation relief. Not only had Helen kindly offered her car so Alyssa could drive to Melville on the Victoria Day weekend, but also for her trip to Jasper in July.

It was on Tuesday afternoon, May 23rd as she was walking to the hospital for her evening shift when she experienced a sudden premonition. On the unseasonably warm spring day her entire body began to tremble with an unexpected chill. What was coming? Her mind racing, Alyssa went through a mental checklist of her family and close friends – her grandmother was well when she left her yesterday, Helen and she had enjoyed an invigorating stroll across the university bridge for breakfast at Louis' Loft this morning, and her delicious homecoming dinner with the Sinclairs last evening revealed their surprising news that they were pregnant again with another baby due in December.

By the time, she entered the hospital Alyssa was breathing normally and had achieved her usual calm demeanour. She gave her full attention to the report at shift change with the name of one of her patients sounding familiar. Deciding to meet him first, she walked into his private room to find him sleeping, and none other than Elaine dozing in the chair beside his bed. A bell in Alyssa's head pealed when she recalled Samuel Hurren was her former loft mate's younger brother. Quietly lifting his chart from the foot of the bed, she slipped back into the corridor.

Against extreme odds, the young man had survived electrocution. Samuel Hurren was a lineman with Saskatchewan Power. He had scaled the sets of brackets arranged in standard patterns that act as hand and foot holds to climb up a utility pole. Unknowingly, when he had reached the top to begin the necessary maintenance and repair, the distribution line was live. As fortune would have it, the high voltage current travelled through his left hip extensor muscles, the muscles that lengthen a person's limbs away from his body. The resultant violent spasm propelled him off the pole, and landed him curled in a fetal position on his right side on a clump of tall grass on the ground.

Miraculously, he had no broken bones, but several ligaments and tendons in both legs were torn as a result of the sudden contraction caused by the electric shock. When the current passed through Samuel's body, marks were left on the skin of his upper thigh, thus indicating the point of contact, while burning the surrounding layers of skin and underlying tissues. Since electricity causes burns where it exits the body, commonly on the feet, which are the 'ground,' he experienced electrical burns on both feet and lower legs. Thus far, the medical team was confident that Samuel had been spared the much more severe burning of his internal tissues and organs, and to date, any apparent long-term neurological damage had not been diagnosed.

Quietly pushing open the door, Alyssa returned into Samuel's room and was replacing his chart when Elaine awoke. Looking dazed, she stared at Alyssa until recognition dawned. "You are NOT welcome here. Leave right now."

Placing her finger to her lips signalling silence, Alyssa motioned to Elaine to follow her out of the room. "Hello, Elaine. I'm sorry about Samuel's accident. Since he's resting, we can talk in the alcove beside the nursing station. I'm his assigned nurse for the evening."

Grudgingly, Elaine accompanied her but the minute they were in the hall out of earshot she said, "I don't want you anywhere near my brother. I'm going to speak to the nurse in charge."

"I'm the charge nurse this evening. I'll be responsible for all of Samuel's nursing care, and when I'm changing the dressings on his feet in order to maintain sterile technique, I'll request you leave his room. Thank you."

Having said all she planned to, Alyssa left Elaine standing and glaring after her while she carried on checking the other patients. She had not had a minute to give Elaine another thought until three hours later when she barged in front of her in the cafeteria queue. "The line starts behind me."

"I'm not interested in getting anything to eat. I intend to talk to you whether you like it or not."

Alyssa detected the animosity in Elaine's voice and rather than allow her to make a scene, she replied, "Why don't you find a table. I'll join you as soon as I've purchased my dinner."

Alyssa was no sooner seated than Elaine said, "So, are you still living in the loft I found for us with that bigoted Helen? The only reason she favoured you over me is because you're a WASP like her, not a half-breed. Since you're in charge, I'm surprised that you didn't assign someone else to look after my brother because you're just as prejudiced as her. I just bet she never told you when I went to say good-bye, she wouldn't let me into her precious house. In fact, she practically threw me off the veranda. "

This was a mistake. I don't remember Elaine being this belligerent. Now how am I going to extricate myself without worsening the situation? Wait a minute – she doesn't expect me to respond, she just wants to vent all her puny sorrows."

While Alyssa hastily consumed her meal, Elaine continued to rant, "Tell me, how many men have you slept with since you spurned me, or did you find yourself a lesbian WASP lover? Are you going to sit there pretending you're deaf and dumb? You always thought you were so much smarter than me, but just guess who discovered why your so-called fiancé deserted you.

To be honest up until I ran into him in Oak Point that first summer I went back home, I'd thought he was nothing more than a figment of your imagination. If you're stupid enough to keep ignoring me, I'll keep his secret fore…"

The more Elaine sounded off the louder her voice was becoming until staff close by were turning their heads to assess what was happening. When Alyssa glanced over to one of the other tables, she noticed Miss Stoughton, the hospital evening supervisor looking at her and mouthing 'Leave now. Call me later.' Whereupon, Alyssa silently rose from the table, gathered her tray, and walked out of the cafeteria leaving Elaine Hurren in mid word.

After allowing twenty minutes for Miss Stoughton to return to her office, Alyssa placed her call. "Hello, this is Miss Rainer responding to your request. Is this a good time?"

"Yes. Care to tell me what was going on between you and the woman you sat down with to have your dinner."

Alyssa narrated Elaine's full name, her reason for being in the hospital, how she had presumably followed Alyssa to the cafeteria that she was the summer relief charge nurse on Elaine's brother's ward this evening, and minimal discreet details of the history between the two of them.

"So, it is very likely Elaine will return to Samuel Hurren's private room. How do you intend to handle this probability, Rainer?"

"Since I had checked with him before I left the ward, I'm confident that unless he pulls his call chord, I can wait until after visiting hours to provide his dressing changes and evening care. I would like to request you to send security to the ward around eight o'clock to ascertain that Miss Hurren has left the premises."

"Very good, Rainer, I'll ask Thomas to clear and then to linger on the ward just in case she may decide to sneak back in, and also to escort you out of the hospital at shift change. In my report, I'll let nursing administration know that for your subsequent shifts, you aren't to be assigned to the surgical ward until Mr. Hurren has been discharged. And, I expect you to keep your wits about you at all times, Miss Rainer. His sister was projecting a great deal of hostility toward you."

❋

At quarter to eight, Alyssa disappeared into the other private room at the opposite end of the ward to attend to Mrs. Rachel Brown, an elderly woman recovering from back surgery. She had estimated that her nursing care would require twenty to thirty minutes, which would make her available for Samuel's more complex treatment after eight o'clock. As she was leaving Mrs. Brown's room, Thomas met her in the hallway.

"It's all clear, Miss Rainer. I escorted the person of interest from Mr. Hurren's room and off the ward when the end of visiting hours was announced over the intercom. I might add she didn't go willingly. I'll keep a sharp eye to make sure she doesn't slip back."

During her time at the hospital, Alyssa had heard vis-à-vis the grapevine that Thomas was on a similar path as her own. He was working his way through university to eventually become a physiotherapist. He was young, of muscular stature, lifted weights in his free time, and had been the evening security officer for at least four years. When he was assigned a particular task, Thomas was as tenacious as a dog guarding his favourite bone. Gathering the necessary sterile supplies, Alyssa was confident that she could now focus on providing optimal nursing care to the youth she had met years ago.

"Good evening, Samuel. I'm Alyssa Rainer. You may remember the weekend I visited your family in St. Laurent. When you're ready, I'll change your dressings and provide a full bed bath."

"Hi, Alyssa, if I may address you by your Christian name, I do recall meeting you, most especially because you were so kind to my mother. Elaine didn't mention you had stayed in Saskatoon, or that you would be my nurse this evening. She was here earlier. Did you have a chance to speak to her?"

"I did. What brought you to Saskatoon and how long have you been living here?"

"Although we met in Portage La Prairie, my wife, Tara, is originally from Saskatoon. When we were starting our family, I applied for a position with SaskPower and was hired by the city. We've a daughter and a son. Tara's parents were delighted, my mother not so much, when we moved and their grandchildren would be close to them."

As Alyssa soaked and removed the bandages from the second-degree burns on Samuel's feet and ankles, she continued to engage him in lively conversation. The procedure was beyond a doubt painful, but while he was telling her stories about Meredith and Ben, about his boyhood in the small Métis community, and his career as a lineman, he scarcely winced. Before Alyssa was finished, she was already regretting that she would not be able to continue his nursing care and follow his recovery. She understood Miss Stoughton's rationale, since the last thing she wanted was any further encounters with Elaine.

Recognizing that sleep would reclaim Samuel soon after his comforting bed bath and back rub, Alyssa decided to communicate her well wishes and good-bye to the brave young man. "I'm sorry we had to meet again under such dire circumstances. Last September I became a fulltime university student, but I've maintained my connection with the hospital so I could work as a relief nurse throughout the spring and summer. Since I substitute wherever I'm sent, I may not be assigned to your ward again. I want to thank you for sharing your entertaining stories, and to express my sincere regards for your speedy and full recovery, Samuel."

"I'm sorry to hear that Alyssa. It was clever of you to get me talking about my family and myself. I hardly realized you were removing my dressings, which usually hurt so much that other nurses give me an analgesic before starting. Would you tell me honestly if you think I'll be able to walk again?"

"Not only will you walk, Samuel, but also with your positive attitude, determination, and courage, I envision you running around and bicycling in Kinsmen Park with Meredith and Ben. I extend my blessings to you and your family." With tears in her eyes, Alyssa wrapped her arms around Samuel in a farewell hug, an action she had hitherto never considered in her nursing career.

The subsequent spring, Alyssa perused the article on the front page of the *Star Phoenix* featuring the SaskPower lineman who had been electrocuted a year ago that day. She was thrilled with the story and the large coloured photo of Samuel Hurren walking in Victoria Park with his daughter and son on either side holding his hands. The narrative detailed that Samuel was now in training for an administrative position with the Saskatchewan Power Corporation following his remarkable recovery. He had regained full use of his body, and although he was seven inches shorter with a hunched back, one of his greatest joys was spending hours in the city's parks with his family.

~49~

The next morning, Kathleen came along pushing Craig in the carriage. She had taken the long way around and her son was having his nap. Soon the three women were comfortably seated on the sunny veranda enjoying coffee and cinnamon buns.

"How could you just walk away? After years of dying to know what happened to your fiancé, the love of your lie, you left when Elaine was on the verge of spilling her guts, pardon my English, Helen."

"No worries, Kathleen. I couldn't have said it better."

"Pretty obvious neither of you have met Miss Stoughton. When she gives an order, your response is immediate."

Alyssa had in fact spent a restless night pondering the same question, still not believing that she had not at least queried Elaine before departing. "Not for one minute did I think that she was telling the truth. Years ago I had read about Oak Point, and the chance she would have encountered him in that remote hamlet is highly improbable. She was being so obstreperous that I appreciated the evening supervisor's directive."

When Craig awoke, Helen immediately gathered him into her loving arms before laying him down to change his diaper. Staving off his breast-feeding for as long as possible, she then handed him to Kathleen. "While she's nursing Craig, would you please help me prepare lunch, Alyssa? It's such a lovely day we'll eat outside. Craig can lie on his blanket and catch some rays like the rest of us."

Two hours later, Alyssa left early to have an extended walk before heading to the hospital for her shift. Her mind was still in turmoil about Elaine's behaviour last evening. During the years she had known her, she never displayed the slightest tendency to being confrontational. Could her bitterness and anger still stem from her ongoing thwarted love for Alyssa? It had been three years, more than enough time to move on and find someone else to love. As Alyssa neared the facility though, she heeded Miss Stoughton's advice becoming alert and observant.

Her evening shift on medicine had additional challenges since the older heavier patients required extra nursing care, unlike most of those on surgery who were more independent and on their way to recovery. When Alyssa went for her break, she kept a sharp eye that Elaine was not lurking in the cafeteria before sitting at a table with several of her colleagues. She had only begun to consume her dinner when a young man asked if he could claim the last chair directly across from her.

Glancing up on the verge of affirming his request, her heart almost stopped. The man was Eric Easton's double. Her voice betrayed her and all she could do was stare.

Standing and waiting for her response he said, "Do I know you?"

With effort, Alyssa at last articulated, "I'm sorry. No, we haven't met. For a moment, you reminded me of someone I used to know. Please have a seat. I'm Alyssa Rainer."

"Thank you. My name is Adam Burke. I think that I might have noticed you earlier on the medical ward when I was visiting my grandmother, Louise Thomas."

"This is my first evening on that ward and I'm just getting to know the patients. Has she been in the hospital very long?"

"She was admitted with a stroke about three weeks ago. I'm sorry to say I haven't visited her as often as I would have liked. I'm in my final year of articling at Stark & Marsh Chartered Accountants, and I just finished writing the qualification examinations last Friday. If I pass, my convocation will be in October, and I hope my grandmother will be well enough to see me graduate."

"I'm a graduate student at the university and only work summer relief, but I think that I'll be assigned to her ward for some time. I assure you that I'll do whatever I can to nurse her to a full recovery. Speaking of which, I'd better resume my duties."

"Say, you wouldn't join me for brunch at the Broadway Café tomorrow around eleven o'clock? I've one day off before I return to work after those gruelling exams."

Wow. Adam Burke, you sure don't waste any time and yet why not?" Alyssa thought as she acknowledged that her shock had changed to attraction within the half hour, and she sensed it had been mutual. "Okay. I'll see you in the morning."

Waiting for Adam in the café the irony that the first man she had considered dating since Eric was the splitting image of him, was not lost on her. Was that the reason she had accepted his impromptu invitation, or was she indelibly attracted to dark handsome men with deep brown eyes? At any rate, Adam Burke was not only appealing to look at, but also he was intelligent and hardworking since he was pursuing a career in chartered accounting. And, it was long past time for Alyssa to interact with members of the opposite sex.

Alyssa was relieved that Adam arrived. Conversation was lively, breakfast was delicious, and lingering over a third cup of coffee, he said, "While she's in the hospital, I've been taking care of my grandmother's small bungalow which is a little farther down on Broadway. If you've time, maybe you could follow me and help water her plants?"

"I've an hour before I need to get ready for work, so tell me her house number in case I lose you in traffic."

Walking up the short sidewalk to the front door, Alyssa noticed that tulips were blooming, while peonies and poppies were starting to burst forth with buds, although the surrounding earth was parched. "It looks like the grass was recently cut, but the flowers are sorely in need of watering. Do you look after the yard work, as well? I think we should find the hose and also water the outside flora."

Once they finished the outside watering and ventured into the house, Alyssa found that the indoor plants had met a similar plight. "Is this your first time to your grandmother's house since she was hospitalized? If you're going to save her plants, you'll have to come every two or three days until they recuperate. It's obvious to me that your grandma is fastidious about her home and her gardening. She would be very disappointed if everything was not maintained until she could return."

"I'll admit I was so busy studying that I didn't make it over, but now I'll come as often as you recommend. She does pay someone to cut her grass, although he clearly didn't think to water her flowers, which are her pride and joy."

When they were at the door getting ready to leave, Adam said, "Thank you for coming with me. I've little doubt now I needed your help. I didn't even see the condition of her garden until you mentioned it. Grandma would be devastated if she came home to find her flowers dead." Suddenly,

Adam took Alyssa into his arms and bestowed a long lingering kiss on her mouth. Initially, she was surprised and then found herself responding with the same intensity, before she gasped, "I have to leave, or I'll be late for my shift."

Later that evening, Alyssa was on her way to provide Mrs. Burke's evening care when Adam opened the door. "Hi, did you not hear the announcement that visiting hours are over?"

"Grandma mentioned you were her nurse so I waited to ask you when you can help me with her plants again. Could you meet me at her house on Saturday around noon?"

Chuckling, Alyssa replied, "It's a brave man who defies Thomas' ire by remaining in the hospital beyond his broadcast to leave the premises. I'll hike across the Broadway Bridge on my morning walk on Saturday and meet you at your grandma's house, but now you need to make a rapid exit."

"Okay. I'm on my way, but before I go I just want to tell you that Grandma thinks you're the best nurse on the ward."

❋

Allowing approximately an hour to walk to Mrs. Burke's home, Alyssa arrived just as Adam's blue Chevrolet Malibu pulled up in front. "Well, we're certainly on the same time clock." He said, opening the door. "Why don't you put these cokes in the fridge and look after the indoor plants while I water outside."

Less than ten minutes later, Adam came into the house to retrieve two of the bottles and asked, "Do you want a glass with ice, or is this okay?"

"Thanks, the bottle is fine. Have you finished watering the flowers already? On such a nice day why don't we sit outdoors?"

After drinking half the coke in one gulp, Adam steered Alyssa to the sofa and said, "I want to pick up where we left off."

Scarcely having time to place her drink on the coffee table, Alyssa was enveloped in Adam's arms and being kissed passionately. Experiencing a feeling of déjà vu she thought, *Not only does he look like Eric, but also he behaves exactly like him.* Overcoming her initial surprise, she found her body responding as he began to unbutton her blouse and to fondle her breasts. Her ardour was peaking when Alyssa realized that she had to slow their fervour.

"We have to stop."

Groaning, Adam murmured, "Not now. I'm too aroused. Just this once, let me love you."

Abruptly, Alyssa pulled away and broke their embrace. Standing up and moving toward the door she said, "No. I can't take that kind of a risk." Straightening her clothes, Alyssa was gone.

Instead of going home, she strode up the street and headed to Victoria Park. She was desperate to walk. Never before had her body and her mind been in such a state of turmoil. Alyssa was vibrating with longing. It had taken all of her willpower to leave. Only her overpowering fear of pregnancy had stopped her. She could not deny that she yearned for Adam as much as he desired her. She wanted him to devour her, to thrust into her as deep as he could. If the memory of how her mother ruined her life had not surfaced at the last moment, she would have been consumed by her passion.

It took the better part of an hour before Alyssa was calm enough to start walking the six blocks home. And, she needed to hurry. In little more than an hour she was due on the ward. How fortunate that Helen had prepared a full breakfast, almost as though she had known. Alyssa would grab an apple and some cheese to consume on her way to the hospital and buy dinner in the cafeteria.

After report, Alyssa went to Mrs. Burke's room and cautiously opened the door. Not for a minute did she think that Adam would come to the hospital after their encounter, but to be on the safe side, she would check on his benevolent grandmother first. Then she could devote her attention to the three new admissions and become familiar with their nursing needs. Other than a quick thirty-minute supper break, Alyssa was quite happy to be run off her feet and to have her mind occupied. By the time her shift was about to end, her equanimity was returning. With any luck she would be tired enough to fall asleep when she went to bed.

It was not to be. Work had held her proclivity for analysis paralysis at bay, but as soon as she was out the door of the hospital the wheels of her mind began churning at full speed. What had happened to her moral compass? How could she engage in sexual intercourse with a man she had only met four days ago? Had her long suppressed feelings for Eric Easton surfaced to haunt her, to attest to the error of her decision? Was her overactive brain playing tricks on her because Adam Burke was his doppelgänger? Or, was she trying to disprove Elaine's accusation that she was a lesbian? Had her desire to have a child heightened since she met Kathleen and became Craig's godmother, along with the awareness that her biological clock was ticking?

Time was passing. Alyssa's queries just kept coming. Would she ever see Adam again? How could she stop his advances? Did she want to? What could she do to control an amorous encounter in the event that there was a repetition? She had come to learn over years of asking, there were always many more questions than answers and what she needed to determine was how she could monitor the situation. As sleep was about to engulf her, Alyssa resolved that her first action tomorrow morning would be to arrange a fitting for a diaphragm.

~50~

Four days later when Alyssa stepped out of the stairwell to the third floor, she nearly knocked Adam over. "Hi, I was hoping to intercept you. I've missed seeing you. I can't get you out of my head. When can we meet again? Come on, Alyssa. You can't keep ignoring me. I know that you're as drawn to me as I am to you."

"Hey, what is this – twenty questions? I interrogate myself enough that I don't need to be answering you. Now please excuse me. I don't want to be late for report."

"I don't mean to interfere with your work. Just help me water Grandma's plants at noon tomorrow." And Adam was gone.

Was running away from each other going to become their modus operandi? As it would transpire, the opposite soon proved to be true. Their attraction was magnetic. The next day they were no sooner in the door of Mrs. Burke's home than they were all over each other. As they were dispensing with their clothing in the hallway, Adam murmured, "I came prepared today so you don't need to worry." Alyssa decided not to disclose that she was wearing a diaphragm with spermicide and felt confident that with dual protection there should be zero risk of an unwanted mishap.

Following their initial coupling when they all but devoured each other, they relaxed and became more playful in exploring one another's body. Some time later, Alyssa was slipping into peaceful oblivion when Adam suddenly leapt up from the bed in his grandmother's guest room and said, "We better get going. It's nearly two o'clock. I've an appointment with a business client in thirty minutes. Aren't you working an evening shift?"

"I've two days off so I'll make the bed and tidy up. Say hello to your Grandma if you have a chance to visit her."

Once Adam was on his way and Alyssa had returned the bedroom to its original condition, she decided to have a bath. She was on the verge of turning on the water when she looked at her face in the mirror. What was she doing? First she copulates in her elderly patient's guest bed, and then she intends to wash away the secretions of her reprehensible activity in the sparkling clean bathtub. What had come over her? All her life, Alyssa had tried to do what was right, and now because of a man, she was turning her back on her moral principles. Within five minutes, Alyssa Rainer was dressed, out the door, and on a soul-searching hike amongst the trees in the nearest park.

Striding toward the grove of conifers, Alyssa's mind was assailed with guilt. True to form, there could not be a hint of pleasure without her mother's legacy rearing its ugly head, with the subsequent retribution. Walking into the woods she dared to ask herself, *But, was what we did so wrong? We're both consenting adults, not causing harm to anyone, other than taking advantage of his grandmother by using her home, although that's on Adam. We are only human, behaving as humanity has from time immemorial. It was so exhilarating. I've never felt this alive in my entire life. When I climaxed I transcended beyond the confines of my body and my mind, soaring to the centre of my being.* Strolling deeper into the forest, Alyssa's soul became suffused with contentment.

And, so Alyssa and Adam met time and time again for two or three trysts every week during the month of June. They neither went out for a date – to a restaurant, a theatre, a park, nor did they ever talk about social pursuits. They had no time for anything or anyone else. Their only activity was between the sheets. Perhaps, if Alyssa had not left for a three-week vacation at the beginning of July, the intensity of their liaisons might have lessened, but when she returned they resumed with heightened passion. If either wondered about their unhealthy obsession with sex, it was never discussed. Their rendezvous did not appear to interfere with the other aspects of their respective lives. It was when Alyssa curtailed her evening shifts at the hospital to continue her graduate studies at the university at the beginning of September that their clandestine affair abruptly ended.

Throughout that summer, neither Helen nor Kathleen could ascertain what had seized Alyssa so tightly in its grip. Whatever it was, she was lost to them by early June and she was sorely missed. One morning after she bathed Craig, Kathleen was walking along Spadina Crescent when Helen called to her. "Well, hello two of my favourite neighbours. Your timing is perfect. I've been gardening since Alyssa left to tutor her students, and I'm thirsting for a cup of tea. Won't you join me?"

"It'll be my pleasure. I was hoping you were available because I would like to pick your brain about what's happening with Alyssa. She hasn't stopped in after her tutorials for over two weeks. I'm beginning to think that I've done something to tick her off."

"At least, I can put your mind at ease about anything you might have done, or I'm also guilty of the same offence. I've started preparing a full breakfast because she never has time for a bite to eat before she gets ready for her evening shift. She flies in the door at the last minute, has a quick shower, changes into her uniform, and is gone. We only see each other if I wait up for her to return, and at that hour our conversations are less than illuminating. So, I can honestly say that I don't have the slightest notion about what is occurring with her. Though I'm becoming concerned, Alyssa doesn't appear to share my disquietude. She has an aura of satisfaction that I've never before attributed to her."

"Do you suppose that Alyssa is getting it on with a man?"

Laughing, Helen replied, "I love your directness, Kathleen. I'll admit that it has crossed my mind several times, but why hasn't she told us? As her confidantes, we surely would be the first to know."

"Maybe, Alyssa's so smitten that she's decided not to communicate with us, should our paths ever cross again. Good for her. I've often wished she would meet a fellow and go out on dates."

"One of my qualms is that she might not come to Banff with me at the beginning of July. I don't feel confident about driving all that way alone, and this summer Mariah and Steven are coming to visit Marjorie and me shortly after Alyssa leaves for Jasper. I could take the bus, but I'm hoping Alyssa might divulge her news while we're together on the road."

❋

Following her return from visiting her grandmother on September 3rd, Alyssa became focused on finishing her course work and completing the thesis for her master's degree. When her uncharacteristic behaviour during the summer ceased as quickly as it had begun, her lips remained sealed. To Helen and Kathleen's incredulity, Alyssa never said anything to either of them about what had consumed her for three months. The two women continued to speculate whenever in each other's company, but they never could unearth the answer to appease their curiosity.

On the morning of the last Saturday in September, Helen arrived to babysit Craig while Kathleen and Alyssa were having a girls' day out. Hope springs eternal. During luncheon at the Garden Court Café, Kathleen was determined she would elicit the information that Helen and she had been hypothesizing about ad nauseam. "How are you adjusting to the rigours of being a fulltime student after your summer fling?"

Alyssa had come to know and appreciate Kathleen's candour, and until she met Adam she would have openly responded. It was neither that she did not trust her friend nor that she feared she would be judged if she disclosed the reason she had been so elusive during the past months, but rather because Alyssa did not fully grasp herself what had happened. Had it just been a summer frolic? She had not seen or heard anything from Adam since the last day of August, the Thursday before she left to visit her grandmother. As it was, they had had a quick tryst before he dashed out the door leaving her to tidy up the mayhem. Alyssa stayed on to ensure everything was in its place, the bed made as neatly as she would in the hospital and the flowers inside and out had been thoroughly watered.

It was not until her Saturday evening shift a week later that she discovered Mrs. Burke had been discharged. Then, and only then did it dawn on Alyssa that at no time had she and Adam exchanged telephone numbers or addresses. They always arranged their next liaison at the hospital. How could they have been so careless? Or, was that the way Adam had restricted their interactions? No, that could not possibly be true. He was as enamoured with her as she was with him. They just never found the time to write down their vital information. They had assumed they would continue to see each other when he came to visit his grandmother.

It could not happen again. Adam had often expressed his love for her. Surely, there was more, much more to their relationship than sex. Could she have been deceived? Was she that naïve, that stupid? Alyssa's only consolation was that she had chosen not to breathe a word about her dalliance to either Helen or Kathleen. Now the more she thought about her possible lack of judgement, the more unlikely she ever would. Alyssa had never been so mortified in her life. When at last she did respond to Kathleen she said, "I'm glad to be back studying at the university."

Alyssa would not know the full extent of her betrayal until October 20th. She had arranged her course schedule to finish Friday morning, thus enjoying a free afternoon before working evening shifts on Saturday and Sunday. She was coming in the door when Helen said, "Here she is now. Wait a minute, Kathleen. I'll be along right after lunch to take Craig for a carriage ride on this nice Indian summer day so you can rest."

"Alyssa, I'm so relieved you're home. I awoke this morning with a dreadful flu. I can't possibly accompany Darren to the Convocation Ball this evening. Could you please throw your glad rags on and be his date this evening for the dinner and ceremony. We weren't going to stay for the dance, but I'm sure Darren would escort you around the floor if your heart so desires."

"You sound horrible, Kathleen. Are you sure Darren will want to go when you're sick? Wouldn't he prefer to keep you company and take care of Craig?"

"It's the first time he's the designated presenter. He has to be there and I would rather he didn't have to show up alone."

"I don't know if I've anything appropriate to wear. My minimalistic wardrobe hardly includes fancy clothes, although come to think of it, I do have the bridesmaid's dress that I never wore when I didn't make it to Susan's wedding. Let me try it on, and I'll get back to you."

When Alyssa located the A-line lime green satin long gown with the brocade top still protected by the cellophane bag at the back of her closet where it had hung for six years, she brought it forth and carefully removed it from the wrapping. Additional searching located the satin heels that had been dyed the same colour. She decided to have a quick shower before trying it on and to her delight the frock fit perfectly, as did the shoes. Standing in front of the full-length mirror in the loft, Alyssa was suddenly overwhelmed with nostalgia.

Had her failure to return to Manitoba for Susan and Bryan's nuptials been the beginning of her propensity for severed friendships? Until she had entered nursing training, Alyssa did not have any friends, although she was certain her three years of socialization had surmounted that particular challenge. Yet, a few years later, Alyssa had lost contact with all of them and now was on the verge of facing another shattered relationship with a man she genuinely thought loved her. Would she ever get it right?

Coming out of her reverie, she heard Helen calling to her from the bottom of the stairs. "I left your lunch on the table, Alyssa. I ate without you because I'm anxious to relieve Kathleen. Did you find something to wear?"

As Alyssa began to descend the short stairway, Helen exclaimed, "My goodness, Alyssa, you look enchanting. What a lovely gown. That colour is exquisite on you. At first glance, I envisioned Cinderella entering the ballroom. Shall I tell Kathleen that you have found suitable attire to accompany Darren this evening?"

Even Darren stopped and stared when he arrived. Helen had loaned Alyssa her emerald earrings and necklace and to complement her accessories, Alyssa had donned an exquisite gold ornate bracelet, which Helen had never seen. She had been more assiduous about curling her hair, and applying her makeup than was characteristic of her in the six years she had resided with her. But, then she was usually dashing off to work or the university. Helen could not recall if she had ever paid such attention to her personal appearance. Wondering whether Alyssa realized what a stunning young woman she was, Helen decided to snap several photos to preserve an image of her beauty.

Before continuing on the way to the university, Darren drove Helen to King Crescent. She was spending the evening with Kathleen to bathe Craig and get him ready for bed after he had been nursed. Pulling the car up in front of the door, Darren said, "Thank you ladies for being such kind friends. Kathleen managed to eat some chicken noodle soup, but she sure doesn't have her usual energy. She appreciates you coming, Helen, and she sends her gratitude, Alyssa, for accompanying me to the convocation. Little did she know that my date would be the belle of the ball?"

Helen and Darren's effusive comments regarding her appearance surprised Alyssa. If the truth were told, even she was a little amazed that she could clean up so well. It was when she was getting ready for the evening she realized that other than for Cheryl's wedding, she had not been out for a formal dress occasion during the six years she had lived in Saskatoon. But, then what would she have worn? She saved every penny she earned to pay her living expenses, summer vacations, and any university costs not covered by her scholarships and bursaries. How fortunate she still had her bridesmaid gown and shoes. Although Alyssa was sorry Kathleen was feeling too poorly to attend, she was secretly thrilled she had been given the opportunity to shine at such a prestigious event.

Entering the ballroom, Alyssa was dazzled by the lights and decorations. She relied on Darren to guide her to their designated table. Directing her to a vacant chair, he remained standing to make the introductions of the six individuals already seated at the round table for eight. Before he began, Alyssa could not believe her eyes and then she did not want to believe her ears. "This is Mr. Adam Burke and his wife, Candace…" No doubt, Darren had continued to speak, but she did not hear another word. If she thought she had been dazed when she was coming into the festive room, now she was stunned. When Alyssa did not reply, Darren carried on with the salutations. Some time later, she found herself seated by a young man whose name she had not heard.

Slowly, Alyssa began to recover. Her shock turned to anger. She glared across the table, but Adam was intently concentrating on a conversation with his wife. What was she going to do? What could she do? Become more of the fool that she already was by reacting? Then Darren's words, "the belle of the ball" resonated in her head. Alyssa knew precisely how she would behave.

Alyssa Rainer rose to the occasion. Within minutes, she transitioned from being stunned to becoming stunning. Throughout dinner, she was charming and vivacious as she captivated the guests seated close by with her spirited tête-à-têtes. Their merriment was soon attracting the attention of the celebrants near them. Many others began to wish that they were seated at her table. Who was that ethereal looking young woman in the lovely ball gown? Long before the celebration would come to an end, the women and men gathered at table number nine would remember the Convocation Gala of October 20, 1972 as an evening of enchantment. That is, bar one.

Long after that evening of revelation, Alyssa felt authenticated by characteristics she had not realized she possessed. As she waited in the car when Darren went in to collect Helen and drive them home, she reached a significant resolution. Possibly for the first time in her life, Alyssa was determined not to take ownership for another person's behaviour and beat herself up because of what had happened. She was not responsible for Adam Burke's deception that he was a married man with a very pregnant wife. He had neither worn a wedding ring nor was she a mind reader. He had initiated all their liaisons and subsequent trysts at his grandmother's tidy home under the subterfuge that he was free from marital commitment. Alyssa was innocent – he was a bird of prey and she his quarry.

Alyssa had read about characters in novels that were considered unlucky in love. Perhaps, she had met individuals who unfortunately shared that particular fate. Even if she had not, she certainly would qualify. First it was Eric Easton, then Elaine Hurren, and now Adam Burke. Strike Three.

~51~

The years glided by in harmony and peace. Helen could not do enough to support Alyssa in her quest to complete her Master of Arts program in English Literature and graduate in the spring of 1973. If Alyssa had permitted her, Helen would have stopped charging room and board. She no longer thought of Alyssa as her boarder, but rather as her much-loved daughter. And, not for one moment would Helen Symonds ever doubt whether Alyssa's feelings for her were reciprocated in full measure.

When Mariah had chosen to pursue a residency as a Cardiologist in Victoria, Helen expected she would return to Saskatoon to begin her practice. Once she met and then married Steven though, the course of her life changed. Helen considered relocating to British Columbia, but as much as she enjoyed the more temperate climate and the City of Victoria whenever she visited she always felt hemmed in by the ocean and the mountains off in the distance. Helen had been born and raised in Saskatoon. Her soul yearned for the pristine silence of the wide open prairie.

Still, if Mariah had ever telephoned with news that she and Steven were becoming parents, Helen would have moved to Victoria in a heartbeat. But that call never came. She spent several weeks with them over the Christmas season, and they would get together every summer either in Banff or Saskatoon. At first, Helen had been so disappointed when grandchildren did not appear to be on the horizon, but now that she was god grandmother to Craig, and his impending sibling, she could not be enticed to the coast.

It did not require much imagination for Helen to know how bleak her life would be without Alyssa and her friends, Kathleen and Darren Sinclair.

❋

When she returned to university in September, Alyssa elected to begin studying German to meet one of the requirements for her subsequent doctoral program – demonstrated proficiency in a language other than English. She was highly motivated to become competent enough to be able to speak to her grandmother in her much preferred language. During dinner one evening she said, "I'm hoping that by Christmas I'll have acquired sufficient words to be able to carry on a conversation with Grandma in German. Won't she be surprised?"

"What a lovely Christmas present that will be for her. I'm astounded that you didn't learn to speak German when you were growing up given the amount of time you spent with your grandparents."

"My mother forbad Grandma and Grandpa to speak to us in German. I've always resented that although she is perfectly fluent in the language, she couldn't be bothered to teach me."

Helen had difficulty comprehending how any mother would not have been thrilled to have such an intellectual daughter and not want to promote her learning in any subject. More and more she understood why Alyssa was only fond of her grandmother, and seemingly could care less whether she saw or heard from her mother, and even her sisters. It was then that an idea began to form in Helen's fertile mind. "Do you think that you could teach me to speak German, Alyssa? We could practice while we're taking our evening strolls after dinner."

"What a capital idea. We would learn together and both acquire a second language."

Helen decided to wait before she clarified the rest of her scheme to Alyssa. Just as long as she elucidated it in its entirety before she took the train to visit her grandmother for Christmas.

✻

The following morning enjoying coffee with Kathleen on her back deck while she nursed Craig, Helen said, "I'm so excited about becoming a student again after all these years. I've always believed that it's healthy to keep learning regardless of my age. Alyssa and I are going to become conversant in German."

"Presumably, you'll be studying during evenings and weekends, and I'm wondering if Alyssa would be okay if I joined you. Darren can spend more time bonding with Craig, because I'm desperate for some mental stimulation before I start to feel like a human marsupial."

Chuckling, Helen replied, "I'm certain Alyssa will enjoy teaching both of us. It's been a while since just our threesome has been together without Craig at the centre of our shared mothering. We're starting this evening about seven o'clock. Wear walking shoes."

Throughout the pleasant months that autumn, the three women could be seen strolling along the river walk falteringly articulating words in German. Fortunately, Alyssa had a phenomenal memory, and could recollect many of the conversational German phrases that her grandmother had spoken over the years to enunciate correctly for Helen and Kathleen. Before long, Alyssa was surprised by all the words she could dredge from her subconscious that she must have acquired whenever she eavesdropped on her grandmother and mother's dialogues. When they returned for Peppermint tea around Helen's dining room table, they focused on the linguistic components of the German language.

The threesome laughed, they cried, on occasions they came ever so close to swearing, but eventually they began to consider that they were starting to make progress. When winter arrived and her baby was imminent, Alyssa and Helen walked along the back lane to Kathleen's home to continue their evening studies. Alyssa recognized her grandmother's dialect was different from that spoken by her German professor; but of course, she would express herself in the vernacular with which she was familiar. Alyssa was already imagining Grandma's surprise when she began speaking to her in her first language during their Christmas visit.

The friends were gathered around Helen's table on the Wednesday evening before Alyssa was to depart on the Thursday noon train for Melville. They were replete following a sumptuous pre-season turkey dinner with all the trimmings, and had finished opening presents when Helen retrieved an additional gift and card from under her tree. "Alyssa, could you please give this to your Grandma, and read my card to her before your mother arrives. I may be speaking out of turn, but this year I've included an invitation for her. I've wanted to meet your grandmother for years. I'm asking her to spend a week or ten days with us in May for your convocation. I thought you could drive to Melville before the actual date, and bring her to Saskatoon."

"That is so thoughtful, Helen. Grandma attended my Registered Nurse graduation, and she still talks about how grateful she was to be invited. And, I've a request for you. Would you plan to travel with me, and spend a day or two with Grandma in her home to get to know her and absolve her feelings of indebtedness? She has always believed that giving is to be reciprocal, and will be considerably more comfortable about coming back with us."

Helen and Elizabeth were kindred spirits. When Alyssa arrived that Thursday before Christmas, she had greeted Grandma in German, and then asked her how she was feeling. Her grandmother was so surprised she almost forgot to envelope her in her accustomed hug. "Oh, Grandma, you should see the look on your face. Not only am I learning to speak your language, but I'm also helping Helen and my Australian friend, Kathleen. We get together three or four times every week to practice, and I always hear your voice in my head whenever we're talking to each other."

"Your grandfather would be proud of you. He never got over his disappointment that your mother would not speak German to his grandchildren when you were growing up. Grandpa always believed she did it out of spite, for a decision we made for her years before any of you were born. Now come to the table. You must be hungry, and I have cooked your favourite smoked sausage and perogies."

Far from the first time, Alyssa wondered what they had done, but from experience she had learned that regardless of how hard she might try, her grandmother would never reveal a family secret. As soon as they had finished cleaning the kitchen, Alyssa sat down with her grandmother on the chesterfield in the living room. "I've a gift and a special card for you from Helen. If you want, you can leave your present under the tree until Christmas, but she would like me to read your card now."

After Alyssa read Helen's Christmas card, and Elizabeth's invitation to journey to Saskatoon and stay with her for Alyssa's graduation, her grandmother became very quiet. At last she said, "Your landlady is asking me to come to her house with you for a week? Helen must be a good Christian woman to invite a stranger into her home and feed her for such a long time."

"By the time we're on our way back to Saskatoon, you and Helen will no longer be strangers. When I come to Melville on Thursday, May 17th to pick you up, she is travelling with me and will stay in your home until Sunday when we'll return to Saskatoon. You'll have a chance to welcome and to cook for her, just like she'll be doing for you."

"I am glad Helen is coming to me first. Although your grandfather and I went to Regina many times, I was only in Saskatoon twice and neither was for a nice time. One of the happiest days in my life was going to your graduation as a registered nurse. I cannot believe you are graduating again, this time from a university. Maybe, we will even be able to look around the city because so many people have told me that Saskatoon is much prettier than Regina."

"Other than when I went to Regina with you and Grandpa, I haven't returned but I agree that Saskatoon is very beautiful. You can view the South Saskatchewan River from Helen's lovely home. So, you will come then, Grandma?"

"Will you and Helen help me to find a nice dress to wear?"

Giving her revered grandmother a huge hug, Alyssa said, "Of course, we shall. You'll be the best dressed member of my family to attend." Elizabeth realized that she was the only one of her granddaughter's family to be invited to her university graduation. She was overwhelmed by the honour.

The months passed quickly. The two aging women were equally excited about meeting one another, and both began preparations well in advance. On the designated date, Alyssa and Helen had an early breakfast and were on the way when facing the rising sun still presented a challenge to driving. They planned to reach Melville in time to lunch with Grandma, and then to drive her to Neudorf to visit with Grandpa's youngest sister. Their shopping excursion would occur on the following day when they would take Elizabeth to her favourite dress shops in Regina to purchase her ensemble for her first ever viewing of the exquisite greystone Collegiate Gothic architecture of the University of Saskatchewan.

As soon as Alyssa stopped the car on Third Street in front of the two-bedroom stucco bungalow, the front door was opened. By the time they were outside, her grandmother was on the walkway coming toward them. Alyssa gave Helen a nudge to go ahead. Elizabeth hugged her because that was how she greeted others, especially women near her age. Warmly accepting her embrace, Helen introduced herself in German, and expressed how happy she was to make her acquaintance. No doubt during this visit, Grandma was expecting Alyssa to talk some German with her, but it had never crossed her mind that her English speaking guest would also know her language. Seeing the astonishment on her face, when she was ensconced in her grandmother's arms, Alyssa said, "Helen and I have become much more fluent these past five months."

During lunch, Helen said, "I've seldom asked for more than one serving of soup in my life, but then I've never eaten any as tasty as your chicken and dumplings. May I please have another ladle, even though I intend to save room for your sumptuous looking apple coffee cake?" When she was presented with a generous slice that had been warmed in the oven with thick farm cream, Helen's taste buds were in ecstasy, "I'm not sure I'll ever be ready to leave your kitchen, Elizabeth."

Alyssa had known from the moment Helen had spoken her gracious words that she was endearing herself to her grandmother. During the hours they spent together in the shops in Regina, Elizabeth had found an attractive floral dress. When Helen chose to gift a beautiful broach, Alyssa envisioned the two women enriching each other's lives for many years to come. By Sunday morning when they were preparing to leave for Saskatoon, even a stranger observing them would have considered that the two senior ladies must have been friends for the better part of their lives. Her grandmother had astounded Alyssa. She had neither seen her so comfortable nor so conversant with anyone, much less with a person she had met only days earlier.

When they were ready to embark, Helen offered the front seat to Elizabeth, who said, "Why do we not both sit in the back so we can visit without hurting our necks." And converse they did, taking turns speaking in their respective language until both were practicing new words. Alyssa not only recognized how excited her grandmother was about her upcoming graduation, but also appreciated that Helen's feelings were similarly aligned. Until the last days of her life, Alyssa would believe these two women whom she loved beyond measure more than made up for the love she had never received from her mother. Being a planner, Alyssa was considering asking Helen to return to Melville with her for her September trip to enhance their budding camaraderie.

The women arrived home close to three o'clock, and had scarcely unpacked the vehicle when the doorbell rang. Kathleen had heard so much about Alyssa's grandmother that she had been counting the hours until she could meet her. "Hi, Alyssa, I hope I'm not rushing your return, but it is our customary tea time, isn't it?"

"Welcome, Kathleen and Lindsey. Oh, let me hold my second godchild before my grandmother sees her. She loves babies and although she has twenty grandchildren, she's always the first person in line to cuddle them. Helen is showing Grandma where she'll be sleeping. Helen has kindly moved to one of the bedrooms on the lower level so she doesn't have to climb stairs. They'll be right out with our afternoon tea. Did you leave Craig at home with Darren?"

When Kathleen greeted Elizabeth in German, she had some difficulty with her Australian accent, but did not display the slightest surprise. As it was, she was much more interested in the baby, and instantly asked Alyssa to relinquish the infant to her. Once she was comfortably seated on the veranda near the table with the baby in her arms, she was content to drink her tea and listen to the other women catching up on the news. Lindsey slept in Elizabeth's loving embrace for nigh onto two hours with nary a peep. It was Kathleen who disrupted the tranquility of the day when she said, "I was going to wait until you all came back with me for the barbeque Darren has planned, but I want you to have some time to digest what occurred while you were away. Alyssa will not be the only one of our little family to be pursuing her Ph.D. come the autumn."

Helen and Alyssa stared at Kathleen with surprise. But, before either could speak she continued, "Darren has been accepted to begin his Doctorate of Philosophy at the University of Minnesota in the Twin City of Minneapolis this September. I never mentioned his plans before because I didn't want to concern you unnecessarily. I've my own reservations about leaving my nest in Saskatoon encircled with you two lovely birds. Fortunately, Lindsey's a much more contented baby than Craig ever was, and is already sleeping twelve hours straight through the night. I'm not nearly as dependent on my surrogate mothers, but still I don't know a single soul a thousand miles away in the United States. I've a long ways to go before I come to terms with this major change in our lives."

Helen was the first to speak, "You can't possibly take our babies so far away. How are we going to manage without them and you? At the very least, please assure us that you'll be coming back to Saskatoon."

"Darren and I have reached a compromise. I have his word along with an awesome gift that in three years we'll be returning to 1108 King Crescent. The University has guaranteed him a full professorship when he graduates, and he has promised that I can become the general contractor to build the house I've designed. With an inheritance from his beloved aunt, Darren surprised me with the deed to the property four doors down from us. We'll live in the small house on the lot while our two-storey cedar home is being constructed. As much as we'll miss you, Helen and Alyssa, as long as you stay in place, we'll all be together again. In fact, depending on when you convocate with your Ph.D., Alyssa, we might even arrive back in time to attend."

~52~

For their patience the women at Spadina Crescent were rewarded with another baby. The three years passed more quickly than any of them on either side of the border between Canada and the United States could have believed. The women had telephoned one another on special occasions – birthdays, Christmas, New Years, and whenever loneliness was an issue. At last the Sinclair's return was imminent. One beautiful Sunday afternoon at the beginning of September near three o'clock, Helen, Elizabeth, and Alyssa were seated on the veranda when they spotted a woman pushing a baby carriage with one small child tagging along while another followed on a tricycle. At first glance they thought it could be Kathleen, but no. Whereas Craig could be the tricyclist, and Lindsey could be the little girl helping her mother with the perambulator, it was too big to be transporting her doll. The closer the troupe came though, the more familiar they looked until finally Alyssa rose from her deck chair and dashed down the stairs.

"Kathleen, it is you. We were hoping, but were deceived by the carriage." Helen arrived just as the two friends released each other from a huge hug, and Kathleen turned to embrace her. Peering into the carriage, Alyssa suddenly exclaimed, "Helen, look it's a baby."

The moment Helen heard Alyssa she reached in and brought forth a beautiful infant dressed in pink. "You never breathed a word that you were pregnant. How old is she and what's her name."

Full of merriment, Kathleen replied, "I wanted to surprise my two best buddies with a special gift. You missed so much of Lindsey's infancy and when I discovered I was pregnant last September, I decided that I wouldn't say anything. Elise was born on May 27th and although not as content as Lindsey so she'll need your motherly love, but perhaps not as much as Craig."

"You precious darling, I couldn't imagine a more delightful present should I live to be a hundred. The entire time you were gone, I kept envisioning Lindsey growing and surpassing all her childhood developmental stages, and I was not with her. Thank you for giving me the chance to be young again."

"I also appreciate another opportunity to play with your children." As the years had passed, Alyssa was coming to terms with the very real possibility that she would never have a child of her own. When at last, she had owned how her emotions had dictated her reckless sexual behaviour with Adam Burke; she had critical lingering doubts about ever trusting herself with another man. All her life she had strived for scrupulous self-control, yet by their second encounter and then every time they were together, she responded with unbridled passion. Alyssa still could not believe her unprecedented conduct. Analysis paralysis ad nauseam had finally confirmed her judgment that because Adam was his spitting image, to attribute her ardour to her long suppressed feelings for Eric Easton.

Alyssa regained her focus in time to hear Helen say, "What time did you get home? We could have helped you unpack and settle."

"The morning we started out from Minneapolis we drove to Winnipeg to spend a day with Darren's mother. Yesterday we left late in the afternoon so the kids would sleep during the evening and didn't get home until midnight. Fortunately we were all so exhausted that other than Elise, whom I brought into bed to nurse, everyone slept until after nine. Darren went to Macdonald's for breakfast sandwiches, juice, and coffee to get us on our feet."

"Where is Darren now?"

"I sent him to the grocery store with a lengthy list so I could enjoy afternoon tea with my closest friends, and give you time to cuddle your surprise gift. You've no idea how much I missed you these past three years. This is but the beginning of my recompense for Darren taking me away from you."

"Kathleen, please telephone the poor man and invite him to come for dinner. We were hoping you would arrive home sometime today. We've a plump chicken and garden vegetables roasting in the oven, with pumpkin pie for dessert."

For the past two years during the month of August, Helen accompanied Alyssa to spend a week with her grandmother in Melville. After enjoyable sojourns, the women had planned that since Alyssa's convocation was the upcoming September, Elizabeth would journey to Saskatoon and stay with Helen. Although she would turn eighty in April of 1976, she insisted that if Alyssa could drive her back and forth, she would come. When her granddaughter identified that this time she was graduating with her Doctorate in English Literature, the only word Elizabeth had heard was 'doctor.' Throughout her life, she revered the men in starched white coats who had cared for her family. Surprised she said, "Alyssa, I did not know you were studying to be a doctor. Now you can look after me when I am sick."

Knowing that her grandmother had misunderstood and would be embarrassed, Alyssa gently explained, "If I were with you when you were ill,

Grandma, I could give you nursing care, but I am not becoming a medical doctor. During all my years of studying, I've taken classes to become a doctor of English, and I'm hoping to get a teaching position at the university when I graduate."

"You will be helping others like me to speak better English? Your grandfather would be so proud of you, Alyssa, if he only knew you have spent all these years learning how to teach people to talk the right way. He always wanted me to learn the language of this country when our children were in school and I was too stubborn, but now you are going to become a teacher. When you come to see me you can teach me."

With a flash of insight, Alyssa realized that for the past three years both she and Helen had been so intent on improving their German they had neglected to reciprocate by helping her to enunciate in English. "Oh, Grandma, how could we have been so insensitive, especially me. I know that Helen sometimes did have you practice saying equivalent English words to her, but I never did. I've always known that you say some English words backwards and mix the two languages together when you are speaking, but I love you too much to have ever corrected you. Besides, I liked figuring out what your words were, but not anymore. From now on whenever I ask you to translate in German, I'll have you speak my word in English."

Helen invited Elizabeth to visit for at least two weeks during Alyssa's graduation on September 10th. Alyssa had left early on the preceding Saturday morning, and they arrived back in Saskatoon on the Sunday afternoon in time to meet the Sinclairs' new baby. Kathleen suspected that Alyssa's grandma was as excited about holding Elise as she was about coming to her second convocation at the university. From that moment three years ago, when Alyssa had placed Lindsey into her grandmother's waiting arms, Kathleen had intuited the purity of the elderly woman's love for children of all ages. She continued to be mystified by how such a loving mother could ever have raised a physically abusive daughter.

Giving her a warm hug, Kathleen said, "May I still call you Grandma? It's so nice to see you again, but I'm sorry to say I've forgotten most of my German without anyone to practice with these past three years."

"Now that you are home I will speak to you in German, while I hold your new baby. Do you know Alyssa is going to be a teacher of English and help me learn to speak properly?"

"Your speech is just fine to me. Your actions speak much clearer than any words. We're all so happy that you have come to be with Alyssa for her graduation again. Darren's ceremony was near the end of August and as soon as we were packed, we started our journey home to be back in time. How have you been when we were away?"

"I am tired now after that long drive, but I always sleep well in Helen's home. I am not going to miss a minute of Alyssa's celebration. She is the only one of my twenty grandchildren to become a doctor."

Holding Elise in her arms, Elizabeth became still remembering Alyssa's graduation when she had become a registered nurse. Dressed all in white her granddaughter had looked like an angel, and when she walked on the stage carrying an armful of bright red roses, Elizabeth had shed tears of joy. For a woman who had loved flowers her entire life, she would not have believed anyone could be more beautiful.

It had been ten years ago. Now Alyssa had asked her to her second graduation from the University of Saskatchewan. In her reminiscence, Elizabeth suddenly thought about Ernest and how excited she had been when he left home to attend this same school. Her eldest son had only one more year of study before he graduated when he had defied his parents, learned to be a pilot, and two years later had been killed in the war. Alyssa was just like Ernest when he had been a boy – head always in a book, could hardly wait to start school, eager to study, and excelled at learning. Following his death,

Elizabeth could never have imagined that she would be honoured with an invitation to the beautiful university in Saskatoon not once, but twice.

When Alyssa was young, Elizabeth had intuited that she was different from her siblings. Her three sisters were long since married and had children of their own, but she would wait a long time before any of them visited her. Elizabeth often wondered if Alyssa would ever find a husband and have a family. Although she knew that she was being selfish, she was glad she was still single. Beyond a doubt, Elizabeth knew how much happier her life had been these past years because of Alyssa.

The morning celebratory ceremony was long and boring, as convocations tend to be, with graduates waiting to be called onto the stage to receive their academic hoods. Alyssa explained to her grandmother that this year she would be in the last group to meet the university's chancellor, president, provost, and faculty members dressed in regalia. Once she had been hooded and crossed the stage she would have officially graduated with her Doctorate in English Literature. There was one individual in the audience who paid rapt attention, her ears straining to hear the pronouncement of every name.

Only Alyssa knew. Her grandmother had never attended school, she could neither read nor write in the English Language, and she did not know the alphabet. She waited and waited until at last she heard her granddaughter's name. Elizabeth had felt that Alyssa's nursing graduation with her pristine white uniform contrasted by a dozen brilliant red roses could never be eclipsed. Still, when the Chancellor of the University of Saskatchewan made the announcement, "Ladies and Gentlemen, I present Doctor Alyssa Elizabeth Rainer" Elizabeth thought that her heart would burst with sheer bliss.

~53~

Long before defending her dissertation, Alyssa had been apprised that there were no positions for instructors available within the English Faculty for the upcoming fall semester. She was only too aware that she should be seeking employment with other universities across the country, but still she was hesitating. Alyssa loved Saskatoon, her Alma Mater, Helen, her friends, and most of all, the proximity to her beloved grandmother. How much time did she have left? How determined were Alyssa's mother and uncle about Grandma leaving her house to move into St. Paul's Old Folks Home in Melville? Over the past ten years, Elizabeth and her granddaughter had become even closer, and Alyssa wanted to continue visiting her in her own home in the spring, autumn, and during the Christmas season for as long as possible.

Alyssa accepted a teaching assistant position as well as two individual tutorials – one with a master's student, and another with a Ph.D. undergraduate experiencing difficulty with her dissertation. Although she would have far preferred to teach, Alyssa could guide the learning of small group classes in which she discussed the material from lectures and readings in detail. With two or three shifts every week at City Hospital, she could comfortably meet her monthly financial requirements with a few dollars to spare. Never having had a surplus of money in her life over the years, Alyssa had become skilled in the art of parsimony.

As so often happens, one person's misfortune is another's joy. The semester had barely started when the professor of the Introduction to Creative Writing ENG 120 was diagnosed with a rare form of cancer. Recognizing that they would require someone who was a quick study, the faculty immediately asked Alyssa to instruct the course for both semesters. Suddenly, she was reminded of a word that had fascinated her when she was learning German, a word that is a combination of two nouns, and one she was not likely to ever forget. Whereas she had never been the type of person to experience *schadenfreude* – any joy over harm or misfortune suffered by another – she was known for being readily available to assist in times of need. Alyssa accepted, received the professor's syllabus, and began her preparations two weeks following her convocation.

In the beginning it was a race with Alyssa barely grasping enough for each session of the required curriculum and strategies for writing original fictitious short stories, poetry, and creative non-fiction, to stay ahead of her full cohort of students. She instantly contacted her nursing supervisor to identify her necessary shift reduction to one evening per month, and spent the balance of her time studying the course content. The more Alyssa delved into the subject matter though, the more enthralled she became with a hypothesis for the potential of dynamic authentic storytelling. By November she was considering the possibility of including creative techniques to unfold the narrative of a story, and wrote her own syllabus for her second semester.

With her course examination scheduled for Thursday, December 16th and Helen's early family Christmas dinner for Sunday the nineteenth, if Alyssa were to finish marking her students' papers, she determined she could not leave for Melville until at least the subsequent Wednesday. During Helen's most recent telephone call to Alyssa's grandmother, a practice she initiated years ago, Elizabeth had explained her daughter and second husband were driving to see her this year, and that Norman and his wife were hosting dinner. From the minute of Helen's disclosure, Alyssa knew that something was afoot. She said, "This is definitely the year for me to be with Grandma while my mother is visiting. I would not put it past those two to gang up on her about going into the old folks' home."

By arriving two days early, Alyssa planned to help her grandmother put her house in tiptop shape, and then use the pristine condition as one of the reasons to refute the necessity for her to leave. Because to argue was at the pinnacle of Alyssa's purpose to curtail her mother and uncle's blatant intentions of appropriating Grandma's home. She had lived by herself for years, planted, harvested, and canned a large vegetable garden every season, managed her laundry and cleaning, and could prepare a full meal for any guests within a half an hour of their spontaneous arrival. So, what would this active, capable woman do within the confines of a nursing home? It would be a prison that would not only break Grandma's heart, if not her mind, but also Alyssa's.

Before Emily and Earl rang the doorbell, Grandma had asked Alyssa to stay seated in the living room while she greeted them at the back door. Although she thought that her grandmother was trying to shield her from her mother's usual tirade whenever the two of them were in the same room together, she was astounded by what actually occurred. Listening intently, Alyssa heard, "Come in for lunch, but leave your valises in the porch. You will be staying with Norman and Freda this time because I have Alyssa visiting me."

"What are you telling me, Mother? We always have that small second bedroom of yours. Why would Miss High and Mighty be sleeping there when you have a sofa?" Emily snapped as she brushed by her mother to confront Alyssa. "You little shit disturber. Just what the hell do you think you're doing?"

Coming up behind Emily and Earl who had of course tagged along, Elizabeth surprised all three of them with her totally uncharacteristic behaviour when she pointedly said to her daughter, "Many years ago your father bought this house in Melville for me, and before he died he put it in my name. It is my home. I will say who sleeps here and who does not. You are welcome to eat at my table and to visit me if you can stop yelling at Alyssa, otherwise you can leave now for your brother's. He already has his letter from Mrs. Schmidt's grandson, my lawyer, and knows that neither of you can make me leave this house until I am ready to go. Here is your letter."

In her fury, Emily refused to even acknowledge her mother, much less take the letter, as she turned to Alyssa, and shouted, "All this is your fault. For your whole life, you've been nothing but a troublemaker. Come on,

Earl, we're going to bring Norman to straighten these two out." Following passively behind her, he grasped the large brown envelope that Elizabeth thrust at him. After Emily and Earl had charged out the door, she locked a newly attached deadbolt.

During the entire exchange, Alyssa was too incredulous to express a single word. She could not believe what she had just seen and heard. Never in her life had Alyssa observed such a manifestation of her Grandma's formidability. She was still pinching herself when she was asked to come to the table. "After we have eaten our lunch, I will tell you what I have done. We have lots of time because they will not be back."

When Alyssa sat down at the table for lunch, she chose the chair opposite the kitchen window so she could observe the stairs up to the back door. She was nervous. Any minute she expected Norman and Emily to be pounding on the door to be let in. They would be furious. As astonished as Alyssa was by her grandmother's defiance, she knew that her domineering children would never allow their aging mother to thwart their burgeoning plans to institutionalize her. After a few minutes, Grandma serenely asked, "Why are you not eating your borsch, Alyssa? You always say I make the best soup. I told you not to worry. I do not think we will see them again."

It was to be a day of surprises. As soon as they washed the dishes, Grandma poured each of them a glass of orange cordial before disappearing into her bedroom. When she returned she moved her chair so that she was seated beside her. She placed a similar brown envelope in front of Alyssa. "Your Helen is a good friend to me. When I was in Saskatoon for your last graduation, she helped me to learn how I could stay in my home. The first thing she told me to do was to hire a lawyer and that was easy because my friend, Mrs. Schmidt, in the WI at our church has a grandson who is a lawyer in Melville. Karl is a nice young man and always speaks German to me, but he will talk to you in English after the Christmas service tomorrow."

Alyssa was so intrigued she was speechless. Sipping her drink she waited for Grandma to continue. "You see, Helen explained to me that if I could afford to, I could pay someone to cut my grass in the summer, shovel the walk in the winter, have a woman to help me with cleaning, and even take me shopping for my groceries whenever I needed to go to the store. With all that help, I could live in my own home, do my gardening, have company every week, and still go to the Women's Institute meetings. Why would I want to leave?"

At last, Alyssa found her tongue. "Good for Helen. What a dear friend she is to you. I'm sorry, Grandma that I never thought about her excellent suggestions. But, do you have the money to pay these people?"

"Now that is the funny thing. When Karl spoke to Norman's lawyer, he said he had been telling him I have lots of money in the bank, and could spend more if I wanted because every year after the harvest the amount keeps growing. Yet, Norman always told me to watch my spending unless I wanted to run out of money and end up in the poor house. You know, Alyssa, I believe your uncle has been saving most of the money your grandfather said was to be mine, so he could have it all when I die. Just because I cannot read or write English, he must think I am slow, or else losing my mind."

Beaming, Alyssa said, "I'm so proud of you, Grandma. When I return to Saskatoon, I'm going to give Helen the biggest hug for everything that she has done for you. Now you can live here for the rest of your life."

"Karl wrote letters to all of us – your mother, your uncle, you, and me, and mine is in German so I can read it whenever I want. Here is yours. You must keep it in a safe place, but Karl is keeping both a German and English copy locked in his office. I want you to read yours now, Alyssa."

Taking a drink of cordial, Alyssa carefully opened the envelope. Karl had prepared a very thorough document outlining the plans that had been implemented immediately to facilitate her grandmother remaining in her home until she chose a different mode of living. She was ecstatic with his methodical approach, but was stunned when she read that she was the legal beneficiary for Elizabeth's house and all her ensuing private property. "Thank you, Grandma, but you can't leave your home to me. Can't you just hear what the rest of this family are going to say and do?"

Smiling at her favourite granddaughter, Elizabeth said, "You are the only one who will ever know what I did with *my house*. I understand you will need to sell it because you have to teach English at your beautiful university, but before you do, you can go through and take whatever you want. I have not heard or seen Norman and Freda since they received Karl's letter. I think we are going to have the nicest Christmas just the two of us because the rest of them will still be too angry to see you and me. After the church service tomorrow morning, we have been invited to Mrs. Schmidt's for lunch. You will meet Karl and his young family. Then when we come home, I have a small duck waiting in the fridge ready to roast for our Christmas dinner."

Their subsequent four days were filled with the peace, hope, and joy of the true Christmas spirit and in the simplest of moments love shone brightest between Elizabeth and her granddaughter. On the eve of Christmas they attended the candlelight service at St. Paul's Lutheran Church at 238 3rd Avenue East. The first church constructed in Melville was built in 1907, and its heritage value lay in the Gothic Revival architecture. This style was exhibited through the building's tall vertical proportions, central steeple, bell tower, rose window, and pointed-arch windows. The historic significance was also reflected in the traditional integrity and beauty of the chapel's interior. The intricately carved alter piece, decorative wood panelling flanking the organ, the wainscoting bordering the chapel, and the two stained glass windows in the sanctuary combined to create an interior typical of churches built in the early twentieth century.

In her childhood, the beautiful church two doors up the avenue from her grandparents' home was the one and only place of worship that Alyssa had ever entered. She loved going to the service, which was completely in German and although she only understood occasional words, she felt sacrosanct within the confines of the chapel. Mostly though, Alyssa was captivated by the size and heavenly sounds emanating from the magnificent pipe organ. Ever since her beloved grandfather had introduced her to classical music, Alyssa's soul would transcend with the timbre of the sacred repertoire of St. Paul's Lutheran Church.

~54~

The years were flying by much too quickly. Of all the changes that can occur within a five-year period, none were more apparent, although expected than those within the Sinclair family. Their three children were growing by leaps and bounds, each progressing through the appropriate stages of development – starting elementary school, learning to swim and skate, joining Beavers, Cubs, and Brownies with Elise being continually frustrated, and all too often acting out because of the age difference between her and her older siblings, which prohibited her from attending.

In the midst of all these parental responsibilities and activities, the Sinclairs moved to an even smaller house four doors further down the street. Kathleen became the general contractor for the construction of their large two-storey cedar house at 1108 King Street, which she had designed years ago. As soon as the snow had melted in April of 1977 the vacated structure on the lot was demolished, and the basement of the new home was excavated with careful preservation of most of the large existing trees.

How Kathleen was able to cope with the myriad of tasks facing her on a daily basis was beyond Alyssa's comprehension. She had long ago concluded that as their children grew and developed, every parent must experience an increasing capacity for dealing with their escalating responsibilities. Aside from the fact that her biological clock was ticking, Alyssa was becoming less and less certain that she would have the patience, aptitude, or endurance to raise a child, and especially during the early totally dependent years. Still, she did enjoy being with Lindsey and Craig, in particular, and many hours of her free time were spent engaging them in appropriate activities to relieve some of Kathleen's parental duties.

Nonetheless, once again the real heroine was Helen. She truly was a remarkable person. Although Alyssa rarely thought about Elaine, she did acknowledge that she would be forever indebted to her for the introduction to a woman she now loved beyond measure. In the autumn, it would be eleven years since she had been the recipient of Helen Symonds' affection, generosity, and grace, and she could not imagine not coming home to 1154 Spadina Crescent East. Alyssa was far from alone. The Sinclair family were eternally grateful to Helen, never more so than the many months required during the construction of Kathleen's architecturally designed dream home. Whereas Alyssa set aside as much time as her teaching schedule permitted, Helen was available from the dawn of every day for childcare, meals, and a place to escape until the project was completed.

To her amazement, Alyssa's position at the university underwent a dramatic transition following her initial two semesters of instruction. During her end of year review, the dean of the English faculty apprised her that the results of her students' evaluations were more auspicious than any she had read in a long time. Dr. Wingate summarized some of their written comments – her classes are mesmerizing, she has a magnetic intellect, totally captures your attention, she is a natural born storyteller – with what Alyssa speculated was a hint of sarcasm. Her suspicion was confirmed when she asked, "So tell me, Dr. Rainer, were you just first time lucky, or do you suppose their remarks are a true indication of your abilities?"

How can I possibly answer a question like that from the head of the department? She thought as she considered an appropriate response. "At best, I would prefer that my students' evaluations are a fair reflection of my competence."

"Well, let's hope that they are. Dr. Graham will not be returning for the fall session. I'm appointing you her temporary replacement. Be prepared for a busy summer. You'll be lecturing the Introductory Creative Writing ENG 120 again, and you can prepare your own syllabus, if you prefer, in addition to the Advanced Creative Writing: Fiction ENG 366, and ENG 365.6, a Creative Writing Workshop. Dr. Graham's syllabi for both 366 and 365.6 will be made available to you subsequent to this meeting. Congratulations, Dr. Rainer, on a successful first year of teaching at the University of Saskatchewan."

Walking home from the university, Alyssa was in a trance. She could not believe that she would be a sessional lecturer after only one year since graduating from the university. Once again, she was aware of the impact that *schadenfreude* could have upon a person's life whether or not she chose to experience any joy. The reality was that her good fortune was because of Dr. Graham's misfortune. When the legacy of guilt instilled into Alyssa's heart and mind by her mother's abusive behaviour threatened to rear its oppressive head, she reverted to the centring technique that she had practiced for years.

By the time she walked across University Bridge, Alyssa's characteristic optimism resurfaced as she reflected upon the perspective that she had been provided with a golden opportunity. As soon as she reached home, she would peruse the syllabi, ascertain the extent of course preparations, and then determine how she might need to alter her plans for the summer. Helen and she were planning to drive to Melville on the second Sunday in May for at least a week or more, depending on how Grandma was feeling. Since Mariah and Steven were coming to Saskatoon, and bringing Marjorie with them during the month of July, their annual trip to Banff had been cancelled. What Alyssa had yet to decide was the duration of her visit to Jasper.

It did not take long for Alyssa to recognize the scope and depth of work that lay ahead of her. On the other hand, in all her years of gainful employment, this position would be the first job where she could earn enough to support herself. She would no longer need to divide her time and energy providing tutorials and accepting teaching assistant positions, but rather she could focus exclusively on lecturing her assigned courses. Alyssa recognized the merit of working one or two shifts every month at City Hospital to maintain her Registered Nurse credentialing. Her journey had been time-consuming and arduous, but at last she was achieving her lifelong dream.

When the fall semester began, Alyssa was delighted that the majority of students she had taught the previous year had enrolled in her new course and workshop. There was little doubt she was initially challenged by the curriculum requirements, although she found it reassuring that she knew and had the trust of so many of the class. As she and perhaps her students anticipated, with experience her confidence increased. Alyssa quickly re-established her inimitable style of spellbinding instruction by integrating the process of dynamic storytelling as a foundation for learning and teaching. Once again, her approach captivated her students, tapped into their existing knowledge, and made their educational experience magical.

Still, if one were to inquire what motivated students to return to Dr. Rainer's classes, it was doubtful that any could specifically provide an authentic answer? In fact, after her second year evaluations were completed, and students were lining up for Alyssa's third year fall courses, Dr. Wingate did ask an impressive number of random learners. Not a single individual was able to identify what it was that distinguished Dr. Rainer's lectures from other professors though, overwhelmingly it was expressed that she was the best teacher they had ever had. Even Alyssa was beginning to question when her balloon would burst.

Although Dr. Martha Graham had retired from the university, Dr. Wingate did not have the slightest intention of changing Dr. Rainer's temporary appointment from a sessional lecturer to an assistant professorship. She was far too young and aside from her outstanding performance on student evaluations, what had she accomplished in terms of writing or research? What Dr. Wingate did determine however, was that she would discontinue the ENG 365.6 Workshop, and include an additional session of ENG 366 for her to teach. Furthermore, once classes were underway come September she planned to sit in on a number of her lectures to conduct a critical assessment of Dr. Alyssa Rainer's lectures.

The first time she arrived without warning, which Alyssa realized was a godsend. To her surprise, Dr. Wingate stayed for the entire fifty minutes and although she would never breathe a word to that effect to Dr. Rainer, she had enjoyed the class. She must have been tired because when the buzzer sounded, it was as though she was awakening from a trance. Yet, Dr. Wingate did remember the essence of all that had been taught. A week later she returned fully rested, but experienced a similar feeling of arousing from a spell at the end of the lecture. Was Dr. Rainer that mesmerizing? How had she captured her attention so completely?

One day mid-October when Dr. Wingate came back with a woman whom she introduced as a colleague from the University of Alberta, alarm bells began to ring in Alyssa's head. What was the dean trying to prove? Were her instructional methods problematic? She was on the verge of second-guessing herself and reverting to her all too often characteristic pattern of analysis paralysis. At the last minute however, Alyssa decided that come what may, she would be herself and focus on her propensity of being truly present with her students.

If Dr. Wingate was surprised when Dr. Snyder approached Alyssa and congratulated her, she would be dumbfounded when she subsequently received her request for a secondment of Dr. Rainer to lecture a Creative Writing course at the University of Alberta during the spring semester of 1980. Would Dr. Wingate come to rue her decision not to appoint Alyssa as an assistant professor, the entry-level to become a tenure-track member of the faculty?

~55~

During the two weeks Alyssa spent with her grandmother over the Christmas season, she had been concerned by how she was observably failing and had immediately called the doctor. When Dr. Gottfried was not available, she readily accepted an appointment with his new associate, Dr. Mathias Fischer. The young man was kind and gentle with Grandma speaking German unless he needed Alyssa to answer a specific question. He completed a thorough physical examination, and then requested his nurse help Elizabeth with a urinalysis.

Dr. Fischer asked to speak to Alyssa within the confines of his office. "Dr. Rainer, I think that your grandmother's health is declining primarily because of her advancing age. I noticed that she'll be eighty-five in a little more than three months, and like so many farmwomen of her generation she has worked physically hard all her life. Her heart is weakening. Although I can prescribe medication to make her more comfortable, I'll essentially be prolonging the inevitable. You say that your grandmother still lives in her own home with a caregiver coming in daily. Is it feasible for her to remain there, with possibly additional help, or should I initiate arrangements for a care facility?"

"Thank you, Dr. Fischer, for your consideration that Grandma be given a choice. I'm visiting for the next two weeks, and I'll finalize arrangements for Maria to live with her when I must return to Saskatoon for the winter semester. The two women are members of the same church, have been friends for years, there is a guest bedroom, and my grandmother has the finances to reimburse her for any assistance that she requires. I'm also a registered nurse and as soon as I finish lecturing at the university in early May, I plan to care for Grandma in her own home until the start of the fall semester."

❋

At the beginning of May of the subsequent spring, when Alyssa had completed her sessional commitments with the University of Saskatchewan, she and Helen drove to Melville. At the end of January as soon as Helen returned from Victoria, Alyssa had despondently apprised her that her beloved grandmother was suffering from heart failure. Helen shared Alyssa's deep sorrow, praying that Elizabeth would survive throughout the winter and she would see her dear friend once more. Helen had overheard Alyssa earnestly speaking to her estranged mother and uncle on the telephone, and secretly wondered if they would visit their mother while she was still alive.

The last four years had been difficult for Alyssa. She was torn between her determined commitment to support her grandmother's choice to remain living independently in her own home, and how it had alienated Elizabeth's offspring, and presumably Alyssa's siblings. Any attempt at an amicable resolution with her mother and uncle had failed miserably, and she bore the burden. Dear God, how would Alyssa feel if Elizabeth were to die without reconciliation? She dare not ask. Helen Symonds had long ago accepted that there were many more questions than answers in life. She vehemently vowed that she would be there for Alyssa regardless of what it might take.

Before they departed, Helen said, "I intend to return home by train and leave the car for you during the summer. I've spoken to Kathleen, and she's more than willing to loan me her prized green Gremlin whenever I need a vehicle. I suspect that in the event either of us requires transportation, my options will be more favourable than yours. Also, I want you to know, Alyssa, that until my family visit in July I've few plans for the summer. For as long as you would like, I'm prepared to stay and help, equally as much for my own selfish reason of spending time with Elizabeth. You and your grandmother are part of my family. I love you both dearly."

Whereas Alyssa was surprised by how frail Grandma had become, Helen was profoundly disheartened. The three women had spoken on the telephone every Sunday over the past four months, but Elizabeth's voice had given little indication of her debilitating condition. She had always been so happy to talk with Alyssa and Helen that she had not restrained her joy.

Invariably, they called in the evening and now they learned that she tended to rally following dinner. Still, Elizabeth rose early each morning and although she no longer prepared the food, she sat with Helen and Alyssa at her kitchen table for every meal, eating a small portion. Grandma often fell asleep in her easy chair where she sat with her crocheting, but was reluctant to leave her company to return to her bed.

It was soon apparent that even though Elizabeth did not have much energy, during his weekly visits, Dr. Fischer confirmed neither did she experience much pain. She chatted with Maria in the mornings when she came by to see her, and during the hours she was awake she enjoyed visiting with her granddaughter and friend. Neither Alyssa nor Helen could believe how serene Elizabeth was as she spoke often about her faith in Jesus, about joining Rudolph in heaven, and about seeing all her loved ones who had gone before her. At first, both of the women were deeply bereaved when she was so peaceful about dying, until collectively they came to realize that the sadness and grief was theirs, not Elizabeth's.

Nonetheless, knowing how difficult it would be for Alyssa, Helen remained in Melville for five weeks before she said her final farewell and hugged Elizabeth one last time. She held her tears until she was on the train, and then began to weep openly. Prior to arriving at the station where Kathleen was meeting her, Helen had regained her composure. The subsequent evening, she telephoned Alyssa and Elizabeth and thereafter called every day without fail. Although Elizabeth always said a few words to Helen, Alyssa would communicate later that her grandmother was eating and drinking less, sleeping longer periods, and becoming increasingly tranquil with each passing day.

Alyssa had little doubt that her grandmother found her constant presence soothing. She often wondered how Grandma had singularly looked after her grandfather until he died at home in his own bed. Elizabeth had devoted her entire life to caring for others. Alyssa was serenely grateful for this opportunity to be with her now during her remaining days. She was not only aware her grandmother was dying, but also knew that the timing could be critical. If it should become necessary, Alyssa would delay returning to the university on an extended bereavement leave for as long as Grandma was alive.

❋

She would never know what had awakened her in the wee hours of Sunday, August 2nd, her grandfather's birthday. The previous evening when she had been helping Grandma to bed before gently laying her down, Alyssa held her in an ensconcing hug, similar to the many she received throughout her lifetime from this loving woman. Early in the morning, Alyssa had risen from her bed, crept into her grandmother's bedroom, and lightly taken hold of her hand. After some time had lapsed she heard a soft voice, "Alyssa, you are with me. I always knew you would nurse me."

"I'm here for you, Grandma. I didn't want to bother you. I just happened to be awake so I decided to come and check on you."

With a quiet calm her grandmother whispered, "Come closer to me, Alyssa. Look at my bright red poppies ..."

Sitting down on the edge of the bed and leaning toward her, Alyssa felt a sensation of release. In her heart, she knew that her grandmother was gone. Alyssa's soul was suffused with bliss. Not with sadness.

❋

During the many hours of the three months she stayed with her, whenever Grandma had been sleeping, Alyssa quietly sorted through her personal possessions, mostly crocheted items and photos, and carefully packed them away in strong cardboard boxes. She was appreciative that Helen had had the foresight to leave her their vehicle. She stored the packages in the trunk of the car, which she kept in the garage.

The Women's Institute, along with the pastor of the church were invaluable in arranging Elizabeth's funeral. Under no circumstance would Alyssa have ever allowed any altercation or disturbance to tarnish the celebration of her grandmother's life. She decided that Helen and she would sit with Grandma's friends during the service. Should any of her family members want to speak to them, Alyssa had determined that they would wait until they approached them. No one came. At the internment, Helen chose to remain seated in the car. When the crowd had dispersed, and Grandma was laid to rest beside Grandpa, Alyssa Rainer paid her final respects to both of her cherished grandparents. Neither Alyssa nor Helen would be back this way again.

The following day, Alyssa and Helen took all of the women from the WI who had been closest to Elizabeth to a luncheon at the King George Hotel, and then brought them back to her home to choose whatever they wanted as remembrances of their friend. Later that afternoon, Alyssa drove to Yorkton to meet with a real estate agent who had been recommended by Dr. Fischer. Once she acquired the woman's unconditional commitment she would only accept an "As-Is" Sale, including all remaining contents, and had understood that prior to her listing of the house, she was welcome to take whatever captured her fancy, she returned to Melville. In the morning as the sun was peeping over the horizon, Alyssa and Helen started for home.

~56~

The denizens of Saskatoon were enjoying a glorious Indian summer. Much to her surprise at the beginning of September, Alyssa received an invitation from Dr. Snyder to journey to Edmonton for the Thanksgiving weekend. It was almost a six-hour drive between the two cities, and she was on the road by three o'clock on the Friday afternoon. Dr. Margaret Snyder had made a reservation for her for three nights at the Varscona Hotel on Whyte Avenue, identifying that a number of specific activities were scheduled for Saturday and Sunday.

Arriving shortly after nine o'clock, Alyssa was registering when the desk clerk handed her an envelope. Once she was comfortably seated in the lounge chair in her room, she opened the epistle, which only heightened her inquisitiveness. Without providing any more information about the purpose of her invitation than she had offered during her telephone call, Dr. Snyder had written she would meet Alyssa in the lobby at ten o'clock to begin their morning with breakfast. Having only consumed Helen's prepared lunch of a roast chicken sandwich and oatmeal cookies in the car while driving, she would be ready for a nourishing meal.

Alyssa awoke early and enjoyed two cups of coffee in her room before dressing and taking the stairs to the lobby. Spotting the dean seated in a chair glancing at a magazine, she approached and said, "Good morning, Dr. Snyder. Thank you for meeting me."

"You're welcome, Alyssa. Please call me Margaret. I hope you're hungry because we're within walking distance of the best breakfast eatery in the city. I even managed to locate a meter on the street so my parking is good for two hours."

The women were soon seated and after ordering began to engage in small talk. If Alyssa had not been so tired from her six-hour drive, preceded by a busy day of lecturing, she doubted whether she would have slept last night. However, her curiosity had resurfaced the minute she awakened and even though she was dying to ask, she realized how prudent it was to wait until Dr. Snyder introduced the reason for her coming to Edmonton. When Alyssa thought that she was on the verge of broaching the subject she asked, "Do you enjoy attending the opera, Alyssa?"

"I love listening to opera, but I've never had a chance to be in attendance for a live performance. Saskatoon did initiate an amateur company in 1978 and has offered several light operas, although I've yet to be present."

"Excellent. I've two tickets for Edmonton Opera's opening production of Vincenzo Bellini's *Norma* at eight o'clock. We'll have dinner at a delightful restaurant in one of our famed old family homes close to the Northern Alberta Jubilee Auditorium located near the university. Now, I would like to suggest that we select one of the multitudes of hiking trails in Edmonton's river valley and enjoy our glorious Indian summer weather. I think that we'll drive to Hawrelak Park and embark on our walk from there."

Ever optimistic, Alyssa was confident that she would soon be enlightened. After walking for nigh onto two hours on scenic paths through beautifully treed areas, they returned full circle to the parking lot, with no reference as to why she was being feted to participate in some of her preferred activities. Once they were again in the car, Margaret said, "Are you ready for coffee and a light snack at the Faculty Club before I drive you back to your hotel?"

The weekend was becoming progressively enjoyable. They were comfortably seated in front of a large picture window in the club, sipping coffee while eating freshly baked scones with strawberry jam and clotted cream, when Margaret came to the point. "The University of Alberta has approved the addition of an undergraduate major in Creative Writing in the Bachelor of Fine Arts degree program starting in the fall semester of 1982. Dr. Rainer, I accessed the Curriculum Vitae that you submitted last year to lecture the pilot summer course, along with the outstanding student evaluations, and proposed you as a candidate for the assistant professor responsible for preparing the syllabi and lecturing the classes. Before October 23rd the University's Board of Governors awaits your decision regarding your pending professorship."

It was not until Alyssa was driving home that the full impact of Dr. Snyder's offer struck her like a bolt out of the blue. Could synchronicity be presenting Alyssa with a perfect resolution to a dilemma that was becoming ever more imminent? Might her acceptance of the position evolve into a simultaneous occurrence of two significant events in which both of their needs would be met? For the past decade, Mariah had been asking her mother to relocate to Victoria. Alyssa had lived with Helen in her beautiful home for fifteen years, and could not imagine residing in the City of Saskatoon should she move away.

She had no sooner opened the front door at Spadina Crescent than another invitation was in the offing. She heard Helen say, "Do you have a minute, Mariah? Alyssa has just arrived and if you wish, you could ask her yourself."

"Thank you, Helen. Happy Thanksgiving Mariah to you and Steven. How are you?"

Following a few moments of chitchat, Mariah said, "Steven and I would like to invite you to come to us during the Christmas season. Mum and you could plan to arrive on the same flight, and you're welcome to stay until you need to return to the university."

"That's thoughtful of you, Mariah. I'm deeply missing my grandmother. Kathleen has invited me to share Christmas day with her robust family, although I anticipate that I might not have the emotional energy to join them. I've never been to Victoria, and I would very much enjoy being with your undeniably calmer family. I'm delighted to accept, thank you."

When Alyssa replaced the telephone in its cradle, Helen asked, "Must you unpack right away, or do you have time for coffee and a bite to eat? The salads are prepared, the pumpkin pies are baked, and the cream whipped for us to take to Kathleen's. Of course, I'm dying to hear about your weekend."

"I'm sorry, Helen. I've left you to be responsible for our contribution to Thanksgiving dinner, but I didn't stop on the drive back so I haven't eaten since breakfast."

"Excellent. I've just brewed a pot of coffee. Since I was making pies, I also baked your favourite cinnamon buns loaded with raisins and brown sugar."

Walking into the cozy kitchen, it was apparent that Helen had been waiting for Alyssa. The table was laid and along with the delectable buns were slices of cheddar cheese to add a touch of protein to the snack.

❄

It was a Christmas of change. It was a season of moving on. Neither one would ever have dreamt of leaving The City of Bridges when Elizabeth was still alive. Now, was each staying for the other? While she was enjoying her repast, Helen waited patiently. Alyssa was not trying to take a page out of Dr. Snyder's book when she choose to delay imparting her news by asking some questions before sharing the highlights of her weekend, but rather that she needed an indication of Helen's intentions. "Driving along the highway, I wondered what you would have prepared this trip for my homecoming. You never disappoint, Helen, and as is my wont, I've been rehearsing how I'll manage to adjust. I've been aware for some time that Mariah and Steven are eager for you to live in Victoria. If I'm not being too audacious, may I ask what you're planning in the near future?"

An uncharacteristic silence descended. Unknown moments elapsed before Helen blurted, "Where will you live? Oh, Alyssa, I'll miss you more than you could imagine. Will I ever see you again if I choose to move to the coast?"

Alyssa rose from her chair, walked to where Helen was seated, and enveloped her in a hug. "You're forever in my heart, Helen, and I certainly can imagine. I'll visit you every spring, autumn, and winter, specifically during Christmas, because as you know, I've a well-established pattern of being with the people I love during these three seasons of the year. As it happens, I'll not have nearly as far to travel therefore, we may see each other more often."

"I'm not following you, Alyssa. How would you be closer to me?"

Then moving her chair beside Helen's, Alyssa shared the excitement, the events, and the job offer that had transpired during her two quick days in Edmonton. "I've yet to provide my decision to Dr. Snyder. I know that both of us are hesitant about bringing our fifteen marvellous years of living together in your lovely home to an end. I also realize that it is much more difficult for you, and the last thing I would ever do is abandon you. If I choose to accept the professorship at the University of Alberta, I wouldn't be leaving Saskatoon until either the end of May, or even June. Should you elect to sell, I suspect that spring would be an opportune time to put your house on the market. I'll stay with you until you're ready to leave."

"My dearest, Alyssa, you have presented me with an ideal solution. Congratulations, you must have impressed Dr. Snyder last summer for her to recommend that you be hired as an assistant professor. I've often wondered why you haven't received that honour at our university and if I'm not speaking out of turn, I think that it is because of Dr. Wingate. I'll sell, but only to kindred souls who will enjoy my home and location as much as you and I always have. We'll depart together and say our farewells until you visit me in Victoria."

"And, let's keep our simultaneous decisions secret until we arrive to spend Christmas with Mariah and Steven."

~57~

Spring was in the air, and the stars aligned in the firmament. The quick sale of her grandmother's house had been finalized by the end of last November, with the proceeds transferred to Alyssa's bank account. Helen adamantly refused to accept her offer to buy her half share of the four-door Honda Accord Sedan they had jointly purchased in 1980, and which she had unilaterally made the decision to register in Alyssa's name. It then dawned upon her that for the first time in her life, she had the finances for a down payment on a house. On the morning of April 8th after the realtor telephoned with urgent news of a home that had come on the market and was the perfect property for her, Alyssa embarked upon another 'first' and booked a flight that evening to Edmonton for the Easter long weekend.

Characteristically, she had done her homework, perused the smaller communities within the vicinity of Edmonton, and after Christmas had telephoned a realtor to begin the search for a two-bedroom home in St. Albert that would fit her specified price range. Alyssa loved Sheila's English accent and arranged to meet her on Good Friday morning after she had attended Mass, for brunch at the Bruin Inn. When she walked into the historic hotel on the northwest corner of Perron and St. Anne Street, a chic black haired woman hailed her immediately. "What are you doing here? I'm expecting to meet a Dr. Alyssa Rainer?"

Surprised at seemingly being recognized, Alyssa replied, "That's who I am, although I must say I'm astounded by your welcome."

"And, I'm amazed because you're the spitting image of my neighbour. That's why I greeted you so rudely. You're her exact double, and I couldn't imagine what she was doing here when she had been planning to drive to Jasper with her husband and two children for the Easter weekend."

"I must have very common features. You couldn't imagine how many times people have acknowledged me with your precise observation."

"No worries. Thank you for agreeing to leap on an airplane for Edmonton on such short notice. The existing mortgage on the property that I mentioned has a locked-in rate of ten percent until 1988, and could be assumed before it is foreclosed on by the Toronto Dominion Bank. I neither know how the couple managed to negotiate the extended term, nor why they decided to steal away in the middle of the night like gypsies."

"I've little familiarity with mortgages, except that they are steadily on the rise. Is there any chance that this house meets my specifications?"

"That's the incredible thing. It's a small two-bedroom home with an attached one-vehicle garage wedged in on an unusual lot between an oversized bungalow and a large four-level split, as though it was an afterthought. The address is 78 Beaverbrook Crescent on a quiet cul-de-sac not far from here and when we've finished eating, I'll show it to you. As I discussed yesterday, we're lucky that it's a holiday weekend, because by Tuesday the house will likely be sold, but now optimistically to you. What you may also find appealing is that with the owners' swift departure in the dead of night, their stylish new furniture remains in place."

Alyssa had no sooner stepped through the front entrance than a sensation of serendipity engulfed her. She stood rooted to the spot as she glanced around the foyer, into a cozy kitchen with four high-backed white chairs positioned around an oval table, and the adjacent living room with a brick fireplace. Two wing chairs attracted her attention compelling her to come and sit. Moving toward one, Alyssa observed that the furniture, walls, and carpet were all earth tone colours in contrast to the pale green flooring, counters, and walls of the kitchen. Alyssa scarcely needed to continue any farther to realize that the house, colour scheme, and well-coordinated furnishings suited her tastes. Once she viewed the master bedroom with an ensuite partial bathroom, the smaller adjoining bedroom, the full bath, and the basement, she was ready to make an offer.

"What's the amount of the existing mortgage and the required down payment? How far is it to the University of Alberta and what's the projected driving time?"

"Appropriate questions, indeed, but the critical factor is how long will it take you to arrange your financing for the eight thousand dollar down payment?"

"Well, Sheila, this is only my second trip to Edmonton, and synchronicity emerges once again with two circumstances that are seemingly meaningful coincidences, yet they do not have a causal connection. I'm referring to subjective experiences, which of course you couldn't possibly know about; although what will be of interest to you is that I have the full amount of the down payment in my bank account. What is our next step?"

Chuckling, Sheila replied, "You're quite right, Dr. Rainer. I've always considered that I have a considerable grasp of the Queen's English, but I'll admit I haven't the slightest idea what you're talking about, although it is wonderful news. Why don't we sit in your soon-to-be kitchen and begin the paperwork?"

Since Alyssa had taught her last class at the University of Saskatchewan on Wednesday, April 7th she had not booked her return flight to Saskatoon until after the Easter weekend. By the afternoon of Tuesday, April 13th when she departed the Capital City of Alberta, Alyssa Rainer was the proud owner of her own home at 78 Beaverbrook Crescent.

❋

Their odyssey had begun months ago when Helen unexpectedly arrived home from her daughter's on Thursday afternoon, January 7th one week after Alyssa's scheduled return. On their way back from the airport, Helen said, "Not that I think I need to explain, but one morning after you'd left, Alyssa, I awoke asking myself what I was doing in Victoria when in a few months, I'll be living here permanently. I realized that I wanted to spend as much time with you before our respective relocations, and besides we've considerable work to do. When I told Mariah about how you sold your grandmother's house, she recognized the merits of emulating your practice."

"Thank you, Helen. Since we'll have substantially more time than when I put Grandma's house on the market, we'll start the process of sorting, clearing, and downsizing tomorrow. Once I've decided what personal possessions I'll take with me, I'm at your service."

As the long winter months passed, the women drew even closer as they prepared for their departures from Saskatoon. When Alyssa returned from Edmonton in mid-April, Helen contacted a realtor to put her house on the market, with Alyssa experiencing all of Helen's ambivalent feelings. The subsequent weeks were soon bursting with preparations, promises, joy, tears, memories, and farewells. Yet, both accepted that their life changes were inevitable. When Kathleen appeared morning after morning as soon as she had her children away to school to assist with their labours, the three long-time friends worked, laughed, reminisced, and cried together.

The well-maintained attractive home at 1154 Spadina Crescent East overlooking the South Saskatchewan River was listed on May 3rd, the sale was completed by May 7th, with a possession date of May 31st. When Mariah decided that she wanted to be with her mother in their ancestral home one last time, she and Steven flew to Saskatoon for the Victoria Day weekend. Although it was too soon to pack what possessions Helen was choosing to take with her, Steven finalized the arrangements with a small moving company, while the women prepared a farewell barbeque for Saturday evening and invited the Sinclair family.

Nostalgia kept creeping into the celebratory activities every time family and friends were gathered, there were many moments when each and every one would fade away, and become lost in memories. Prior to their return flight on Monday, Helen apprised her daughter that she and Alyssa were driving to St. Albert for the night, and then on to visit Marjorie in Banff when they departed Saskatoon the morning of the last day of the month. After they had returned to Alyssa's home, she would fly to Victoria from Edmonton and telephone with her arrival time.

During the last week of May, the three women were as inseparable as teenage schoolgirls. Every moment when Darren could be with their children, Kathleen joined Alyssa and Helen for coffees, strolls, lunches, and heart-to-heart chats that invariably lasted late into the evenings. On Saturday the Sinclairs hosted yet another send-off barbeque. When the bewitching hour was fast approaching, Kathleen encircled Alyssa and Helen in her arms and said, "I'll say good-bye now, because I know that both of you'll want to have time for shared reminiscences, plans, and emotional leave-takings. Enjoy dinner in the Garden Court Café at The Bessborough tomorrow, and safe travels to the best friends a girl could ever have."

~ 58 ~

Life has a way of creating patterns that propel a person along until the ground again becomes firm under her feet. Alyssa and Helen had had a relaxing soul-satisfying week in Banff with Marjorie before each embarked upon her new path. Other than a lunch meeting at the Faculty Club on Tuesday, June 15th with Dr. Snyder to confirm the syllabus and finalize the course, she had no commitments, with the exception of her two-week planned vacation at the Patricia Lake Bungalows until the middle of August. Even before Helen left, Alyssa had been wondering what she would do with nearly two months of unscheduled time on her hands after sixteen years of studying while juggling employment at the hospital, and during the past five years at the university.

From an early age, Alyssa had recognized that she was defined if not by work, than by accomplishment, while constantly striving to achieve her ever-increasing personal goals. By the time she was in elementary school, she was already alienating her siblings and classmates alike with her competitive need to attain the highest marks. Now, after twelve years of postsecondary education, her limited socialization skills had atrophied until she was totally estranged from her entire family, could count Kathleen and Helen as her only remaining friends, and had not been in a relationship with a man since that debacle with Adam Burke.

When Alyssa had learned to read at five years of age, books became her first love – her escape, her solace, her constant companion, and her everlasting joy. She had always been a solitary person preferring to pursue the tranquility of nature, rather than interacting with her siblings even when at last their mother allowed them to play after the innumerable farm chores were completed. When she enrolled in nursing training and her classmates became intent upon socializing her, it had not been an accident that Alyssa would arrive at parties with her perpetual book in hand.

In the soft glow of twilight the evening she had arrived back from driving Helen to the Edmonton International Airport, Alyssa was seated on the cozy front veranda of her newly purchased home feeling introspective. Why had she always been so reclusive? Was some serious soul-searching in order? Would she ever truly accept her favourite directive from the Desiderata – *Beyond a wholesome discipline, be gentle with yourself. You are a child of the universe no less than the trees and the stars; you have a right to be here*. Alyssa managed to hold her tears until she returned to her car after hugging Helen at Departures, but then had to wait several minutes before she was ready to safely drive home. Why could she not permit herself to be heart-broken when saying good-bye to a woman whom she loved much more than she ever had her own mother? Deciding that this would hardly be an auspicious time for a critical analysis of her true feelings, beliefs, motives, or actions, she went inside and retired.

Returning to her veranda the next morning with her second cup of coffee, Alyssa's mood was considerably more optimistic. She would not deny how much she was going to miss Helen, Kathleen, her children, and several of her colleagues from the hospital and the university, but the time had come for her to move on from Saskatoon. And, there would be no shortage of people to meet. She could begin with her neighbours, and within weeks she would be back on campus with new faculty members, and of course, her students. If the truth were known, Alyssa could always find a plethora of activities in which to participate, so why now would she be any different just because she had relocated to another city?

Within the week before she was scheduled for her lunch with Dr. Snyder, Alyssa had discovered walking paths through several ravines in her immediate vicinity, and had begun to explore Riverlot 56 Natural Area. Then she remembered strolling in Haverluk Park, and also contacted the City of Edmonton for a comprehensive map of its trail system. While partaking in the beauty of St. Albert, she contemplated driving back to Manitoba until she realized that she had lost touch with everyone she had previously known, with her mother's address the only one she could verify. What would motivate Alyssa to drive over six hundred miles to visit with her alienated parent?

Their business was finished and they were nearing the end of their luncheon, when a woman approached the table. "Hello, Margaret, I didn't intend to interrupt you, but when I recognized your guest, I wanted to express my greeting." Turning toward Alyssa, she said, "Hello, I'm not sure you'll remember me. We met at a meeting for the Canadian Cancer Society almost two years ago. Are you and your family enjoying St. Albert? As I recollect, you have two school age children."

"I'm sorry. I only moved to St. Albert two weeks ago, and during the first I was away in Banff. You must be thinking of someone else."

"That's so strange. You could be her identical twin. At the time, I was a member of the Edmonton Cancer Board and had attended the St. Albert branch meeting, specifically to meet with you. You had volunteered to be the new Education Coordinator, and were embarking upon a comprehensive Cancer Awareness Programs for Primary and Secondary Schools. In addition, you consented to coordinate In-Service Workshops, and if available, local Television Programs for the General Public, with the Canadian Cancer Society's extensive Educational Curriculum. I can remember being very impressed with the scope of your commitment and energy. My term with the Edmonton Board came to an end a few months later. I'm sorry, but I can't recall your name."

"It certainly is uncanny. You're already the second person who has presumably met me in St. Albert. My realtor was convinced that she not only knew me, but also those two children to whom you allude. What I'm finding peculiar is that although you've acknowledged me, you can't remember my name, nor did the realtor ever mention what my 'double' was called. How unfortunate to have such a common face, yet a forgettable moniker? At any rate, I'm Alyssa Rainer. I've recently been hired by the university to lecture the new Creative Writing courses in the Bachelor of Fine Arts Program."

"Hello, Alyssa. Welcome to the University of Alberta. I'm Natasha Nash, head of the Biology Faculty. I've little doubt that in time you'll come to realize that you've been hired by perhaps the most personable dean on campus. I'm sorry about your mistaken identity, and now I'll let you two continue. See you later, Margaret."

Before their luncheon was over, Margaret invited Alyssa to a faculty barbeque at her home on Saturday evening, June 26th. As it happened, it would the first of many delicious meals she would savour in her dean's beautiful house on University Avenue on the south side of the North Saskatchewan River in Edmonton. Natasha was invariably in attendance and during that initial evening, in addition to meeting her colleagues, Alyssa was on her way to developing an enduring friendship with her. Perhaps, she was more relaxed with Natasha because she was in a different faculty, and Alyssa did not feel she needed to be as circumspect with her as she should be with Margaret. Years would pass though, before Alyssa realized that Natasha was Margaret's partner so discreet were the two women in each other's presence when socializing.

~59~

The academic year was upon her before she could believe it. She scarcely slept the night before her initial class, and could not believe how nervous she was about lecturing a course that she had been teaching for several semesters. Alyssa arrived on campus very early, and for just a moment considered going to the small English faculty lounge before heading straight to her lecture hall. Another cup of coffee after the two she had consumed at home on an empty stomach was not a sound idea if she did not want to have the jitters. Opening the door to the vacant theatre and walking around the still quiet spacious room, she began to feel calmer by the time she reached the whiteboard at the front.

For the umpteenth time, Alyssa reviewed the class lists, and was once again pleased she had the maximum number of registered students in both of the sessions. Not for the first time, she wondered how the dean had arrived at the numeral of forty-eight. Could it be because it was divisible by 2, 3, and 4 for the small group work when the students were to critique the original writing by their class members? She began by writing a quotation by Francesca Lia Block, an American author of adult and youth literature, and poetry, in large letters on the board, "Telling your story is touching. It sets you free." By the time the first small cluster of students began to file in, Alyssa was ready.

The introductory class came and went. The buzz from the students as they lingered on their way out the hall was encouraging. When the room emptied, Margaret appeared at the door and asked Alyssa to join her for a coffee. "I was surprised to see your car in the parking lot when I drove in this morning. I'm usually the first one, at least from the English department, to arrive. Did you have time for breakfast, or would you like to get a bite to eat before your afternoon group?"

"Truthfully, I was too uptight to consider consuming food this morning. Now I'm starving."

"Excellent. I must confess that I don't have much of an appetite at the start of the day, but I thoroughly enjoy brunch. Shall we return to the breakfast eatery on Whyte Avenue?"

On the way to the restaurant, Alyssa wondered if it was happenstance that Dr. Snyder had sought her out at the end of the hour because she was genuinely interested in affirming with her professor how her opening class had been received. She had been apprised since she was new, as was the course, initially they would schedule mentoring meetings every week. Eventually, their reviews would taper to once per month. She remembered Natasha's remark during their unusual introduction about Dr. Snyder's affability, and although it was early in the relationship, Alyssa was inclined to agree. In all the years she worked for Dr. Wingate, not once had there been any socialization and precious few appointments between them.

Then it was Friday. She had taught her two sessions three times, and facilitated an introductory creative writing workshop. Overall, Alyssa was pleased with her inaugural week in the English Department at the University of Alberta. At the end of each day she had been tired, although it was a positive feeling of fatigue that she readily overcame by walking the Braeside and Forest Lawn ravines as soon as she returned home. Her evenings were solitary and relaxing as she always had an entertaining novel to read following a home prepared meal, and a perusal of her subsequent day course curriculum.

One week became two, then three, then a month. Alyssa was meeting her colleagues in the faculty, and even started to accept invitations for drinks or evening meals after work. All the years she lived in Saskatoon, she invariably left campus as soon as she had finished her specific responsibilities. Her social life had been fulfilled by Helen, her long-standing neighbours, and Kathleen with her energetic family. Throughout her life, she had always favoured a select number of friends to a large group of people, and true to herself, she would once again seek to establish choice relationships with a few. It would take time, but then, Alyssa had always been reclusive, although seldom lonely. In the interim, she would curtail any feelings of isolation by pursuing her preferred activities – nature hiking, cross-country skiing, tennis, strength training, reading, and listening to classical music.

Before long, the highlight of Alyssa's weekdays was her interactions with her students. Every day delving deeper into the curriculum, each of them was becoming convinced that they did have a story to tell and were focused on incrementally acquiring the fundamental principles of creative writing. Their enthusiasm and commitment were infectious, and the fifty minutes passed much too quickly for both teacher and learners. Fortunately, Alyssa did not need to dash off for another immediate class. Students started to linger, to ask questions, and to share their passion with a professor who they soon realized possessed that extraordinary gift of being truly present with them.

As Christmas was approaching, it would have been fair to acknowledge that there was nary a student in Professor Rainer's Introductory Creative Writing class who did not appreciate that ENG 120 had been scheduled as a full year course. Furthermore, it was surprising how many of the registrants were inspired to explore their creativity, to apply acquired writing strategies, and to begin word by word to tell their story over the holiday season.

The sheer expectations of the department and of herself during the initial semester had been daunting, and she was ready for the two-week break. On the Saturday evening before her Monday morning flight on December 20th to Victoria, Alyssa attended The Nutcracker with Dr. Snyder and Natasha. She had never been to a live performance of a ballad. The beauty, grace, intricacy of the dancing, and Tchaikovsky's sublime musical score captivated her. When she had arrived home, she succumbed to sweet repose.

⁂

The week of Christmas in Victoria was heart-warming. Helen was the first to reach her at the airport and while enveloping her in a hug said, "Alyssa, you have no idea how much I've missed seeing you these past months."

"We would have a draw. You can't imagine the number of times I opened my front door anticipating to be greeted by you. Living in this beautiful city though appears to be agreeing with you. I'm sure you're finding the much more clement weather easier to pursue outdoor activities at this time of the year."

"Yes, I do prefer Victoria's weather. You look wonderful. I can hardly wait until you bring us up to date."

Following a delicious lunch at Mariah and Steven's, Helen drove Alyssa to her one-bedroom condo. Once they were inside, Helen said, "I'm glad you decided to stay with me instead of with Mariah in her spacious home. She'd offered me her other guest room, but I wanted to have you to myself for this short period of time. I knew that you would travel light and I think you'll find my sofa comfortable."

"Thank you, Helen. I appreciated Mariah and Steven's hospitality last year, but they're so busy and I don't like to impose. Also, I'm hoping that during the three days before Christmas you and I can do some touring around Victoria."

The week sailed by. Bright and early the next morning following a quick breakfast, Helen handed her car keys to Alyssa, and they were off to travel one of the most picturesque routes in Canada. They embarked upon the Malahat Drive at the Goldstream Park, located in the northern part of Victoria on Highway #1, and travelled up towards the beautiful rugged region with steep cliffs along the eastern coast of Vancouver Island. The road was constructed hugging the Seaside Mountains, and they stopped at scenic lookouts that afforded spectacular views overlooking the Saanich Peninsula and the San Juan Islands before gradually carving through the thick woods of Arbutus, Douglas Fir, Maple, and Red Cedar. When they arrived at MacMillan Provincial Park, home to a famous 157-hectare stand of ancient Douglas Fir, Alyssa and Helen exited their car to amble in the old-growth forest known as Cathedral Grove.

The unseasonably warm weather persisted, and the subsequent day they were on their way to the Butchart Gardens in Brentwood Bay. With a former limestone quarry as her canvas, Jennie Butchart envisioned landscaping a sunken garden haven in its place, overflowing with lush greens and colourful blooms. Her creation was begun in 1912, and in 1939 when grandson Ian Ross was gifted the Gardens on his 21st birthday, he transformed them into a world-renowned 55-acre display garden that is still privately owned and operated by the family. Even during the winter the unique setting, surrounded by majestic conifers and seasonal decorations adorning the gardens, was exquisite. After a hearty luncheon in the Blue Poppy Restaurant, Helen and Alyssa strolled about until the sun was creeping below the horizon before returning to the cozy condo.

All too soon it was time for Alyssa to leave. On Christmas Eve, the two adventurers had joined Mariah and Steven for a light dinner before the family attended the Candlelit Service at Christ Church Cathedral. As soon as they had entered, Alyssa was drawn to the magnificent pipe organ and was immediately transported to St. Paul's Lutheran Church in Melville. This was the time of the year when she missed her grandmother the most. Still, she believed that her beloved grandparents were now together, and Alyssa would be forever grateful that Helen's family had taken her into their hearth and home. Their weeklong celebrations had been overflowing with hope, peace, joy, and love. Prior to Alyssa departing for the airport, the two women had finalized their plans for Helen to fly to Edmonton during the middle of May, before they journeyed on to visit Kathleen and their godchildren in Saskatoon.

❋

Who could have telephoned her over the Christmas holiday? She noticed that the red light on the answering machine on the small table in the foyer was blinking as soon as she opened her front door. Hitting the button, Alyssa was surprised to hear Dr. Snyder's voice, "Alyssa, I hope that you had a wonderful time in Victoria. There has been a development, and I'd like to meet on Wednesday for lunch at the Faculty Club. When you return, could you please confirm? Thanks."

Wondering what could have happened in a week, Alyssa did not linger about replying. If she were truthful she experienced a pang of alarm, and was disappointed that she would have to wait for any information when she discovered that her response initiated a game of telephone tag. She left her message and proceeded into her bedroom to unpack. What could be so urgent that the dean needed to see her before classes resumed? Had something untoward been written in the student evaluations that she had submitted at the end of midterm?

Alyssa was awake early enough on Wednesday morning to drive the short distance to Riverlot 56 Natural Area for a quick cross-country ski before getting ready for her meeting. Exercise always invigorated her body and her mind. Over the past two days, she had had a sinking feeling that she should be prepared for a possible problematic circumstance. As soon as they had ordered, Dr. Snyder dispensed with the small talk and said, "Your students evaluations were not only incomparable, but also the majority of the registrants are petitioning for a full course in advanced creative writing to be available by the fall semester. I've never experienced such an outstanding and collective student response in all my years as a university dean. Congratulations, Alyssa."

"Thank you, Dr. Snyder. I'm at a loss for words."

"Well, Dr. Rainer, the real question is what are we going to do about the students' request? To be fair to you, since I've had some time to contemplate, might I share a proposal that has come to mind?"

"Yes, please."

"I began by rereading your syllabi for the Introductory Creative Writing Course, and for the Creative Writing Workshop to review the objectives. By the end of the course, the students have acquired basic approaches for writing short stories in original fiction, creative non-fiction, and poetry so that they have a portfolio of polished writing in three genres. What if the advanced course curriculum focused on specific techniques for writing successful fiction, such as character creation, dialogue, narrative strategies, prose style, and plot development for a full length novel? Participants would need to be prepared to have their narrative discussed by the professor and their fellow students in a workshop atmosphere. In essence, we would springboard from the introductory course and build a continuum with the syllabus of the workshop to develop the advanced course."

"Brilliant. I'm sorry, Dr. Snyder, I didn't realize I was saying that out loud."

Pausing to enjoy several bites of her salad, Margaret replied, "Thank you. Since I plan to assign you full responsibility for the course preparation and the subsequent instruction, I need you to think very carefully about how achievable my expectation to add an Advanced Creative Writing Fiction Course is within nine months, Alyssa?"

Silence lapsed as both women ate lunch. When their coffee was served, Alyssa said, "Dr. Snyder, I'm honoured that you're offering the new course to me. As you can well imagine, my mind is racing with the potential requirements and demands of having it ready by the start of the fall semester. Nonetheless, I believe that I can manage my time, energy, and commitment to be lecturing the first class of students in September."

~ 60 ~

Her life was unfolding beyond any flight of imagination. She was soaring above the hallowed halls of higher learning. It was a fantasy. Could nine years have come and gone since she had relocated to Edmonton? As a rule, Alyssa scarcely paid attention to the passage of time. She was more mindful of the consequential moments and connections that were developing from the patterns she was creating in her life. She still visited Helen on two or three occasions every year, journeyed to Saskatoon to spend long enjoyable days with Kathleen and her adolescent family, and made her annual junket to the Patricia Lake Bungalows. Alyssa had broadened her horizons venturing farther and farther in search of spectacular hiking trails throughout the Rocky and Kootenay Mountains. Interestingly, Alyssa always travelled west, never once taking a trip east beyond the Saskatchewan border.

One Tuesday Alyssa arrived home to find an invitation in her mailbox that came as a total surprise. When she opened the envelope she was stunned. How had Rachel ever managed to find her? Twenty-five years could not have passed since they had graduated from Brandon General Hospital School of Nursing. Inside was an invitation for a reunion to be held August 15th to 18th at Clear Lake in Riding Mountain National Park in Manitoba. Alyssa was about to toss it into the wastebasket when she jerked her hand back. Maybe, she should consider going? It might be enjoyable to visit and reminisce with her classmates from training days. The timing was perfect. She could make a quick trip to Manitoba, and still enjoy ten days in the Radium Hot Springs and Fairmont area before returning to prepare for the fall semester.

Memories of the week for two consecutive summers when she had been Susan's guest at her aunt's cabin at Clear Lake came flooding to the forefront of her mind. They had experienced such a bonding time. Neither before nor since had Alyssa felt so close to a girlfriend as she had during those vacations each July. She had had many regrets about losing touch with Susan, and perhaps a spark of their friendship could still be rekindled. Alyssa picked up the telephone to call The Arrowhead Family Resort in Wasagaming, the main townsite and booked a guest room for the designated dates. For reasons she could never identify, she decided not to return the reply envelope choosing instead to just arrive.

The morning she embarked dawned bright and clear with every portent of a hot summer day. Alyssa left on Wednesday planning to spend the afternoon and evening with the Sinclair family on the proviso that she and Kathleen would not visit into the wee hours. She wanted to insure an early start on Thursday so she would arrive with plenty of time to settle in before the barbeque that was scheduled for five o'clock. She was looking forward to the drive into Riding Mountain National Park, the forested parkland standing in sharp contrast to the surrounding farmland, and including the three different ecosystems, which converged in the area – grasslands, upland boreal and eastern deciduous forests. Alyssa was aware of the plethora of hiking trails within the park, but seriously doubted that little, if any time would be available to explore them.

As she neared the resort for the first time, Alyssa wished she drove a less conspicuous car than her fire engine red Honda Prelude. From a distance, she could see a group of women mingling on the grassy area surrounding the parking lot and if they were her former classmates, she could hardly effect a subtle arrival. As soon as she opened the door and stepped out of the vehicle, Alyssa could hear murmurings, which soon became clearly articulated words – "Has she come for the reunion," "Can't have, I don't recognize her," "No, she isn't one of us," "You know, she does look vaguely familiar," "I know who she is." Rachel said as she started to walk toward the newcomer.

"How nice you could join us. When I didn't receive a reply, I wondered if the invitation had reached you."

"Hello, Rachel. It's lovely to see you. How did you ever manage to find me?"

"You remember my cousin Lynda, don't you? Years ago she married and although it didn't last long, she kept his surname. On one of her visits she told me that she had registered in a course at the University of Alberta, but like most everything in her life, she didn't finish the classes. I suspect that she was hardly on campus long enough for you to even place her. She did however, recollect your name and apparently checked out your personal information in the course syllabus. Her name now is Lynda Johnson."

"Interestingly, I do recall the name since she's the only student who has ever left, but in all honesty, I can't say that I recognized her. Thank you for solving that mystery, but then you were ever resourceful. Thanks also, Rachel, for coming over to chat. I think that you've made my reception warmer."

The words were scarcely out of Alyssa's mouth when she heard, "I don't believe it. You didn't actually deign to come back to Manitoba."

Could that be antipathy she was hearing in Susan's voice? Surely she had not continued to harbour feelings of resentment because Alyssa had not made it to her wedding twenty-five years ago. Knowing that how she replied within the next few moments could determine not only Susan's reaction, and that of many of the other women, but also colour the entirety of the reunion, Alyssa chose her words insightfully, "Susan, how nice that we finally meet again in the very place where you invited me for my first vacation. I've never forgotten how special you made me feel for that one week in July during those two consecutive summers."

"Well, finally you've made it to a reunion. It has taken you long enough."

❋

Other nursing classmates were now approaching Alyssa to welcome her back into the fold. She chatted happily with all who came, many of whom she had to pause to identify, although she was still feeling that she had dodged a bullet with Susan. What could possibly have motivated her to respond with such rancour after all these years?

The barbeque was fun resonating with the gaiety of women's voices and peals of laughter, which did become more subdued with the shadows of twilight finding them gathered around the bonfire now in clusters of their closest friends from training days. Alyssa gave Susan a wide berth choosing to stay near Rachel, who as always was popular with most of their class. Eleven o'clock was approaching when Alyssa edged away, grateful that her room was at the front of the resort, and retired to her private accommodation.

There were raised eyebrows when she had been asked who her roommates were, but she had been reticent about answering.

When she closed her door, she breathed a sigh of relief. After setting up the coffee pot for the morning, she completed her forty-minute upper body stretching and strengthening routine, enjoyed a candlelit bath, and slipped into the comfortable bed. By the time the sun was coming over the horizon, Alyssa had drunk her coffee, and was on the path into the woods where she had so long ago confided the history of her mother's abuse to Susan. She was returning just as the class was walking in small groups to Smitty's for breakfast, and she joined in with scarcely anyone being aware. The rest of the day was smooth sailing. Alyssa was beginning to think that she had made a sound choice in renewing her nursing friendships.

The Class of 1966 were on the verge of finishing dinner, after taking innumerable photos, and were standing ready to leave Boston Pizza when Susan approached her, seemingly with the precise purpose of instigating a diatribe. Alyssa would never know what triggered her outburst, although in retrospect she did wonder if she had consumed too much wine. She was as surprised as was everyone near enough to witness it.

"Well, Miss High and Mighty, are you going to slink off to your room early again tonight? It's your own fault you're all alone, but of course it is also your fault that you lost Eric Easton. If you hadn't been so stubborn and could have listened to me for once, you would be married and have children and grandchildren just like the rest of us. But no, you had to go to Saskatoon and waste your life at some university, instead of coming to Winnipeg. You had to be different. You always thought you were so bloody smart, but you know what, you're still as stupid and clueless about life as you ever were."

Before Susan could catch her breath to resume, Alyssa spoke in a soft calm voice, "I never allowed myself to believe that there was only one ending for my life's story."

"Now, what the hell do you mean by that? Who talks like that? Who even thinks like that? Go back to your Ivory Tower and books, Dr. Alyssa Rainer."

Casting an incredulous glance at Susan in the ensuing silence, Alyssa turned and walked out of the restaurant.

❋

With a Styrofoam cup of coffee in her hand, Alyssa was in her Prelude driving out of the park when the sun was appearing over the tops of the bountiful conifers. How fortunate that she had asked Kathleen not to expect her to stop on her return trip. She only planned to pick up lunch at a drive-through in Saskatoon before continuing on to St. Albert by evening. Alyssa loved driving and when the morning warmed, she opened her sunroof and turned on a CD of Verdi's Rigoletto. She had spent more time and energy than she cared to remember fretting about the estrangement from her family to now deliberate over being alienated from Susan. It was doubtful that she would ever return to another reunion or to see her again. Within two days, Alyssa would be in Fairmont and the mountains would bring peace to her soul.

~61~

Years ago when Alyssa had the Advanced Creative Writing Course on the academic calendar within nine months, Margaret Snyder outright acknowledged to herself that she was a thief. She had intuited that Dr. Alyssa Rainer was inimitable during the afternoon Dr. Wingate had invited her into the aspiring professor's class. She was spellbinding. The hour had been magical. Yet, Deborah was seemingly oblivious of her mesmerizing propensity for captivating the students. Alyssa was a master storyteller. She instinctively understood that stories are a tool to convey information, to augment analytical thinking, to tap into existing knowledge, and because listeners became so engaged they remember, to create linguistic bridges to effective learning and teaching. Truthfully, Margaret very much doubted that Alyssa herself was cognitively aware of her magnetism.

Shortly after Alyssa joined the faculty, she started to be called the Dean's Pet and rightly so. When she first arrived, Margaret included her in several social activities, both alone and with her partner, Natasha because the young woman virtually did not know a soul in Edmonton. Soon though, she came to realize that she was interacting with Alyssa as much because of her personal appeal as to alleviate her isolation. As time passed the upper echelons of the university began to press Dr. Snyder to require Alyssa to take on research, writing, and administrative functions to become eligible for tenure. Margaret's intuition again surfaced. She understood beyond a doubt that those responsibilities would perpetrate the Peter Principle and render a natural born teacher incompetent. As pressure mounted, Margaret became increasingly focused on a singular quest.

It was inevitable that Margaret and Natasha had come to meet and love Helen. In the beginning, she flew to Edmonton to visit and travel with Alyssa every May and August, and the four women interacted on several occasions during each trip. The autumn when Helen turned eighty-one was the first time that she decided not to journey to Alberta, which probably had prompted Alyssa to drive to Manitoba and attend the ill-fated reunion. Thereafter, Alyssa drove to Victoria in the spring, and booked a flight for Christmas to stay with Helen in her condo twice annually. Each year, Alyssa knew her physical health was progressively failing, although her mind was still as sharp as a knife. It was not until the past Christmas when Helen had reached her ninetieth birthday that Alyssa began to fear her imminent demise.

Millennium celebrations had come and gone, albeit scaled down not to overtire Helen, and she had rallied to enjoy a festive dinner at Mariah and Steven's. During the balance of her week in Victoria, Alyssa never left the condo.

Then it was May 2001, and Helen was dying. Mariah was on the telephone, "Hello, Alyssa. My news is not good. Mum has had another myocardial infarction early this morning, and she is much weaker. She's asking for you. How soon can you come?"

"I'll be on the evening flight. I'll call Dr. Snyder to let her know and then telephone the airport."

❋

The airplane touched down at nine o'clock. Alyssa was at Helen's bedside in her condo an hour later. Mariah was sitting with her mother who had just fallen asleep. "As the hours wore on Mum's vital signs stabilized. She did eat a light meal, and as you can see, is sleeping peacefully now. Some time ago we engaged a caregiver to be with her throughout the day, and I have been sleeping on this cot at night. If you're up to staying with her tonight, Alyssa, I would appreciate a sound sleep in my own bed."

"I've come exclusively to be with your mother. Margaret and Natasha send their regards, and I've been given a carte blanche to stay as long as I'm needed. I've little doubt my nursing skills are rusty, but my love for Helen will carry me through. My only reservation is that I do not interfere with your caring for your mother."

The clock was nearing eight when Helen opened her eyes. Glancing toward the chair and seeing her she uttered, "Oh, my dearest Alyssa, you're here. I knew you would come to nurse me."

"Good morning, Helen. A team of wild horses could not have kept me away. Shall I bring you a cup of tea before your morning wash?"

Slightly raising the head of the bed, Alyssa went to the kitchen and returned carrying a tray with tea and light biscuits. "I always believed that my grandma and you were kindred spirits, Helen. Both of you thoughtful, loving women waited for me to provide your nursing care until I could be free to come to you. Margaret and Natasha send their love and their blessings for me to be with you."

"Yes, Elizabeth was as dear to me as an older sister. I learned so much from her gentle heart and ingenuous soul that I've chosen to follow her lead. When you came into my life, I acquired another daughter. I've arranged with Mariah and Steven, who are in complete agreement, for you to receive my condo when I'm no longer in need of it."

Alyssa was stunned. What could she possibly say?

✵

One day became another and another until Alyssa had comforted and cared for Helen for a week. As soon as the frail woman had surrendered to a restful sleep, she would quietly open the patio doors and be seated on the deck until Helen started to stir. With Alyssa's assurance, Mariah released the health care aide from hire and the two women provided all of her essential needs. Helen was fading. She was sleeping more and more and eating less and less, with dehydration becoming apparent. Mariah and Alyssa discussed the possibility of starting an intravenous and came to accept that it more for them because of their need to prolong the inevitable, than for Helen. Early in the evening of Alyssa's eleventh day in Victoria, Helen Symonds slipped away to join her beloved Ray in the hereafter. Her birth and adoptive daughters consoled each other, both having rejoiced in Helen's motherly love.

~62~

Not again. It could not occur yet another time. It was beginning to unnerve her. How many doubles could she have? Whatever had happened to the concept of individuality? Now a third incident since she moved to Alberta. Alyssa finished the workshop early, an approach she never once considered at the university. Half of the participants had not returned after lunch and those who had kept referencing the wall clock. She had had enough of trying to pique their interest, much less involvement on a beautiful spring Friday afternoon.

Alyssa would never have consented to offer an introductory creative writing workshop at MacEwan College during the last week in May 2004, except that Dr. Snyder had made the request. After it opened in 1993, she had driven by City Centre Campus stretching along 104 Avenue for seven blocks from 105 to 112 Streets, with the plethora of buildings connected through a pedway system on the second floor. Nonetheless, Alyssa had never ventured inside the complex with the eclectic groupings of architectural influence, which she quite frankly found bizarre in its entirety.

Until the end of her career and beyond, Alyssa would be indebted to Dr. Margaret Snyder for the success of her unprecedented quest on her behalf. Shortly after Alyssa returned from Victoria, before the Dean embarked upon her mission to take on the University Administration all the way to the Board of Governors, she had scheduled a full day retreat off campus for just the two of them. After she had verified that Alyssa did not have aspirations to conduct research, to pursue postdoctoral studies, or to climb the corporate ladder of the university, Margaret turned her focus to the writing of literary works. "I consider my next question to border on rhetorical, but I need to confirm my deeply held belief that you're not interested in authoring books before I elucidate my plan to you. Are you?"

Following considerable thought, Alyssa said, "I think that storytelling is implicit in both the art of writing and of teaching. I prefer lecturing because it is interactive, dynamic, and captivating to engage and share with learners, thereby observing and understanding the impact on students – a void that is seldom filled with readers. Because teaching requires auditory and visual involvement from listeners, they learn to organize their mental representation of what it is I'm instructing, to explore the essence of language, and to express their own thoughts. Choosing to follow the solitary pursuit of writing could never have comparable appeal for me."

Dr. Margaret Snyder could not have received a more definitive affirmation. Alyssa's insightful response validated her perception of the rarity of her teaching aptitude. She was now ready to petition the University of Alberta hierarchy to not only grant tenure, but also to indemnify no age limit to her professorship.

☸

The room at MacEwan had been tidied, and Alyssa was in the hallway locking the door when she heard, "Oh, my God. How long has it been since we got together? It's so nice to see you."

Standing in front of her was a younger woman of her height, sturdier build, blonde hair, and beaming as though they were long lost friends. "I'm sorry. You must be mistaking me for someone else."

"Come on. Surely you remember me? Bonnie Berkley. For years we had lunch at least once a month. When my two girls were little you took them out on many excursions, which I appreciated because you gave me a much-needed break. Okay, we lost touch after you were transferred to Millwoods, whereas I lucked out and was sent to Jasper Place. But, you couldn't have been so annoyed that you totally blocked us from your mind. I've been a psychologist for years, and of course, I've studied how some clients can do that, but why would you? What are you doing on campus anyway?"

Wow, this woman is insistent. She is actually becoming irritated. Am I glad that none of the participants decided to linger. How can I convince her? What a good thing that most of her colleagues seem to have left for the day?"

"I must be on my way. My parking metre has expired and I don't want a ticket."

"You're not going to give me the brush-off. Who do you think you are, Mrs. High and Mighty?"

Not that phrase again. What was it about her that inspired others to confer that label? But, enough was enough. "I'm leaving this building right now whether it is by my own volition, or if I have to call security."

Could there be a parallel universe, also known as parallel dimension, alter universe, or alternate reality – a hypothetical self-contained realm of existence, co-existing with one's own? Did a person lead an alternative life in parallel universes that existed concurrently, but which did not intersect? Are dreams of unfamiliar people and situations glimpses into that other reality? Were there times when Alyssa's parallel dimensions had criss-crossed? Was it possible she could have been living the life that Kathleen Sinclair and three women within the vicinity of Edmonton had alleged for her? But, why had not one of them acknowledged her name? Had Alyssa ever asked? And, then there was Adam Burke? She had little doubt that her choice at undeniably her major crossroads had created a ripple effect that changed every instance of her life onwards. Could Kathleen, Sheila, Natasha, and now Bonnie have known Alyssa Rainer's alternate self – whoever she was called – from the other path, which she had not chosen?

~63~

Why had they drifted apart? When both Alyssa and Helen left Saskatoon in the spring of 1982, Kathleen had felt abandoned. Her three children were away at school and developing an ever-widening circle of friends. During the intense years of nurturing them while constructing their home she had had precious little time for socialization, other than with her two close friends on Spadina Crescent. Still, even if she could count a multitude of women in her circle, Kathleen knew that she would never be able to recreate the cocooning she had experienced during those years with Alyssa and Helen.

Instead of lessening, Kathleen's parental responsibilities only changed when her family became teenagers. As much as she would have liked to accept Alyssa's invitations to spend a few days with her in St. Albert, there was always one reason or another why she could not get away. Nonetheless, Helen and Alyssa journeyed back to Saskatoon every May to visit with the Sinclairs, and their bond had always been renewed. However, when Helen reached her eighty birthday in 1990, it spelled the end of her sojourns to the city where she had lived her life. Alyssa arrived in August of the following year on her way to a nursing reunion in Manitoba, but thereafter her travels were always westward, never again east.

Years passed, and Kathleen's caring shifted to looking after Darren's mother whom they had relocated from Winnipeg, as well as making annual trips back to Australia to see her aging mother. Life was getting in the way for both friends. Now during the month of May, Alyssa drove to the west coast to spend at least two weeks with Helen and flew to Victoria for the Christmas season. Kathleen and Alyssa did however enjoy long telephone conversations on a regular basis. On one of those calls, Kathleen had jokingly said, "I knew I would hear from you today, Alyssa. You've a refined clairvoyance sense. Are you aware that whenever I want to talk to you, I begin to think about you and sooner or later during the day, you act on my telepathic message?" History seemed to substantiate Kathleen's premise when Alyssa realized that she invariably initiated all of their telecommunication.

Kathleen's one and only trip to St. Albert had arisen because of a tragedy. Alyssa opened her front door the moment the telephone began to ring. When she heard it was Kathleen, she interjected, "Well, you're quite the psychic yourself…" until she registered the alarm in her friend's voice. "What wrong?"

"Thank you for being home. Can I come? Elise's best friend is in critical condition at the Burn Unit at the University of Alberta Hospital. I need to be with her. Belinda has no one else. I can't believe the police haven't thrown her estranged husband in jail. I'm afraid he'll follow her."

"Kathleen, please take some breaths. Of course, you're welcome. When are you starting on your way?"

It was three o'clock on a Wednesday afternoon in July. Alyssa was returning from her two weeks at the Patricia Lake Bungalows. She had nearly decided to stay until the weekend when not for the first time and far from the last, her intuition had guided her home.

"I'm leaving as we speak."

"I'll be here waiting for you. Please drive safely."

Alyssa did her unpacking and started her laundry before she dashed to the Safeway to replenish her groceries. Although, she was piqued by curiosity she had decided not to heighten Kathleen's distress by quizzing her. Alyssa had long ago realized that Kathleen was a caregiver. With her bustling family, she had never sought employment outside their home and soon began to look after other families and friends in need.

It would have been beyond the capability of any human being to alleviate Kathleen's angst and despair during her five days in St. Albert. There was little question that she could find any peace, much less pleasure, could forget why she had come, or that she would ever want to relive the dreadful experience by returning. Belinda's husband had accosted her in her backyard just as she was about to pour lighter fluid over charcoal briquettes for a barbeque. The man grabbed the can from her, doused Elise's beautiful friend over her head and upper body with the contents and lit her afire.

The horrendous incident involving Belinda that resulted in extensive burns, internal trauma, and appalling disfigurement had a devastating and lasting effect upon Kathleen. Other than a curt call to identify she had arrived home safely, Alyssa did not hear a word from Kathleen for weeks. She intuited that she needed to be left alone in her anguish. Alyssa yearned to provide emotional support, but she knew that she must wait for Kathleen to reach out to her. Near the end of August when she read in the *Edmonton Journal* that Belinda had been flown to the University of Saskatchewan Hospital to be closer to family and friends, she telephoned Kathleen. When no one answered, she left a message that she was driving to Saskatoon.

Never before had Alyssa been so ill received at 1108 King Crescent. Instead of the ornate oak door being opened with a cheery hello, Alyssa heard a voice call out, "Come in. The door is open." Entering the foyer, she was surprised by the shambles in the adjacent living room and when she glanced around the corner, the piles of papers on the dining room table. Kathleen was the first person to see her. She exclaimed, "I didn't know you were coming?"

"I called leaving a message that I was on my way. You look exceedingly busy so perhaps you haven't had a chance to listen to it."

"We were at the hospital all morning and have just got home. I wish you hadn't made the trip, Alyssa. I can't cope with you at this time."

"I'm in Saskatoon for meetings with the university for the next two days, and I'm booked into the Sheraton. I've only dropped by to see how you are, Kathleen. I'm worried about you."

"Well, you have very good reason to be. Elise and I have taken charge of proving the case against Belinda's husband who is outrageously claiming he's innocent, that it was an accident, and unbelievably the police have yet to arraign him. Whenever we talk to them they tell us that they're investigating, but so far there is no evidence against him. Why the hell would Belinda inadvertently pour lighter fluid over herself and then light a match? It's insane. He's as free as a bird while Belinda lies in agony in the hospital. We have to find proof, get character witnesses to testify against him, apply enough pressure to make him confess, so the evil bastard is thrown into jail. Whatever it takes, Elise and I won't quit until we've succeeded in getting justice for Belinda. Please wait and let me get in touch with you. I promise to telephone you when we have him behind bars."

The drift between the friends had widened until they were ships lost at sea. Alyssa respected Kathleen's request, but when weeks became months, years, she feared that the women were overwhelmed with the enormity of their unachievable undertaking. How could they possibly prove that Belinda's husband had deliberately torched her? There were no witnesses. It was her word versus his. It was beyond Alyssa's comprehension what justice would accomplish for Belinda. Nothing could ever reverse her extensive mutilation nor make right the terrible wrong done to her.

Alyssa waited and waited until she began to second-guess herself. Could she have misunderstood what Kathleen had said? As a true friend should she reach out? If there had been any accuracy to Kathleen's long-held claim that whenever she wanted to talk to her she would simply think about her, and Alyssa would telephone then clearly her thoughts were never focused on her. The Christmas card that year was written and presumably sent by Darren.

When the telephone call came, years later, it was Darren on the line. "Kathleen has been diagnosed with breast cancer. Because the growth is in her lymph nodes it had gone undetected for a long time. She's scheduled for a radical mastectomy tomorrow at the University Hospital."

"Oh, Darren, I'm so sorry. I'll start out tomorrow morning and be there when Kathleen comes out of surgery."

"Kathleen doesn't want any company right now. I made the decision to ring and let you know. I'll call again when she is well enough to see you."

Alyssa waited. A month later when neither Darren nor Kathleen telephoned she rang them, but had to leave a message. Once again it was Darren who eventually called, "Thank you, Alyssa, for the card and beautiful bouquet of flowers you sent Kathleen. She has come home from the hospital, although she'll soon be returning as an outpatient to begin intensive chemotherapy."

"Thank you, Darren, for returning my message. When may I come to visit Kathleen?"

"I'm sorry, Alyssa, but she's still not receiving visitors. She wants to be finished with her treatment and recover before she sees anyone, except the kids and me."

"What is going on, Darren? Kathleen has been my closest friend for years, and suddenly I can't come to be with her when she is ill."

"It's her choice. She won't see any of her friends here in Saskatoon either, not even her Tae Kwon Do mates with whom she has been involved every day for years. Her brother was ready to fly here from Australia to spend time with her. She told him not to come. I've no idea why Kathleen is responding the way she is, Alyssa, but I accept her decisions."

❋

Eventually, Kathleen did telephone Alyssa and over time after several strained conversations, they did begin to re-establish some semblance of their previous camaraderie. But, although the women were exchanging calls on a fairly regular basis, there was never any mention of Alyssa venturing to Saskatoon, if not to stay with, at least to see Kathleen. At that juncture in her career, Dr. Snyder had proposed that the English Faculty at the University of Alberta develop a Masters of Fine Arts in Creative Writing program, and Alyssa was to play a dominant role. Honoured to be one of the professors selected for the pioneering project, which challenged her creativity over the course of subsequent years, she devoted herself to the implementation of the innovative degree.

Nonetheless, Alyssa continued to sorely miss Kathleen and try as she might, she could not understand why she had become increasingly secluded during the seven years that she had been battling cancer. Had she failed her friend? Should she have been more insistent about supporting her? Was she the reason that the relationship between the lifelong friends had become non-existent? Unbelievably, Alyssa had only seen Kathleen once briefly in her front entrance in the fourteen years that had passed since she had made her fateful trip to St. Albert.

Finally at the beginning of August, 2011, Alyssa arose one morning, threw together a change of clothes, grabbed a MacDonald coffee and egg muffin, and drove to Saskatoon. After she had checked in, she telephoned the Sinclair residence. "Hi, Kathleen, it is nice to hear your voice. I've returned for meetings at the university and have just registered at the Sheraton. I would like to take you and Darren out for an early dinner."

With verbal support from Darren audible in the background, Kathleen finally consented. When she arrived at the much-loved home at 1108 King Crescent, Alyssa had to take several minutes before she could exit her Prelude. Other than that she was thinner, her pale blond hair had turned white, she had a distant look in her eyes, and she spoke in a softer voice, Kathleen appeared remarkably healthy. They drove to a small family restaurant that was cozy. They were well ahead of the crowd. They conversed, reminisced, laughed, cried, and were comfortable when intervals of silence descended upon the three friends. When they returned home, Kathleen suggested a relaxing stroll first by Helen's, and then along the South Saskatchewan River until they reached University Bridge. Twilight was creeping upon the horizon when Alyssa ensconced Kathleen in one of her grandmother's hugs for prolonged moments.

❋

No, it could not be. Darren was on the telephone. "Alyssa, I'm calling to tell you that Kathleen has chosen to discontinue her chemotherapy. She's in palliative care." It was the beginning of November, not three months beyond her impromptu drive to Saskatoon.

"I'm leaving right now."

"Please do not come. Kathleen is saving her precious energy and time for Craig, Lindsey, Elise, and me – no one else."

In early afternoon of November 22, 2011, Darren made his last call to Alyssa. "Kathleen died peacefully this morning. Her choice was to slip away without any closure to her life."

~64~

It is true that we love the ones we are near. The three women had become close friends over the years, which every elderly person knew sped up when nearing the finish line. They most often met in St. Albert at Alyssa's, as much because they had also come to love the satellite city, as that they did not want to appear to be gathering too frequently at Margaret and Natasha's home with its proximity to the university. The trio had season tickets to the symphony, ballad, and opera and were seen seated together at every performance.

When Christmas had been approaching the year Helen died, Alyssa was lost. She was still grieving her beloved friend. She could not imagine travelling to Victoria to spend the week alone in the condo she had inherited. On one of her hikes in Riverlot 56 a thought flitted across her mind, *What if I asked Margaret and Natasha to join me for the holiday season*? As soon as she arrived home she rang their number. Margaret answered the telephone and after the usual introductory dialogue, Alyssa said, "I would like to invite you and Natasha to book a flight with me to the west coast and spend Christmas in my condo? Mariah always asks about both of you since Helen shared commentary about her many visits with you in St. Albert. I know she and Steven would love to meet you."

"What a lovely gesture, Alyssa. Do you have adequate sleeping space in a one-bedroom condo?"

"During all my visits with Helen, I was perfectly comfortable sleeping on a wide sofa in the living room, which I assure you, I'll be again. I actually don't want to be in Helen's room, preferring that you and Natasha occupy it. There is an ensuite bathroom adjacent to her bedroom, and we can draw straws regarding the timing of the use of the shower or the bathtub in the main bathroom. I'll store my clothing in the hall closet, which Helen had fitted with a small chest of drawers. There is a heated closed-in patio where we can enjoy our morning coffee on sunny days. The weather is often clement enough, even in December during the afternoons to soak up rays on the deck overlooking the back garden."

"It sounds divine. Let me consult with Natasha, and I'll let you know."

The minute Margaret confirmed that they would be delighted to fly to Victoria; Alyssa placed a call to Mariah. "How are you doing? I can only imagine how much you must miss your lovely mother."

"Thank you, Alyssa. Both Steven and I think about her daily. I hope you're telephoning to let us know to expect you for the Christmas season. We would be very disappointed if we didn't have one family member seated at our table."

"The acorn never fell far from the tree. Thank you, Mariah, for your incredible hospitality throughout the years. As it happens, I've just received confirmation that Margaret and Natasha have accepted my invitation to sojourn with me in Victoria this Christmas. They look forward to meeting you."

*

Over the course of the subsequent eleven years, the colleagues spend two weeks every Christmas in Victoria. At the end of the academic year in May, 2012 when Dr. Margaret Snyder and Dr. Natasha Nash decided to retire as the deans of their respective faculties, Alyssa hosted a drop-in gathering in her backyard at 78 Beaverbrook Crescent. The afternoon proved to be a testimony to the respect and admiration that both women had garnered from every member of their faculties over the many years of their tenure. The invitation had specified between one and five o'clock, but guests had started arriving shortly after noon and had continued until the supper hour.

When at last the four remaining well-wishers were on their way, the retirees sought a comfortable chair on the deck to unwind while Alyssa disappeared into her home. She returned with a tray of refreshing drinks and two bulky coloured envelopes. "What a wonderful tribute to the two most acclaimed deans at the University of Alberta. There is little doubt that I'm going to need time to adjust to not seeing you on campus. Now that we have a moment of peace, I've a gift of gratitude for all that each of you has given to me."

Margaret was the first to respond. "What's this, Alyssa? Your party has been more than enough. You've always been my present to the English faculty."

"Your friendship has meant the world to me." Natasha chimed in.

When they opened their small packages, both stared in disbelief. Enclosed inside was a gold key with a tag, which read, "To our condo in Victoria."

✵

The spring when Alyssa turned seventy she reached the decision to semi-retire. For the past three years when she had been returning to St. Albert at the end of her Christmas vacation, she had acknowledged to herself she was envious that Margaret and Natasha were staying longer to escape Edmonton's inclement winters. Still, Alyssa continued to delight in teaching, and she particularly enjoyed autumn on the prairies. Subsequently, she elected to lecture the fall semester of the Introductory Creative Writing course to launch the enthusiastic first year students, before journeying to Victoria for the balance of the winter months.

In the spring of 2018, Dr. Alyssa Rainer announced her full retirement from the University of Alberta, Faculty of English.

Epilogue

Springtime in Victoria, the capital city of British Columbia is exquisite. The "Garden City" is located in a temperate sub-Mediterranean climate zone, and mild weather arrives very early in the season compared to the rest of Canada – as soon as mid-February. Alyssa not only enjoyed walking outdoors in more clement weather, but also was delighted that she did not need to shovel snow for an additional two or three months.

For as long as Alyssa owned the condo, she neither removed nor supplemented any furnishings, major items, or even kitchenware to what Helen had bought when she purchased it. Once Mariah had taken out her mother's personal belongings – clothing, mementos, and jewellery, she had simply presented Alyssa with the legal papers and the key. Over the years that Margaret and Natasha had wintered in Victoria they restored Helen's beautiful floral garden in the yard to its original state, to the extent that they had to hire a gardener to maintain it when they returned to Edmonton.

On the first day of April, her grandmother's birthday, in the spring of 2019, Alyssa was seated on the cedar deck at the back of her condo gazing upon an array of blooming flowers in her enclosed yard. She was in a reflective mood, specifically about how suited she had been for a career in academia. She was well aware of the phrase from George Bernard Shaw's *Man and Superman* written in 1903, "Those who can't do teach." Nevertheless, instead of considering the words a source of irritation, Alyssa had always appreciated that she was much more proficient with work requiring studying and reasoning rather than with practical or technical skills. She had pursued teaching for her love of literature and stayed for the love of her students. Alyssa often thought that she developed healthier relationships with relative strangers than with family or friends.

As occurred on occasion, fleeting thoughts of Eric Easton flitted through her mind. She genuinely hoped that he had found happiness, and had reared the children who were seemingly important to him. Did Alyssa regret the path that she had chosen? There could be no denying that often she had led a solitary life pursuing years of education, and many activities – travelling and hiking in the mountains, cross-county skiing, and riding many of the ever-increasing number of biking trails – by herself. Had her recurring distrust of people been the reason all but a few left? Still, buoyed by her lifelong faith, Alyssa Rainer was never alone.

Even so, Alyssa was not beyond wondering, "What if…?"

CPSIA information can be obtained
at www.ICGtesting.com
Printed in the USA
BVHW070038130123
655956BV00001B/3